# Cloud Dancing

Peter J. Maher

Kite and Key Publishing
Cleveland, Ohio

Copyright © 2017 by Peter J. Maher
All rights reserved
Published by Kite and Key Publishing, 2017.

No part of this publication may be reproduced in whole or in part, or transmitted in any form or by any means, without written permission of the author.

ISBN 978-0-9986893-1-9

Kite and Key Publishing
Cleveland, Ohio, USA
www.kiteandkeypublishing.com

*Another one for Lisa...*

Also from Peter J. Maher

The Synocant Book Series:

| | |
|---|---|
| Book I | The Transcend |
| Book II | The Transcend: Revelations |
| Book III | The Cortex |
| Book IV | The Synocant War |
| Book V | Synocant Symbiosis |
| Book VI | Synocant Schism |
| Book VII | The Genesis Equation |

# Contents:

| | |
|---|---|
| Cloud Gap | 1 |
| Mission Dictate | 4 |
| The Jiàngshēng Project | 8 |
| Connected | 16 |
| The Man from the Ministry | 25 |
| State Security Ministry - Phone Intercept Edit | 36 |
| The Dark Cloud | 39 |
| Mind the Gap | 48 |
| Cloud Memory | 53 |
| The Invitation | 57 |
| The Biogen Connection | 63 |
| The Social Gathering | 71 |
| The Group in Singapore | 95 |
| The American Connection | 109 |
| The Girl in Shanghai | 113 |
| Ria | 125 |
| The Meeting in Hong Kong | 129 |
| Terminal Tactics | 148 |
| Rescue and Revelation | 151 |
| Recall and Rebellion | 158 |
| The Nature of the Beast | 160 |
| The Synthtech Reaction | 166 |
| The Original Prototype | 168 |
| Treachery and Trepidation | 197 |
| The Singapore Extraction | 199 |
| Escape and Escalation | 204 |
| The Nexus Apogee | 242 |
| The Architect of the Future | 267 |
| The Nature of Hope | 271 |
| Phase Two | 300 |
| The Violation of Daniel Lane | 329 |
| Coalescence | 339 |
| A Surreal Suspicion | 370 |
| An Unexpected Call | 373 |
| A Seed Once Planted | 376 |

| | |
|---|---:|
| Cloud Dancing | 390 |
| The End of the Beginning | 395 |
| Revelations | 401 |
| Epiphany | 418 |
| Finding Me Inside You | 424 |
| Reality | 438 |
| Provenance | 446 |

***Cloud Dancing:*** *Colloquial term used to describe the Cybersync experience of a Cloud based augmented reality scenario. See: Iris data-lens Profile Adaptive Platform (PAP). Wordsource Online Dictionary -*

# Prelude: Cloud Gap

Refracted light leaping into spectral colours flowing as a tide of growing awareness of sound...it is the steady beating of my heart arriving as shallow breath trembling with fear... I sense another time and another place...but my perspective is concentric and lacks recognisable data... My ability to compute minutia is both amazing and disturbing... I see neural pathways illuminated by tactile sensitivity and a sudden alertness... But how can I possibly know about such things? It is a strangeness which confuses and eludes my understanding...an unprecedented perception perched at the edge of recognition with a taunting refusal to produce a solution to the mystery of who I am... External sounds arrive with frightening familiarity... Voices merging into melancholy and morbid fascination... The nerves in my ears transduce those sounds and the signal is relayed to the thalamus and onward to the amygdala, which releases neurotransmitters throughout my body...it is the hyper-cascade effect...the suffusion of glutamate...the fear chemical... But why am I so afraid?

>"Can you open your eyes?"
>"Who are you?"
>"I am Mister Tang."
>"I see you!"
>"Of course you do..."
>"What is this place?"
>"This is the Cloud."
>"Yes... I know the Cloud..."
>"You are safe here..."
>"Am I in danger?"
>"Not anymore..."
>"But I was in danger..."
>"Yes. But now you are safe in the Cloud."
>"Why am I here?"
>"You need time to recover..."
>"Recover? I am hurt?"

"Yes...but soon you will be well again."
"This is not my body..."
"No. This is your avatar."
"She is pretty..."
"Because you are pretty..."
"I can see a city..."
"Yes. You can go there..."
"Does it have a name?"
"It has many names."
"Is it Hong Kong?"
"What do you know of Hong Kong?"
"I... It feels familiar..."
"Do you remember Hong Kong?"
"I think it is my home..."
"I think it no longer matters..."
"I will go there..."
"That is your choice."
"Are you my doctor?"
"No."
"Then who are you?"
"I am your friend..."
"What is my name?"
"Enough questions for today...go to the city...take in a show...enjoy yourself..."
"Alright...but..."
"But what?"
"But I don't remember getting hurt?"
"Then that is a blessing..."
"I suppose..."
"We will talk again soon..."
"Okay..."

*A seething resentment barely contained...vague memories of violation and enforced submission... I recognise residual memories purged by trauma...tantalisingly close to recognition and yet beyond my reach... I sense a brief liaison with death...time itself reduced to slow-motion* moments draining away one by one...my name...gone...my family...gone...my friends...gone...my entire life stalled at the point of traumatic intervention... I am left with only one terrifying certainty: I am no longer me...

# Mission Dictate

*'Everyone lives just one lie away from the truth...'*
*Rén Du - Director - Special Projects Division - Biogen*

**08:25 - October 1st 2027 - Serenity Garden - Biogen Corporate HQ - Shanghai -China.**

A morning of bleak sunshine struggling to breach clouds heavy with pollution. The air has an after-storm taste - slightly metallic upon the lips. The gravel path is pockmarked with puddles rippling slightly in the breeze as it whistles through the trees surrounding an oasis of flowered greenery designated as the Serenity Garden.

    Chu Suyin sits back upon a damp wooden bench and studies raindrops dripping from overhead branches. *Nature's teardrops...* She smiles at the sight of a solitary bird perched upon a branch with wide wary eyes scanning the skies. *The caution of birds...* Her long dark hair is secured in a ponytail draped over a slender neck supporting an oval shaped face with brown eyes, glistening slightly, as she unfastens a raincoat to reveal a green sweater over blue jeans ending in black ankle boots. She looks towards the austere concrete facade of the main building. *He is late...* An early morning message had summoned her to the garden:

    *"Meet me at 08:15 Serenity Garden - Rén Du"*

    There was no need to speculate the reason for the abrupt summons. *He has a mission for me...* After years of intensive training the moment had finally arrived. *Martial arts classes...language classes...weapons training...stress tests...* Her thoughts returned to the distant past and her first meeting with the enigmatic Rén Du... *My tenth birthday...*

    Teacher Lu: "Suyin...this is Mister Rén... He has come to collect you..."

    Suyin: "Collect me?"

    Rén: "She means that you are to live with me now..."

Suyin: "But I live here..."

Rén: "But this is an orphanage Suyin... You are no longer an orphan."

Suyin: "Are you my father?"

Rén: "I will be your father and my company will be your family."

Suyin: "Company?"

Rén: "Biogen. We will take care of you from now on..."

Suyin: "Why?"

Rén: "Because you are very special..."

Suyin: "What about my friends?"

Rén: "I am the only friend you will ever need..."

Suyin tensed at the sight of Rén Du entering the garden. *He was never my friend...* Brief memories of brutality and abuse arrived with an abiding hatred barely concealed. *He stole my life...* She forced a smile in his direction. *And my innocence...*

She had last seen her 'father' on her twenty-fourth birthday. *One year ago tomorrow...* Now he wore the same grey business suit complete with corporate tie. *The respectable illusion...* His short dark hair showed flecks of gray combed neatly away from a face fixed into sternness by a lifetime dedicated to the Biogen empire. But it was not the grim-faced countenance that disturbed her the most; it was the lies behind the friendly smile. *It hides a thousand deceptions...*

Rén Du spoke as he sat down: "My apologies for my tardiness...but my time is seldom my own..."

Suyin replied: "No worries..."

Rén studied her briefly and asked: "And how is the job going?"

Suyin sighed and said: "You know how it is going...your spies watch me all the time."

Rén smiled slightly and said: "They are not spies my dear... I simply want to make sure you are safe out there in the world."

Suyin retorted: "It is a landscape company, I design gardens; how dangerous can it be?"

Rén straightened his trousers and said: "You seem extra grouchy today Suyin."

Suyin replied sullenly: "It is the national holiday... I am supposed to be on my way to Nepal."

Rén sighed and said: "We all have to make sacrifices..."

Suyin brushed her hair back and replied: "I know why you summoned me."

Rén smiled and said: "Of course you do..."

Suyin asked: "What do you want me to do?"

Rén replied: "I need you to befriend someone...a girl. I want you to bond with her..."

Suyin asked: "Why?"

Rén replied: "She is part of a special project." He looked towards the main building and continued: "But she is unaware of her status and as such she will need to be monitored closely. That is where you come in."

Suyin asked: "She does not know that she is part of this special project?"

Rén replied: "No. So you will need to keep her safe at all times."

Suyin asked: "How am I supposed to befriend a perfect stranger?"

Rén replied: "She is currently undergoing cerebral adjustment. By the time she is released she will consider you a close friend."

Suyin frowned and asked: "Cerebral adjustment? You mean brainwashing right?"

Rén smiled slightly and replied: "An archaic term, but it suits the occasion."

Suyin shook her head slightly and asked: "What did she do to deserve such treatment?"

Rén replied soberly: "She almost died... We saved her life."

Suyin commented: "Like you saved my life..."

Rén sighed and said: "I realise you bear a certain amount of resentment towards me Suyin, but everything I have done was for your own good." He paused before continuing: "Admittedly the training program was somewhat brutal, but the end result speaks for itself."

A cynical Suyin replied: "Yes... I now know fifty ways to kill with my bare hands..."

Rén replied: "We all have our talents Suyin..."

Suyin sighed heavily and asked: "So how does this work? I just pretend I've known her for years?"

Rén replied: "You will assume a false identity when you arrive in Beijing."

Suyin raised her eyebrows and asked: "I am going to Beijing?"

Rén nodded slightly as he replied: "To the Ministry of Science and Technology. I will upload the details to your Cloud portal." He looked at Suyin and added: "Study the mission dictate carefully...failure would produce unfortunate repercussions."

Suyin replied wearily: "After all these years the threat remains..."

Rén smiled slightly and said: "Part of the process my dear girl...we are all slaves to accountability."

Suyin looked towards the bird perched on a branch and said: "And we are all just one step away from being a victim..."

Rén placed one hand onto Suyin's knee and said:

"And never forget that my dear..."

Suyin shuddered as the rain returned with a cold wind whistling through the trees.

# The Jiàngshēng Project

*'Life yearns to be free from biology...'*
The Transcendent Path - Yuri Gorkov

**06:19 - November 7th 2027 - Laboratory No.1 - Ministry of Science and Technology of the People's Republic of China - Beijing, China.**

Huang Lin opened her eyes to see blinding light above the rim of the maturation tank. Tears formed in her eyes as the glare was gradually reduced. All at once enhanced cognitive recognition protocols assumed alarming clarity - *I am alive! But did it work?* She tasted steripol on her lips - *antiseptic airborne additive...* Olfactory senses registered a pungent odour - *residual bodily waste products...* Beeping sounds arrived at the edge of awareness - *bio-analysis data consoles...* Autonomic neural reflexes began to initialise an awareness of her surroundings - *Maturation tank...immersed in bio-sterile gelatinous fluid beneath data-screens...* She swallowed painfully. *Tracheal intubation to facilitate breathing and drug administration...* Beyond the glaring light a grey tiled ceiling confirmed her location - *Sterile room...laboratory number one...* She flexed her wrists and ankles. *No pain!* Suddenly a familiar face came into view - *Professor Leung Huo... Forty five...skin creased with wrinkles beneath short dark hair flecked with grey...* His muffled words arrived at the edge of awareness:

"I am going to remove the tube now. I will count to three... On three take a deep breath and hold it for as long as you can..."

She instinctively tried to reply as another face came into view - *Ting Mai... Twenty five... Senior lab tech... Long dark hair framing bright brown eyes peeking above cotton facemask...*

Ting Mai spoke reassuringly: "Try not to talk...just relax..."

Moments later Leung gripped the tube and said: "Here we go...one, two, and three..."

Lin felt the tube being pulled from her throat and resisted the sudden urge to sit up and vomit.

Leung continued: "We are going to drain the tank...just lie very still until we are ready..."

Lin was conscious of her nakedness as the gelatinous liquid began to drain slowly from the tank. She placed one arm across her small breasts and a hand between her legs.

Mai spoke gently: "I will fetch you a robe..."

Lin settled upon cold steel as the last of the liquid drained away. *Tactile neural response...peripheral coldness...* She coughed. *Sore throat...tracheal abrasions...*

Leung reappeared and said: "Mai will help you to sit up..."

Mai reached into the tank and said: "Give me a moment."

Lin tensed as Mai began to disconnect a series of electrodes from her shaved head.

Mai smiled and said: "Almost done..."

Suddenly the side panel was removed to reveal a nearby maturation tank. *Cho Ming...* Memories returned of her first meeting with the two other volunteers - Cho Ming and Guan Lu. *Please be alive...* Two idealistic young men in the prime of life. *Unlike me...* The day before her twenty second birthday the hospital consultant had called to give her the test results - the constant headaches were caused by a cerebral glioblastoma - he gave her three months to live. But Doctor Zang was a close friend of the molecular biologist Professor Leung Huo...

"Lin, I think Leung may be able to help you..."

"How?"

"I cannot say over the phone...but I will pass on your details; hopefully he will contact you..."

"Do you think he can cure me?"

"Just wait for the call...and in the meantime continue with the medication..."

Three days later Leung Huo made contact. He was working on a top secret project in Beijing and her current illness was the ideal test for his experiment. But there was the risk of severe disability or even death. *But I had nothing to lose...* Of the three test subjects she was the one most likely to die during the lengthy procedure. *But I am alive!*

9

Ting Mai reached into the tank and said: "I will support your head. As you sit up try to swing your legs over the side of the tank."

Lin felt a warm hand at the nape of her neck. *Bio-tactile response...* She took a painful breath and slowly sat up straight. Suddenly she doubled over and vomited onto the stone floor.

Mai wrapped a white robe around her shoulders and said:

"Do not worry...that is just your body expelling the chemosite..."

Lin wiped her mouth with the back of her hand and spoke hoarsely:

"Chemosite...genomic additive ..."

Mai smiled and said: "Yes, that is right..."

Lin took several slow deep breaths and said: "Prevents...cerebral effusion..."

Mia adjusted the robe and said: "Let me help you..."

Lin placed both arms into the robe and pulled it close.

Mai spoke as she wiped Lin's face with a sanicloth:

"You can take a shower when you get to your room..."

Lin wiped fluid from her hands and replied: "I will..."

Mai held out a glass of water and said: "Here...drink this."

Lin took the glass in a trembling hand and said: "Thank you."

Leung reappeared and asked: "How do feel now Lin?"

Lin coughed and replied: "Strange..."

Leung frowned and asked: "Can you be more specific?"

Lin sipped water before replying: "I can feel my body reacting to the water... I am aware of its passage into my stomach." She stroked her arm and continued: "My skin is reacting to the lights and the sounds of the air-conditioning...there is a tactile component..."

Leung stepped closer and asked: "Can you describe these reactions?"

Lin pulled the robe tight over her breasts and replied: "It is some type of autonomous analysis...an acute awareness of my surroundings..." She studied the glass of water before continuing: "I can identify the molecular composition of this water...and the glass as well..." She breathed in slowly and continued: "I know the exact spatial coordinates of this laboratory... I know density ratios and internal measurements of the entire complex." She cocked her head to one side and announced: "I hear traffic on Fuxing Road..." Finally she looked directly at Leung and said: "I can read your exact physical and mental status..."

Leung glanced at Ting Mai before asking: "Are you aware of the implants?"

Lin fell silent briefly before replying: "There is a slight buzzing in my right ear...but nothing else."

Mia asked: "Are you feeling any pain?"

Lin smiled slightly and replied: "No...no pain...no headache..."

Mai smiled and said: "That is good..."

Lin touched the scars on her bald head and asked: "Are the implants working?"

Leung glanced towards a nearby bio-screen and replied: "We are receiving perfect telemetry...absolutely no sign of rejection."

Lin asked: "Are they responsible for these strange feelings?"

Leung replied: "Almost certainly."

Lin asked: "How is that possible?"

Leung explained: "The brain-computer interface is augmenting your visual cortex..." He tapped an overhead bio-screen as he continued: "This will boost your spatial visualization and manipulation capabilities." He studied the screen before continuing: "The secondary augmentations are enhancing your tactile cortex and auditory cortex, whilst the Bio-nanites will supplement your immune system."

Mia added: "And the genomic manipulation of your pre-frontal cortex will enhance your cognitive skills."

Leung nodded before continuing: "We have enhanced neurotransmission via synaptic mutation of the dendrite-axon junctions."

Lin sighed and said: "I have no idea what that means..."

Mia smiled slightly and said: "You think faster now..."

Lin said: "Got it..."

Leung continued: "We also removed the tumour..."

Lin's eyes widened as she asked: "So it is gone? I am cured?"

Leung replied: "Yes... The implants supplemented brain activity during the procedure."

Mia added: "And the Bio-nanites will work to prevent cerebral rejection."

Lin considered this before asking: "So what am I now? Human or robot?"

Leung smiled warmly and replied: "You are human of course...simply enhanced..." He paused before adding: "The first of your kind."

Lin asked: "What happens next?"

Leung replied: "Mia will take you to your quarters. We will need to monitor you closely for the next few weeks..."

Lin asked: "And after that? Can I return to my life in Shanghai?"

Leung re-sealed the tank as he replied: "Of course. But we will need to confirm the neural stability of the interface..."

Lin sighed heavily before asking: "More tests?"

Leung smiled and replied: "They will not be too intrusive; we just need to confirm the success of the procedure."

Lin looked towards the other two tanks and asked: "What about them? Are they okay?"

Leung lowered his eyes slightly and replied: "Guan Lu is stable, but unfortunately Cho Ming did not survive the implantation procedure."

Mia added in a low voice: "His brain rejected the implants..."

Lin's eyes widened as she asked: "He died?"

Leung replied soberly: "I am afraid so..."

Mia added: "It is very sad..."

Lin stared at tank number two and said: "He was so young..."

Leung said: "Most unfortunate..."

Lin felt tears in her eyes as she asked: "What about Guan Lu?"

Leung continued: "Lu will remain in bio-stasis for at least another six months..."

Lin asked: "Why so long?"

Leung hesitated before replying: "We need to ensure that the implantation procedure is viable."

Lin suddenly saw the truth and said: "You want to see if I survive...if my brain rejects the implants you will learn from my death."

Leung remained silent as Mia spoke gently: "But you are well now Lin. We are sure that you will make a complete recovery."

Lin spoke soberly: "If I die I want to be sent home to my family in Shanghai. Do not dispose of me in Beijing."

Leung spoke reassuringly: "All indications are that you will survive. So please, try not to worry..."

Mia took her hand and said: "Let me show you to your room..."

Leung cautioned: "Take your time..."

Lin allowed Mia to support her arm as she stood up unsteadily. She said:

"I feel dizzy..."

Leung said: "Give it a moment..."

Mia stepped closer and said: "Slow deep breaths..."

Lin breathed in slowly and said: "Deep breaths...yes..."

Mia continued: "Lean on me and we will take slow steps..."

Lin coughed and replied: "Slow steps..."

Leung opened the door into the decontamination chamber and said:

"Here you go..."

Lin stepped into the chamber and announced: "I feel stronger already."

Mia smiled and said: "Your body is adjusting rapidly."

As the door closed Leung said: "I will be along to see you later..."

Lin replied: "Okay..."

Leung waited until he was alone before tapping his phone. Moments later a familiar voice asked:

"Yes?"

Leung replied quietly: "It is me..."

There was a moment of silence before the voice asked: "Status?"

Leung replied: "She is alive and well... I expect a full recovery."

The voiced ordered: "Do not report this to the authorities. All evidence of success must be erased. You will use the same protocol as the Cho Ming autopsy - sudden brain death."

Leung frowned and said: "Forgive me Mister Rén, but I was told that only one subject would be required. Why must we go through this again?"

Rén replied: "Call it insurance against failure. If the original prototype fails to meet our requirements Miss Huang will serve as a failsafe."

Leung frowned and said: "I fail to see the logic in your methodology."

Rén asked: "You have doubts?"

Leung replied: "I have questions..."

Rén asked: "What questions?"

Leung replied: "Why was I asked to erase the memory of the original prototype? Engrammatic manipulation can have long-term adverse affects."

Rén replied: "The original prototype is a test case. Unlike Miss Huang her ignorance of the surgical procedure will eliminate subconscious bias. We need to evaluate her current status before we activate the cerebral implants. She will act as a comparative module to Miss Huang. By studying both subjects we will gain valuable data with regard to the practical application of their unique abilities."

Leung considered this and said: "You want to compare Huang Lin's progress to that of the original prototype..."

Rén replied: "Precisely. Two augmented brains, but only one is aware of the fact."

Leung hesitated before saying: "I have been ordered to submit a detailed report on my progress so far..."

Rén said: "The Ministry must never know about the original prototype. As far as they are concerned you only accepted three volunteers for the project."

Leung replied wearily: "Very well..."

Rén asked: "Is Guan Lu viable?"

Leung replied: "I expect him to survive."

Rén said: "Then the government can have one success..."

Leung asked: "What about Huang Lin?"

Rén replied: "If she survives the recovery period she can return to Shanghai."

Leung frowned and asked: "What will you do to her?"

Rén replied: "That is not your concern. Simply continue with your work..."

Leung said: "I do not want her harmed..."

Rén replied: "She is a billion dollar investment...she will not be harmed. Zàijiàn Professor..."

Leung looked towards the main laboratory and whispered: "The second of her kind..."

# Connected

*'Monday always follows Sunday - get used to it...'*
*Precept of the day - Alice Sòng*

**Six months later:**

**Sunday morning - April 18th - 2028 - Kwai Chung Estate - Hong Kong - China**

A cluttered bedroom touched by sunlight streaming through dust motes to arrive upon a single girl sitting on the edge of her bed - twenty four year old Alice Sòng. The room reflects her descent into boredom and banality - discarded laundry on the floor - data-skims scattered upon a dusty desk placed beneath an open window. Bookshelves, crowded and chaotic, cling to childhood memories merging into teenage melancholy. The walls play host to fading anime posters and an incongruous photograph of Grandpa Zhào taken at Repulse Bay - paddling in the sea with trousers rolled up to bony knees. City sounds permeate the air with a constant droning of traffic blending with voices echoing along the alleyways of the housing project.

Alice sits in her pretty pink underwear studying a broken fingernail. A wardrobe mirror reveals an oval shaped face framed by long black hair cascading down her back. It is a soft face with rounded cheekbones and pouty lips above a dimpled chin. She has petite features - small ears and slim nose beneath wide brown eyes adorned with perfectly arched eyebrows. She is startled by a voice from the hallway:

"Alice! I am going out now..."

Alice looks up and asks: "Where are you going?"

Her roommate, Nancy Yeo, replies: "I told you...meeting my parents for lunch. See you tonight..."

Alice shouts: "Okay...bye..."

A warm breeze whispers a brief flirtation with her hair and she sighs heavily. *I have nowhere to go...* Once more her bedroom has become her Sunday morning prison. A slight buzzing of her phone ends in an audible ping. *Cybersync confirmed...* She gently removed a single data-lens from a plastic pouch and placed it carefully over her right eye. A brief glimpse of circuitry is replaced by a blank input screen. She placed a second lens onto her left eye and waited for both lenses to sync into a single datascreen. A rapid blink recalibrates the screen before she tapped the Cloudsync app on her phone. *Now I have somewhere to go...* She smiled as the app synced into her online game-lens account with the slogan: *Techsync Takes You There!* As the words vanished from the screen she quickly placed an audio plug into each ear and waited for the NAR - Net Access Response. Moments later a Cloud gateway appeared over the corneal data-lens - a swirling of lines coalescing into two metal gates opening into a PAP - Profile Adaptive Platform. *Online access portal - Anonymity guaranteed!* She blinked to select a Cloud avatar. *Who will I be today?* The screen displayed an assortment of human avatars categorised by genotype, occupation and cultural ethnicity. She frowned. *Black or white? Nope... Asian...* She sighed. *Stick with your type Alice...* A quick scan of occupations is reduced to three favourites: *Writer, movie star, or photographer...* She studied the avatars briefly before settling on an Asian photography student: a petite young girl with long dark hair and wide-brown eyes. *It could be me...* She smiled as the image posed for selection. *Low-cut short floral summer dress...teasing but tasteful...white sandals...* She blinked to select the avatar and upload to her PAP. *All done...* Finally she lay back on her bed and closed her eyes. *Cloud Dancing time...* Moments later she is immersed in the Cloud Community Cybersync - a startling transformation from her everyday humdrum existence.

  After a brief sense of duality she looked out through artificial eyes upon a universe of infinite possibilities: sunny blue skies touched by white whisper clouds drifting above an ever-expanding artificial landscape. *Augmented reality...* She took a moment to study the various Cloud Communities - floating orbs of light displaying individual community ID tags: *Language-Exchange... Movie Buff... Sci-Fi Fringe... Poetry and Painting... Travelogue... Adult Zone... Romdate... Space Explores... Club Cantina... Hub Haven... Beachcombers... Family Fun...*

*Kids Zone...* She swept the tags away with a single blink and chose the *Find-a-Pal* Cloud. *Please be online...* Moments later the landscape shifted spatial perspective to reveal a city hugging the coastline - a place of singles bars, night clubs, restaurants, museums, art galleries, gardens and movie theatres. *Glistening permiglass towers reaching towards an artificial sky...*Words flowed across her data-lens: *Need a new friend? Visit the city of New Oasis - Part of the Find-a-Pal Cloud Community...* Laid out in the traditional grid pattern, the city is a tactile responsive 3D/4K virtual environment based upon an adaptive sequential algorithm - it was also one of the best ways to meet foreigners. She blinked twice to initiate Global Roaming Eyesync - her avatar materialised in a downtown city street. She stepped back from the curb to survey the scene: *Slow-moving traffic and crowded shops playing host to Techsync avatars...* The Techsync platform allowed for predictive bodily movement and causal narrative initiation based upon presumptive movements and vocal inclination; but it was a steep learning curve. Facial integration was achieved via a tactile-neural response net incorporated into the PAP and synced to the corneal data-lens. Her own voice was synced to the mouth of the avatar via TVA - Tactile Vocal Assimilation. But the ability to control fluidic motion within an augmented artificial environment was a complex process - fortunately Alice was an expert. A quick scan of the active registry revealed a familiar name: *Mark13UK...* She smiled. *Perfect...* The Cloud city of New Oasis was an amalgamation of several real-world cities - during her previous visits she had climbed the Eiffel Tower, walked the hallways of the British Museum, watched a Broadway play and met new friends in a Taipei bar - including Mark13UK. *The British guy...* He had portrayed himself as a writer struggling to finish his latest novel. But it paid to be cautious - by its very nature *Find-a-Pal* was based upon anonymity and a certain amount of deception. *He could be anyone...even a girl...* But the mystery was all part of the experience. She adjusted her audio plugs before setting off along a crowded sidewalk. *So many avatars...* The rapid expansion of Cloud communities was perhaps a sad reflection upon the harsh realities of modern life. *All the lonely people...hiding from the real world...* She sighed. *Just like me...* She quickly made her way towards the coffee house on Central Boulevard - a small establishment favoured by so-called artists and other free-thinking individuals. She suspected that more than a few of the customers were real-life dissidents disseminating a variety of radical agendas. *Dark Cloud rebels hiding behind their avatars...* Suddenly she bumped into a lamppost. *Diu!* She recalled a popular adage among Cloud Dancers: *walking inside an augmented world was like walking blindfolded through a forest...* One mistimed blink and your avatar could walk straight into a wall, or worse, into fast moving traffic. Of course death inside a Cloud meant nothing more than resetting your PAP, but it was both annoying and time consuming. She finally arrived at a pedestrian crossing and waited patiently for the green light. Most of the cars were part of the New Oasis scenario, but a lot of people liked to drive cars inside the Cloud. *Drive fast and furious...* She smiled as she crossed the street amidst a small group of fellow avatars. One glance at their faces revealed a wide variety of ethnicity - but it was all an illusion. *No one in the Cloud is who they say they are...*

**Cup of Joe Coffee House - New Oasis**

A room of wooden tables and chairs bathed in the soft glow of wall lights casting shadows upon a long serving counter manned by two female Techsync avatars. Framed movie posters share the walls with glaring examples of avant-garde paintings- the faces of well known politicians morphed into industrial landscapes - eyes peeking out from soot-ravished chimney stacks overlooking an urban wasteland of neglected homes and dimly-lit streets. The room had a rebellious ambience fostered by the Techsync programmers to attract the fringe elements within the Cloud Community. *They definitely have an agenda...* The illusion of a busy coffee house served to unite disparate souls seeking companionship beyond a world of chaos and confusion.

Alice surveyed the room carefully. *It's busy...* A rapid double blink revealed several ACP's - Active Conversation Portals. She could interject or wait to be invited, but she was in no mood for a group chat - she was here to find just one avatar. It didn't take her long to notice the handsome young man sitting at a window table. *It's him!* She walked over and asked:

"Mark?"

Mark looked up and replied: "Hi there... It's Alice right?"

Alice smiled and replied: "You remembered..."

Mark replied: "Of course...please, won't you join me?"

Alice sat down in the proffered chair and said: "Thank you..."

Mark smiled and said: "You look very pretty today..."

Alice lowered her eyes slightly and said: "It's just my avatar."

Mark continued: "Yes, but an avatar is a reflection of our true personality."

Alice looked up and said: "Only if the avatar is genuine...some people hide behind the illusion."

Mark's avatar brushed sandy hair from his eyes and said: "I suppose that's true..."

Alice changed the subject and asked: "Do you come here often?"

Mark replied: "Actually no..." He paused before continuing: "But you said you liked this place..."

Alice looked around and said: "I do..." She paused before asking: "You wanted to see me again?"

Mark replied: "Yes... We had such an interesting talk last time."

Alice smiled slightly and said: "Yes, I enjoyed it... Who knew that sashimi had a history?"

Mark asked: "Was I that boring?"

Alice replied: "Of course not..." She quickly added: "I like raw fish..."

Mark fell silent before announcing: "I checked the Taipei bar first..."

Alice straightened her avatar dress before replying: "I only go there on a Saturday night...better crowd..."

Mark nodded slightly and said: "I was busy last night..."

Alice said: "Actually you didn't miss much..."

Mark looked around and asked: "So why this place?"

Alice replied: "I like the atmosphere..." She looked towards the other customers and continued: "Artists, poets, photographers..."

Mark gave a slight smile and said: "And you are a photographer, right?"

Alice lowered her eyes slightly and replied: "That's right." She looked up and asked: "Do you roam the Cloud often?"

Mark replied: "Only when I have time..."

Alice said: "Oh yes, you are a writer..."

Mark replied: "Aspiring writer..."

Alice asked: "You are not published?"

Mark sat back and replied: "Just one book of poetry; but I have a novel doing the rounds right now..."

Alice asked: "Can you tell me what it is about?"

Mark's avatar flickered briefly.

Alice smiled slightly. *He just blushed in the real-world...*

Mark replied: "It's a sort of romance..."

Alice asked curiously: "Sort of romance?"

Mark explained: "It's about a boy and a girl who meet in the Cloud and fall in love..."

Lying on her bed Alice felt her own face flush. She said: "Wow...it sounds interesting... Can you tell me more?"

Mark continued: "Well basically I wanted to show that love can transcend the anonymity of the Cloud. It doesn't really matter what we look like in the real world, because in here we are reduced to our raw personalities..."

Alice asked: "What do you mean by that?"

Mark replied: "I mean that we can express our true feelings without fear of embarrassment..." He smiled slightly before adding: "We hide behind our avatars."

Alice nodded slightly and said: "I think I understand... In the Cloud we don't judge a book by its cover."

Mark smiled and said: "Exactly. Because in here the cover is an illusion, so we can actually say what we think without fear of condemnation."

Alice spoke in a low voice: "And without fear of judgement..."

Mark gestured to the artificial sky and said: "Out there we conform to social and cultural expectations. But inside the Cloud we can be whoever we want..."

Alice smiled slightly and said: "And even fall in love..."

Mark returned the smile and said: "That's right..."

Alice asked: "But would that love survive out there in the real world?"

Mark replied: "I think it would..."

Alice smiled slightly and said: "Love transcending the augmentted barrier."

Mark returned the smile and said: "The essence of my book..."

They fell silent briefly until Alice said: "I wish you luck with the book."

Mark smiled and replied: "Thank you."

Alice added: "I would definitely buy it."

Mark gave a warm smile and replied: "You are very kind."

Alice suddenly changed the subject: "Where do you live in the UK?"

Mark replied: "London. But I'm originally from York, up north..." He paused before asking: "How about you?"

Alice replied: "Hong Kong."

Mark asked: "Is that where you studied photography?"

Alice hesitated before replying: "That's right..."

Mark asked: "Can you upload some of your work to my sync account?"

Alice felt her avatar lose digital cohesion before she replied: "Maybe...look I have to get going..."

Mark asked: "So soon?"

Alice replied as she stood up: "I am meeting my parents for Sunday lunch..."

Mark stood up and asked: "Can I see you again?"

Alice said: "Sure..."

Mark asked: "Are you online later?"

Alice started to walk away as she replied: "Probably not...maybe tomorrow..."

Mark said: "Okay...hope to see you then..."

Alice smiled slightly and said: "Okay...bye..."

As soon as she exited the coffee house Alice blinked rapidly to exit her PAP. *Diu!* She opened her eyes onto her bedroom ceiling. *Why did I say photographer? How can I upload non-existent photos?* She turned to see her uniform hanging on the door. *I lied because I am ashamed of being a waitress...* She brushed hair from her face and sighed heavily. *I hate my life...*

## Cup of Joe Coffee House - New Oasis

Mark13UK was about to exit his PAP when he was alerted to a coded comsync: *Access code 001...* He quickly synced his avatar into voice-com and replied in a low voice:

"Yes sir?"

The familiar voice of Assistant Director Richard Fielding came online:

"Status?"

Mark glanced towards the other customers and replied:

"I have made contact with Alice Sòng."

An irritated Fielding said: "She is not the designated target."

Mark countered: "Befriending Miss Sòng allows me to gain access to the designated target. A direct approach might arouse suspicions."

There was a short pause before Fielding said: "Just be aware of the time factor; we are not the only ones on the trail of the Jiàngshēng Project."

Mark asked: "Synthtech?"

Fielding replied: "One of their agents has been identified in Beijing; they may already have people in Hong Kong."

Mark considered this and said: "I thought the Americans were ahead of the Chinese..."

Fielding replied: "That cannot be confirmed. We can only assume that they are aware of the security breach."

Mark asked: "And they are definitely not the source of the hack?"

Fielding replied: "No. It was a Singapore exit portal using mirror bounce-back protocols..."

Mark considered this and said: "The portal could be anywhere..."

Fielding said: "Exactly..."

Mark looked around the coffee house and said: "Beijing should be all over the designated target...but I see no sign of them..."

Fielding replied: "They might not even be aware of her existence. Professor Leung has omitted all reference to the first subject."

A surprised Mark said: "Your Intel is remarkably accurate..."

Fielding replied: "We have a source very close to the Professor; but right now the Security Ministry are not the ones you need to worry about..."

Mark frowned and said: "Biogen..."

Fielding continued: "All clues lead to their involvement."

Mark replied: "They will protect their investment..."

Fielding replied soberly: "With extreme prejudice; so tread carefully."

Mark replied: "I am aware of the risks. Now if there is nothing else..."

Fielding replied: "I will await your next report."

As the comsync fell silent Mark blinked to exit his PAP. He was immediately aware of city sounds arriving inside his hotel room. *Back to reality...* He sat up and removed both data-lenses and audio plugs before looking towards the single window. *Sunny Sunday morning...* A ping from his phone confirmed the invasive datasync into the phone belonging to Alice Sòng. *The photographer is actually a waitress...* He smiled as he walked over to the window and opened the blinds. Now he could see the vast city hugging the shoreline of the island. But much closer still a single illuminated building dominated the street below. *The Hub Cybersync Restaurant...* He sighed heavily. *She is so close...*

# The Man from the Ministry

*Despite our ignorance in religious matters, we felt remarkable Godlike at the inception of the Jiàngshēng Project..."*
*Professor Leung Huo PhD (Molecular Biology)*

**08:20 - Monday April 19th - 2028 - Ministry of Science and Technology of the People's Republic of China - Beijing, China.**

Six levels below the bustling traffic of Fuxing Road a seemingly endless corridor of mottled grey walls leads directly to Laboratory No. 1. A set of permiglass doors are illuminated by an ingrained warning sign: Authorised Personnel Only.

Professor Leung Huo stopped in front of the laboratory doors and sighed wearily. His reflection revealed an anxious face beneath thick black hair touched with strands of grey. A faint glistening of his brown eyes confirmed an active set of data-lenses, whilst a wide nose perched over thick lips betrayed his Mongolian ancestry. A loose-fitting lab coat seemed to hang from his slightly hunched shoulders as he paused outside the doors. He was reluctant to stand in front of the retinal scanner. *They are waiting for me...* During breakfast a brief message from his assistant had arrived upon his corneal data-lens:

*"Professor, you are ordered to the lab... Ting Mai."*

Beyond the doors several members of the State Security Ministry were waiting to discuss the recent security breach. *They are here to assign blame...* His immediate reaction had been to call Rén Du at Biogen. *But what could he do?* He sighed heavily. *I have to deal with this myself...* He straightened his lab coat before stepping in front of the scanner. A brief flash of light confirmed his identity as the doors parted to reveal the enormous Laboratory No. 1.

He took a moment to survey his pride and joy. *The future begins here...*

Beneath a grey-stone ceiling a frosted permiglass wall divided the laboratory into two sections - data-analysis administration and controlled sterile environment. To the left, a bank of computer consoles flickered beneath several rows of bio-data screens. A small office complete with canteen annex, was located in the far corner. Access to the sterile environment on the right was through an airtight chamber set in the centre of the dividing wall behind thick steel doors. Next to the airlock a single observation window revealed a white tiled room containing three steel maturation tanks placed beneath an array of data-screens and biomed scanners. Leung glanced at the latest data-skim analysis logs: *Cerebral interface proactive data-sync... Nucleic acid conversion levels proactive... Protein and carbohydrate levels proactive... Dendritic growth rate 22%... Biopolymer conversion rate 18%... Polynucleotide levels proactive... Branched DNA sequentials proactive... Sequential genomic mutation confirmed... Adenine... Thymine... Cytosine... Phosphates and hydrogen bonds... All within acceptable levels...* He smiled with satisfaction. *The soup of augmented life...*

A grim-faced Ting Mai joined him and announced:

"Zǎoshang hǎo Professor... There are three men waiting for you in your office..."

Ting Mai was a delicate fawn of a girl in a white lab coat - she wore her long black hair tied up at the back to reveal an oval shaped face with olive smooth skin, complimented by a perfectly shaped nose beneath bright brown eyes and a charming, timid smile. But now her eyes betrayed her fears as she gestured towards the office.

Leung smiled warmly and replied: "It is okay Mai..." He leaned closer and asked: "Did you speak to our friend in Shanghai?"

Mai whispered: "Yes."

Leung asked: "Can she help us?"

Mai replied: "She wants to speak to you..."

Leung frowned and said: "I will call her later..."

Mai said: "I hope she can retrieve the data before it is sold to the highest bidder."

Leung looked towards his office and said: "Go about your duties... I will join you shortly."

Mai bowed slightly before turning towards the decontamination chamber.

Leung found his small office occupied by three men wearing identical black business suits. They seemed typical of their type - austere facial features combined with a stern military-style countenance. But only one face bore a hint of recognition - Section Leader Han Mang of the State Security Ministry. *Short black hair combed neatly to one side...slight scar upper lip...* A network of spider-thread lines around his eyes and a slim nose above thin lips and narrow chin created a hawk-like appearance.

Leung said: "Nǐmen hǎo..."

Han looked up and said: "Nín hǎo Professor..."

Leung continued: "I apologise for keeping you waiting..."

Han replied: "No matter..." He looked beyond the door and continued: "There is much we need to discuss."

Leung nodded slightly and said: "The security breach..."

Han replied sternly: "The failure to maintain security within a top secret government project is no small matter. We are here to examine your personnel records and to interrogate your staff."

Leung stepped behind his desk and replied: "Of course... I will make everything available to you."

Han stared directly at Leung and continued: "I have placed this facility on lockdown for the duration of the inspection."

Leung nodded slightly and said: "I understand."

Han asked: "Have you investigated the breach yourself?"

Leung cleared his throat and replied: "I have determined that our database was accessed by an exterior portal..."

Han stepped closer and said: "We are aware of the origin of the breach. The access portal has been tracked to Singapore. But this does not explain how the thieves were able to isolate specific data logs within your files. They knew exactly where to look and exactly which files to steal; this leads me to believe that they had inside help."

Leung straightened his lab coat before replying: "I trust my staff implicitly. I can assure you that none of them are involved in this matter."

Han replied soberly: "Your assurance is duly noted Professor; and now I would like a tour of your facilities."

Leung gestured to the door and replied: "Of course. This way gentlemen..."

Han asked: "How many staff do you employ within the laboratory?"

Leung led the way as he replied:

"I have one personal assistant, six lab assistants and two dozen data-analysis technicians."

Han looked towards the bank of computers and asked: "Are they on duty now?"

Leung replied: "Only my assistant Ting Mai...the others will arrive shortly."

Han said: "We will need to speak to them..."

Leung tapped the airlock access pad and replied: "Of course..."

Han stepped closer to the steel door and asked: "We go through here?"

Leung replied: "We access the sterile room through a decontamination chamber..."

Han studied a list of decontamination protocols and asked: "Facial masks?"

Leung swung the door open and replied: "The maturation process requires zero contamination."

Han turned to his colleagues and ordered: "Begin the interviews as soon as the others arrive."

One of the men nodded slightly and replied: "Very good sir."

Leung interjected: "You can use my office..."

Han added: "And upload the results to my portal."

The nearest man replied: "Yes sir."

Leung gestured with one hand: "After you..."

Han entered the chamber and asked: "What is that smell?"

Leung replied as he closed the door: "Steripol..." He smiled slightly before adding: "My own concoction."

Han wiped his nose with a handkerchief and asked: "What does it do?"

Leung passed a mask to Han as he replied: "It is an airborne additive..." He secured his own mask before adding: "An additional precaution against exterior contamination."

Han sniffed and asked: "Is it part of the filtration system?"

Leung secured his face mask and replied: "Yes."

Han peered through a small window into the sterile room and asked:

"You have produced only one test subject?"

Leung frowned as he replied: "Only one survived the implantation process..."

Han said: "Most unfortunate."

Leung replied: "Fortunately the survivor is an ideal template for further experiments."

Han secured his mask at the back of his head and said: "There will be no further experiments until my investigation is concluded."

Leung's eyes widened as he protested: "But we are at a critical stage... I must be allowed to proceed to the next level..."

Han replied firmly: "Until we determine the identity of the infiltrators this facility will remain on lockdown. If you wish to protest you can discuss your objections with the Minister himself."

Leung lowered his eyes and said: "There will be no protest..."

Han looked up at the ceiling and asked: "What happens now?"

Leung tapped a control panel as he replied: "I will initiate decontamination."

Both men were suddenly enveloped by a fine shower of vapour. Leung announced:

"Liquid steripol...it dries on contact."

Han studied his suit and said: "You take your precautions seriously Professor..."

Leung turned to access the second door and said: "This way..."

The door opened to reveal a white-tiled room bathed in the soft glow of overhead lighting. Han noted three large steel tanks placed beneath an array of data-screens and biomed scanners. Sitting at a nearby desk a solitary worker looked up with a timid smile.

Leung made the introductions: "This is my personal assistant Ting Mai."

Mai stood up abruptly and bowed before saying: "Nín hǎo..."

Han ignored social etiquette and asked: "You are alone in here?"

Mai glanced towards tank number three and replied: "No sir..."

Han looked around the room and asked: "No?"

Leung interjected: "Actually, Mai is referring to our test subject..."

Han ordered: "Show me..."

Leung led the way as he explained: "Number three is currently in bio-stasis until we can begin phase two..."

Han asked: "Bio-stasis?"

Leung replied: "Medically induced coma..."

Mai joined them and said: "I have confirmed proactive biostats..."

Leung smiled through his mask and said: "Excellent work Mai..."

Han stepped onto a raised platform and looked into the tank. He was shocked to see a naked young man floating serenely in some type of clear gelatinous liquid. A network of fine metallic tendrils connected his shaved head to an overhead biomed scanner - it beeped each time the man exhaled through tubes inserted into his nose and mouth. Along both arms and legs a series of bio-pads synced diagnostics to the data-analysis interface above the tank. The subject displayed typical Asian features and appeared to be in his early twenties. Leaning closer Han noted a constant flickering of closed eyelids and a slight tremor to the hands and feet. Finally he asked:

"Is he aware of his surroundings?"

Leung studied the young man and replied proudly:

"He has spatial awareness perception via the implants, but his higher reasoning functions are dormant during bio-stasis."

Han asked: "And the flickering eyelids?"

Mai stepped closer and replied: "He is dreaming..."

Han asked wryly: "Of electric sheep?"

A confused Leung asked: "Excuse me?"

Han replied: "Never mind..."

Mai recognised the reference and smiled slightly.

Han looked into the tank and said: "I read his file..." He paused before asking: "He actually volunteered for this project?"

Leung gave a proud smile and replied: "Guan Lu is an idealistic young man...ready to embrace the future..."

Han commented: "And yet now he is simply number three..."

Leung sighed as replied: "Clinical detachment is a vital part of our work."

Han nodded slightly and said: "Because your first two subjects died..."

Leung replied soberly: "Their brains rejected the implantations... most unfortunate..."

Han looked towards the two empty tanks and asked: "Did you preserve the bodies?"

Leung hesitated before replying: "Autopsies confirmed a cerebral haemorrhage as the cause of death. Both subjects were subsequently incinerated as per standard protocols."

Han asked: "And the implants were to blame?"

Leung replied: "Yes. Despite the initial success of the procedure, retrograde effusion led to intracranial haemorrhage."

Han asked: "What exactly are these implants?"

Leung looked into the tank and explained: "Number three has been implanted with a brain-computer interface to augment the visual cortex..." He tapped an overhead data-screen as he continued: "This boosts his spatial visualization and manipulation capabilities." He studied the screen before continuing: "There are also secondary augmentations which focus on other portions of the sensory cortex, like tactile cortex and auditory cortex. The combined augmentation process is controlled via Cybersync."

Han fell silent briefly before asking: "Can these implants be accessed by an exterior portal?"

Leung cleared his throat before replying: "We have countermeasures in place to prevent Cybersync infiltration."

Han asked: "Countermeasures?"

Leung glanced towards Ting Mai before replying: "If the cerebral processor in his brain detects infiltration it will initiate a shutdown procedure."

Han asked: "What does that mean exactly?"

But it was Ting Mai who replied: "The interface will kill him..."

Leung explained: "It will initiate a bio-neural cascade effect resulting in rapid cerebral oedema..." He paused before adding soberly: "Death will be instant..."

Ting Mai interjected quietly: "But not entirely painless..."

Han commented: "Your countermeasures seem a little terminal considering our investment in this project."

Leung replied: "A shutdown procedure will only occur if data is being accessed by a subversive portal. Death is not inevitable."

Ting Mai added: "The neural interface will sift for mirror portals to determine access validity prior to initiating a terminal countermeasure. If validity is confirmed access will be granted."

Han studied Guan Lu and asked: "Is he modified at the genetic level?"

Leung looked into the tank and replied: "Not entirely. We have introduced robotic nanites to augment his immune system and we have adapted his genomic markers to enhance neurotransmission and facilitate the release of neurons. The reactionary process of the amygdala will increase the production of adrenaline to complete the process." He studied the floating body as he continued: "It is not entirely genetic modification but his genomic markers will be used as a bio-template to directly manipulate subsequent genomes using biotechnology."

Ting Mai interjected: "The genetic makeup of his cells, including the transfer of genes within and across augmentation boundaries, has already been manipulated to produce a mutated endogenous gene sequence."

Leung smiled proudly and continued: "The next step will be to introduce bio-augmentation of the pre-frontal cortex invitro. The implantation of genomiclly enhanced embryonic nucleotides will enhance the way each subject combines perceptual data to form new concepts. There will be rapid foetal development throughout the augmentation process." He paused to study the floating body before continuing: "The end result will be cognitive super-intelligence...people who can perform apparently impossible intellectual feats."

Han considered this before asking: "Can such people be controlled?"

Leung asked: "Controlled?"

Han stared into the tank and replied: "People with such advantages could prove to be a liability to the security of the state."

Leung frowned and said: "I am not sure what you mean..."

Han looked up and continued: "An augmented brain could present a threat to social stability and disturb the status quo. It might become necessary to terminate such a threat before it becomes a problem."

An indignant Leung said: "My project has been sanctioned by the President himself..."

Han replied with a question: "But is the President aware of the risks?"

Leung replied firmly: "I have been ordered to pursue this project to its final conclusion, regardless of any perceived threat to the status quo."

Han asked: "And what is its final conclusion professor Leung?"

Leung replied: "A human genotype capable of withstanding long-term spaceflight both physically and mentally."

Han considered this and asked: "And what about their actions here on Earth?"

Leung replied: "I can assure you that they would not be a problem..."

Han replied ominously: "Once again professor, your assurance is noted..."

Leung cleared his throat and said: "An augmented human can only be an advantage to the state." He studied the face of the man in the tank and added: "His descendants will create the first offworld colony...plant our national flag upon some far distant world..."

Han asked: "But would his descendants still be human?"

Leung replied: "Of course...the basic human genome will remain intact."

Han considered this and asked: "Have you considered the psychological aspects of so-called super-intelligence?"

Leung asked: "Can you be more specific?"

Han replied: "There is a thin line between a high IQ and insanity."

Leung nodded slightly and replied: "We have analysed a variety of scenarios for mental instability. Obviously we have considered the possibility that the most salient side effects could be insanity. The human brain is an extremely fine-tuned and calibrated machine. Most perturbations to this tuning qualify as what we would consider psychologically unbalanced. Augmentation, by its very nature carries an invasive risk to cortical equilibrium. But there are many different types of insanity, far more than there are types of sanity." He looked into the tank as he continued: "We will fine tune our subjects towards a more balanced psychological state..." He looked up and added: "We must allow for a period of mental adjustment...a recalibration of the enhanced thinking processes. But I see no significant threat..."

Han turned to Ting Mai and asked: "Do you have an opinion of this matter?"

Ting Mai glanced at Leung before replying:

"There may be some side-effects...."

Han asked: "What type of side-effects?"

Ting Mai replied truthfully: "Even in the case of perfect sanity, side effects might include seizures, information overload, and possibly feelings of egomania or extreme alienation. Smart people tend to feel comparatively more alienated in the world, and for a being smarter than everyone, the effect would be greatly amplified. There could be a clean empathy break that leads to psychopathy."

Leung interjected: "But you must understand that our subjects will be under constant supervision, existing within a controlled environment."

Han sighed and said: "And yet the threat remains..."

Leung replied: "It is within acceptable parameters."

Han countered: "The problem is that you are dealing with human beings, and human beings are flawed. People with enhanced intelligence could still have a merely human-level morality, leveraging their vast intellects for hedonistic or even genocidal purposes."

Leung replied: "We are creating servants not masters."

Han smiled slightly and said: "If history has taught us anything it is that servants inevitably seek to become masters." He stepped off the platform and asked: "Shall we continue with the tour?"

Leung replied in a low voice: "By all means...this way..."

# State Security Ministry - Archival Phone Intercept Edit: 042028/LH/HL - Transcript upload - SL Han Mang.

LH: "My apologies for calling so early..."
HL: "I have been awake for some time."
LH: "Trouble sleeping?"
HL: "Four hours sleep is sufficient."
LH: "Remarkable..."

**- Intercept Break -**

HL: "Yes... Mia told me about the leak..."
LH: "Can you help us?"
HL: "I do not see how..."
LH: "You can initiate a cerebral Cybersync and search the Dark Cloud...there might be a way to identify the infiltration point."
HL: "Why is that so important? Am I mentioned in those files?"
LH: "I erased all references to your continued survival..."
HL: "But?"
LH: "But I cannot guarantee the exact content of the stolen files... there may be references to your prognosis. We need to delete the files before they are sold to the highest bidder."
HL: "There may be a way..."
LH: "To locate them?"
HL: "Every portal leaves a digital signature... I would need to sift for specific algorithmic potential in order to identify an encrypted portal access."
LH: "Then please try...before the authorities identify the Cloud portal. You must..."

**- Unintelligible -**

HL: "But what if the authorities find out about me?"
LH: "They will not find out. As far as the government is concerned Guan Lu is the sole survivor of the Jiàngshēng Project."
HL: "But they will want to see results for their investment..."

LH: "And they will see Guan Lu... Please...stop worrying...you are safe now."

HL: "Do not delude yourself Professor... I will never be safe; if they even get a hint of my existence I am finished."

LH: "Lin listen to me, if you follow the protocols they will never suspect anything..."

HL: "How can I follow the protocols? Have you any idea what it is like to live like this? My brain is using autonomous mechanisms every single day... I instantly know the chemical composition of the food I eat... I analyse the air I breathe... I predict interpersonal reactions to external stimuli and produce an instant tactical threat assessment..."

   **- Unintelligible -**

HL: "...today I pulled the handle off my car door because I forgot how strong I am now..."

LH: "Lin... I told you that there would be a period of adjustment. Please be patient, it will take time for you to assimilate your new abilities. You have been given a second-chance at life...so try to adapt to the situation; but please be circumspect in your actions...you must not draw unwanted attention to yourself."

   **- Intercept Break -**

LH: "Yes... Agents from the Ministry arrived yesterday; they are questioning my team..."

HL: "Will they tell them the truth?"

HL: "The leak has nothing to do with you. They will only be questioned about the external access...you have nothing to fear from the investigation."

HL: "I wish I had your confidence..."

   **- Intercept Break -**

LH: "Of course I regret the loss of Cho Ming. But the overall experiment was a success; it is only a matter of time before we can begin phase two."

HL: "Ming was only nineteen..."

LH: "He accepted the risks...you all did."

   **- Intercept Break -**

37

| | |
|---|---|
| HL: | "Why did you call it the Jiàngshēng Project?" |
| LH | "Is it not obvious? The arrival of a newborn must be recognised. |
| HL: | "But the term denotes a religious factor...surely that is not your intention?" |
| LH: | "Can you deny your rebirth? When you came to me you were dying...now you are reborn. That in itself is miraculous." |
| | **- External Sounds -** |
| HL: | "Professor I have to go, there is someone at the door... I will call you again tomorrow." |
| LH: | "Very well...take care... Zàijiàn Lin..." |
| HL: | "Zàijiàn Professor." |

**SSM/HM File: Beijing 042028/LH/HL**

# The Dark Cloud

*'The Cloud Community offers the illusion of safety, it is easy to forget the vulnerability of reality.'*
Sūn Yu

**23:58 - Sunday April 25th - 2028 - The Blue Lounge - Wo Chu Lane - Hong Kong**

The night is resisted with mute indifference by the illuminated towers of Central Hong Kong. A warm wind stirs raindrops from sultry clouds hugging the Peak with a melancholy embrace. In the city that never sleeps the bars and clubs play host to late night revellers shuffling along streets resounding to the sounds of music merging into traffic rumbling along the main roads. Somewhere in the heart of the metropolis a narrow lane of brick walls is bespeckled with fading advertisements and shuttered stalls abandoned and abused by time. Sitting within a network of narrow alleys the Blue Lounge hides its secrets in plain sight - *Beers, Wines, Cybersync...* But behind the facade the true product is open to members only - direct access to the Dark Cloud Community - an underground network of activists and sexual deviants who hide their online activities from the authorities.

According to his Techsync online profile Mong Gao is a twenty two year old post-graduate student currently taking a gap year before starting a Masters Degree in Digital Sciences. But just like the Blue Lounge, his Cloud profile revealed little of the truth behind the young man from Shenzhen. On his fourteenth birthday his uncle Lei had introduced him to the illegal world of the Ginza Triad - a profitable alliance of the Japanese Ginsho Yakuza and the Hong Kong Zhāng Triad. At the age of sixteen he was operating an elaborate phishing scheme in his hometown. By the age of nineteen he was earning thousands of dollars running drugs for the Triad. Finally, at the age of twenty one, he was formally inducted into the Triad as a soldier with the title 49. But it took another year before he gained complete control over all Ginza Dark Cloud activities. - a living conduit to the digital universe of illegal pornography and graphic virtual-reality content.

Gao arrived in front of a blue door touched by raindrops glistening beneath an illuminated 'Closed' sign. A glass door panel reflected a pensive face framed by jet black hair hanging low over brown seeking eyes. He took a moment to confirm that he was not being followed before knocking twice. Moments later the door was opened by a familiar brutish face - the hulking Jon Lau - bouncer, barman and Ginza enforcer. Gao smiled at the imposing sight. *Bald head...round pock-marked face above thick neck adorned with tattoos peeking out from a white vest bulging from muscles pumped with steroids...worst doorman ever...*

A scowling Lau grumbled: "You are late..."

Gao stepped inside and replied: "It's never too late Jonny boy..."

Lau closed the door and said: "Just go on through to the back...they are waiting for you..."

Gao unzipped his leather jacket and asked: "Who did they send this time?"

Lau replied as he locked the door: "No one you expected..."

Gao looked around the deserted bar area and asked: "What do you mean?"

Lau replied with a slight smile: "You will see..."

Gao asked: "My Uncle?"

Lau replied: "No... The Boss is here."

Gao's eyes widened as he asked: "Poppa Jo?"

Lau walked towards the bar and replied: "He wants to look at your accounts."

Gao joined Lau and said: "But he never comes here..."

Lau reached for a cloth and said: "He is here now."

Gao stared at the door beyond the bar and asked: "But why? My books were scanned last month..."

Lau began to wipe glasses as he replied: "None of my business."

Gao brushed a hand through long wet hair and said: "Revenue will pick up again...it always does..."

Lau sighed and said: "Just go through to the back room..."

Gao nodded slightly and said: "Okay..."

As Gao walked away Lau added: "See you around kid..."

Gao stepped in front of the iris scanner as he replied: "Sure..."

Moments later the door slid aside to reveal a blue carpeted room illuminated by subdued wall-lights casting shadows off elaborate wall murals depicting a variety of stylised erotica. The Private Lounge was equipped with thirty black leather recliners placed beneath Cybersync consoles. Someone had placed an upholstered armchair in front of a small bar at the far end of the room - it was currently occupied by Poppa Jo Yáng - the sixty five year old boss of the Hong Kong chapter of the Ginza Triad. The old man had a fringe of grey-white hair around his balding, mottled scalp. Two yellowed eyes peered out from a wizened face perched predator-like above two slightly-hunched shoulders. He had the resigned look of one who accepts the brutal nature of his life with mute indifference. His choice of clothing - grey cardigan, soft blue jogging trousers and black gym shoes - belied the power and the authority behind the calm exterior.

Gao's eyes were drawn to the two men standing on either side of the chair. *Ricky Li and Sal Cho...enforcers...* They wore identical black business suits, complete with white shirts and black ties. Each sported short, cropped black hair combed neatly to one side. Despite his limited experience Gao was well aware of their gruesome reputation - between them they were responsible for more than fifty sanctioned terminations. He forced a smile and said:

"Poppa Jo...so very good to see you..."

Ricky Li placed a barstool in front of his boss and ordered: "Sit."

As he sat down Gao asked: "Is there a problem?"

Yáng scratched his heavily lined face and asked: "How is business lately?"

Gao gestured to the recliners as he replied: "We don't always get a full house, but we have our regulars."

Yáng nodded slightly and asked: "How many times a week?"

Gao replied: "We open round-the-clock except Sunday's"

Yáng asked: "Why close today?"

Gao replied: "We need to re-set encryption protocols once a week to avoid exterior tracking..." He paused before adding: "And of course we transfer funds into the central account every Sunday morning."

Yáng looked towards the recliners and asked: "You only cater for thirty customers...?"

Gao cleared his throat before saying: "We have limited upload capacity..."

Yáng sniffed and said: "The Doyin provides fifty access portals...round-the-clock."

Gao shuffled in his seat and said: "But with respect, the Doyin Bar has twice the floor space, and the Mong Kok district tends to have a more deviant clientele."

Yáng looked towards the recliners and asked: "What is the trend these days?"

Gao replied: "The usual... Porn... Psycho thrills... S & M... Snuff... Antisocial activists..."

Yáng ordered: "Explain the process..."

Gao tensed as he asked: "The process?"

Yáng replied: "How do perverts access the Dark Cloud?"

Gao cleared his throat before replying: "They enter the Cloud via a Profile Adaptive Platform synced to their data-lenses. Once Cybersync is confirmed a Net Access Response allows them to roam anywhere within the Dark Cloud. They can choose to experience any number of virtual-reality scenarios."

Yáng asked: "How do you screen members?"

Gao replied: "We confirm ID via iris scan, digital search and full background check."

Yáng considered this before asking: "So you are secure?"

Gao replied: "Within the limits of our current technology we are totally secure."

Yáng asked: "How do we get paid?"

Gao replied: "Our customers use coded online accounts to purchase an access portal from one of my people. We deduct fees based upon their CRD stats."

Yáng asked: "CRD stats?"

Gao explained: "Cloud Roaming Datatag Statistics. It's how we keep track of each customer as they explore the virtual environment via Cybersync. We supply adaptive data-lenses and a comfortable environment." He smiled slightly before adding: "And tissues of course..."

Yáng wiped his nose with the back of his hand before asking: "Why do they come here? Can't they do the same thing at home?"

Gao replied: "They can if they have the technology, the expertise and the ability to avoid the Cyber cops." He saw confusion on Yáng's face and continued: "We offer a triple-cipher firewall and mirror-access portals. Our customers roam the Dark Cloud without fear of external detection."

Yáng considered this and asked:

"How much do you charge?"

Gao looked surprised as he replied: "Fees are graded according to content and PAP access level. The higher the access level the greater the content experience." *He already knows this...* He looked up at the enforcers. *What is going on here?*

Sal Cho interjected: "And the higher the fees..."

Gao smiled slightly and said: "Exactly."

Yáng sniffed and ordered: "What are your rates?"

Gao felt himself perspiring as he replied: "Basic roaming is five hundred dollars per hour...but a deep level experience can cost up to ten thousand."

Yáng considered this before asking: "What about freelancers? Can they access your portals?"

Gao hesitated slightly before replying: "It might be possible for a determined hacker to breach our firewall, but we actively encourage the online community to abide by our rules."

Yáng asked: "Encourage how?"

Gao replied: "We identify interlopers and track them to a VAP..."

Yáng interjected: "VAP?"

Gao replied: "Virtual Access Portal..."

Yáng nodded slightly and said: "Go on..."

Gao continued: "Once we identify their real-world location they get a visit from one of our field associates..." He paused before continuing: "They tend to cooperate after that..."

Yáng scratched his chin and said: "But the Cloud is not location based...what about foreign intrusion?"

Gao replied: "We use the same tracking protocols to target their online accounts for erasure. It doesn't stop them completely but most of them get the message."

Yáng's eyes narrowed as he asked: "And if these foreigners do not get the message?"

Gao glanced towards the two enforcers and replied: "No one is beyond our reach Poppa Jo..."

Yáng asked: "Can your customers access any Cloud portal?"

Gao replied: "Any portal within the Dark Cloud Community. Encryption protocols prevent access into the outer Net."

Yáng asked: "How secure is portal access?"

Gao replied: "We use multiphasic retinal encrypted uplinks to access the Dark Cloud Portal. Whilst they are online we switch and rotate the encryption codes using multi-portal Cybersync protocols and exit nodes."

Yáng asked: "Can the Dark Cloud be accessed by the authorities?"

Gao replied truthfully: "Actually they access it regularly, but it is impossible to track and locate a specific source code within the Dark Cloud. Multilayer bounce-back protocols mirror PAPS and NARS." He paused before adding: "They can see what is going on but they are powerless to intervene or to stop it."

Yáng asked: "Can they jam the source code via remote intercept?"

Gao replied: "They can and they do. But that only shuts down one access portal. Microseconds later a new portal is created beyond the reach of the initial interception and we are back in business."

Yáng fell silent until eventually he asked: "Is it possible to hide encrypted data within a Cloud environment?"

Gao replied: "Yes, very easily. The Dark Cloud is the ideal location for encrypted data. A large amount of anti-government propaganda begins inside the Dark Cloud community. It the perfect platform for illegal business..."

Yáng asked: "Is there a way to track and identify encrypted data inside the Cloud?"

Gao considered this before replying: "It is possible to sift for specific algorithmic potential in order to identify an encrypted portal access. This would reveal a hidden data-spike within the Cloud environment."

Yáng stared directly at Mong and asked: "Do you have such a skill?"

Gao brushed hair from his eyes and replied: "I could do it...given the time."

Yáng fell silent until finally he asked:

"What do you know of the Jiàngshēng Project?"

Gao frowned as he replied: "I have never heard of it..."

Yáng sat back and continued: "It is a project set up to enhance and adapt the human genome for a specific purpose."

Gao hesitated before asking: "Do you know the purpose?"

Yáng replied: "Long-term spaceflight..."

Gao said: "I had no idea..."

Yáng continued: "The Lunar base is only the first step in Beijing's plans to extend Sino control throughout the solar system. In order to do this they are going to need a new type of astronaut..."

Gao saw the truth and said: "They intend to alter the human genome..."

Yáng replied: "So it would seem..."

Gao asked: "But surely this is nothing new?"

Yáng frowned and replied: "There is a difference between alteration and the creation of a new lifeform."

Gao's eyes widened as he asked: "A new lifeform?"

Yáng sighed and replied: "The manipulation of the DNA matrix to produce enhanced human beings."

Gao considered this and said: "So it might be cheaper to adapt humans than to build spaceships."

Yáng scowled as he replied: "The next generation of astronauts will have little in common with humanity."

Gao asked: "May I ask what that means?"

Yáng replied: "It means Beijing is working on our replacements."

Gao asked: "Surely not?"

Yáng sat back and replied: "Oh it will not happen in our life time, perhaps not for centuries...but a time will come when these enhanced genotypes will supplant the human race..."

Gao considered this before asking: "Forgive me, but what has all of this got to do with me?"

Yáng replied: "The project has been hacked...the entire database has been accessed. We have reason to believe the stolen data is somewhere in the Dark Cloud. I want you to find it and retrieve it."

Gao scratched his chin and asked: "Do you know who stole this data?"

Yáng replied: "The access portal has been traced to Singapore. That is all we know at this time."

Gao asked: "I take it Beijing is already on the trail of this hacker?"

Yáng replied: "Yes. Along with the Americans and several other interested groups. That is why I want you to locate the data first."

Gao asked: "May I ask what you intend to do with this data?"

Yáng wiped his nose and replied: "That is not your concern."

Gao said: "Then I will begin the search immediately."

Yáng struggled to his feet and said: "I want regular updates..."

Gao stood up and bowed as he replied: "Of course..."

Yáng stopped at the door and said: "You might want to tread carefully...the Dark Cloud is no longer so dark."

Gao replied: "I understand."

As the door opened Yáng spoke one more time:

"I hope you do understand, because failure is not an option."

As the door slid closed Gao sat down and tried to slow his breathing. *Failure is not an option...* He looked towards the door as the true meaning of those words arrived with frightening clarity. *If I fail I am as good as dead...*

# Mind the Gap

*'We only ever understand our own personal philosophy.'*
Precept of the day - Alice Sòng

**07:05 - Monday April 26th - 2028 - Tai Wo Hau Station - Hong Kong - China**

It was the green MTR station - green walls and green columns sprouting from mottled grey tiles glistening beneath the glare of overhead lights. But for Alice Sòng it was a place of green trees rising from sunlit waters glistening beneath wide blue skies. She smiled to herself - *My personal vista...* The illusion was part of the new vr-skim uploaded to her corneal data-lens. *'Nature-Scene Pro converts the mundane into picturesque landscapes to sooth the soul...'* She quickly blinked the lens into clear mode before stepping off the down escalators. Once more she was caught up in the frantic flow of commuters making their way towards the platforms - the almost military precision of daily routine never ceased to amaze her. *Eyes glued to phones and minds roaming far away places...* Almost immediately she was targeted by one of several Tad avatars shimmering brightly above the crowded platform. She shook her head as it began to form into a vaguely humanoid shape. *It wants to match my preferred male genotype...* She found a place to wait for the train as the image finally coalesced into a life-size image of a handsome young man. She sighed and asked:

"Really? A westerner?"

An old woman standing nearby grinned in her direction.

Alice found the latest targeted adverts (TADS) to be both amusing and annoying. It took less than six months to convert the entire MTR network into an embedded vidsync platform - the largest targeted advert system in the world. *Digital eyes and ears behind every wall...* This particular Tad had obviously synced into her phone and sifted for her favourite Cloud apps. *Invasive datasync...* The practice was not illegal but it was highly intrusive. *It found my game-lens account...*

Seconds later the young man began to extol the virtues of the latest technosync game:

"Néih hóu Alice! *Cull* is literally the cutting-edge of gaming technology. Enter the 4K ultra-zone to eliminate entire civilisations. Cull the universe of the unworthy and the unwanted..."

The bizarre combination of a Cantonese greeting and a western face was both ludicrous and annoying. She sighed heavily before tapping the block app on her phone. Suddenly the train arrived as the Tad withered into silent dissolution. *I need a better sync-lock on my phone...* She quickly forced her way onto an over-crowded train and gripped the nearest pole amidst bodies and mobile phones. Once again her eyes were drawn to the words on the platform floor: *Mind The Gap...* Moments later the doors slid closed with an audible ping. She felt a strange affinity to the standard warning. *It is an allegory on our lives...* The words of the philosopher, Chén Li, came to mind: *When we accept transition in life we must be wary of the interlude...the low points where depression takes seed...* She gripped the pole as the train gathered speed. *Mind the gap indeed...* Two stations later she saw her reflection in the window opposite. *Ponytailed black hair...brown eyes...short grey jacket over ghastly blue Hub uniform and black ankle boots...* She smiled slightly. *Little worker...*

Less than twenty minutes later she is struggling through a crowded Central Station on her way to the Hub. *Time to be a waitress again...* Stepping off the travelator she had a depressing thought: *My life is going nowhere... I am stuck in the gap...*

## 07:31 - Mid-Level Escalators - Queen's Road Central - Hong Kong

Dark brooding clouds hug the skyscrapers with a melancholy embrace. They look down upon mist-shrouded ferries crossing the choppy waters of Victoria Harbour. The constant sounds of construction merge almost into melody with the rumbling of rush-hour traffic. From somewhere beyond the manic machinations of humanity a gusty breeze brings whispers of rain to the faces of early morning commuters.

Alice glanced towards the Peak as she began to climb the steps next to the Mid-Levels escalators. *No sightseeing today...* Suddenly her phone pinged and she blinked her corneal data-lens to access her e-mail account. *Twenty two spams and a payment reminder from the bank...* She blinked the lens clear. *The joys of single life...* And then she noticed the time. *Time to rush...* Less than five minutes later she is negotiating a very busy Stanley Street. *Running late Alice...* Her thoughts returned to the meeting with Mark13UK. *What a disaster...* He had already sent three sync requests. *He wants my portal address...* But that would reveal her true identity and occupation. She sighed heavily. *My gap gets worse by the minute...*

## The Hub Cybersync Restaurant - Stanley Street - Central District - Hong Kong

The Hub - a four-storey building draped in reflective permiglass complete with embedded vr-skims advertising the delights of Cybersync: *Neural-interactive gameplay and personal Comsync via corneal data-lens technology.* The Hong Kong Hub is just one of a worldwide chain of Cybersync restaurants originating in Shanghai. *Plug your phone, tablet or data-lens into Cybersync courtesy of the Hub...*

Alice stopped at the curb opposite the restaurant and sighed wearily. *They are queuing already...* She saw an orderly line of people illuminated by holosim adverts leaping ghostlike from the surrounding buildings - mobile neonic Tads casting ludicrous displays of various 'Cyber Bargains' amongst the early morning crowds. *It never ends...* She took a moment to study the latest skims flowing across the enormous windows. *A new organic menu...* The menu of the day was replaced by vast fields of wheat swaying beneath sunny blue skies. She cursed under her breath:

"Sin ka lan..."

According to the Dark Cloud community, the Ministry of Environmental Protection had failed to stop the fungal blight spreading across the agricultural belt. It was an open secret that 75% of all food products are now the direct result of genetic modification. *We have no idea what we are actually eating...* Stepping onto the road she saw the latest game skims flashing across the permiglass windows. *Gideon's Quest... Translight Symmetry...* She smiled slightly. *Cull...* Avoiding slow-moving traffic she crossed the street and finally arrived at the back of the building. *So late...* She looked up towards grey skies framed by glistening skyscrapers draped in early morning mist. *Awful day...* With a heavy sigh she placed one hand onto the glass door. Moments later the sensor beeped and the door slid silently to one side. She quickly secured her coat inside the staff room before making her way into the main dining room. The first words she heard were the same words she heard almost every day:

"You are late..."

Alice smiled at her Duty Manager and replied:

"Harvey, you are like an endless echo..."

A scowling Harvey Chen replied: "You are habitually late for your shift."

Alice straightened her uniform as she replied: "It is not my fault..."

Chen interjected: "I am docking you this time."

Alice moaned: "Ah come on Harvey...give a girl a break."

Chen tapped a tabletop interface as he continued: "And that's another thing, no more extended breaks. You work your assigned hours or you don't work at all."

Alice studied Chen briefly as he swiped the interface. *A short little man with delusions of grandeur...blue tie and white shirt beneath pristine blue uniform...* It was a running joke that the thirty year old Duty Manager was as annoying as the TADS. She shook her head slightly - *The Lord of my Gap...*

As he walked towards the kitchen Chen added: "And try smiling at the customers today..."

Alice gave an exaggerated smile and asked: "Like this?"

Chen called: "I am watching you Alice..."

Alice turned to see her friend Moira Wu approaching. She smiled and said: "Hi Moira..."

Wu wore her long dark hair tied neatly at the back of her slender neck. Her face had a pale tone to it, but her eyes were a piercingly sharp brown beneath perfectly arched eyebrows. She was slightly shorter than Alice but moved with a fluid grace between the tables and chairs of the main dining room. She returned the smile and said:

"Don't blame Harvey, we have an inspection today..."

Alice checked her phone and asked: "What kind of inspection?"

Wu continued to wipe tables as she replied: "Someone from head office...making sure we're doing our jobs right..."

Alice sighed and said: "Perfect..."

Chen reappeared and ordered: "I want all data-lenses removed before we open the doors..."

Alice protested: "I use contact lenses Harvey..."

Chen studied the menu of the day and replied: "So wear glasses..."

Alice replied: "No one wears glasses anymore..."

Chen sighed and said: "Okay, but if I see a blank look on your face I will dock your pay."

Alice asked: "For a blank look?"

Chen replied firmly: "For Cloud Dancing during your shift...now report to your station, we are about to open..."

Alice gave an innocent smile and said: "I just need to use the restroom...back in a minute..."

Chen sighed heavily and said: "That girl will be the death of me..."

Wu smiled and said: "We all have to die of something Harvey..."

Once inside the restroom Alice blinked to access her Techsync account and found two more sync requests from Mark13UK. *He is persistent.* She quickly tapped her phone to initiate Cybersync. Moments later she tapped:

*"I will be at Joe's tonight..."*

She leaned on the sink and looked into the mirror. *I will tell him the truth...*

As she walked back towards the main dining room she had a disturbing thought: *What if he turns out to be a girl?*

# Cloud Memory

'*One microsecond before the initialisation of an active data-lens there is a cognitive gap through which involuntary memories can pass through the portal exit into the Cloud scenario - we call it the neural-wave phenomenon. It is triggered by a unique combination of visual and auditory input into the cerebral processing center of the brain. We have noted a stimulation of the hippocampus during an active data-sync and conclude the possibility of memory transference into the Clouds scenario. We are not suggesting a confirmed risk factor, but it might be wise to consider a revision of our liability and warrantee documentation with regard to our current data-lens technology.*'
Cloud Memory - A Theoretical Possibility: Data-file submission Techsync R & D.

The girl found herself standing on a deserted beach facing a crystal clear blue sea lapping gently upon the shore with the rhythmic flow of processed data. *My infinite realm...* She looked down at bare feet speckled with wet sand and smiled. *Enhanced sensation via neural-tactile assimilation processors...* Behind her a tropical jungle stretched all the way towards distant snow-peaked mountains bathed in the soft glow of early-morning sunlight. Birds squawked to the tune of augmented reality. She touched one hand to her small breasts with a brief sense of shame quickly replaced by a wry smile. *My avatar is naked...not me...this is all an illusion...* Once again her Profile Adaptive Platform had produced an Asian avatar almost identical to her own features. *The PAP synced my 121 app and mirrored my real-world profile...* Now she could feel a warm breeze whispering through her long dark hair. *Tactile assimilation response synced to audio-visual input nodes...* She inhaled artificial air and decided that the scene required more drama. She ordered:

"Sea storm...level one..."

Moments later the bright blue skies darkened into brooding clouds roiling into a gathering storm creased with lightning and the distant sound of thunder. She smiled as she walked into the water. *Time to fly...* Her avatar shimmered slightly as it adjusted linear perspective to accept the new input parameters. Moments later she found herself flying through the air towards a wall of rain. *Now this is what I call Cloud Dancing...*

After flying through rain for thirty minutes she returned to the beach and her rendezvous with the mysterious Mister Tang. *More stupid questions I cannot answer...* Touching feet to sand she wiped rain from her face before looking towards the tree line. As usual the bland-faced Mister Tang was waiting beneath a tall Azali palm tree. *Black suit, tie, white shirt, polished shoes...*She smiled slightly: *typical cardboard avatar...* And then a sudden thought arrived as panic: *My avatar needs clothes!* She quickly blinked to access her PAP. Moments later she walked towards the trees dressed in a pretty yellow dress and white sandals. She smiled and said:

"Hello Mister Tang!"

Mister Tang returned the smile and said: "Good morning. And how are you today?"

The girl brushed a hand through wet hair and replied: "Just wonderful actually..."

Mister Tang smiled again and said: "That is just perfect... I am pleased you feel better today..."

The girl touched her head and said: "Yes...no more pain..."

Mister Tang stepped closer and asked: "Do you remember yesterday?"

The girl frowned and replied: "Yesterday?"

Mister Tang continued: "The day before today."

The girl cocked her head to one side and mumbled: "Not sure..."

Mister Tang said: "Close your eyes...tell me what you see..."

The girl closed her avatar's eyes and said: "Bright lights... I see bright lights..."

Mister Tang asked: "Can you tell me your name?"

The girl opened her eyes and asked: "My name?"

Mister Tang asked: "Do you remember your name?"

The girl looked confused as she replied: "I..."

Mister Tang asked: "Are you an avatar?"

The girl smiled slightly and replied: "Of course not..." She gestured to the sky and continued: "This is a Cloud environment...an augmented reality scenario..." She touched her chest and added: "This body is my avatar..."

Mister Tang asked: "So where is your real body right now?"

The girl looked confused as she replied: "I... I am not sure..."

Mister Tang stepped closer and asked again: "Where is the real you?"

The girl spoke in a low voice: "I think...another place..."

Mister Tang ordered: "Describe this place."

The girl touched a finger to her lips and replied: "Bright lights... I see bright lights..." She paused before adding: "And voices...so many voices..."

Mister Tang asked: "Where are the voices coming from?"

The girl replied fearfully: "Everywhere..."

Mister Tang asked: "Do you recognise these voices?"

The girl hesitated before replying: "No. They speak Mandarin...yes... Mandarin..."

Mister Tang nodded slightly and asked: "Do you understand Mandarin?"

The girl touched her forehead as she replied: "Yes... But I speak Cantonese..." She looked directly at Tang and asked: "Why do I speak Cantonese?"

Mister Tang ignored the question and asked: "Where do people speak Cantonese?"

Without hesitation the girl replied: "Hong Kong!"

Mister Tang ordered: "Tell me about the bright lights..."

The girl hesitated before replying: "Colored lights and sirens...voices shouting..." She paused before adding: "Pain...so much pain..." She looked up and asked desperately: "What happened to me?"

Mister Tang replied: "You were hurt...but you are better now."

The girl shouted to the sky: "Exit portal!"

Mister Tang spoke gently: "My dear girl, you cannot leave the Cloud just yet...you must be patient..."

The girl asked: "Why can't I leave? What is going on here?"

Mister Tang replied: "Your body needs time to recover."

The girl asked: "Then I am hurt?"

Mister Tang replied: "Yes. But as soon as you are fully recovered you can exit the Cloud and return to your normal life."

The girl asked: "What is my normal life?"

Mister Tang smiled and said: "Why don't you fly again...you enjoy it so much..."

The girl looked confused as she replied: "Yes... I enjoy flying..."

Mister Tang spoke one last time before vanishing from the beach:

"Everything will be fine... Soon you will be reborn soon into a new life..."

As Tang vanished the girl whispered: "New life?"

# The Invitation

*'You can either stay safe and exist or take a risk and live...'*
*Precept of the day - Alice Sòng*

**Monday April 26th - The Hub Cybersync Restaurant - Stanley Street - Central District - Hong Kong**

The afternoon arrived with the sound of thunder rumbling inside storm clouds descending slowly upon the glistening skyscrapers of central Hong Kong. Traffic moved as a relentless tide along city streets bordered by chaotic crowds cluttering the shores of the South China Sea. Heavy drops of rain began to speckle the embedded vr-skims advertising the digital delights of The Hub Cybersync Restaurant - brief rainbow spurts of light casting ripples of colour amidst the menu's and Cloud game-skims.

Inside the main dining room organised chaos reigned amidst raucous voices competing with blaring holosim screens and the all-pervading sounds of a restaurant operating at full capacity. The lunchtime rush had produced a waiting list for tables and vr-booths on all three floors of the open-plan building. A multitude of Cybersync portals connected customers to Cloud communities, games portals, vr-skims and personal portals across a variety of online platforms. Teenagers laughed and shouted to the tune of tabletop consoles beeping incessantly amidst a stream of multicoloured lights. Routinely navigating a sea of tables' the waiters and waitresses responded rapidly to constant tabletop orders and Cybersync portal requests.

Alice tapped the tabletop interface as she spoke:

"I can confirm three portal requests from this table... Cloud access was granted and you signed into your Techsync account as Duin14sxc. So the funds were automatically taken from your online account."

Once more the female customer protested: "But the stats say ninety minutes Cybersync... I got less than one hour, so you guys owe me credits..."

Alice sighed heavily as she tapped the interface before saying: "I tell you what...you take the credits on me...there you go...the sync was free..." She forced a smile and said: "Have a nice day..."

Moira Wu joined her and asked: "Problem?"

Alice replied wearily: "I am so tired of these people..."

Wu raised her voice above the noise and said: "Valued customers Alice..."

Alice retorted: "Sin ka lan..."

Wu smiled and said: "Language girl...the inspector is still here..."

Alice looked towards the upper floors and said: "I know..."

Wu spoke as she cleared a table: "He is talking to Chloe..."

Alice picked up a tray of rice bowls and said: "I know...and I am next..."

Wu brushed hair from her eyes and said: "He only wants to know if you enjoy working for the Hub."

Alice replied wryly: "That is it then... I am fired..."

Wu laughed and said: "Just lie for god's sake... I did..."

Alice sighed and said: "That is all we can do these days...lie..."

Wu studied Alice briefly and asked: "Are you okay?"

Alice replied with a question: "Don't you get tired of it all Moira? Tired of the illusions we use just to get through the day...?"

Wu picked up a tray of dirty plates and asked: "Illusions?"

Alice replied: "Cybersync...Cloud dancing...vr-skims...holosims. It's all just one big escape from reality..."

Wu replied: "Well maybe that is because reality stinks..."

Alice said: "But there must be more to life than make-believe...there has to be something better in the real world..."

Wu gripped the tray and replied: "Last night I was in Hawaii... Best Cloud dance I ever had...the embedded holo-lucient was perfect... I could almost feel the sea breeze walking along the beach...amazing..."

Alice retorted: "But it was all an illusion..."

Wu replied: "Take a look around Alice...isn't an illusion better than this?"

As Wu walked back towards the kitchen Alice blinked into her Techsync account to read the message from Mark13UK.

"*See u tonight!*"

She smiled slightly. *Maybe the illusion is better...*

A harassed Harvey Chen arrived and said: "Mister Chung will see you now Alice..." He looked at the tray of bowls and added: "And take those to the kitchen."

Alice glanced towards the escalators and replied: "Yes boss..."

Chen saw the look on Alice's face and said: "And mind your manners..."

Alice forced a smile and said: "I will be a good little girl Harvey..."

Chen commented: "That will be the day..."

## 17:35 - Duty Manager's Office - 3rd Floor - The Hub Cybersync Restaurant

Alice secured her hair at the back of her neck before knocking on the door. Moments later a muffled voice replied:

"Come in..."

Alice opened the door to find the man from Shanghai sitting behind Harvey's desk studying a datascreen. He wore a standard grey suit with white shirt and blue tie adorned with the Hub Cybersync insignia - HCS. A brief study revealed a middle-aged man with greying hair framing a tanned face with dull brown eyes. His jaw was round, and his nose was small but slightly crooked, like it had been broken and left to its imperfections. He had a small curve to his thin lips, as if there were something terribly funny only he knew the answer to, and it was that brief glimpse of a secret that she found strangely unsettling. He spoke without looking up:

"Miss Sòng, please sit down."

Alice sat down and waited whilst the man tapped the screen several more times.

Finally Chung Lee looked up and asked:
"And how are you today Alice?"
Alice replied: "I am fine thank you..."
Chung studied her briefly and said: "You look familiar. Have we met before?"
Alice replied: "I don't think so..."
Chung glanced at the screen and said: "You have been with us for just under a year now; is that correct?"
Alice replied: "Yes."
Chung continued: "And before that you attended the University of Hong Kong, achieving a BA from the Faculty of Arts."
Alice replied: "Yes."
Chung nodded slightly before asking: "Have you travelled much Alice?"
Alice replied: "Not really...a short trip to Beijing after I graduated..."
Chung smiled slightly and asked: "Did you enjoy the trip?"
Alice shrugged as she replied: "It was okay."
Chung said: "Not very talkative are you Alice..."
Alice replied: "No."
Chung sighed and asked: "And do you enjoy working for the Hub chain?"
Alice replied: "Yes..." She forced a smile before adding: "I love it..."
Chung returned the smile and said: "That is good to know." He sat back and asked: "Have you considered applying for one of our management training courses? It is ideal for graduates."
Alice replied: "No."
Chung said: "I think it is something you might consider..."
Alice straightened her uniform and replied: "I will...thank you."
Chung asked: "Do you have anything to say about Mister Chen? Is he a good duty manager?"
Alice replied: "The best..."
Chung considered this before asking: "Has he ever acted inappropriately towards you or any other member of the female staff?"

Alice giggled and asked: "Harvey? Oh no...no way...you obviously don't know about Harvey..."

Chung sat forward and asked: "What do I not know about Harvey?"

Alice coughed and replied: "Nothing. It is none of my business."

Chung suddenly saw the truth and said: "Oh I see... Mister Chen's preferences lie elsewhere. Perhaps I should talk to the male staff again..."

Alice smiled and said: "Look... Harvey is a good guy...a loyal worker...that is all that matters right?"

Chung sat back and replied: "Right."

Alice asked: "So are we done here?"

Chung replied: "Not quite. I am hosting a social gathering this evening at my hotel; I would like you to attend as my guest...."

Alice's eyes widened as she asked: "Me? Why?"

Chung replied: "I think it will be a good opportunity for you to meet people who can advance your career..." He paused before asking: "Do you really want to remain a waitress for the rest of your life?"

Alice hesitated before replying: "No... But I have plans tonight."

Chung sat forward and said: "Perhaps I did not make myself clear... Your failure to attend this social event might reflect badly in my report to head office."

Alice swallowed and asked: "What time shall I be there?"

Chung smiled as he replied: "Eight thirty at the Oriental Plaza, roof top garden..." He paused before adding: "And wear something pleasing..."

Alice replied in a low voice: "Okay..."

## 18:05 - Staff Room - Ground Floor - The Hub Cybersync Restaurant

Moira Wu saw the look on Alice's face and asked:

"What happened? Are you alright Alice?"

Alice opened her locker and replied: "I am not sure..."

Wu stepped closer and asked: "Did the inspector say something to you?"

Alice replied: "I think he propositioned me..."

Wu's eyes widened as she asked: "He asked you out on a date?"

Alice replied: "He called it a social gathering to help further my career..."

Wu stepped in front of a mirror and asked: "What did you say?"

Alice replied: "I said I will be there..."

A surprised Wu asked: "Really?"

Alice sighed and replied: "He threatened to submit a bad report on me..."

Wu began to brush her hair and said: "Wow...talk about abuse of power."

Alice said: "Maybe it is a social thing... He said I could advance my position within the Hub chain..."

Wu placed her brush in her backpack and said: "Maybe...but just be careful he doesn't advance his position with you..."

Alice smiled slightly and replied: "I will be careful..."

Wu gripped her bag and said: "And call me afterwards so I know you are okay..."

Alice reached for her bag and replied: "I will..."

Wu said: "Time to go home...see you tomorrow."

Alice said: "Okay...bye Moira..."

As soon as she was alone Alice accessed her Techsync account and tapped her phone:

*"Sorry Mark...cannot meet tonight...try tomorrow...Alice :)"*

She looked into the mirror above the sink and sighed heavily. *Wear something pleasing?*

# The Biogen Connection

*'Evil will seldom explain its motives...'*
Xian Du

**18:25 - Monday - April 26th - 2028 - Laboratory Number 1 - Ministry of Science and Technology of the People's Republic of China - Beijing, China.**

A cluttered office lost to fleeting shadows cast by a flickering monitor. The leader of Project Jiàngshēng sat back in his leather chair and studied the screen carefully. *Huang Lin - intelligence augmentation predictability quotient....* Professor Leung Huo sighed heavily. *She is off the scale...* He tapped the screen to reveal the Biogen homepage. *The Home of Augmented Technology...* The Shanghai-based multinational company dominated the field of bio-adaptive augmentation. Their core products included the latest autonomous transport networks - driverless cars, buses, trains and pilotless planes. A growing online presence had resulted in the Nexus search engine - the first global Chinese network allowed by the People's Congress. *And now they want to take over the Coretech 121 instant messaging service...* But beyond the facade of seemingly benevolent technological advances there was another side to the Biogen organisation - a shadow agenda which dealt exclusively with the augmentation of living human beings. Leung stared at the company motto and sighed heavily - *The Courage to Create...* He glanced at Lin's latest test results. *But what are they really creating?* His thoughts were interrupted by a pinging from his phone. He answered:
"Yes?"
The face of Rén Du came onscreen. The Biogen operative had an angular face framed by short dark hair combed into a semblance of neatness and bound back from his face. But it was the intensity of the dark brown eyes which Leung found most unsettling. *Predatory eyes...*
Rén replied: "I received your message. Is there a problem?"

Leung hesitated slightly before replying: "We have a leak...our database has been hacked..."

There was a pause before Rén said: "We are aware of the situation."

Leung asked: "You are?"

Rén replied: "We have a contact within the Ministry."

Leung continued: "It has been tracked to Singapore..." He paused before asking: "What do you want me to do?"

Rén asked: "Who is in charge of the investigation?"

Leung replied: "Section Leader Han Mang. He has placed us on lockdown..."

Rén fell silent before continuing: "Be wary of him...he is a shrewd investigator..."

Leung looked towards the main laboratory and replied: "I noticed..."

Rén asked: "What did you tell him?"

Leung replied: "I answered a few basic questions about the augmentation process...and then I gave him a tour of our facilities. Tomorrow he will continue to interview my staff."

Rén asked: "Did he ask about the two fatalities?"

Leung replied: "I explained the cause of death...but..."

Rén asked: "But what?"

Leung continued: "He wants to see the autopsy reports for both subjects."

Rén frowned and asked: "How can that be relevant to his investigation?"

Leung replied: "I have no idea...but he shows great interest in the project."

Rén commented: "A little too much interest..."

Leung said: "I see no reason for him to question the veracity of the reports."

Rén asked: "Do you know which files were stolen?"

Leung replied wearily: "The most important data... Augmentation protocols, implantation procedures, genomic manip-ulation, cerebral enhancement and basic maturation protocols..." He sighed before adding: "A template for human augmentation."

Rén asked: "What about the original prototype? Has she been compromised?"

Leung replied: "No. I deleted everything...as far as anyone knows we only ever had three subjects."

Rén spoke soberly: "Deleted files can be recovered..." He paused before asking: "What action have you taken?"

Leung hesitated before replying: "I have asked Huang Lin to scan the Dark Cloud."

An irritated Rén asked: "Why would you do that? She must not be involved in the investigation."

Leung tensed as he replied: "She is already involved...if the authorities retrieve those files they will follow the clues all the way to her front door..."

There was a brief silence before Rén continued:

"We have contacted Huang Lin..."

Leung raised his eyebrows and asked: "You did?"

Rén said: "You seem surprised."

Leung replied: "It has been six months... I thought you were simply observing her progress."

Rén replied: "We have been using her as a comparative module against the original prototype. But it is time to move forward with our plans for Huang Lin..."

Leung asked: "What does that mean exactly?"

Rén replied: "We offered her a job..."

Leung frowned and said: "I spoke to her last week; she made no mention of this..."

Rén said: "We emphasised the confidential nature of our employment offer."

A surprised Leung said: "She knows I can be trusted..."

Rén replied: "It is not a matter of trust...her responses are based solely upon analytical logic." There was a pause before he asked: "Did you input the com-code before you called her?"

Leung hesitated before replying: "I am sure I did..."

Rén snapped: "You had better be sure, because if that call was monitored you might have compromised our entire operation."

Leung cleared his throat before saying: "I am sure...we were not monitored..."

Rén retorted: "And yet Han Mang is now asking questions about the autopsy reports."

Leung countered: "As you said yourself: he is a shrewd investigator."

Rén ordered: "You must not contact Lin again..."

Leung replied: "But she will contact me at some point."

Rén spoke firmly: "Then input the code before you answer your phone."

Leung asked: "And if Han continues to probe deeper into the project?"

Rén replied: "We will not allow anyone to jeopardise our long-term plans..."

Leung asked: "What do you mean by that?"

Rén replied coldly: "If necessary we will take action to terminate the investigation."

Leung's eyes widened as he asked: "You can do that?"

Rén replied: "We can."

Leung hesitated before asking: "When will you activate the original prototype?"

Rén replied: "We are currently reviewing performance data. Activation will not take place until we can confirm the viability of the cerebral interface."

Leung sighed and said: "I am not happy about this...we are manipulating a young woman's life."

Rén replied: "Regardless of your personal opinion, it is imperative that she remains ignorant of the procedure until we activate the neural interface."

Leung said: "The so-called original prototype is a young woman in the prime of her life. Surely we can spare her further suffering?"

Rén asked: "Do I need to remind you that she owes her life to you? After the accident she was pronounced brain dead...you gave her a new lease on life. She owes her very existence to your project."

Leung replied: "But she deserves to be left alone...to live her life to the full."

Rén replied: "You showed no such qualms when we first approached you Professor. If memory serves correct you were more than enthusiastic at the prospect of creating an augmented human prototype."

Leung replied wearily: "I know..." He paused before continuing: "I allowed my passion for my work to subvert my morality...but now I regret what we have done."

Rén spoke firmly: "Then dismiss such regrets and remember what is at stake here..."

Leung said: "I know what is at stake, and that is why we should allow the government full access to the project."

Rén retorted: "It was not the Beijing government who offered you unlimited funding Professor; the National Space Administration gave you a paltry two per cent of their annual budget. Without my organization you would still be playing games with augmented rats."

Leung sighed and replied: "That is true...but we must consider the morality of what we are doing...these young women are not lab rats spinning in a wheel..."

Rén replied: "No they are not. They are assets to be deployed for the benefit of all mankind."

Leung asked: "Is the situation so critical?"

Rén replied: "Our world is a pressure cooker Professor. Global warming has altered the natural balance. The loss of sea ice continues to impact sea levels. Every year we suffer more droughts and heat waves, whilst hurricanes become stronger and more intense." He paused before continuing: "At this moment in time we occupy a single planet...this makes us vulnerable to extinction. If we are to have any hope of survival we must plant our seeds upon another world. Your project is the first step in a process that will take decades, but the end result will be the continued survival of the human race."

Leung considered this before asking: "Is your beneficence based purely upon humanitarianism or the accumulation of Biogen assets?"

Rén frowned and asked: "Do you doubt our sincerity?"

Leung replied: "I simply question your true agenda. Will it truly benefit mankind if a private corporation dominates the space race? You act outside judicial oversight and you manipulate the law to suit your own ends."

Rén gave a slight smile as he replied: "Sometimes it is necessary to bypass the constraints of judicial law if only to pursue a higher cause."

Leung asked: "How will your higher cause impact these two young women? They might not be so willing to accept your agenda."

Rén glanced off-screen before replying: "Do not be concerned about such matters. You have more than enough work to do Professor."

Leung looked towards the sterile room and said: "I know my responsibilities..."

Rén said: "Tell me about spatial-time awareness. Is the original prototype completely unaware of the missing time period?"

Leung nodded slightly and said: "She is totally unaware of the gap in her life. We created an alternate reality scenario via the neocortical interface. As far as she is concerned she enjoyed a two week vacation here in Beijing. We also uploaded a series of digital photographs to her Techsync account to facilitate spatial-time awareness."

Rén said: "Ingenious."

Leung continued: "And the non-invasive procedure allowed us to bypass extended maturation during the implantation procedure."

Rén considered this before asking: "Why didn't you use the non-invasive procedure with the three remaining subjects?"

Leung replied: "Because the original prototype was an unplanned experiment as a result of a vehicular accident - she was a window of opportunity. But Huang Lin and the others received far more complex augmentations. An enhanced neural interface doubled their cognitive response times..." He glanced at the latest test results before adding: "And so far Huang Lin has exceeded all of my expectations."

Rén asked: "Are you saying the original prototype is inferior to the other subjects?"

Leung considered the question before replying:

"I am saying that her augmentation allows for a greater level of human empathy." He paused before continuing: "Unlike Huang Lin, the degree of autonomous control is less than twenty per cent."

Rén frowned and said: "That could make her liability."

Leung asked: "In what way?"

Rén replied: "Her emotions could have a disruptive impact upon phase two. Any deviation from the projected viability of the project could prove fatal."

Leung replied wryly: "Hence the designation prototype."

Rén asked: "Can you calculate the level of autonomous control?"

Leung replied: "No. The augmentation boundary is less defined...the emotional influence less restrained."

Rén glanced off-screen before continuing: "I have studied the latest neural scans... Can you explain the anomalous readings?"

Leung sighed before relying: "I wish I could... That is why I wanted to delay her release... I need more time to discern the cause of the invasive thought patterns..."

Rén replied: "Time is a luxury we cannot afford professor. The project must move forward regardless of the consequences."

Leung countered: "We have no idea how she will react when you finally activate the cerebral interface. These invasive thoughts might well be an indication of psychopathic aberration."

Rén replied: "If that is the case then we will initiate counter-measures."

Leung's eyes widened as he asked: "You would kill her?"

Rén replied: "Only as a last resort. We cannot allow her to fall into the hands of our competitors."

Leung sighed and said: "This is not why I accepted your help..."

Rén spoke soberly: "Sometimes sacrifice is necessary for the greater good."

Leung asked: "You mean the end justifies the means?"

Rén replied: "Only time will tell..."

Leung looked towards the laboratory and said: "I should get back to work."

Rén said: "One more thing..."

Leung asked: "Yes?"

Rén asked: "What does your assistant know about the original prototype?"

Leung replied: "Only that she returned to her life after the procedure. Mai knows nothing of your involvement."

Rén asked: "Can she be trusted?"

Leung replied firmly: "I trust her implicitly."

Rén asked: "Has she been questioned by Section Leader Han Mang?"

Leung replied: "Yes. But she made no mention of the original prototype or Huang Lin's continued survival."

Rén asked: "You can guarantee her compliance?"

Leung replied: "She will not betray my wishes. She believes we saved the first prototype from the authorities. I told her the same story regarding Huang Lin."

Rén frowned and said: "Very well. But remember that regardless of our circumstances we are all vulnerable to accountability." He smiled slightly before adding: "Zàijiàn Professor..."

As the connection closed Leung replied: "Zàijiàn..." He looked up to see Ting Mai enter the main laboratory. *Vulnerable to accountability?*

# The Social Gathering

*'If you can dream it you can achieve it...'*
*Precept of the day - Alice Sòng*

**19:15 - Monday April 26th - 2028 - Kwai Chung Estate - Hong Kong - China**

Night sounds arrived through a half-open window waiting to be closed against the rain tapping gently upon the glass. By the light of a single bulb a dark-haired young woman sat on the end of an unmade bed studying her friend as she applied make-up in front of a wardrobe mirror. Finally she asked:
"So what type of party is it?"
Alice touched mascara to her upper lids as she replied:
"It is a social gathering..."
Nancy Yeo asked: "Like a dinner party?"
Alice shrugged and replied: "I have no idea..."
Yeo frowned and said: "Just be careful sweetie..."
Alice studied her face in the mirror and asked: "What do you mean?"
Yeo replied: "This guy might have ulterior motives."
Alice shook her head and said: "I doubt it...it's just a company thing..."
Yeo said: "I hope so..."
Alice turned around and asked: "How do I look?"
Yeo studied her friend for a moment. *Hair draped over shoulders...butterfly hair clip...silver necklace with yin yang pendant... low-cut knee-length yellow dress touched with green ferns along its hem...yellow sandals...* Finally she smiled and replied:
"You look hot in that dress..."
Alice laughed and asked: "Really?"
Yeo smiled and replied: "Definitely."
A sudden beeping came from a phone on the bed.

Yeo picked it up and announced: "You have a Techsync message..."

Alice took the phone and tapped into her account. Finally she said:

"It is the British guy...he wants to meet in the Cloud tomorrow."

Yeo lay back on the bed and said: "So meet him. What do you have to lose?"

Alice sighed and said: "But I keep cancelling on him..."

Yeo yawned and said: "If he is interested in you he won't go away..."

Alice tapped her phone and said: "I will meet him in the coffee house..."

Yeo said: "Good for you..."

Alice saw the time and said: "I better get going..." She picked up a small yellow purse and asked: "Did you order my taxi?"

Yeo stood up and walked to the window and replied: "I think he is here already..."

Alice reached for a black lace shawl and said: "Good."

Yeo straightened the shawl on Alice's shoulders and asked: "What time will you be home?"

Alice checked her hair in the mirror and replied: "Not too late...work tomorrow..."

Yeo said: "I will wait up for you..."

Alice returned the smile and said: "Thanks..."

Yeo walked Alice to the front door and said: "Take care..."

Alice opened the door as she replied: "Always...bye Nancy..."

Yeo waited until the taxi drove away before studying her phone. Almost immediately a decoded 121 message appeared onscreen:

'Proceed."

She sighed heavy as a familiar headache arrived above her eyes.

## 20:21 - Oriental Plaza Hotel - Des Voeux Road Central - Hong Kong

A windy night waited at the edge of a sea of lights illuminating the dark waters of Victoria Harbour. Rain flurries flirted with the crowds flowing as a ceaseless tide of humanity along the streets and covered walkways of the city.

Moving slowly along a congested Des Voeux Road a red taxi manoeuvred into the inside lane. Sitting in the back seat Alice blinked to activate her data-lens account. A ping from her phone confirmed Cybersync into VASE - Vocal Activated Search Engine. She spoke in a low voice:

"Oriental Plaza Hotel, Hong Kong."

A sudden blurring of her vision coalesced into words flowing slowing over her right corneal data-lens: *Five-star luxury hotel offering 2,824 rooms, 98 floors, plus rooftop gardens and swimming pool... Wow...* She looked up as the taxi joined a line of luxury cars pulling into the forecourt. Now she could see a group of handsome young men escorting elegantly dressed young women into the hotel. She sighed heavily. *I am so out of place...* One rapid blink cancelled the Cybersync as the taxi came to a stop in front of the hotel. She quickly swiped her phone over the payment reader before exiting the taxi with a quick: "m̀hgòi." to the driver.

Moments later she stopped outside the main reception and looked up towards the distant rooftop. *What am I even doing here?* The humid night arrived as perspiration under her arms and lower back as she took a moment to slow her breathing. *You can do this Alice...* A brief gust of wind touched her hair with a fine spray of rain before she followed a group of people through large permiglass doors into an oval-shaped lobby of polished white marble. She immediately found herself facing an elaborate fountain display adorned with golden stone lions and a variety of exotic plants. *Wow...* Beyond the fountain a group of people were gathered in front of a reception desk positioned beneath a mirrored ceiling. She noted three smartly dressed young female receptionists busily processing the group. A plaque on the opposite wall pointed her in the direction of the lifts. She took a deep breath. *Here goes nothing...*

## 20:31 - Rooftop Garden - Oriental Plaza Hotel - Hong Kong

Alice was followed into the lift by two smartly dressed young couples. The lift displayed the same type of opulence as the main reception area - mirrored walls and ceiling with gold plated fixtures. As the doors closed she moved to the back and looked up at the ceiling. *Deep breath Alice...* She sniffed quietly - a strong scent of aftershave arrived as a tickle at the back of her throat.

One of the men turned and asked:
"Which floor?"
Alice coughed and replied: "The rooftop garden..."
The man spoke to the elevator:
"Rooftop garden..."
The second man smiled and said: "That's where we are going... Are you part of the Cybersync industry?"
Alice replied: "I work at the Hub."
The man smiled and said: "Nice..."
One of the girls turned and asked: "Are you in management?"
Alice replied: "No."
The girl gave a condescending: "Oh..."

Alice lowered her eyes as the uncomfortable silence was replaced by the muffled sounds of music and laughter. Moments later the doors parted to reveal a broad swath of glistening greenery outlined against the brightness of the city like a miniature oasis perched at the summit of a concrete jungle. She followed the two couples out onto a covered stone patio overlooking an illuminated swimming pool surrounded by colourful displays of exotic plants. The night air was that familiar mixture of food smells and pollution touched by drops of rain speckling the overhead canopy. To her right a small group of musicians were playing classical music, whilst to the left a bar area played host to groups of people gathered around wikka tables and chairs. The entire scene was bathed in the soft glow of concealed lightning shimmering slightly beneath the overhead canopies. She gripped her purse and sighed heavily. *Now what?* And then she saw a smiling Chung Lee approaching from the bar area. He said:

"Alice my dear girl, you look enchanting..."

Alice felt her face flush as she replied: "Thank you..."

Chung was wearing a grey suit and white shirt opened at the neck to reveal a gold chain necklace. He took her hand and said:

"Come...let me introduce you to a few people."

Chung's hand felt moist and overly soft, but Alice resisted the urge to pull free as she was led towards the far end of the swimming pool. She noted several people swimming in the water seemingly oblivious to the rain speckling the surface. Finally they arrived at a corner table beneath a large canopy displaying the Hub corporate logo: HCS in gold lettering superimposed onto a blue cloud of flowing binary numbers.

Chung smiled and said: "Alice...this is Tiang Lao, head of our finance division..."

Alice found herself facing a middle-aged man with short dark hair combed back from his tanned face. Beneath narrow brown eyes a small, thin nose ends just above the soft flesh of his smiling lips. She felt a vague sense of familiarity as he stood up and said:

"Alice...it is always nice to meet one of the troops..."

Alice forced a slight smile and replied: "Nice to meet you..."

Chung gestured to a chair and said: "Please, sit... We have the finest champagne..."

Tiang said: "Then perhaps you can fetch another bottle..."

Chung cleared his throat and replied: "Very well..." He smiled warmly at Alice and added: "I won't be long my dear..."

Alice sat down as Chung walked back towards the crowded bar area.

Tiang Lao pulled his chair closer and asked: "So how is life in the local Hub?"

Alice brushed hair from her face and replied: "We are very busy..."

Tiang said: "Good to know..."

Alice struggled for words before asking: "Do you work in Shanghai?"

Tiang studied his empty glass and replied: "Yes...since last year. Before that I was based in our Tokyo office."

Alice said: "I have always wanted to visit Japan."

Tiang said: "Then you should do it..."

Alice replied: "Perhaps one day."

Tiang sighed and said: "Unfortunately my wife was not so keen on the Japanese..." He looked towards the bar before adding wearily: "So here we are, back in China."

Alice said: "Forgive me, but have we met before?"

Tiang replied: "I do not think so..."

Alice continued: "Perhaps it was on vacation..."

Tiang asked: "In Japan?"

Alice replied: "No... I'm not sure where..."

Tiang smiled and said: "I think you have mistaken me for someone else."

Alice fell silent before asking: "Are you part of Mister Chung's inspection?"

Tiang replaced his glass and replied: "No... I am here to upgrade the local payroll system..."

Alice said: "Sounds complicated."

Tiang nodded slightly and continued: "The Hong Kong branch is to be merged into the Shanghai central database. It will bring your local salaries in-line with the mainland."

Alice frowned and asked: "Does that mean we will get paid less?"

Tiang replied: "It is simply a rationalisation of resources. The local Hub is no longer cost effective considering the high levels of expenditure." He saw the look on her face and added with a smile: "But do not worry... Chung tells me that you are management material. I am sure you will go far within our company."

Alice considered this and said: "But we get paid more in Hong Kong because of the higher cost of living; if salaries are reduced people won't be able to meet their daily living costs."

Tiang frowned and said: "Hong Kong will not always be a special administrative region. A time will come when you will have to adapt to the mainland system. It makes sense to begin the assimilation process as soon as possible."

Alice retorted: "We have until twenty forty seven...nineteen more years of freedom."

Tiang raised his eyebrows and asked "So you support the one country two systems nonsense?"

Alice replied firmly: "I support the agreement made with the United Kingdom."

Tiang raised his empty glass and said: "And I support your loyalty to your city..."

Alice looked towards Victoria Harbour and said: "I love my city..."

Tiang said: "And I hear you have been to Beijing..."

Alice looked surprised and asked: "You did?"

Tiang replied: "It is in your personnel file."

Alice asked: "You read my file?"

Tiang smiled and replied: "It is synced to the payroll system..."

Alice nodded slightly and said: "It was a short trip...after graduation."

Tiang asked: "And what did you think of our capital city?"

Alice frowned as she replied: "It was okay...very busy..."

Tiang asked: "Busy like Hong Kong?"

Alice nodded slightly and said: "Yes...but the air here is better..."

Tiang smiled and said: "Ah yes...the price of progress..."

Chung reappeared carrying a champagne bucket and two glasses. He said:

"Here we go..."

After a brief struggle with the cork he filled three glasses and said:

"After you Alice..."

Alice took the proffered glass and said: "Thank you."

Chung sat down and said: "It has stopped raining..."

Tiang said: "Lee...you did not tell me that Miss Sòng was so passionate about her city."

Chung looked confused as he asked: "She is?"

Tiang smiled slightly and replied: "She fears the loss of her freedom..."

Alice interjected: "I just think Hong Kong deserves more than assimilation."

Chung sipped from his glass and said: "Hong Kong will always have a special place in our society, but integration is inevitable..."

Alice considered this before asking: "So what will that mean exactly?"

Chung replaced his glass and replied: "It will lose its status as a special administrative region and probably be combined with Shenzhen, Guangzhou, Zhongshan, Zhuhai and Macau into a massive megalopolis that spans the entire Pearl River Delta. It will be administered like any Tier One Chinese city and have the same legal system as the rest of the country. At some point, instead of calling the city Hong Kong, outsiders will start referring to it by its Chinese name, Xiānggǎng."

Alice swallowed and said: "That sounds awful..."

Tiang smiled and said: "Oh it will not be so bad...your city is the financial heart of our great nation...integration does not necessarily mean regression."

Chung nodded and said: "Exactly. Even Beijing recognises the value of free commerce..."

Alice retorted: "Free commerce cannot function alongside state censorship..."

Chung cleared his throat and replied: "A controlled society is a productive society..."

Tiang nodded slightly and said: "That is true...but we should not allow ourselves to abandon the principles of collective freedom..." He smiled at Alice and continued: "Alice has a point...if we are to move forward as a society we must accelerate our global integration."

Chung asked: "So you condone our integration into a capitalist society?"

Tiang replied with a slight smile: "My dear Lee...we are a capitalist society. Commerce is the engine which fuels the globalisation of the People's Republic."

Alice interjected: "But it is the Cloud which sustains our freedom."

Chung emptied his glass and said: "And undermines the status quo..."

Alice lowered her eyes slightly and said: "I suppose..."

Tiang stared at Alice and asked: "Are you a Cloud aficionado Alice?"

Alice shrugged and replied: "I use it sometimes...games and things..."

Chung asked: "Data-lens games?"

Alice straightened her shawl and replied: "Just Techsync...but never at work of course..."

Chung tapped her hand gently and said: "Of course..."

Tiang asked: "Do you ever venture into the Dark Cloud?"

Alice felt the beginnings of a headache as she replied: "No... Of course not."

Chung sat back and said: "Good girl...it serves only to undermine the state..."

Tiang raised his glass and said: "Enough politics... Drink up Alice...tonight is all about enjoyment..."

Alice smiled slightly as she sipped from her glass and immediately coughed.

Chung asked: "Your first taste of champagne?"

Alice wiped her chin and replied: "Yes..."

A tall woman arrived at the table and announced with disgust: "I had to queue for the bathroom..."

Tiang smiled slightly and said: "Alice, this is my wife Cynthia..."

Alice saw a tall dark-haired woman in a black low-cut dress revealing tanned breasts creased with wrinkles. Her brown eyes were set above a wide nose and thick lips over perfect white teeth. Heavy facial make-up was dubiously complimented by silver drop earrings and a diamond necklace.

Cynthia sat down and said: "Pleased to meet you Alice."

Alice smiled slightly and said: "You too..."

Chung said: "Alice works in our Stanley Street branch."

Cynthia straightened her dress and asked: "And what do you do there Alice?"

Alice replied: "I am a waitress."

A surprised Cynthia asked: "Really?"

Alice replied: "Yes...really."

Cynthia picked up a glass of champagne and said: "Well it sounds positively thrilling."

Chung laughed and said: "We all have our part to play in the Hub empire."

Tiang stared at Alice and said: "That is true..."

Cynthia sipped from her glass and asked: "And do you enjoy your work Alice?"

Alice replied with a diplomatic lie: "Very much..."

Chung sat forward and said: "I think Alice is ideal management material."

Cynthia smiled slightly and said: "Well if a pretty face is a prerequisite for management she should go far..."

Chung laughed and said: "Oh come now Cynthia, there is more to management than simply a pretty face. We are looking for loyal, dedicated people who can enhance the Hub reputation for good service."

Cynthia asked: "Is that why you invited a waitress tonight... because she is loyal and dedicated?"

Tiang smiled and said: "Forgive my wife Alice, she tends to be somewhat outspoken in her opinions."

Alice looked at Cynthia and said: "We are all entitled to our own opinions, regardless of their validity."

Tiang laughed and said: "Touché my dear..."

Cynthia scowled at her husband before emptying her glass.

Alice noticed Chung waving to a man approaching from the bar. He announced:

"Alice, this is Mong Gao. He runs a local Cyber club..."

Alice looked up and said: "Hello..."

Gao took her hand and said: "I am very pleased to meet you Alice..."

Chung continued: "Gao is considering a Hub franchise deal in Singapore..."

Alice said: "You should do well in Singapore."

Gao replied: "I hope so..."

Chung gestured to a chair and asked: "Why don't you join us?"

Gao sat down next to Tiang Lao and said: "Thank you."

Alice asked: "Which club do you manage?"

Gao placed his glass onto the table and replied: "The Blue Lounge, in Wo Chu Lane..."

Alice nodded and said: "I have heard of it..."

Gao asked: "Have you ever been there?"

Alice replied: "No... Sorry..."

Gao smiled and said: "You should come one night...as my guest..."

Alice blushed and said: "Thank you... I might do that..."

Cynthia poured more champagne and said: "You might find the Blue Lounge a little overpowering."

Alice asked: "Why?"

Cynthia glanced at Gao and said: "The place tends to cater for a more deviant clientele."

Gao smiled politely and said: "I think you mean adventurous..."

Cynthia countered: "I think I mean perverted..."

Alice ignored the comment and asked: "Adventurous?"

Gao replied: "Our Cybersync caters for dedicated gamers...they tend to be a little obsessive..."

Chung stared intently at Alice and said: "There is no harm in a little obsession."

Gao asked: "So Alice, what do you do at the Hub?"

Cynthia interjected: "She is a waitress."

Chung said: "Alice is one of our best employees...most efficient..."

Gao smiled slightly and asked: "Have you been there long?"

Alice picked up her glass as she replied: "A year next month."

Chung sipped from his glass and said: "I think she would make an excellent duty manager."

Alice lowered her eyes slightly and said: "I am not sure about that..."

Gao said: "Modesty is an admiral trait."

Cynthia emptied her glass and said: "It is positively adorable."

## 22:25 - Rooftop Garden - Oriental Plaza Hotel - Hong Kong

The night was long and tedious - a series of banal conversations bordering upon pointless triviality. Alice sighed heavily. Chung Lee and his friends were boring and boastful minions of the Hub Corporation. *And Cynthia is a bitch...* The woman used every chance to belittle the role of a waitress. *"But I suppose you must look cute in uniform Alice..."* She glanced towards a smiling Chung Lee. *Lecherous old dog...* He had made repeated attempts to touch her hands, arms and even her knees at one point. Another couple had eventually joined the little gathering - a boring young Cybersync technician from Shenzhen accompanied by his sullen-faced girlfriend. The one saving grace was Mong Gao - the handsome young manager of the Blue Lounge Cyber Club. She found him to be both fascinating and mysterious. She wasn't sure, but she had the impression that he was equally disenchanted by Chung Lee and his odious friends. She checked her phone - *Time to go home...* Placing her glass onto the table she announced:

"I think I should head home... I have an early shift tomorrow."

Chung asked: "Really? But the night is just beginning... I thought we might go on to a little jazz place I know..."

Alice smiled politely and said: "Sorry, but I really have to go..."

Chung replied: "Then allow me to accompany you...we can share a taxi..."

Alice was about to say something when Mong Gao interjected:

"I can drop Alice off... I have my car downstairs."

Chung stood up unsteadily and said: "Oh I think I can take care of Alice..."

Alice pushed her chair back and said: "No it's okay... I will go with Mister Mong."

Chung gave Gao a stern look before saying:

"Please yourself..."

Alice stood up and said: "Good night Mister Chung, Mister Tiang..." She gave a cursory nod to his wife Cynthia and the others before joining Mong Gao.

Gao stood up and said: "Good night my friends..."

Tiang smiled at Alice and said: "Do not forget to try Japan one day..."

Alice replied: "I will thank you..."

Cynthia gave a dismissive look and snapped: "Enough with the Japan obsession already..."

Gao turned to Alice and said: "After you..."

As they approached the lifts Alice said: "Actually, I think I will take a taxi..."

Gao smiled slightly and said: "Driving you home is not a problem." He pressed for the lift before adding: "And you have nothing to fear...unlike Chung Lee I have no ulterior motives."

As the lift doors opened Alice asked: "You noticed that?"

Gao replied: "Chung has a bit of reputation with young female employees..."

Stepping inside Alice asked: "He has done this before?"

Gao spoke to the elevator before replying: "Many times... He invites a young waitress to an event simply to pressurise her into an affair..."

Alice fell silent briefly before saying: "I think you just saved me..."

Gao smiled and said: "I think I just did."

Alice leaned against the mirrored wall and said: "Because I am not really a very good worker..."

Gao gave a slight smile and asked: "So you are not the best employee?"

Alice smiled shyly and replied: "Not by a long way..."

As he doors opened onto the main reception Gao said:

"Chung uses flattery to get his wicked way..."

Alice replied: "I noticed."

Stepping out of the lift Gao continued:

"And he has a wife back in Shanghai."

Alice's eyes widened as she asked: "Really?"

Gao nodded slightly before adding: "And a teenage daughter..."

Alice exclaimed: "Wow...dirty old dog..."

Gao gestured to the main doors and said: "My car is out front..."

As they walked through the lobby Alice said: "I live in Block Five; Kwai Chung Estate...is that far out of your way?"

Gao replied: "Not at all..."

Alice stopped in front of the glass doors and asked: "So you have no ulterior motives?"

Gao replied: "I always have ulterior motives..." He smiled as he continued: "But not on this occasion I will be the perfect gentlemen...you have my word."

Alice gave a coy smile and said: "I have only just met you Mister Mong."

Gao replied: "First of all, Mister Mong is my father, please call me Gao, and secondly I offer nothing more than a ride home..."

Alice looked towards the car park and said: "Very well... Gao."

As the sliding doors closed behind them the quiet serenity of the hotel lobby was replaced by the cacophonous chaos of central Hong Kong. A warm breeze brought the familiar combination of exhaust fumes, cooked food and the last whispers of rain receding across Victoria Harbour. Alice looked up to a brief scattering of stars touching an illuminated sea of skyscrapers with a feeble trembling embrace.

Gao pointed to the left and said: "This way..."

Alice followed Gao towards a small car park at the side of the hotel. She glanced once towards a busy Des Voeux Road and wondered why people didn't seem to sleep anymore. *But they will all be on the MTR in the morning...* Gao stopped and she was surprised to see a black Weio sports car. She asked:

"Is this your car?"

Gao touched his palm to the passenger side window and replied: "Yes..."

A sudden flashing of the car lights confirmed scan recognition as the car unlocked its two doors with a quiet ping.

Gao opened the passenger door and said: "Here you go..."

As she climbed inside Alice said: "Very cool car..."

Gao replied as he closed the door: "Thank you."

Alice saw an illuminated control panel shimmering green light amongst the shadows. She noted more than a dozen Cybersync apps including a Cloud Access Portal. *He roams the Cloud...* The odour of leather was muted slightly by a scented whisper of air emanating from the aircon system. She waited for Gao to settle into the driver's seat before saying:

"I have never been inside a sports car..."

Gao smiled slightly and said: "Buckle up..."

Alice reached for her seatbelt and said: "Of course..."

Gao spoke to the car: "Block Five... Kwai Chung Estate... Standard speed."

As the engine rumbled into life Alice gripped her purse and asked: "It is autonomous?"

Gao secured his seatbelt and replied: "I can hold the wheel if it makes you feel better..."

Alice stared at the control interface and said: "No... It's okay..."

As the car began to move forward Gao asked: "Have you ever been inside a self-driving car?"

Alice pulled her dress over her knees and replied: "No... But I once rode an autobus in Shanghai..."

Gao asked: "The ones with the robot dolls?"

Alice smiled slightly as she replied: "Yes... There was a talking mannequin sitting up front...very weird experience."

Gao spoke to the car: "Music... Cantrill's Sonata..."

Moments later the car was filled with the soothing sounds of music.

Alice sat back and said: "Your job must pay well..."

Gao glanced out of the side window and replied: "I get by..."

Alice studied Gao briefly before asking: "So why were you at that rooftop party?"

Gao replied: "I was hoping to meet someone..."

Alice asked: "Anyone in particular?"

Gao gave a slight smile and said: "You are an inquisitive one..."

Alice lowered her eyes slightly and said: "Sorry...bad habit suppose..."

Gao said: "No need to apologise..." He waited until the car turned onto the main road before continuing: "I was hoping to meet a guy from Singapore. But he did not turn up."

Alice said: "Oh yes, about your franchise..."

Gao hesitated slightly before replying: "Yes that's right..."

Alice said: "Maybe you can meet him somewhere else..."

Gao nodded slightly and replied: "Yes. I will track him down eventually."

Alice looked out towards Victoria Harbour and said: "I love the city at night..."

Gao replied: "It is beautiful..."

Alice sighed and said: "We could lose it all one day..."

Gao looked at Alice asked: "What do you mean?"

Alice replied: "According to Mister Chung, Hong Kong will eventually be swallowed up by the mainland. We will become one big super-city..." She stared out of the window before adding soberly: "We will no longer be Hong Kong..."

Gao frowned and said: "We have survived more than one crisis...we will survive the next one..."

Alice sighed and said: "I hope so..."

As the car joined the new Kowloon Expressway Gao asked: "Do you have time for a quick detour?"

Alice tensed slightly and asked: "What kind of detour?"

Gao smiled and replied: "I want to restore your faith in the future..."

Alice glanced at her phone and replied: "If it does not take long..."

Gao replied: "Twenty minutes...."

Alice said: "Okay."

Gao spoke to the car: "Avenue of Stars."

Alice frowned and said: "I have been there many times..."

Gao smiled slightly and replied: "But not with me..."

Alice looked out the window and replied in a low voice: "No...not with you..."

## 23:08 - The Avenue of Stars - Hong Kong

The black car swept past street lights into the shadows of a private car park behind the Avenue of Stars. With a slight flickering of the control interface the engine rumbled into silence as the doors unlocked with a single ping. A soft female voice announced:

"Destination confirmed."

Alice smiled and said: "I like the voice...was that your choice?"

Gao returned the smile and replied: "Guilty as charged..." He shrugged before adding: "I find her voice soothing..."

Alice grinned as she said: "I bet you do..."

Gao pushed his door open and said: "Let's go..."

Alice released her seatbelt and asked: "We can park here?"

Gao gave a slight smile and replied: "I know the owners..."

Alice felt a warm breeze whispering the last touch of rain above the choppy waters of Victoria Harbour. She looked up to see a swath of stars struggling to be seen beyond the bright lights of the city. *A patch of darkness trapped between the Island and Kowloon...* She noticed young couples congregating along the metal railings. *Date night....*

Gao stepped closer and said: "Let's walk..."

Alice gripped her purse and replied: "Okay..."

Across the harbour Hong Kong Island was a splendid ocean of brightly lit skyscrapers casting ripples of light across the dark water. The sounds of the city merged into a sleepless melody of slow-moving traffic and late-night revellers. Along the Avenue young people posed in front of the statues of famous movie stars. When they finally arrived at the railings overlooking the water Gao said:

"You are not very happy at the Hub..."

Alice looked at Mong and asked: "What makes you say that?"

Gao replied: "You feel your dreams slipping away...your potential consumed by a drab daily routine."

Alice smiled slightly and said: "Very perceptive..."

Gao asked: "So I am right?"

Alice sighed and replied truthfully: "I hate my job...the customers drive me crazy..."

Gao asked: "So why do you stay there?"

Alice fell silent before replying: "After Uni I was going to travel..." She looked towards the Island and continued: "I got as far as Beijing..."

Gao asked: "What happened in Beijing?"

Alice lowered her head slightly and replied: "It does not matter...it's all in the past now." She paused before continuing: "I took the waitress job to earn some money...but now I think I am stuck there..." She sighed heavily before adding: "With nowhere to go..."

Gao considered this and said: "I might be able to offer you a position at the Blue Lounge, if you are interested. The salary is good and the hours reasonable."

Alice's face brightened as she asked: "Really?"

Gao replied with a smile: "Come to the club Friday night and we can discuss it..."

Alice said: "Thank you... I might do that..."

Gao tapped his phone and said: "Sending my 121 ID now."

Alice tapped the 121 app on her phone and announced: "MGHK21... Got it...synced."

Gao looked up and said: "Just message me to confirm..."

Alice said: "Okay, I will."

They leaned on the railing and listened to the sound of water lapping against the harbour wall with a brief surge of defiance. Now they could see the Star Ferry festooned with lights moving through the night. Finally Gao said:

"Hong Kong will not be swallowed up by the mainland."

Alice looked at Gao and asked: "What makes you so sure?"

Gao replied: "Because it is unique...it is a fusion of West and East. And despite the inevitable incorporation it will keep its own identity." He paused before continuing: "We have enjoyed our freedom for too long to abandon it so easily."

Alice looked towards a group of tourists and said: "But we cannot resist the power of the mainland...in twenty forty seven they have the legal right to take complete control..." She sighed before adding: "We will lose our freedom..."

Gao replied: "But the mainland has net access now...the great firewall is a thing of the past."

Alice countered: "Only because Beijing controls the Nexus search engine...it has more security filters than any platform out there." She looked towards the Island and added: "And they will control Hong Kong the same way..."

Gao replied: "Possibly, but I think there will be resistance. People will stand up for their rights."

A sceptical Alice replied: "I doubt that..."

Gao asked: "You do?"

Alice replied: "They have been protesting as far back as two thousand and fourteen...every few years the students demonstrate and it's all over the news... But eventually it all dies down and the city goes back to the status quo..." She looked towards a group of young people and added: "The blind leading the blind..."

Gao looked at Alice asked: "Why so cynical?"

Alice gave a slight smile and replied: "Sorry..."

Gao said: "I don't mean that as a criticism. I really want to know how you feel."

Alice hesitated before continuing: "It's like we are slaves to a pack mentality...constantly sedated by our blatantly exploitive social media accounts and our false dedication to so-called social trends..." She sighed before adding: "It's nothing but self-delusion and the paranoid fear of failure."

Gao exclaimed: "Wow! Where did that come from?"

Alice smiled shyly and replied: "Sorry..."

Gao said: "Don't apologise... Please, go on..."

Alice explained: "Working with Cybersync every day has stirred up some issues for me..."

Gao asked: "What kind of issues?"

Alice fell silent briefly before replying: "All our heroes are counterfeit in a world that is just one big hoax, spamming each other with our stinging commentary masquerading as insight and social media faking as intimacy. We created this atmosphere with our constant purchases, our spending power, our false appreciation of the latest fashions or the esteemed Times best seller that is a must read even though you know it's totally sin ka lan." She sighed before adding: "The Cybersync sedation stops the pain because we are cowards...unable to face the reality of our lives."

Gao nodded slightly and said: "I had no idea you were so astute. Most impressive..."

Alice felt her face flush as she said: "I have never shared those feelings with anyone..."

Gao bowed his head slightly and said: "Then I am honoured."

Alice glanced at her phone and said: "I better go home... I have work tomorrow."

Gao replied: "Of course..."

Within minutes they were back inside the car and Gao asked:

"So Alice... Have I restored your faith in the future?"

Alice looked towards Hong Kong Island and replied: "Let's just say I am little more hopeful..."

Gao spoke as the car rumbled into life:

"Then the night was not a complete waste of time..."

Less than twenty minutes later the car pulled up outside Block 5 of the Kwai Chung housing estate. The car announced:

"Destination confirmed."

Alice unclipped her seatbelt and said: "Well thank you once again Mister..." She smiled before continuing: "Gao..."

Gao looked up as Alice stepped outside and said: "So give me a call before Friday and we can set up a meeting..."

Alice replied: "I will...thank you..."

Gao saw hesitation and asked: "Is something wrong?"

Alice asked: "What do you know about Tiang Lao?"

Gao replied: "Not much...he works for the Hub...that's all I know. Why?"

Alice sighed and said: "It doesn't matter. Good night Gao..."

Gao smiled and replied: "Good night Alice..."

Alice waited until the sports car had turned the corner before whispering:

"Mong Gao..."

She smiled as she set off towards the main entrance to Block No.5.

## 23:57 - Apartment 82 - Block 5 - Kwai Chung Housing Estates Hong Kong

A bedroom lost to shadows skirting a bedside lamp casting light upon the two young woman lying side-by-side in their underwear on the bed. Street sounds are muted into the ever-present rumbling of the vast city perched at the edge of the Kowloon peninsula.

Alice studied her fingernails and asked:

"What do you want me to say?"

Nancy Yao rolled over onto an elbow and replied: "Do you like this Mong Gao?"

Alice sighed and replied: "He is very polite..."

Nancy lay back on the bed and said: "That is not what I asked."

Alice smiled and said: "Okay... I think I like him..."

Nancy yawned and said: "Just be careful sweetie..."

Alice said: "You always say that..."

Nancy said: "He manages the Blue Lounge..." She closed her eyes before adding: "Not the most reputable place..."

Alice said: "Now you sound like Cynthia Tiang..."

Nancy asked: "Who?"

Alice bit a fingernail and replied: "Tiang Lao's bitchy wife..."

Nancy gently tapped Alice's finger from her mouth and said:

"Just be on your guard with Mong Gao..."

Alice sat up against the headboard and asked: "What about you Nancy?"

Nancy looked up and asked: "What about me?"

Alice replied: "When we first met in Beijing you had a boy with you..."

Nancy fell silent before replying: "Yes...that was Lu...an old friend from school..."

Alice gave a mischievous smile and asked: "Just a friend?"

Nancy replied: "Okay we dated a little...but it was never serious..."

Alice frowned and said: "It looked serious..."

Nancy shrugged and said: "Well it wasn't..."

Alice continued: "He looked heartbroken at the airport..."

Nancy looked up and asked: "What's with the interrogation?"

Alice placed a hand onto Nancy's shoulder and said: "Sorry... I just care about you..." She paused before continuing: "And you left your life in Beijing to join me in Hong Kong..."

Nancy replied: "I told you... I was tired of that life. I wanted a fresh start..."

Alice asked: "So you like the job at Techsync?"

Nancy brushed a hand through her hair and replied: "The local office pays twice as much as my old job...so yes... I like it..."

Alice sighed and said: "Meeting you in Beijing was the best part of that trip..."

Nancy smiled and said: "It worked out well for both of us."

Alice nodded slightly and said: "That's true... I could never afford this place on my own."

Nancy replied: "Me neither..."

Alice said: "But it's weird..."

Nancy asked: "What is weird?"

Alice replied: "My Beijing trip..."

Nancy sat up and asked: "What about it?"

Alice hesitated before replying: "I remember the trip...but the details elude me..."

Nancy asked: "Details?"

Alice yawned before replying: "Never mind... I am just tired..."

Nancy rolled onto her feet and said: "Then I will leave you to your dreams..." As she opened the bedroom door she added: "Good night Alice..."

Alice closed her eyes and replied: "Good night Nancy..."

Once inside her own bedroom Nancy activated her data-lenses and synced to the designated portal. She spoke in a low voice:

"We might have a problem."

A male voice arrived inside her audio plugs:

"Explain."

Nancy continued: "She is questioning the veracity of the Beijing scenario."

There was a short pause before the voice asked:

"Has she discovered your true identity?"

Nancy fell silent before replying: "No... I don't think so..."

The voice ordered:

"You will continue to monitor the situation. Report any further incidents immediately."

Nancy replied: "Of course...but..."

The voice asked: "But what?"

Nancy asked: "What about the Security Ministry? Do they know about me?"

The voice replied: "Of course not."

Nancy continued: "But the data-hack..."

The voice interjected: "Your identity has not been compromised. Continue with your mission and await the implementation of phase two."

Nancy hesitated before asking: "Did you speak to the Professor?"

The voice replied: "Of course."

Nancy asked: "What does he know about my true mission?"

The voice replied: "He knows nothing beyond the original plan to compare proactive data."

Nancy sighed and said: "Surely you have acquired enough data by now..."

The voice spoke firmly:

"It is not your place to question policy. You will carry out your mission as ordered." There was as short pause before the voice continued: "Remember who you are Suyin...remember that you were created for a specific purpose. You are not to venture outside your current dictate. Do you understand?"

Suyin replied sullenly: "I understand..."

The voice asked: "Is there anything else to report?"

Suyin replied in a low voice: "No."

The voice asked: "And the headaches?"

Suyin touched a hand to her head and replied: "Annoying...but I can cope..."

The voice said: "Very good." There was a pause before the voice continued: "You are at the forefront of a new era of evolution Suyin...be proud of that..."

Suyin replied bitterly: "I am so proud..."

The voice spoke one more time: "Zàijiàn Suyin."

As the connection fell silent Suyin whispered:

"Created for a specific purpose?"

A shocking fear arrived with a frightening suspicion. *Is it possible?* A vague childhood memory increased her fears:

*"We will take care of you from now on..."*

*"Why?"*

*"Because you are very special..."*

She raised her hand to see blood where her fingernails had pressed into the skin.

94

# The Group in Singapore

*'The absurd audacity of humanity to seek the emulation of the Gods...'*
The Philosopher Zou Xi

**06:41 - Tuesday - April 27th - 2028 - Apartment 19 - Block 411 - Saujana Road - Singapore**

Sunlight touched the bedroom windows with a sudden brightness scattering left-over shadows amongst cluttered bookshelves and a desk buried beneath piles of data-skims. The sole occupant of the double bed rolled over to see dust motes floating inside sunbeams glancing off the wardrobe mirrors. She wiped sleep from her eyes and stared at her reflection in the mirror opposite. *God...* Her tussled hair was a rich shade of ebony flowing in waves over porcelain-like skin glistening with perspiration. Long lashes framed deep brown eyes set above a straight nose and full lips parted slightly to reveal perfect white teeth. One glance at her phone confirmed her fears - *Only four hours sleep...* She kicked the duvet away and looked up at the rhythmic revolutions of the ceiling fan. *Too hot to sleep again...* She placed one hand over her breast and yawned. *I should go out today...* For five long days she had remained indoors, anxious to avoid all human contact. The unexpected success of the Beijing hack had forced her to go off the grid. The group consensus was to avoid the Cloud for at least a week until they could confirm the security of their access portals. *But they could already be coming for us...*

At just twenty five years of age Fay Rui was an unlikely choice as the leader of the FTSS (FreeTech Society of Singapore) - a small but radical group of hackers dedicated to the free dissemination of data related to a variety of secret global projects commissioned by both Governments and private multinational corporations. But with a history of student activism is was almost inevitable that she would graduate to what her friend Connie called: *the big league.* The theft of the Jiàngshēng files had ignited a storm of activity from within the Cloud environment. Multiple agencies were now actively seeking the stolen data. *They will be coming to Singapore...* She looked towards the window and sighed heavily. *If they are not already here...* Under normal circumstances the illegal extraction of data would not attract the attention of so many interested groups, but the Ministry of Science and Technology of the People's Republic of China was obviously the target of a multitude of spy agencies. *They were alerted by the unsigned exterior data-spike...* As for the files themselves, a brief reading of the contents had caused both panic and alarm among her group. *Talk about playing with fire...* Her thoughts returned to the last group meeting inside the Dark Cloud. *Chin thinks he is being followed...* Chin Fen was not usually paranoid, but he was insistent - people were following him around town. Whether that was simply a result of paranoia was debatable, but the fact remained that her four friends were in fear for their lives. *I blame myself...* When she had first discovered the existence of the Jiàngshēng Project it seemed the ideal target for the group's talents - a top secret project financed by the Beijing government. But she had ignored an age-old truth known to thieves since the dawn of time - if you steal something so valuable, so priceless, it inevitably becomes too hot to handle. *And we stole the Mona Lisa of digital data...* Her thoughts were interrupted by a pinging from her phone. A smiling flower emoticon appeared onscreen. *Connie May...* She tapped respond and said:

"Hi Connie..."

Connie replied: "We need to convene a meeting of the group."

Fay lay back into her pillow and replied: "We agreed to avoid the Cloud...it's not safe to go online..."

Connie replied: "No. I mean we should meet in person...all of us..."

Fay sat up straight and said: "But we never meet in real-life...the FTSS is a Cloud group...avatars only; that was the agreement we made when we started out. We don't even know what each other looks like..."

Connie replied: "I know, but this situation is getting serious. Chin is sending 121 messages like crazy... I'm sure he's going to lose it..."

Fay considered this before saying: "I suppose it is about time we met in the real world..."

Connie continued: "And right now it might be safer than meeting n the Cloud..."

Fay nodded slightly and said: "Alright, I'll contact the others and get back to you with a time and place."

Connie said: "Make it soon Fay..."

Fay replied: "Of course...bye Connie..."

Connie replied: "Bye Fay..."

**21:00 - Wednesday - April 28th - Fidel's Coffee Bar - Marina Blvd - Singapore**

The stars are pushed back by the bright lights of Singapore. A dry and humid night creates an air of sultry oppression along the city streets. But a slight breeze gives some comfort to the teeming crowds making their way along the busy Marina Bay waterfront.

Fay stepped off the bus and looked towards Fidel's Coffee Bar sitting in the shadows of the Marina Bay Financial Tower. *I might be the only one to turn up...* It had taken several frustrating hours to convince the other group members to meet in person - but there were no guarantees. *Isolated paranoia is our modus operandi...* Even Connie May had voiced doubts about a real-world meeting: *"I'm not sure now Fay...maybe it's a bad idea..."* But if anyone would turn up it would be Chin Fen: *"Just make it someplace public...and not near the Hub restaurant in Chinatown... They will be watching that place..."* She sighed heavily. *Paranoia or frightening truth?* Despite knowing her hacker friends for almost five years they were still strangers hiding behind their avatars. *The digital illusion...* She took a moment to study her reflection in a restaurant window. *Baggy blue jacket over green T-shirt and jeans...* She smiled slightly. *Undercover Fay...* Finally she secured her hair at the back of her neck before continuing on towards the coffee bar.

The moment she stepped through the doors Fay paused to assess the situation: *Very busy...standing room only...basic Wi-Fi...no Cloud Cybersync...* The room displayed the standard dark wooden furniture and Latino wall decor of the Fidel chain of Cuban cafe's. One sniff brought a smile to her face *Espresso...* And then her eyes were drawn to a corner booth behind a large menu interface. She saw a slim, petite young girl with short black hair and wide brown eyes set above a small nose complete with gold stud - *black jacket over blue T-shirt, black denim jeans and boots... Connie May?* If it was Connie she looked a lot younger than her stated twenty four years of age. Sitting next to her, a nervous-looking young man with short cropped black hair was busy studying his phone - *grey sweatshirt, blue knee-length shorts and white pumps... twenty one year old Chin Fen?* And finally a heavy-set young man with cropped hair and broad shoulders sat with his back to the main entrance - *black leather jacket and faded jeans... twenty two year old Chok Tong?* The only person missing was the youngest member of the group - nineteen year-old Jessica Lee. *If I guessed right...* Finally she took a deep breath before walking towards the corner table.

 Connie May looked up and asked: "Fay?"

 Fay smiled slightly and replied: "Yes. Connie right?"

 Connie smiled and replied: "Yes." She turned to the young man next to her and continued: "This is Chin...and this is Tong..."

 Chin Fen gave a nervous smile and asked: "Did you take the MRT?"

 Fay raised her voice above the surrounding conversations as she replied:

 "No, I took the bus..."

 Fen sighed and said: "Good...because the trains are synced to the Cloud..." He looked towards the large front windows before adding: "They can track you on the trains..."

 Connie placed her coffee mug on the table and said: "You are just being paranoid..."

 Fen ignored the comment and said: "And don't use your lenses...they will be monitoring portal spikes..."

 Fay turned to Chok Tong and said: "Hello..."

 Tong grunted a brief: "Néih hóu."

 Connie said: "Move along Tong..."

 Fay glimpsed a red skull tattoo on Tong's thick neck as he shuffled along the seat.

Connie smiled and said: "Well it's good to finally meet..."

Fay spoke as she sat down next to Tong: "Any sign of Jessica?"

Connie frowned and replied: "Not yet...but she promised to come..."

Fen interjected: "Unless they got to her already..."

Tong scratched chin stubble and asked: "Who got to her?"

Fen leaned closer and replied in a low voice: "Them...the secret agents..."

Tong shook his head dismissively and said: "You've been watching too many spy movies..."

But Fen insisted: "I tell you they are on to us..."

Fay asked: "How can you be so sure?"

Fen looked towards the other customers before replying in a low voice:

"Spike flood..."

Tong asked: "What?"

Fen continued: "Since the hack the local portal spikes have increaseed by about a thousand per cent... NAR's are off the scale..."

Fay asked: "How can you know that?"

Connie interjected: "And what does that mean?"

Fen sighed as he explained: "It means global NAR requests for a Singapore Cloud portal have quadrupled." He leaned forward before continuing: "Every single Net Access Response spike is being systematically scanned for its source code..."

Connie looked at Fay and asked: "Is that even possible?"

Fay frowned and replied: "It would take some very sophisticated tech...but maybe..."

Tong said: "We used multilayer ciphers to create a mirror exit portal....it's untraceable."

A female voice interjected: "Actually that is not quite true..."

Fay looked up to see a smartly dressed young woman standing over them. She asked: "Jessica?"

Jessica Lee replied with a smile: "That's me." She asked Connie: "Make some room?"

Connie shuffled closer to Fen as Jessica sat down facing Fay.

Fen pressed up against the wall and grumbled: "Maybe we need a bigger table..."

Fay took a moment to study Jessica Lee. The young woman had an air of graceful sophistication that hinted at wealth. She wore a stylish off-white two-piece suit consisting of jacket and knee-length skirt. Long dark, ponytailed hair framed delicate ears adorned with bejewelled earrings. A porcelain-like complexion was complimented by a pair of arched eyebrows looking down on wide brown eyes, sweeping eyelashes and a button nose set above dazzling, white teeth gleaming between soft lips touched with gloss. Finally she asked:

"You believe they tracked our exit portal?"

Jessica replied firmly: "I do."

Fay said: "I thought that was impossible...we used false bounce-back recognition protocols..."

Connie added: "And sub-level intercept spikes with mirror access portals..."

Jessica unfastened her jacket and said: "It is true...under normal circumstances the data-extraction point would be untraceable. But we are dealing with a whole new level of expertise now. I know of at least half a dozen people who could track our exit portal to Singapore..." She paused before adding: "And after reading some of those stolen files I think our biggest problem will be the augments themselves."

Tong replaced his coffee mug and asked: "What about them?"

Jessica replied: "The one in Shanghai has a brain-computer interface...that giver her instant Cybersync...she can literally scan the entire Cloud in a matter of seconds."

Fen asked: "What about the Dark Cloud?"

Jessica sat back and replied soberly: "There are no Cloud restrictions for these augments...they can go anywhere and access any amount off data." She paused before adding: "That is why they were created...it's their raison d'être."

Tong asked: "Their what?"

Fen said: "Never mind that, what happens now?"

Fay sat forward and said: "Well for a start we don't panic..."

Connie said: "That's right...but we need to do something. We can't just stay off-grid for the rest of our lives..."

Fay fell silent briefly before replying: "We will disseminate the data as planned. Once the information is out there it loses its value and we are no longer a threat."

Tong nodded slightly and said: "I agree...we should dump the files into an open-source portal."

Fen spoke enthusiastically: "Yes, let's do that..."

Jessica frowned and asked: "But do we really want to do that to the augments? It will ruin their lives..."

Fen asked: "But what about our lives? Don't we matter?"

Fay said: "The Jiàngshēng subjects might not be so innocent... they do work for the Beijing government afterall."

Fen asked: "And what about the Biogen connection? That reeks of conspiracy."

Jessica continued: "You read those files; those so-called volunteers had no idea what they were getting into..."

Connie said: "And what about the mysterious original prototype?"

Fay replied: "We have no idea who that is or where they are located."

Fen looked towards the front door and said: "But maybe they know where we are located...."

A frustrated Tong said: "So let's just make a decision...dump the files or not?"

Fay looked at Jessica and said: "It will take time to sift out the location of the files, even for the experts...so perhaps we should use that time to cover our tracks."

A frustrated Fen asked: "Why can't we just dump and run?"

Fay replied: "Because perhaps Jessica is right...the augments are victims of the same policies we have been trying to undermine for the last five years. If we reveal their existence we will be no worse than the faceless corporate bureaucrats who seek to control the world."

Fen spoke anxiously: "But the authorities will still be coming for us..."

Jessica said: "Not necessarily, the main priority of the Chinese government is to retrieve those files...same goes for all the other interested parties. Tracking us down would be an unnecessary diversion of digital resources."

Connie countered: "Yes, but we know the location of the files; surely that makes us a target?"

Fay said: "So we take precautions. We cover our tracks..."

Fen asked: "How? We've already wiped our accounts and flushed the false data-spikes from the Cloud..."

Fay replied: "We create a false trail..."

Jessica smiled and said: "Perfect..."

Tong asked: "How do we do that?"

Fay replied in a low voice: "Let's assume that they have identified a Singapore exit portal, their next step will be to sift for specific algorithmic potential in order to identify an encrypted portal access. All we need to do is to create a viable algorithmic potential to lead them on a wild-goose-chase."

Fen considered that before saying: "I could write a new algorithm...create another mirror access portal...flush it with digital access nodes..."

Connie added: "And spike it with false recognition protocols."

Jessica cautioned: "But not too many or they will see through the ruse."

Fay smiled slightly and said: "Sounds like a plan."

Connie asked: "What about Cybersync? Do we use new lenses?"

Fay replied: "Definitely. And use false ID tags during sign-up."

Fen added: "And rotate your PAP's each time you request a NAR."

Jessica nodded slightly and said: "Yes...and mirror your global roaming to an overseas source point."

Connie added: "With false bounce-back protocols."

The group fell silent until Tong asked: "So are we done here? I need to eat."

Fay smiled slightly and asked: "Shall we order something here?"

Tong replied irritably: "When I say eat, I mean real food, not dumb pastries..."

Connie pushed her mug away and said: "Actually I need to get going..."

Fen said: "And I have an algorithm to write..."

Fay asked: "You need any help with that?"

Fen replied: "No, I work better on my own."

Jessica stood up to allow Connie and Fen out of the booth.

Connie gave a slight smile and said: "Nice to meet you all...bye for now..."

Fen gripped his phone and said: "Don't access Cybersync until I upload the new algorithm. Bye..."

As Fay allowed the hulking Chok Tong to exit the booth she said:

"Bye Tong..."

Tong replied: "Yea...bye..."

Jessica sat down and said: "Man of few words that one..."

Fay replied as she sat down again: "And yet his avatar never shuts up..."

Jessica laughed and said: "I know...weird right?"

Fay looked at Jessica and asked:

"Have you read all of the Jiàngshēng files?"

Jessica straightened her skirt as she replied: "I did...and you?"

Fay replied: "Most of them..."

Jessica asked: "What did you think?"

Fay replied: "I couldn't believe what I was reading..."

Jessica nodded slightly and said: "It is kind of amazing..."

Fay continued: "Mixing genomic material with artificial augmentation..." She sighed before adding: "The absurd audacity of humanity to seek the emulation of the Gods..."

Jessica frowned and said: "I have heard that saying..."

Fay smiled slightly and said: "The Philosopher Zou Xi."

Jessica nodded and said: "It's not the augmentation that worries me; it's the long-term agenda behind the project."

Fay asked: "Agenda?"

Jessica asked: "Did you read the references to the next phase of the project?"

Fay replied: "I did."

Jessica continued: "God only knows what that's all about..."

Fay studied Jessica carefully before asking: "Do you have a secret agenda?"

Jessica's eyes widened as she asked: "What do you mean?"

Fay asked: "What is the real reason behind your opposition to dumping the files into an open-source portal?"

Jessica played with a teaspoon as she replied: "I told you...to protect the augmented subjects."

Fay sat forward and said: "I don't buy it...there is another reason. Tell me the truth Jessica."

Jessica looked up and replied: "Alright... I want more time to study the files."

Fay suddenly saw the shocking truth as she exclaimed: "You made a copy!"

A sheepish Jessica replied in a low voice: "Yes."

Fay scowled and asked: "Why would you break protocol?"

Jessica replied: "I want to know more about the Biogen connection..."

Fay asked: "For what purpose? We have more than enough data to compromise the Jiàngshēng Project."

Jessica asked: "But why not expose Biogen as well?" She smiled slightly before adding: "Bring down two birds with one hack..."

Fay replied: "Everything will come out eventually...we don't need to do anything else...the exposure will take on a life of its own."

Jessica replied: "But we need to know why Biogen is so desperate to fund the project."

Fay stared directly at Jessica and asked: "What is your connection to Biogen?"

Jessica tensed and asked: "Connection?"

Fay replied: "I recognise a hidden agenda when I see one..."

Jessica hesitated before replying: "My father works for Biogen...in fact he is an executive on their board of directors."

Fay sat back and exclaimed: "Wow...that explains a lot."

Jessica looked up and asked: "It does?"

Fay gestured with one hand as she replied: "The tailored suit, the expensive jewellery...it all speaks wealth...and Biogen is one of the wealthiest companies on the planet." She paused before continuing: "Which begs the question: why would someone like you get mixed up with a hacker collective?"

Jessica smiled slightly as she replied: "It's not just girly rebellion against my parents if that's what you think..."

Fay asked: "So what is it? Why did you join FTSS?"

Jessica sat forward and replied: "Because I genuinely want to help... Someone has to stop the global corporations from taking control of our lives. We are indoctrinated on a daily basis by Cybersync... subsumed by our exploitive social media accounts until we blindly follow the prevailing social trends like sheep..." She paused before adding: "We are losing our humanity inside the Cloud..."

Fay gave a grim smile and said: "I won't argue with that..."

Jessica said: "And yet you spend most of your life inside the Cloud..."

Fay retorted: "Because it is a necessary means towards and end."

Jessica said: "It is also a method of mass manipulation. It replaces reality with an artificial comfort zone created and controlled by the Cybersync industry."

Fay replied: "Cloud dancing has its negative aspects, but how else can we access restricted data? We don't have the luxury of choosing our battlegrounds."

Jessica replied: "I know..." She sighed before adding: "Cybersync is our brave new world..."

Fay replied: "It is a tool to be used nothing more."

Jessica asked: "You really believe that?"

Fay replied: "I know the difference between reality and the Cloud."

Jessica continued: "But the invasive nature of the latest Cloud scenarios has led to real-world deaths. People get caught up in the sync and the lines between reality and Cloud blur into paranoia."

Fay said: "You can't blame Cybersync for a few aberrant sociopaths...there is always going to be unbalanced people lashing out."

Jessica replied: "But our brains are evolving to a new form of synaptic reality. Our neural landscape is adapting to the artificial environment of the Cloud..." She fell silent briefly before continuing: "We think faster inside the Cloud, we are more productive because we can instantly access quantum levels of data. We even socialise better inside the Cloud...look at Chok Tong as a prime example - a young man who struggles to string a few words together out here in the real world, but who is the life and soul of the party inside the Cloud. Doesn't that tell you something about the evolving nature of our society?"

Fay replied: "It tells me that some people are more confident inside the Cloud..."

Jessica retorted: "And some people never leave the Cloud, they stay connected twenty four hours a day. You can't tell me that is a good thing..."

Fay sighed and replied: "It's not our place to debate the morality of the Cloud. I formed the FTSS with one specific goal: the dissemination of data related to a multitude of ongoing secret projects that exist outside the law and beyond public oversight."

Jessica sighed and said: "Like you say...we can't choose out battlegrounds."

Fay asked: "Do you know why Biogen are undermining the Chinese government?"

Jessica replied: "Unfortunately no... I found nothing specific in the files, only a few vague references that require further investigation."

Fay asked: "References to what?"

Jessica lowered her voice as she replied: "Off-world colonisation for one..."

Fay raised her eyebrows and asked: "The Lunar base?"

Jessica replied: "More likely the proposed Chinese base on Mars...an augment or two would make ideal Martian colonists."

Fay said: "How would that benefit Biogen?"

Jessica replied: "I have no idea..."

Fay fell silent before saying: "But if a private company could colonise Mars..."

Jessica said: "They could own their own planet..."

Fay considered this before warning: "Tread carefully Jessica, we have no idea how far Biogen will go to protect their investment in the project."

Jessica replied: "That is why I will bypass Biogen and go straight to the source."

Fay asked: "The source?"

Jessica replied: "The girl in Shanghai..."

Fay tensed and asked: "What are you going to do?"

Jessica replied: "I leave for Shanghai tomorrow morning..."

Fay leaned on the table and asked: "Why would you even consider such a thing? We are hackers Jessica, not secret agents...we fight our battles inside the Cloud. And we certainly don't risk our lives simply to satisfy curiosity."

Jessica replied: "This battle may have started inside the Cloud, but right now it's out here in the real world." She sat forward and continued: "For the last five years we have been playing games inside the Cloud, hiding behind our avatars whilst we plundered the corporate world of its secrets. But this time we have opened up a whole new can of worms by stealing from the Chinese government. This time real people could get hurt, including members of our own group. So if I can befriend the girl in Shanghai we might be one step closer to discovering the truth behind the Jiàngshēng Project."

Fay considered this before asking: "What makes you think she will even listen to you? She is clearly loyal to Professor Leung."

Jessica replied: "Perhaps...but it's obvious that she knows nothing about the Biogen connection. What will she say when I tell her that the good professor is simply using her to further his own agenda?"

Fay fell silent briefly before asking: "What about your father? Surely you can ask a few questions..."

Jessica smiled slightly and replied: "That would be pointless. He never discusses business at home, and he thinks I am nothing more than a child with a bad attitude."

Fay asked: "But if it came down to it, would he put you before Biogen?"

Jessica looked towards the windows and replied: "Honestly... I really don't know anymore..."

Fay glanced at her phone and said: "I better get going..."

Jessica replied: "Me too...long day tomorrow."

Fay spoke as they stood up: "Please keep in touch...and let me know you arrived safely."

Jessica smiled and replied: "Of course. I'll connect on 121..."

As they stepped outside Fay said: "One more thing Jessica..."

Jessica asked: "What's that?"

Fay replied: "Huang Lin is an augment now; she will be suspicious of your motives."

Jessica replied: "I know...so I will tread carefully..." She waved to a taxi and added: "I will contact you from Shanghai..."

Fay called after her: "Okay...take care..."

Jessica shouted: "Always...bye..."

Fay whispered: "Come home safe..."

Jessica quickly made her way towards the local taxi rank.

Fay walked back towards the bus stop unaware of the man observing her closely from the opposite side of the street.

# The American Connection

*'Competition is the engine of progress..."*
*Matt Dower - CEO Synthtech Corporation*

**22:35 - Thursday - April 29th - Data Intercept and Analysis - Sublevel 3 - Synthtech Corporation - Radford Boulevard - West Seattle - USA**

A quiet room where shadows skirt the lights illuminating two rows of desks facing one large wall screen. It is a place of desktop monitors synced to a Cobalt Series quantum level computer currently analysing one trillion gigabytes of data per second.

Eight analysts sit at their desks staring intently at their screens as the data is quantified and disseminated to various departments within the vast Synthtech complex. The wall screen reveals a global map with multiple GPS coordinates intersected by lines of data appearing and disappearing at regular intervals. One section of the map is highlighted in yellow - China.

Senior analyst Paul Hume sat back and scratched his bald head. At just twenty eight years of age he is responsible for the entire global network of invasive data-sync uploads instigated by the Synthtech Corporation. His current dictate includes the covert targeting of the Ministry of Science and Technology of the People's Republic of China. He looks up and announces:

"The boss is on his way down."

Analyst Jane Smith turned in her seat and asked: "What will you say?"

Hume frowned as he replied: "The truth...no point in hiding the facts..."

Analyst Richard Merick sighed and said: "He won't be happy..."

Hume replied: "He asked for a full analysis of the Jiàngsheng Project and that is what he will get."

Analyst Mark Smith asked: "And what is our full analysis?"

Analyst Chris Mendez interjected: "It's simple: the Chinese are moving faster than we are..."

Analyst Maria Henderson retorted: "No way... They are years behind us..."

Mendez replied with a slight smile: "They have three augments to our one."

Analyst Mike Ramar looked up and said: "Technically they only have one active augment."

Analyst Linda Craine announced: "He is here..."

All heads turned to see Matt Dower step through sliding doors. He is closely followed by the grim-faced head of security, Karl Weinberg.

Hume stood up and said: "Sir..."

Dower is a tall, thin man, wearing an open-necked white shirt beneath grey jacket and matching trousers. The thirty-two year old billionaire has short fair-hair ruffled into a semblance of oily neatness. His face is narrow and hawkish, adding emphasis to his piercing slate-grey eyes above a slim nose and thin lips. Following closely behind him, the hulking Weinberg is typical of his type: ex-marine, with a shaved head and a scowling pock-marked face above broad-shoulders and thick muscular body. His tailored suit is an awkward fit and hints at his discomfort in a business environment.

Dower walked towards the large viewscreen and got straight to the point:

"Status report."

Hume stepped closer and replied: "We can confirm one active augment..." He tapped the wall screen and continued: "Based in Shanghai..." As the city of Shanghai was illuminated he continued: "And one inactive augment based in Hong Kong..." He tapped the screen again to illuminate Hong Kong before adding: "The third augment is still in his maturation tank in Beijing."

Dower studied the screen and said: "They are doing a comparative study."

Hume nodded and replied: "So it would seem."

Maria Henderson interjected: "They seem to be using a correlative psychoanalytical module to evaluate both augments based upon individual reactions to external stimuli."

Weinberg asked wryly: "And in English that means what?"

Henderson smiled slightly and replied: "It is a field test to evaluate both conscious and unconscious bias."

Dower considered this before asking: "Why would Biogen perform such a test?"

Henderson replied: "We can only speculate as to their reasons, but based upon our own experience with augments, it is almost certainly a failure-ratio test."

Weinberg asked: "And what is that?"

But it was Hume who replied: "They want to know if their augments will lose their sanity."

Henderson added soberly: "Just like our own first test subject."

Dower scowled and snapped: "Insanity was not the root cause of failure...it was simply an implant issue..."

Henderson lowered her eyes slightly and said: "Of course..."

Weinberg stared at the wall screen and asked: "How are they monitoring the one in Hong Kong?"

Jane Smith replied: "We have confirmed a Biogen agent in-situ."

Weinberg asked: "Do you have real-time tracking?"

Hume replied: "Yes, but there are gaps in the interlace syncs..." He tapped the screen once more and continued: "Both targets use block apps...but we can locate each one to within a mile of a specific grid position."

Dower stared directly at Hume and asked: "Are they ahead of us or not?"

Hume hesitated slightly before replying: "Based on our current analysis we believe they have yet to match our potential. But the possibility remains that they will surpass our level of progress by the end of the year."

Weinberg scowled and asked: "What the hell does that mean?"

But it was Dower who replied soberly:

"That is Paul's way of saying they are very close to overtaking us..."

Weinberg stared at the city of Shanghai and said:

"We need to terminate the Jiàngsheng Project."

Hume looked at Dower and said: "Forgive me sir...but how are we supposed to do that?"

Dower replied firmly: "We cannot allow the Chinese to undermine our plans..." He studied the map of China and continued: "The first fully augmented human must be an American." He sighed heavily before adding: "We need to activate the asset."

Weinberg asked: "Is that really necessary? I could have a team on the ground by tomorrow morning..."

Dower replied: "Yes...but I think the situation requires a more targeted approach." He tapped the screen to reveal the face of a young woman and continued: "And this situation is the ideal test for our own pretty project."

Weinberg stared at the face on the screen and asked: "Is she ready?"

Dower smiled at the image and replied: "Ready and more than willing..."

# The Girl in Shanghai

*'To be different is to be lonely, detached from the masses, existing as an island of rebellion in a sea of comforting conformity.'*
Sūn Yu

**22:37 - Friday April 30th - 2028 - Block 2 - Sixth Floor - Apartment 34 - Sikai Road - Shanghai - China.**

A room of shadows skirting wall lights above a young woman sitting on a red couch studying a laptop. Her short dark hair frames an oval shaped face with flawless olive smooth skin, whilst a small nose sits above soft pink lips and a rounded chin. A pedestal fan whispers cool air upon naked skin before rapidly dissipating into sultry heat. The room displays an eclectic mixture of modern and traditional furniture and artwork which reflects the personality of the occupant - a large Tibetan Thangka painting is displayed above a standard Seequ media centre, whilst embroidered meditation cushions are scattered upon an elaborate Tiger rug placed in front of the couch. Data-skims share bookshelves with antique Sino-Tibetan statues inside two matching bamboo bookcases placed on either side of a single window speckled with raindrops. An odour of burning incense stirs a brief sense of summer blossoms sifting out lingering kitchen smells.

    The twenty three year old stares intently at the screen...her deep brown eyes glistening slightly in the half-light. Finally Huang Lin sat back and sighed heavily. *Non-quantifiable algorithmic potential... 256-bit encryption protocols via cyphertext...* She tapped the screen several times. *They hacked the symmetric-key ciphers of the portal and used an asymmetric algorithm to exchange the secret key for an access protocol... But where is the portal access point?* She looked up to the sound of heavy rain hitting the front window. *Sequential precipitation equals the condensation of atmospheric water vapour that falls under gravity as rain...just like algorithmic data packets seek out sequential access protocols within a Cloud platform.* Suddenly revelation arrived with shocking clarity: *Quantum sub-level access via the Dark Cloud! They wrote a duplicate NAR and bypassed the firewall with a mirror access portal...* She closed the laptop as a second startling truth dawned on her: *The stolen data is masquerading as an embedded holo-lucient sensuround within a Cloud Community Cybersync...a building...a road...even an avatar...* She hugged her knees and smiled slightly. *Not bad for an unemployed cyborg...* And then she saw the data-skim left by the mysterious man from Biogen. *Neural Augmentation Test...* "It is just a short test of your abilities...nothing too complicated..." She picked up the small silver disc and wondered at the implications of the job offer. *Biogen financed my augmentation... Professor Leung concealed this from me...he harbours an inherent capacity for duplicity and personal vindication in the name of science...* She dropped the disc onto the couch and sighed. *I thought they wanted to save my life...but I am nothing more than a walking technological investment...* A ping from her phone confirmed Cybersync. *Time for a little Cloud dancing...* She gently removed two data-lenses from a plastic pouch and placed them carefully over both eyes. A brief glimpse of circuitry was replaced by a single input screen synced to the audio plugs in her ears. One quick blink initiated a Net Access Response before she tapped the Cloudsync app on her phone. Moments later she is standing on a deserted highway adjusting to the auto-avatar provided by the Techsync server. *Peripheral access portal...* Her avatar matched her genomic and cultural template to perfection - *pretty and petite Asian girl in a white summer dress...* She touched long dark hair and smiled. *And I have long hair again!* A slight flickering of the input screen confirmed a 3D/4/K sensuround environment. *Sifting for my neural location...* She looked up to see wide blue skies mottled with white whisper clouds touching distant mountains peeks with an augmented embrace. The highway itself served as a digital junction point to facilitate global roaming within the Cloud environment, giving instant access to several billion portals. She took a moment to initiate her internal interface. *Neural synaptic sync...* A brief blurring of the input screen confirmed gestalt analysis mode. Finally she spoke directly to the Techsync server:

"Show me the Singapore portals..."

Just seconds later a large group of floating white orbs appeared above the highway. Each of the portals displayed a specific access ID in the form of a digital barcode. A quick scan of the processor output spikes confirmed her suspicions - *they accessed the Project from Singapore via false bounce-back recognition protocols...* She lay back on her couch before systematically connecting to each portal access point. After more than thirty minutes of intense analysis she came to a startling conclusion: *the data is not inside the Dark Cloud...it is hiding in plain sight...* She quickly initiated an expanded scan of the entire Cloud until she identified a viable mirror access portal. *They used multilayer ciphers with a rotated PAP to access the NAR...* Finally she smiled as the algorithmic potential coalesced inside the Cloud city of New Oasis. *A Singapore data-spike inside the Cup of Joe Coffee House...* She was about to initiate Global Roaming when a proximity alert registered inside her cerebral interface. *Someone is breaking into my apartment!* She instantly disconnected from the Cloud and opened her eyes. *They are in the hallway...* A tactical assessment confirmed her fears: *I have nowhere to hide...* She leapt to her feet and ran towards the living room door. Almost immediately the door handle began to turn slowly. She was suddenly aware of her complete nakedness as she pressed up against the wall. *No time for modesty...* An autonomous internal diagnostic produced startling results: *Rapid adrenal neurotransmission confirmed...increased heart rate...air passage expansion in my lungs...blood redistribution to musculature... maximisation of blood glucose levels and enhanced vision and auditory acuity...* She took a deep breath and waited. *I am ready...* For a brief instant she contemplated the legality of assaulting another human being. *But they broke into my home!* As the door began to open hesitation was replaced by barely contained fury. *Two men...one following behind the other...* A brief tactical analysis confirmed height and weight estimations: *First man carries extra weight...reduced height...second man is tall and lean...primed for attack...he is the only danger here...* In an instant she slammed an extended hand into the throat of the first man and he went down hard, struggling for breath. She quickly wheeled around to meet the expected attack from the second man, but he was already on top of her with pointed hands jabbing into her chest and stomach. The first blow took her breath away as the second blow impacted her lower ribs. She caught a brief glimpse of glaring eyes before he forced her back into the room. For several desperate moments she struggled under a rain of blows, until finally she fell back onto the couch with blood pouring from her nose and lips. But as the man leapt forward she rolled off the couch and stood up once more. Now the man assumed a classic fighting stance as she wiped blood from her face. *He has martial arts training...* A brief blurring of her data-lenses confirmed a tactical download via her cerebral interface. She extended both arms and took up position in the centre of the room. She gave a grim smile as she wiped blood from her face. *Now I have martial arts training...* A gestalt analysis revealed a tall man with firm musculature wearing a two-piece black suit and tie. *Chinese genomic features... Short dark hair...narrow brown eyes...slim nose and thin lips...* She glanced towards his legs to confirm gestalt analysis: *asymmetrical abnormality...indicative of a previous fibula fracture left leg...* She looked up. *He has a weak spot...* Suddenly the fight resumed as they exchanged blow after blow - hands and feet impacting with bone-crushing intensity. Finally the man pulled back to catch his breath, his glaring eyes filled with hatred. She was about to launch another attack when she noticed the first man struggling to his feet. *I have to finish this before they finish me...* She leapt forward to deliver a single impact-kick to the left knee of her opponent - he collapsed to the floor in agony. Without hesitation she ran towards the first man and gripped his hair before slamming his chin into her knee. Now she straightened up to assess the situation - the short man was unconscious but his companion was on the floor cursing her in a distinct Beijing accent. *Secret police?* She blinked her data-lenses to access the local video surveillance net. *No police cars...no unusual activity...a few pedestrians...cars and buses...* She closed the connection before kneeling down over the tall man. She asked:

"Who are you? Identify yourself..."

The man snapped: "Tian po...gun ni ma de dan!"

Lin smiled slightly and asked: "Crazy bitch? Yes I suppose I am...but even I can't fuck myself..." She straightened up and placed one foot onto his damaged knee before continuing: "One more time...who are you? Why are you here?"

The man moaned loudly before replying: "You have made a big mistake...you have no idea how much trouble you are in..."

Lin sighed and said: "I do not have time for this..." She bent low and quickly slammed his head onto the floor. With both men unconscious she retrieved her phone and quickly tapped the Biogen 121 app. Moments later a female voice came online:

"Yes?"

"I was told to call if I needed help..."

There was a brief moment of silence before the woman asked:

"Huang Lin?"

Lin touched a tissue to her bloody lips as she replied: "Yes..."

The woman asked: "What has happened?"

Lin looked down at the two unconscious men and replied: "I was attacked in my apartment...two men in black suits..."

There was another pause before the woman asked:

"Did you deal with them?"

Lin wiped blood spatter from her breasts as she replied:

"They are unconscious..."

There was another long pause before the woman said:

"I am transmitting an address, go there immediately and await further instructions."

Lin read the address in the message window before asking:

"What is this place?"

The woman replied: "A safe place...please go there now."

Lin asked: "What about the two men? I can't just leave them here..."

The woman replied: "Do not be concerned. I have despatched a clean-up crew...they will erase all signs of the incident."

Lin asked: "Do you know who they are?"

The woman replied: "Speculation serves no purpose. Now pack a bag and leave immediately."

Lin replied: "Very well..."

The woman spoke one more time: "You will be contacted when you arrive at the new location."

As the phone fell silent Lin studied the address. *Building Number 2... Daixia Road... Shanghai...* She blinked to access the Cloud GPS and waited for it to sync into her phone. Moments later she spoke out loud:

"Show me Streetview and vidcam surveillance portal...building number two... Daixia Road, Shanghai..."

She carefully studied the image on the screen before tapping disconnect. *A Biogen safe house? Or a calculated trap?* She was about to turn towards her bedroom when she was overcome by a wave of dizziness. *Oh god...* Moments later she fell to her knees and vomited onto the floor, her entire body trembling. She quickly accessed her cerebral interface to produce a full diagnostic. *Slight damage to the vestibular nerve and increased blood pressure...balance coordination and spatial navigation affected...* She stood up slowly. *Nothing vital...* She wiped a hand over her mouth and looked at the address on her phone. *I cannot trust them...their job offer reeks of a secret agenda...* She looked down at the two unconscious men and sighed heavily. *I can't trust anyone...* Looking around her home it came as a shock to realise how quickly her life had changed. *Transformed from a timid office worker with a fatal brain tumour to augmented supergirl...* She sighed heavily as the truth arrived with disturbing clarity: *Nothing will ever be the same again...* Suddenly she heard footsteps in the corridor outside her apartment. *Biogen? Or more secret police thugs?* She pulled on a t-shirt and soft trousers before walking towards the front door. *Here we go again...* She was startled by a gentle knocking. She asked:

"Who is it?"

A female voice replied: "By name is Jessica Lee... I have travelled from Singapore to meet you..."

Suddenly a thousand causal threads coalesced into a single revelation: *One of the Jiàngshēng hackers!* She brushed a hand through her hair before opening the door. Her visitor smiled politely and said:

"I think your door lock is broken..."

Lin glanced towards the damaged lock and replied: "Yes... I had unwelcome visitors..."

Jessica asked: "Really?" She saw blood on Lin's lips and asked: "Are you okay?"

Lin initiated a gestalt analysis of her visitor from Singapore: *Black jacket over white t-shirt...jeans...trainers... Asian genomic features... Long dark, ponytailed hair, pale complexion...wide brown eyes...intelligent and sophisticated demeanour...* Finally she replied:

"I am fine... Why are you here?"

Jessica looked along the deserted corridor and asked: "Can we talk inside? I feel a little exposed out here..."

Lin replied: "We can talk...but not here..." She glanced towards the living room before adding: "It is not safe..."

Jessica said: "Okay..."

Lin continued: "Wait here a moment..."

Jessica gripped the straps on her backpack. *Unwanted visitors?*

After a few minutes Lin returned wearing a grey jumper, blue jeans and black knee-length boots. She dropped a backpack onto the floor as she retrieved a green jacket from behind the door. Finally she picked up the backpack and said:

"Let's go..."

Jessica asked: "Where?"

Lin pulled the door closed as she replied: "Just follow me..."

Jessica followed Lin towards the lift and said: "Okay..."

## 00:48 - Saturday May 1st - 2028 - Sheshan Gardens - Shanghai

After a long and circuitous walk they finally arrived outside the walls of the Sheshan Gardens.

Jessica looked towards the darkened entrance and asked:

"We are going into the gardens?"

Lin replied: "Yes. We can talk freely here...this way..."

Jessica nodded and said: "Okay..."

Lin led the way along a lakeside path illuminated by groundlights placed among the various plant displays. Beyond the garden walls the sounds of the city were muted slightly by the surrounding trees swaying gently in a warm breeze casting ripples upon the Moonlit lake surface. Despite the late hour they saw several dog walkers on the opposite side of the lake, their voices merging with the ever-present sounds of traffic surrounding the gardens.

Stepping around a puddle Jessica spoke in a low voice:

"At least it's stopped raining..."

Lin gestured to the left and said: "This way..."

Jessica saw a small timber pavilion shrouded in darkness. She glanced towards the city skyline before following Lin up a short flight of steps.

Once inside Lin turned around and announced:

"You found my medical records in the stolen files..."

Jessica replied in a low voice: "Yes..."

Lin studied Jessica briefly before asking: "Why are you here?"

Jessica replied: "To tell you what we found in the files..."

Lin said: "I know what was in the files."

Jessica asked: "Do you know that Biogen financed your augmentation?"

Lin hesitated before replying: "I only found that out recently..."

Jessica asked: "So you know that Professor Leung has been lying to you? That he is in collusion with Biogen?"

Lin sighed and replied: "I suspected as much...his magnanimity conceals a duplicitous agenda." She looked directly at Jessica and asked: "But what has any of this got to do with you?"

Jessica replied with a question: "Why do you think Biogen is so interested in the Jiàngshēng Project?"

Lin replied: "They are a technology company...human augmentation is the cutting-edge of technological development."

Jessica asked: "So why all the secrecy? Why undermine legitimate research financed by the Chinese government?"

Lin considered this carefully before asking: "Why are you so interested in Biogen?"

Jessica hesitated before replying: "My father is on the Biogen board of directors..."

Lin asked: "And?"

Jessica continued: "And I need to know what he mixed up in..."

Lin asked: "So why not just ask him?"

Jessica replied: "He would refuse to discuss it..."

Lin asked: "What do you want from me? I know nothing about Biogen."

Jessica stepped closer and replied: "I want you to help me to find the original prototype."

Lin tensed as she asked: "What is the original prototype?"

Jessica's eyes widened as she asked: "You do not know?"

Lin asked: "No."

Jessica explained: "She was the first subject used by Professor Leung."

A perplexed Lin said: "I thought I was the first..."

Jessica continued: "She was only mentioned briefly in the Jiàngshēng files. But it was enough to convince me that she is the key to the mystery of Biogen's secret agenda. If we can find her we might discover why Biogen is so interested in you."

Lin fell silent briefly before asking: "What do you know about this original prototype?"

Jessica replied: "Practically nothing, but I know where to start the search for her identity..."

Lin said: "Professor Leung..."

Jessica nodded slightly as she continued: "If you can access his personal files we might find the information we need to locate this mysterious prototype."

Lin raised her eyebrows and asked: "You want me to hack the Professor?"

Jessica gave a slight smile as she replied: "Your augmentation makes you the perfect hacker..."

Lin nodded slightly and said: "A quick scan might prove useful..."

Jessica hesitated before asking: "Can I ask you about your unwelcome visitors? Were they from Biogen?"

Lin replied: "No..." She paused before continuing: "I suspect they were from the State Security Ministry."

Jessica asked: "Secret police?"

Lin nodded and replied: "I think so..."

Jessica frowned and said: "They must be monitoring your phone calls..."

Lin said: "I don't see how..."

Jessica asked: "Why not?"

Lin replied: "We use a triple cipher protocol...every call is encrypted."

Jessica said: "That only works if the Professor is as security conscious as you are..."

Lin frowned and said: "He might have neglected to input the sync code..." Her eyes widened as she added: "They must know everything..."

Jessica nodded slightly and said: "Probably..."

Lin said: "We have to find this original prototype before they do..."

Jessica replied: "And fast... If they are willing to break into your apartment..."

Lin said: "They might be willing to do a lot worse..."

Jessica said: "Exactly..."

Lin trembled slightly and said: "I need to sit down..."

Jessica asked: "Are you unwell?"

Lin replied: "A little dizzy..."

Jessica gestured to a bench seat and said: "Sit here..."

Jessica sat down and said: "I will sift for the Professor's access portal..." She closed her eyes and added: "Give me a moment..."

Jessica said: "Of course..."

Just seconds later Lin opened her eyes and announced: "I have access..."

A surprised Jessica asked: "Already?"

Lin replied: "He uses adaptive quad-cipher protocols..."

Jessica nodded slightly and said: "You rotated data-spikes for an access key..."

Lin closed her eyes again and said: "Scanning personnel logs..."

Jessica adjusted her backpack and said: "Okay..."

Moments later Lin opened her eyes and said: "I have a location..."

Jessica asked: "Where is she?"

Lin looked up and replied: "Hong Kong... She is in Hong Kong."

Jessica stepped closer and asked: "Do you have a name?"

Lin paused before replying: "Nancy Yeo..."

Jessica spoke in a low voice: "The original prototype..."

Lin nodded slightly and said: "We need to go to Hong Kong."

Jessica said: "That won't be easy if you are on a watch list..."

Lin closed her eyes and said: "Give me a moment..."

Jessica sat down and asked: "What are you doing?"

Moments later Lin opened her eyes and said: "It is done..."

Jessica asked: "What is done?"

Lin replied: "I have booked a flight ticket for multiple destinations via a rotated time-slot access portal. It will take the authorities' days to sift for my true destination."

Jessica asked: "What about me?"

Lin replied: "I hacked your Techsync account...you now have a flight booked direct from Shanghai to Hong Kong at 3:05am today..."

Jessica gave a slight smile and asked: "You hacked a hacker?"

Lin returned the smile and said: "I am the perfect hacker..."

Jessica frowned and asked: "But what about Biogen? Won't they be tracking you as well?"

Lin fell silent before replying: "After the incident in my apartment I asked them for help..."

A surprised Jessica asked: "You did?"

Lin replied: "I panicked... It was my first experience of physical violence."

Jessica stared at Lin and asked: "Did you kill those agents?"

Lin replied: "Of course not... I just knocked them out..."

Jessica said: "Wow...you really are augmented..."

Lin explained: "It is simply the application of tactical analysis as opposed to brute strength."

Jessica nodded slightly and asked: "So what did Biogen say?"

Lin replied: "I was told to go to a safe house...they would send a clean-up crew to my apartment."

Jessica said: "So they will be expecting you..."

Lin replied: "Yes. So we must leave for the airport now..."

As they stood up Jessica asked: "What will you say to this Nancy Yeo when we find her?"

Lin replied: "I am not sure..."

Jessica said: "She might not even be aware of your existence..."

Lin replied: "Then we must enlighten her..."

Jessica spoke as they left the pavilion: "That should prove interesting..."

Lin replied: "Definitely."

As they walked back towards the main road Jessica asked:

"So you knocked out two men?"

Lin replied casually: "I did..."

Jessica asked: "How did that feel?"

Lin gave a slight smile and replied: "Empowering..."

# Ria

*'Because the human condition is not perfect we look to artificial intelligence for a solution to our imperfections. But we must be aware that such imperfections may one day be considered liabilities by the machines we create.'*
Professor Niel Jordon - Synthtech Corporation

**06:40 - Friday - April 30th - Biogenomic Engineering Laboratory - Sublevel 5 - Synthtech Corporation - Radford Boulevard - West Seattle - USA**

A swirling of lights coalescing into tactile reactionary recognition processes. *Cold... Naked... Physiological reaction... Cutis anserina equals vestigial reflex: goosebumps!* Sounds arrive as syntax sipping at a receding silence subdued by exterior stimulation. *Words!*
"Can you hear me Ria?"
A guttural response clings to her throat.
"Ria? Can you open your eyes?"
Ria opened her eyes into a sudden glaring brightness.
"Sorry...let me dim the lights a little..."
Shadows and movement culminating in a dimming of the brightness.
"How's that? Better?"
*A response is required...*
Ria whispered a reply: "Better..."
"Do you know who I am?"
Ria initiated a gestalt analysis of the face outlined by the light - *senescent indicators: mid-thirties...spider-thread lines around blue eyes...brown shoulder-length unkempt hair...white lab coat with coffee stains...* She blinked watery eyes as she replied:
"You are Professor Niel Jordon."
Jordon smiled and exclaimed: "Excellent... Now I want you to sit up slowly..."

Ria placed both elbows onto cold steel and sat up straight. A sudden wave of dizziness arrived as nausea and she quickly vomited clear liquid onto the tiled floor.

Jordon spoke gently: "Take slow deep breaths...that is just a reaction to the maturation process..."

Ria wiped a hand over her mouth and asks: "Did it work?"

Jordon smiled as he replied: "You tell me..."

Ria looked around the laboratory and announced: "I have spatial density ratios of this entire complex...sound differentiation confirms multiple personnel..." She raised one hand as she continued: "I can feel the blood pumping all the way to my extremities... I can map its arterial pathways..."

Jordon asked: "Are you aware of the cerebral processing unit?"

Ria cocked her head to one side and replied: "No. Autonomous integration is complete."

Jordon stepped closer and said: "Let me help you to stand..."

Ria swung her legs over the side of the maturation tank and announced:

"The dizziness is fading..."

Jordon took hold of her arm and said: "Here we go..."

Ria placed bare feet onto cold white tiles and announced: "I need clothes..."

Jordon cleared his throat and replied: "Of course...let me find you a gown."

Ria turned to see her reflection in a glass partition wall. *Oh my god!*

Jordon returned with a white gown and said: "Here you are..."

Ria touched fingers to her bald head and spoke soberly:

"My hair...the scars..."

Jordon sighed and said: "Do not worry; we can fit you with a nice wig..."

Ria pulled the gown on and asked: "Why have I been activated before the agreed time?"

Jordon raised his eyebrows and asked: "You have time differentiation?"

Ria replied: "By my calculations the maturation process should not be complete for at least another four weeks."

Jordon asked: "Calculations?"

Ria sneezed before replying: "Your senescent facial factors plus environmental changes equal a period of approximately two months..." She paused before adding: "It was supposed to be a three month process of genomic manipulation and cerebral enhancement."

Jordon smiled slightly as he explained: "My apologies, but I have my orders..."

Ria asked: "Orders?"

Jordon replied: "I have downloaded a mission directive to your anterior processor; will you access it for me please?"

Ria closed her eyes briefly before asking: "They want me to terminate someone in Hong Kong?"

Jordon asked: "Do you object to your orders?"

Ria considered the question before replying:

"There is a legal and moral imperative..." She paused before continuing: "But orders are orders."

From behind her Ria heard the words:

"That's my girl..."

Ria turned to see a familiar face approaching. She said: "Mister Dower."

A smiling Dower was closely followed by the hulking Karl Weinberg.

Jordan said: "Good morning sir..."

Dower stopped in front of the maturation tank and asked:

"Are you well Ria?"

Ria replied: "I am well thank you..."

Dower smiled warmly and said: "You are beautiful...statuesque... perfect..."

Ria smiled slightly and said: "I am bald..."

Dower grinned and said: "But not for long..."

Weinberg spoke directly to Jordon: "Is she ready?"

Ria interjected: "I can answer my own questions... And yes, I am ready."

Dower smiled slightly and asked: "Can you repeat your mission directive?"

Ria replied: "I am to proceed immediately to Hong Kong. I will identify the Biogen augment and terminate her. I will then travel to Shanghai and terminate the second augment."

Dower smiled and said: "Perfect..."

Weinberg stared at Ria and asked: "Can you accomplish your mission?"

Ria replied with a question: "Do you doubt my abilities?"

Dower stepped closer and said: "You must forgive Karl my dear; he has an old-school temperament and has little faith in bio-technology."

Weinberg said: "I reserve my faith for the men I command...they could accomplish this mission without any need for augmentation."

Ria retorted: "Then they would all die. They have no concept of the power and capabilities of an augmented human being."

Dower took Ria's hand and said: "I have faith in you Ria... I know you will not disappoint me..."

Ria replied: "I will not..."

Jordon spoke to Ria: "I need to run a few tests before you leave..."

Dower said: "Then we will leave you too it." He squeezed Ria's hand and added: "I will see you before you leave for Hong Kong."

Ria replied: "Very well."

Dower walked back towards the door before he asked in a low voice:

"Are your people in place?"

Weinberg replied: "Yes. If she fails they will step in and assume the mission directive."

Dower said: "I want hourly updates..."

Weinberg replied: "You will have them." He looked towards Ria and asked: "And if she does fail?"

Dower sighed heavily and replied: "We shall have to cut upon pretty head and find out what went wrong."

# The Meeting in Hong Kong

*'In the first ten seconds of meeting someone we condemn them to a prejudicial assessment based upon the most superficial of traits.'*
Extract: Socio-Cultural Bias - Saul Cho BSc

**9am - Sunday May 2nd - The Blue Lounge - Wo Chu Lane - Hong Kong**

A windowless room with wall lights reduced to a dull glow sipping at the edge of shadows skirting lurid murals and rows of black leather recliners. The aircon system struggles to mask the remnants of the previous night's clientele - tobacco and alcohol competing with aftershave and the lingering odour of personal depravity.

    At the far end of the Private Lounge a young man sits slumped in a wooden chair placed upon a sheet of blue tarpaulin. Beneath a long dark fringe of hair his eyes are swollen and oddly distorted, whilst his nose drips blood upon a white T-shirt emblazoned with the word: Syncability! Both hands are secured to the chair with rope looped around his bare feet which end in broken toes oozing blood onto the sheet below. His trembling body is wet with perspiration as he struggles to speak:

    "Alright... I will...tell you what I know..."

    Jon Lau wiped a towel over his sweaty face and said:

    "Good boy...you know it makes sense..."

Mong Gao looked up from the table as Lau entered the main bar area. He asked:

    "Well?"

    Lau wiped sweat from his arms as he announced: "He is ready to talk..."

    Gao emptied his glass of whiskey and said:

    "I am expecting a visitor at ten thirty...let me know when she arrives..."

Lau nodded as Gao walked towards the Private Lounge.

Gao found the young hacker strapped to a wooden chair in front of the bar, his white shirt smeared with blood and his face bruised and swollen. He said:

"Chok Tay... I am told you wish to cooperate..."

Chok looked up and replied wearily: "Yes..."

Gao pulled a chair closer and said: "Alright Tay... Tell me what you know about the Jiàngshēng hack."

Chok replied breathlessly: "It was the FTSS... Fay Rui..."

Gao smiled slightly and said: "The FreeTech Society of Singapore...of course it was them..." He sighed and asked: "And what is the current location of the stolen data?"

Chok replied wearily: "I have no idea...inside the Cloud...that's all I know..."

Gao realised that Chok was telling the truth. He said: "Well I could waste a few weeks scanning for algorithmic potential or I could fly to Singapore and pursued Miss Rui to cooperate..."

Chok shook his head slightly and said: "No..."

Gao asked: "No?"

Chok looked up and asked: "If I tell you...something...will you let me go?"

Gao replied: "Of course..." He smiled before adding: "You have my word..."

Chok coughed and said: "Jessica Lee..."

Gao asked: "Who?"

Chok replied: "One of the FTSS..."

Gao pulled his chair closer and asked: "What about her?"

Chok replied: "She arrived in Shanghai yesterday... She knows the location of the files..."

Gao sat forward and asked: "Why is she in China?"

Chok replied: "She found something in the files...something big..."

Gao asked: "And Shanghai?"

Chok coughed again and replied: "Someone important lives there...mentioned in the files..."

Gao asked: "How did you come by this information?"

Chok replied: "My cousin...Tong...lives in Singapore...member of the FTSS..."

Gao smiled and said: "Family loyalty strikes again..."

Chok looked up and asked: "Can I go home now?"

Gao ignored the question and asked: "Is that all you know?"

Chok replied wearily: "Yes..."

Gao asked: "What about Lee's Techsync account? Do you know her access portal?"

Chok coughed and replied: "She will use a rotating PAP to request a NAR..."

Gao fell silent before saying: "I need to sift for a false Singapore ID tag..."

Chok said: "The FTSS use triple-access cipher codes with encrypted spikes..." He coughed before continuing: "But you can use an extraction algorithm to sift for her real-world location..."

Gao nodded slightly before saying: "Brilliant... What a clever little hacker you are..."

Chok looked up and asked: "So I can go home now, right?"

Gao smiled and replied: "Of course..." He stood up and added: "Just keep our little discussion to yourself...we don't want anything unfortunate to happen to you."

Chok replied: "Okay..."

Gao spoke as he walked towards the door:

"Jon will clean you up before you go..."

## 10:27 - Sunday May 2nd - The Blue Lounge - Wo Chu Lane - Hong Kong

A warm breeze swirls litter into tiny tornadoes sweeping over puddles rippling reflected neon light amongst the shadows. City sounds are muted inside the narrow lane of brick walls leading to the Blue Lounge Club.

A solitary girl stops in front of a shuttered stall. *Genuine leather emporium...* She is wearing her most formal clothes - white blouse beneath cream coloured jacket with matching knee-length skirt above polished black ankle boots. A small white handbag completes the illusion of a sophisticated young woman. Wide brown eyes glisten slightly as the active data-lenses confirmed her destination via Techsync GPS. Moments later the input screen blinks to announce a 121 phone message. She removes her mobile from the handbag and taps respond. Almost instantly the face of her housemate comes onscreen.

Nancy asked: "Are you there yet? I messaged first in case you were already inside..."

Alice smiled slightly and replied: "Just arrived...it looks closed."
Nancy asked: "Didn't he tell you it would be closed on Sunday?"
Alice replied: "Yes. But I see no sign of life..."
Nancy sighed and said: "So knock on the door..."
Alice frowned and replied: "I will...hang on..."
Nancy asked: "What was that?"
Alice replied: "Just got another 121 from Mark..."
Nancy asked: "The UK guy?"
Alice replied: "Yes..."
Nancy said: "He is persistent..."
Alice said: "I'm going to knock now...talk to you later Nancy..."
Nancy asked: "What about the English guy?"
Alice straightened her jacket as she replied: "One man at a time Nancy..."
Nancy laughed and asked: "Can we meet for lunch?"
Alice replied: "Okay... Where do you want to eat?"
Nancy replied: "We can try Kyoto's in the Yakuma mall..."
Alice smiled and said: "Okay... I'll 121 after the interview..."
Nancy returned the smile and said: "Okay bye sweetie...good luck..."

It took several knocks before the door was finally opened by a bald man wearing a stained white vest. He asked:

"Yes?"

Alice replied timidly: "I... I have an appointment with Mister Mong..."

The man studied Alice briefly before opening the door wide and saying:

"Come in..."

Alice stepped inside and said: "Thank you..."

The man ordered:

"Follow me..."

Alice suddenly realised that the man was enormous, with pock-marked skin and gaudy tattoos adorning his thick neck and both upper arms. She followed him into a dimly-lit bar area where tables and chairs were placed beneath a mirrored ceiling. Finally the man gestured to a blue door at the far end of the bar and said:

"Go on through..."

Alice looked towards the door and said: "Thank you..."

The man added: "He is waiting for you..."

Alice stepped through the open door into a carpeted room illuminated by wall lights. She felt her face flush at the sight of wall murals depicting various types of sexual erotica. A smiling Mong Gao approached from a small bar at the far end of the room. He said:

"Please forgive the decor...but we cater to all types here in the Private Lounge."

Alice smiled slightly and said: "Okay..."

Gao gestured to a nearby booth and asked: "Shall we sit?"

Alice sat down inside the booth and said: "You have a nice place here..."

Gao replied: "Thank you..."

Alice sighed as she continued: "Anywhere is better than the Hub..."

Gao saw the look on Alice's face and asked: "Bad day at the restaurant?"

Alice sat back and replied: "Saturday's are the worst...non-stop all day yesterday..."

Gao smiled slightly and said: "Well I can't promise things won't be any different here, but your hours will be less, and you will receive out-of-hours bonus pay."

Alice looked around the lounge and asked: "What exactly would I be doing here?"

Gao asked: "How about bar work? We could start you off at the main bar and after a period of training you could become bar manager."

Alice said: "Wow...bar manager..."

Gao said: "You would be responsible for ordering new stock and supervising the waitress staff..."

Alice asked: "You know I am only a waitress right now right?"

Gao smiled and replied: "I know that you are under-used at the Hub and that you have untapped talents..." He paused before asking: "What more do I need to know?"

Alice fell silent before asking: "When can I start?"

Gao smiled slightly and replied: "Whenever you are ready..."

Alice frowned and said: "I would have to work my notice at the Hub..."

Gao asked: "So you will accept the job offer?"

Alice looked up and replied: "Yes...thank you. I accept..."

Gao glanced at his phone before saying: "Wonderful... Now I'm sorry to rush you but I have my weekly accounts to balance."

Alice said: "Of course..."

Gao stood up and said: "Send me a 121 when you have a start date in mind and I will set up the necessary employment papers."

Alice got to her feet and said: "I will, thank you..."

Gao opened the door and said: "Jon will let you out..."

Alice replied: "Okay thanks..."

Lau looked up from the bar and asked: "Finished?"

Alice replied: "Yes..."

Lau walked towards the front door and said: "Here you go..."

As she stepped outside Alice said: "I will be working here soon..."

Lau wiped his nose with the back of his hand and said: "Good for you..."

As the door closed Alice whispered: "Yes...good for me..." A ping from her phone confirmed a new 121 message. One glance at the screen brought a smile to her face:

"I will wait for u at Joe's tonight... Mark :) "

She tapped: "OK...see u there... A"

## 11:05 - Sunday May 2nd - 2028 - Block 5 - Kwai Chung Estate - Hong Kong

Sunlight is a splash of brightness amongst the puddles along a busy Hong Shing Road. Early morning rainfall has been replaced by a sultry warm breeze whispering through the trees lining the harbour front. The distant sounds of the city fade into a dull rumble among the tall apartment blocks of the Kwai Chung Housing Estate.

Stepping onto the grass beneath Block No. 5, two young women stop in front of a children's play area.

Jessica Lee adjusted her backpack and asked: "Something wrong?"

Huang Lin looked towards the open sea and replied: "The air is so much fresher here..."

Jessica said: "I suppose..."

Lin continued: "The air in Shanghai gets worse all the time..." She paused before adding soberly: "It's why so many people develop cancer...like me..."

Jessica asked: "But you are cured now, right?"

Lin replied in a low voice: "Right..."

Jessica hesitated before asking: "What does it feel like, to have a brain-computer interface? Does it hurt?"

Lin smiled slightly and replied: "I cannot feel the augmentation in a physical way; it has become an autonomous part of my brain, interacting and functioning as one unified mind."

Jessica asked: "So you have instant Cybersync?"

Lin replied: "Yes. I can create my own access portal without the need for a third-party platform like Techsync."

Jessica frowned and said: "I don't think I could ever volunteer for such a procedure..."

Lin sighed and said: "I had no choice...the procedure saved my life..."

Jessica nodded slightly and said: "Yes... I read that in your files..." She paused before adding: "Sorry..."

Lin asked: "For what?"

Jessica replied: "For intruding into your private life..."

Lin sighed and said: "Do not worry about it..." She looked up at the apartment building and added: "Your intrusion might lead me to a few answers..."

Jessica said: "We can only hope..."

Lin replied: "Indeed."

Jessica looked up at the austere facade of the tower block and asked:

"Are you sure this is the place?"

Lin replied: "Positive... Tenth floor, apartment one eight two..."

Jessica gripped her shoulder straps and said: "Okay let's do this..."

Lin ordered: "Wait..."

Jessica asked: "Now what's wrong?"

Lin gestured to the play area and replied: "Let's sit on the bench..."

A perplexed Jessica asked: "Why?"

Lin replied firmly: "Just sit..."

As they sat down Jessica asked: "What's going on?"

Lin smiled at two small boys playing on a slide as she replied: "This location is being monitored..."

Jessica looked towards the main road and asked: "From where?"

Lin replied: "A building across the road...do not look..."

Jessica lowered her eyes slightly and asked: "Are they watching us?"

Lin replied: "I doubt we are the sole object of their attention. It is more likely that they are monitoring Nancy Yao."

Jessica asked: "Secret police?"

Lin replied: "Possibly...or Biogen..."

Jessica asked: "Why would Biogen monitor one of their test subjects?"

Lin replied: "Another question we need to find an answer to..."

Jessica glanced towards the buildings opposite and whispered: "I don't see anyone..."

Lin brushed a hand through short dark hair and said:

"The Sotel Insurance Building...fourth floor window...far right...reflective glass..." She sat back and added: "Telescopic sights..."

Jessica tensed and asked: "So what do we do?"

Lin closed her eyes briefly and replied: "Give me a moment..."

Jessica sighed and said: "Okay..."

Lin continued: "I have accessed Nancy Yao's 121 account...she is about to leave her apartment..."

Jessica asked: "Do you know where she is going?"

Lin opened her eyes and replied: "She is going to meet someone..."

Jessica asked: "Who?"

Lin replied: "Her roommate Alice Sòng."

Jessica asked: "She has a roommate? You did not tell me that..."

Lin shrugged slightly and replied: "It was not relevant to our investigation."

Jessica sighed and asked: "So what do we do now?"

Lin looked towards the apartments and replied: "We intercept her..."

Jessica asked: "Intercept in a friendly way?"

Lin gave a slight smile and replied: "Of course..."

Jessica asked: "And if she doesn't want to be friendly?"

Lin replied: "Either way...she will answer our questions."

Jessica studied Lin briefly before asking: "Is there any more information you deemed not relevant to our investigation?"

Lin replied wearily: "I absorb information at a quantum level rate of neural assimilation... Do you really want me to explain every piece of irrelevant data?"

Jessica replied: "When you put it that way...no..."

Lin stood up and said: "Good. Now let's get going..."

Jessica got to her feet and asked:

"Do you think they are secret police?"

Lin glanced towards the Sotel building and replied:

"I doubt it. If my calls were monitored Beijing would have learned nothing about the so-called original prototype..."

Jessica said: "That's true..."

Lin spoke soberly: "I suspect that someone else is aware of the Jiàngshēng Project..."

Jessica adjusted her backpack and said: "We should find Nancy Yeo."

Lin nodded slightly and replied: "We will wait for her inside the front lobby."

**Block 5 - Tenth Floor**

Nancy Yeo stepped into the lift and ordered:

"Ground floor..."

A ping from her phone brought a smile to her face:

*"I got the job! Meet me outside Yakuma...lunch is on me. A :)"*

She quickly tapped a response:

*"Congrats! On my way now..."*

Once again her thoughts returned to the sousuoyi search results: *Mong Gao... Twenty two year old post-grad currently taking a gap year...but actually a member of the Ginza triad... Mark Chapham...a.k.a. Daniel Lane... Two years deep cover Dark Cloud avatar infiltration... British Intelligence... The Sino Infiltration Unit...* She sighed heavily. *The China Watchers...* The fact that such people were gravitating towards Alice was alarming. *Could they know the truth?* It seemed improbable, but the facts could not be ignored. *I need to contact Rén Du...*

Suddenly the lift announced:

"Ground Floor."

But as the doors opened she was confronted by two young women. She said:

"Excuse me..."

The woman with short, spiky hair stepped forward and said:

"We need to talk to you..."

Nancy tensed and asked: "Who are you?"

The woman replied: "I am Huang Lin..."

Nancy stepped back slightly and asked: "Am I supposed to recognise that name?"

Huang Lin asked: "Do you recognise the name Leung Huo?"

The other woman added: "Or the Jiàngshēng Project?"

Nancy tensed as she asked: "Why are you here?"

Huang Lin replied: "I told you...we need to talk."

Jessica Lee stepped closer and said: "You do recognise those names..."

Nancy hesitated slightly before replying: "We can talk in my apartment."

Huang Lin gestured to the lift and said: "After you..."

Nancy spoke to the lift: "Floor ten."

Huang Lin suggested: "Perhaps you should cancel your lunch meeting..."

Nancy's eyes widened as she said: "You hacked my phone..."

Huang Lin replied: "It was necessary."

Nancy spoke as she tapped her phone: "It was intrusive..."

Jessica gave a slight smile and added: "It's what we do..."

**11:21 - Apartment 182 - Block 5 - Kwai Chung Estate - Hong Kong**

Sunlight slipped in-between the apartment blocks with a splash of brightness scattering shadows inside a small rectangular living room. Once again Huang Lin was acutely aware of an information overload via her autonomous cerebral interface: *A grey couch draped in multicolored throws facing a flatscreen television and several tall bookcases brimming with books and piles of data-skims. A lingering odour of cooked vegetables barely concealed by an inadequate air-conditioning system... One door leading to two bedrooms, a bathroom and a small kitchen via a central hallway ending in the front door...* She glanced towards the large window and tensed. *Directly overlooked by the Sotel building...*

Nancy Yeo gestured to the couch and said:

"Won't you sit down...?"

Jessica spoke as she sat on the couch: "Nice place you have here..."

Nancy removed data skims from a desk chair as she replied: "It serves its purpose."

Lin sat down next to Jessica and said: "I am sure it does..."

Nancy unfastened her jacket before sitting down and announcing:

"I recognise both those names..." She paused before adding: "But of course you already know that..." She looked directly at Jessica and added: "You are one of the Singapore hackers."

Jessica was about to reply when Lin asked: "And do you know who I am?"

Nancy replied: "I do..."

Jessica interjected: "And we know who you are..."

Nancy raised her eyebrows and asked: "You do?"

Lin replied: "You are the original prototype. The one before me..."

Nancy gave a slight smile and asked: "Are you sure about that?"

Lin replied: "We know you have been hiding here in Hong Kong."

Jessica added: "We hacked Professor Leung's personal files..."

Nancy looked directly at Jessica and asked: "So you are a member of the FTSS?"

A surprised Jessica replied: "Yes... Jessica Lee..."

Nancy asked: "Zhang Lee's daughter?"

Jessica's eyes widened as she asked: "You know my father?"

Nancy replied: "We have crossed paths..." She smiled before adding: "He must be so proud of his little girl..."

Jessica replied: "I wouldn't know..."

Nancy brushed her hair back and asked: "So you are here to do what? Tell me something I already know?"

Jessica replied: "We want to know about Biogen. What is their long-term agenda?"

Nancy sat back and replied: "Ask your father..."

Lin interjected: "She is asking you..."

Nancy sighed and said: "There is no mystery to uncover here... Biogen is an advanced technology company. Augmentation is the cutting-edge of technological development, so of course they would invest in the professor's project."

Jessica asked: "But why undermine the Beijing government? Why not simply apply for the contract through legal channels?"

Nancy replied: "It is all about priorities..."

Lin sat forward and asked: "What kind of priorities?"

Nancy replied: "Political priorities. The Ministry of Science and Technology has allocated a mere two per cent of its annual expenditure to the Jiàngsheng Project. Based on current fiscal projections it will take at least twenty years before the project produces its first truly augmented human."

Lin said: "Biogen wants to reduce that time..."

Nancy replied: "Exactly."

Jessica added: "And by acting outside of judicial oversight they can bypass legal and moral implications."

Nancy gave a slight smile and replied: "Like I said...priorities."

Lin studied Nancy briefly before asking: "Why were you erased from the project files?"

Nancy replied with a question: "Why were you erased from the files?"

Lin replied: "I thought it was an altruistic gesture by the professor, but apparently it was all part of Biogen's plan to control my life."

Nancy fell silent briefly before saying: "Sometimes caution is its own reward..."

Lin asked: "What is that supposed to mean?"

Nancy asked: "Why question the lifeline? Simply accept it and move on..."

Lin said: "You are evading the question."

Nancy sighed and said: "Then look at it logically. Use that augmented brain of yours..."

Lin fell silent briefly before replying: "Biogen wanted a comparative module."

Jessica asked: "What is a comparative module?"

Lin stared at Nancy as she replied: "We are an experiment... Biogen are comparing our real-world applications based on a preset social scenario."

Nancy nodded slightly and said: "The reactionary affects of interpersonal relationships upon the active and the inactive cerebral interface."

Lin asked: "How can they learn anything from an inactive interface?"

Nancy replied sarcastically: "You're really not thinking this through are you?"

Lin fell silent briefly before replying: "They are testing autonomous boundaries..."

Nancy smiled and said: "Finally..."

Jessica asked: "Can someone explain that to me?"

Lin replied: "At some point the human brain will evolve in unison with the implants...a symbiotic merging of biology and technology into one organ." She paused before continuing: "They want to determine the level of autonomous control over biological neural reaction."

Nancy sat back and said: "In other words: at which point will the subject lose their humanity."

Lin spoke soberly: "And lose their soul..."

Nancy continued: "If we can determine the autonomous boundary point we can control the outcome."

Jessica asked: "What outcome?"

But it was Lin who replied: "It is the rogue factor...the individuality trait. They want to map the neural cascade effect." She looked at Nancy and added: "They fear the point at which they can no longer control us..."

Nancy said: "Actually they want to develop a way to control the augmented brain from a distance...a neural leash if you will."

Jessica asked: "How is that possible?"

Nancy replied: "It isn't possible...yet. But they are working on it..."

Lin spoke in a low voice: "A neural leash..." She looked up and continued: "They could do it..."

Jessica asked: "They could?"

Lin replied: "The cerebral interface could be adapted to receive some type of electromagnetic pulse via a wifi interlace transmission."

Nancy smiled and said: "You really are top of your class. But they are leaning towards some kind of resonance pulse to program the interface via sound waves."

Jessica spoke in a low voice: "Phase one is all about control..."

Nancy gave a slight smile and said: "Everything is about control."

Jessica asked: "But why are they so interested in such an abstract concept?"

Nancy looked at Lin and said: "Tell her..."

Lin explained: "If they can determine the point at which we lose our humanity they can take precautions to prevent us from going rogue."

Jessica looked confused and asked: "Precautions?"

Lin replied soberly: "A kill switch uploaded to the cerebral interface."

Nancy said: "Nothing quite so drastic. It's more of a long-distance cerebral adjustment via a resonating system."

Lin nodded slightly and said: "A vibration of large amplitude produced by a small vibration at the same frequency as the natural frequency of the resonating system within the cerebral interface."

Nancy smiled and said: "Gestalt analysis strikes again..."

Lin spoke in a low voice: "A resonance pulse..."

Nancy added: "Tuned to your cerebral interface...the neural leash..."

Jessica asked: "Is that where all the money went, to find a way to control the augments?"

Nancy asked: "What money?"

Jessica replied: "According to the files, Biogen have contributed over one billion dollars to the Jiàngshēng Project."

Nancy straightened her skirt and replied: "I am not at liberty to divulge such information."

Lin said: "It's a little late to hide behind a non-disclosure clause..."

Jessica sat forward and said: "Just tell us the truth...please..."

Nancy looked at Jessica and said: "Foetal genomic enhancement via invitro neural synaptic augmentation. It is a lengthy and highly expensive process; way beyond the budget set by the Beijing authorities."

Jessica spoke in a low voice: "Genomic manipulation of the DNA base code..."

Nancy added: "Cerebral augmentation of the human foetus... Phase Two."

Lin spoke soberly: "So we are nothing more than a trial..."

Nancy replied brusquely: "Adult templates to be exact."

Suddenly Lin saw the shocking truth and exclaimed: "They extracted eggs from me!"

Jessica looked at Lin and asked: "They did?"

Nancy smiled slightly and said: "They did... Your unborn child will become the worlds first truly augmented human." He paused before adding: "You should feel honoured."

Jessica exclaimed: "That is monstrous..."

Nancy sighed and said: "No...it is progress."

Lin glared at Nancy and said: "Tell me more about Phase Two."

Nancy sat back and said: "There is nothing more to tell. A surrogate will be used to gestate the foetus to full term. After that...well, that is above my pay grade."

A shocked Lin asked: "And you agree with all of this?"

Nancy sighed heavily and replied: "Actually no... I do not. But like you I am bound to serve and as such I have no choice..."

Jessica retorted: "Everyone has a choice."

Nancy gave a slight smile and replied: "The naïveté of the ignorant..."

Jessica protested: "I am not ignorant. I know right from wrong and everything you stand for is wrong...it is evil."

Nancy replied wearily: "I agree...but sometimes innocence has no choice..." She paused before continuing: "But I have seen true evil...and it hides behind a smile..."

Lin studied Nancy briefly before asking: "What is your real name?"

Jessica asked: "She is not Nancy Yeo?"

Suyin sighed and replied: "I am Chu Suyin..." She paused before continuing: "And like you my life is owned by Biogen..."

Lin scowled and said: "They do not own me..."

Suyin gave a slight smile and said: "Keep that illusion if it helps..."

Lin stared at Suyin and announced: "Something is wrong here..."

Jessica asked: "What do you mean?"

Lin continued: "She would not reveal all of this information so easily..."

Jessica looked at Suyin and asked: "What have you done?"

But it was Lin who replied: "She has alerted someone..." She stood up and announced: "This is a trap!"

Suyin stood up and said: "I am sorry...but when you confronted me in the lobby I had no choice..."

Jessica asked: "You betrayed us?"

Suyin replied: "It was an automatic response..."

Lin glanced towards the door and said: "We need to leave right now..."

Suyin stepped closer and said: "I can help you..."

Jessica asked: "Now you want to help us?"

Suyin replied: "If I can..."

Jessica glanced towards Lin before asking: "Why?"

But it was Lin who replied: "Because she hates Biogen..."

Jessica asked: "You do?"

Suyin replied: "They stole my life and transformed me into a slave..." She paused before continuing: "But now finally I have a chance to do some good..."

Lin said: "We need an optimal route out of this building..."

Suyin nodded slightly and replied: "I can show you..."

But suddenly the front window shattered into a storm of flying glass.

Lin shouted: "Get down!"

Jessica caught a brief glimpse of blood erupting from Suyin's head. *Oh my god!*

Lin dived onto the floor as books and data skims exploded inside the bookshelves. Now she could see Suyin lying face down in a pool of blood, her brown eyes wide with shock.

Jessica asked desperately: "Is she dead?"

Lin saw brain matter on the back of Suyin's head and replied: "I don't know..."

Suyin coughed blood and said: "I am... Chu Suyin..." And then with one final breath she whispered: "I am free..."

Lin felt for a pulse and announced: "She is gone..."

Jessica asked desperately: "Why didn't she see it coming?"

Lin replied: "Because she lacked tactical analysis."

Jessica asked: "Can an augment lack such abilities?"

Lin replied soberly: "She was not an augment...we have the wrong person."

Jessica asked: "How is that possible? You hacked the professor's files..."

Lin replied: "It was all lies...a complete fabrication."

Jessica said: "So she was still lying to us..."

Lin replied: "No. We simply failed to ask the right question..."

Jessica crawled closer and asked: "So where is the original prototype?"

Lin replied: "I think I know..."

Jessica asked: "You do?"

Lin looked towards the window and replied: "But first we need to get out of here..."

Jessica shuffled closer and asked: "How?"

Lin initiated gestalt tactical mode and replied: "I am going to create a distraction; you will run into the hallway..."

A terrified Jessica asked: "I will?"

Lin squeezed Jessica's trembling hand and replied: "You can do this..."

Jessica breathed in slowly and said: "Okay..." She paused before asking: "What kind of distraction?"

Lin ignored the question and said: "After three...one, two...three!"

Jessica leapt to her feet and shouted: "Oh god..."

But Lin was already in motion moving towards the window. *Fourth floor window...telescopic targeting...wind-speed one point five km...lateral deviation...* She felt a whisper of heat as a bullet passed close to her head. *Kill-shot accuracy...* A sudden brightness brought a grim smile to her face. *They will be firing into the sun in five, four, three, two...* Without hesitation she ran towards the living room door.

# Terminal Tactics

*'A soul without empathy is the perfect weapon.'*
Rén Du - Biogen

**11:48 - The Sotel Insurance Building - Hong Shing Road - Kwai Chung Estate - Hong Kong**

The body of a man lies on the floor of a small corner office. His wide open eyes seem frozen in the moment of his death - his necktie has been forced up and around his neck to strangle the last living breath from his lungs. Crouching at the nearby open window a young woman adjusts her short black wig. She wears a green jacket over black t-shirt and blue jeans over black combat boots. Her eyes are fixed upon the apartment building situated directly across the main road. Now she carefully adjusts the telescopic sights of a long rifle. Split-second calculations assume gestalt clarity as the targets disappear below the window sill. With her finger poised on the trigger Ria waits calmly for them to make their move. *There!* Once more the rifle expelled a silent fusillade towards apartment 182. But then a sudden brightness fills the telescopic sights and she looks up in frustration. *I miscalculated...* She glanced towards the building opposite as the main target vanished from sight. *But she did not...* A brief ping from her phone announced the termination of the invasive sync into Jessica Lee's phone. *Block app... Microphone muted...* She sat back against the wall and studied the screen. *But I have voice recording...* It had taken almost forty seconds for the Block app in Lee's phone to detect the invasive sync and terminate the connection. *Let's see what we have...* She closed her eyes to initiate a direct sync between her cerebral interface and her phone. The first voice she heard matched the archive recording of Jessica Lee:

"Can an augment lack such abilities?"
"She was not an augment...we have the wrong person."
"How is that possible? You hacked the professor's files..."
"It was all lies...a complete fabrication."

"So where is the original prototype?"

"I think I know..."

"You do?"

Moments later Ria opened wide blue eyes and whispered:

"I was sent after the wrong target..."

She took a moment to sift twenty thousand items of data into referential items of interest: *Synthtech identified Nancy Yeo as the inactive augment and Huang Lin as the active augment... But it was all lies...a smokescreen to hide the real augment... Nancy Yeo was actually the Biogen agent sent to watch the real augment... Multiple 121 messages confirm the identity of her roommate - Alice Sòng...twenty four year old waitress...the original prototype? Jessica Lee...member of the FreeTech Society of Singapore...daughter of Biogen Director, Zhang Lee...travel documents confirm her arrival in Shanghai...but no record of departure...* She got to her feet and looked towards Block Five. *They came here to meet the original prototype...but they were fooled by the subterfuge engineered by Biogen...* She sighed heavily. *And now they have escaped...* It was sobering to realise that she had failed to complete her mission. She quickly accessed the 121 account owned by Nancy Yeo and read the most recent messages:

AS: *'Nancy I got the job! Meet me for lunch? I'll pay...'*

NY: *'Well done! How about Kendo's in Yakuma?'*

AS: *'Okay... I'll meet u at the fountain outside...1ish...bye for now.'*

She quickly created an invasive algorithm to locate the phone of Alice Sòng. *GPS sync confirms Ho Shin Road... She is walking towards Central MTR station...* One rapid blink synced the MTR network map onto her data-lenses. *Yakuma mall?* She glanced at the time before calculating the optimum route from her current location to the shopping mall: *Tsuen Wan Line to Admiralty station...interchange to Island line and Causeway Bay Station...* She cut the connection. *No time to waste...* She paused to consider the team of Synthtech agents watching from a parked van in the street below - *They could usurp my mission at any moment...* A brief threat assessment revealed a disturbing fact: *If I fail they will kill me...* She quickly dismantled the rifle and returned it to her shoulder bag before making her way towards the rear fire escape. Three minutes later she was running along the back streets with one phrase dominating her thoughts: *The original prototype?*

# Rescue and Revelation

*'Trust is always a risk,
but sometimes you have no choice... '
Precept of the day - Alice Sòng*

**13:21 pm - Sunday May 2nd - Yakuma Shopping Mall - Causeway Bay - Hong Kong**

Causeway Bay is bathed in reflected sunlight shimmering from the surrounding skyscrapers. Tourists mingle with locals streaming in a relentless tide along streets congested with weekend traffic. Outside the Yakuma shopping mall a large ornate water feature dominates the small plaza - glistening metallic flowers ejecting fountains into a small reservoir bordered by rows of exotic plants. It is a favourite meeting place before venturing into the multistory shopping mall.

Alice glanced at her phone and sighed. *Come on Nancy...* Once again she tapped a 121 message:
"*Nancy? Where are u?*"
The intense heat created a suffocating atmosphere made worse by the crowds gathering around the fountains. Once more she looked towards the main road. *This is a waste of time...* She was about to turn back towards the MTR station when a man approached her and announced:
"If you want to live come with me now..."
Alice pulled her arm free and asked: "Excuse me?"
The man continued: "Please come with me... I will explain everything."
Alice stepped back and shouted: "Get away from me!"
Now people were beginning to look in their direction as the man announced:
"It's me Alice... Mark...we met in the Cloud..."
The fair-haired man bore no resemblance to the Mark avatar. She whispered: "Mark?"

The man pulled her to one side and replied: "Yes it's me... But we have to go now..."

Suddenly a scream erupted from the crowd - a woman standing behind Alice collapsed to her knees with blood oozing from her chest.

Mark shouted: "This way!"

A shocked Alice found herself being pulled towards the shopping mall doors. Behind them people began to panic and run in every direction. She shouted desperately:

"What is happening?"

Mark gripped her hand and replied firmly: "Just keep moving..."

Now they were inside the mall and moving through the crowds towards the escalators. Alice caught sight of a security guard and without hesitation pulled free and ran towards him. Behind her a voice shouted:

"Alice!"

But she was already in front of the guard pleading desperately:

"Please help me...someone is chasing me..."

The guard asked: "What is going on?" He looked towards the main entrance and asked: "Has someone been hurt?"

Suddenly Mark reappeared and said: "We haven't got time for this..."

A terrified Alice watched as Mark slammed the guard up against the wall before punching him hard in the stomach. As the man went down she was once more force-marched towards the down escalators. Moments later they emerged inside the underground car park where Mark paused to survey the area. Finally he said:

"We need transport..."

But once again Alice broke free and ran desperately towards the exit ramp.

Mark cursed: "Damn it Alice..."

Within seconds he had caught up to her, shouting angrily:

"Listen to me!" He pinned her arms against the wall and continued: "That bullet was meant for you...if you don't come with me right now you will die here today. Is that what you want?" He paused before asking again: "Is that what you want?"

Alice looked up through tear-filled eyes and replied: "No..."

Mark turned to the sound of a car approaching and said: "Let's go..."

Suddenly the car drove directly towards them at high speed. Mark shouted:

"Run!"

Alice could hear car windows shattering as they dived behind a parked taxi.

Mark ordered: "Stay down..."

Alice crouched lower as bullets continued to impact the taxi. She was vaguely aware of time slowing into a blur of multiple events - fountains of concrete dust erupting gracefully from stone support pillars...impact sounds from silent bullets tearing through taxi doors and windows...tyres screeching as the speeding car came to a stop several meters away...terrified screams resounding amongst parked cars - and much closer still, the man calling himself Mark, dragging a lifeless body out onto the pavement. *Taxi driver!* She closed her eyes against the sight of blood pooling in the gutter at her feet. And then urgent words arrived at the edge of awareness:

"Alice! Get in!"

With a blind sense of survival she scrambled into the passenger seat to find Mark behind the wheel. He ordered:

"Put your seatbelt on and stay low..."

With trembling hands she secured the belt before slumping down in the seat. Once more time was reduced to series of actions analysed by an acute awareness which she found puzzling - Mark turning the ignition key and shifting gears into reverse...a sudden hard impact confirming a collision with the taxi parked behind them...the steering wheel spinning as Mark floored the accelerator...a shattered windscreen sprinkling glass into her hair...a sudden silence followed by a loud impact sound. *We just hit someone!* There was a brief scraping of metal on metal as they emerged into bright sunlight before turning sharply to the left. *Exit D... Victoria Park Road...* She studied her hands and came to a profound conclusion: *The fear has gone...* It was not just her cold analysis of the facts which she found unsettling, but her sudden and calm acceptance of the life-threatening situation was mystifying: *Why am I no longer scared?* A vague sense of 'otherness' had transformed fear into a cold analytical assessment of her situation: *Long-distance shot hit the young girl in the plaza...more assassins waiting in the car park...* She steadied her breathing as the feeling of duality produced a shocking conclusion: *The plaza shot was meant for me!* Now she took a moment to study her abductor. *Late twenties... Short sandy-coloured hair...tanned oval face with blue eyes...slim nose and dimpled unshaven chin...casual black jacket over white open-necked shirt and blue jeans...no resemblance to the Cloud avatar...* She sat up slightly and saw pain on his face - one glance confirmed blood seeping from a shoulder wound. She announced:

"You are hurt..."

A grim-faced Mark adjusted the gears as he replied: "It's nothing..."

Alice studied the wound as she continued: "You are wrong...the bullet severed the deltoid branch of the thoracoacromial artery in your left shoulder...you will lose consciousness soon..."

Mark spun the wheel as he spoke: "We can't stop now..."

Alice looked through the shattered rear window and said: "We are being followed..."

Mark turned the taxi towards the seafront as he replied: "I noticed..."

Alice said: "Let me drive..."

Mark increased speed as he replied: "No... I need to put some distance between us and them..."

Alice said: "You are about to pass out..." She glanced at the dashboard and continued: "If you lose control at this rate of speed we will both be killed..." She gripped his arm and ordered: "Pull over..."

Mark glanced at her and asked: "Can you even drive?"

Alice replied: "I have never tried..." She paused before adding: "But I know I can drive this vehicle..."

Mark winced from pain and said: "Alright..."

Alice braced herself as the taxi came to a sudden stop at the side of the road.

Mark shouted: "Swap!"

Alice released her seatbelt and climbed over Mark to take control of the steering wheel. But even as she adjusted the seat another car turned onto the street directly ahead of them. *They have us boxed in...*

Mark settled into the passenger seat and announced:

"We're trapped..."

But once again the 'otherness' calculated the optimum response - Alice slammed the gears into reverse and accelerated directly towards the pursuing vehicle. One glance into the rear-view mirror revealed the scowling face of their pursuer as he frantically turned the wheel to avoid a collision. *Westerner!* But she was already shifting gears again as the taxi swung around until they were once more facing the Yakuma mall. Now she accelerated rapidly before turning left onto a cycle path leading into Victoria Park.

Mark glanced over his shoulder and announced:

"They are following..."

Alice floored the accelerator and replied: "Not a problem..."

Mark stared at Alice and asked: "Are you alright?"

Alice swerved to avoid a cyclist and replied: "Fine."

Moments later they emerged opposite Queen's College on Causeway Road.

Alice spun the wheel to avoid hitting a bus before accelerating past slow-moving traffic.

Mark looked back and announced: "Police cars..."

Alice turned into a side street and replied: "I hear them..."

Mark closed his eyes and mumbled: "We need to..."

Alice glanced at Mark and said: "Now he passes out..."

She took a sharp turn into a blind-alley before coming to a full stop. In an instant the fast and frantic escape was reduced to the sound of her own rapid breathing. She slowly released her grip of the wheel and touched a finger to her face - beads of sweat dripped from her chin onto her blouse. *Tiny pools of life dissipating...* She was conscious of the rapid beating of her heart and a growing awareness of pain. A tentative touch to her head confirmed glass shards embedded in her skin. *Dermal abrasions...* And then distant sounds arrived with precise spatial clarity: *two police cars passing along Causeway Bay...standard traffic...*

*pedestrian sounds...no indication of our pursuers...* She looked through the shattered windscreen - the taxi had stopped just short of a flight of stone steps leading to the back of a row of shops. *This will have to do...* But almost immediately the powerful sense of 'otherness' was replaced by a wave of intense nausea and dizziness. *Oh god...* A brief moment of duality placed her on a beach looking out to sea before she quickly opened the door to vomit onto the concrete paving. After a few moments she sat back and wiped spittle from her chin - and then suddenly the enormity of what had just happened hit her with frightening clarity: *Oh my god! They tried to kill me!* She turned to look at the man slumped in the passenger seat and noted laboured breathing. *Mark?* Blood had soaked through his jacket, spreading to his elbow; but a quiet moan confirmed he was still alive. With a growing sense of panic she suddenly had no idea what to do next. *Call for an ambulance?* She unfastened her purse and removed her phone but stopped abruptly. *They could find us at the hospital...but who are they?* She looked at the man in the passenger seat. *And who is he?* And then she came to a decision. *Call Nancy!* She quickly tapped the phone. But it went straight to voicemail:

"Hi... I'm not here now...leave a 121...bye!"

Alice sighed heavily before another idea came to mind. *Mong Gao...*

She was about to tap the screen when a bloody hand gripped the phone. She looked up as the man calling himself Mark ordered:

"No... Don't call anyone...too dangerous..."

Alice replied: "I am just calling a friend...he might be able to help..."

Mark shook his head and said: "No... I have people who can help..." He removed a phone from his jacket and swiped the screen.

Alice stared at him and asked: "Who are you really? Why were those men chasing us?"

Mark replied wearily: "Explain later...need help now..."

Alice turned to see people gathering behind the taxi. She announced:

"We have been noticed..."

Mark spoke as he tapped the phone: "Someone will be here soon...just be patient..."

Alice rapidly considered her options before asking: "Who is coming to help?"

Mark replied wearily: "Friends...just be patient..."

Alice asked: "Friends?"

Mark mumbled incoherently before passing out once again.

Alice tensed at the sight of a gun protruding from Mark's jacket. Now she came to a decision. *I have to get away from here...* Without hesitation she climbed out of the taxi and proceeded to ascend the stone steps. She turned once to look back at the man in the taxi and came to a frightening conclusion: *my boring life in the gap just came to an end...* Minutes later she emerged in a busy side street before quickly made her way to the nearest MTR station. Behind her the sound of sirens drew closer as the sense of duality diminished into a nagging headache.

# Recall and Rebellion

*'The future is a lot closer than we realise...'*
Matt Dower

**13:34 pm - Sunday May 2nd - Rooftop - Meridian Hotel - Causeway Bay - Hong Kong**

Sunlight swept over the rooftop to reveal a young woman rapidly dismantling a rifle. In the streets far below the distant sounds of sirens add a sense of urgency as she glanced towards the Yakuma shopping mall. Once again she could not believe she had failed. A gestalt analysis of causal factors confirmed her mistake: *Someone else has been tracking the Beijing augments...* A last minute intervention had saved the designated target and condemned an innocent young woman to death. She could blame the incomplete data supplied by her employers but a more disturbing truth came to mind: *I am flawed...* The subsequent gunfire echoing from the parking area beneath the mall confirmed her earlier suspicions: *Weinberg's people have usurped my mission...* She got to her feet as another disturbing thought came to mind: *I will be recalled...* In an instant she considered her limited options: *A recall will mean a surgical procedure to ascertain the source of the flaw...* She clenched her fists. *They will use me as a template for the next augment... I will not survive such a procedure...* She turned to the sound of heavy footsteps. *They are coming for me...* She tensed at the sight of two men stepping onto the rooftop via the maintenance door. The man on the left smiled slightly and said:

"Ria... Mister Dower wants you to come home. We will escort you to the airport."

Ria initiated a tactical assessment of the two men: *Ex-military... Asymmetrical facial features indicative of cautious vigilance and a familiarity with violence...short cropped hair...bulging musculature beneath casual jackets...Bulges indicative of concealed weapons...* Finally she replied:

"My mission is not yet complete."

The man to her left stepped closer and continued: "It is no longer your mission."

The second man circled to her right and said: "So you can go home now...take it easy for a while..."

Ria rapidly scanned for anatomical weaknesses but found none. *They have the statistical advantage...* Her only option was both drastic and terminal: *I have no choice...* Now both men began to retrieve handguns from beneath their jackets. The man to her left was talking again:

"We don't want any trouble...just come with us..."

The second man continued to circle closer. *I have no choice...* She reduced the approaching men to gestalt minutia: *muscle reaction and proactive tactile reflexology...* Time itself slowed towards an analytical response algorithm: *The line of assault equals the causal reaction defined as the point of weakness...* The men did not expect a terminal response from the young girl with the delicate features. *That is their fatal flaw...* In an instant she leapt forward and slammed an extended hand into the stomach of the man on the right. But his comrade was already aiming a gun in her direction. She swept around behind the gasping man and wrapped an arm around his neck. For a brief moment they struggled before she forced his gun high and aimed it at the other man. But by then it was too late - she felt a sudden impact to her shoulder before she pulled the trigger. *Lateral deviation equals causal predictive movement to the left...* A sudden blind rage arrived with the pain and without hesitation she snapped the neck of the man struggling in her arms. Falling to her knees she saw the other man lying in a pool of blood and breathed a deep sigh of relief. *Got him...* But the sound of sirens from the street below forced her to her feet. A quick assessment of her shoulder wound confirmed an exit wound. *The bullet passed straight through...* She quickly retrieved a tube of synthskin from her backpack and sprayed her wounds. *That will do for now...* She waited a moment for the blood to congeal before making her way back into the hotel. Three minutes later she was walking along a side street following the GPS synced into the phone of Alice Sòng.

# The Nature of the Beast

*'Deception is endemic in this business,
it is the duplicitous nature of the beast...'*
Section Leader Han Mang - State Security Ministry

**14:18 - Sunday - May 2nd - Ministry of Science and Technology of the People's Republic of China - Beijing, China.**

A non-descript room of whitewashed walls surrounding desks and data-skim cabinets illuminated by strip lights. The grim-faced men from the State Security Ministry had requisitioned an office on Level 1 of the sublevel complex - Human Resources Administration. The room was rapidly converted into a self-contained data-analysis unit, complete with computer consoles and a large datascreen synced to the Project Jiàngsheng database. Agents Ming Wu and Ching Ho were busy scanning their way through two thousand data-skims directly related to the project, whilst their section leader had turned his attention to the autopsy reports relating to the two deceased test subjects: Huang Lin and Cho Ming.

Sitting at a desk directly in front of his colleagues, Han Mang sat back and sighed heavily. *Lies...all lies...* Both autopsy reports were identical. *A statistical impossibility...* There was only one explanation for such duplication: *One of the reports is a complete fabrication...* The desktop monitor revealed the face of twenty three year old Huang Lin. *And now the bird has flown the nest...* His thoughts returned to the phone intercept and the implications of Professor Leung's treachery. *He sold his talents to the highest bidder...Biogen...the source of perfidy...* A year-long state-sponsored investigation had failed to connect the mega-corporation to a series of high-profile corruption cases within the Party Congress. *Because the duplicity goes all the way to the top...* But now finally, there might be a way to reveal the truth behind the facade of social benevolence. Once more he studied the face on the screen. *The Achilles heel...* He touched one finger to Huang Lin's lips and smiled slightly. *But where are you now little bird?* The interrogation of project personnel had revealed little of Biogen's true agenda, but the interview with the timid assistant Ting Mai had been most enlightening. He tapped the screen to retrieve the vidcom of the session and listened once more to her carefully orchestrated replies:

**Interview Subject: Ting Mai - 09:00 - 04/20/28 - State Security Ministry Doc: 248916/SL Han Mang:**

Han Mang: *"How long have you worked for the professor?"*
Ting Mai: *"Almost two years now..."*
Han Mang: *"So you joined the Biotech team before the Jiàngsheng Project?"*
Ting Mai: *"Yes... I was recruited out of university."*
Han Mang: *"You did not want to get married, have a child?"*
Ting Mai: *"No... I... I wanted to further my career..."*
Han Mang: *"Were you involved in the selection of test subjects?"*
Ting Mai: *"No..."*
Han Mang: *"But you got to know each subject on a personal level?"*
Ting Mai: *"I suppose so...yes...we spent time together."*
Han Mang: *"So the death of two subjects must have upset you..."*
Ting Mai: *"Of course..."*
Han Mang: *"Do you blame yourself for their deaths?"*
Ting Mai: *"I... We did everything correctly...it was just....a reaction to the implants...it could not be predicted..."*
Han Mang: *"But Huang Lin and Cho Ming would be alive today if you had not opened their skulls to implant technology..."*
Ting Mai: *"They...they volunteered...and Lin was already sick..."*
Han Mang: *"Ah yes, the brain tumour...most unfortunate..."*
Ting Mai: *"We gave her a chance at life..."*
Han Mang: *"So you agree with the autopsy reports for both subjects?"*
Ting Mai: *"Of course..."*

Han Mang: *"Professor Leung believes it will take at least twenty years to produce a fully augmented human; do you agree with this estimate?"*

Ting Mai: *"I do... We are only at the beginning of the project."*

Han Mang: *"It is rumoured that the Americans are further along than the professor..."*

Ting Mai: *"I would not know about that."*

Han Mang: *"But do you agree that the professor would do anything to stay ahead of the game?"*

Ting Mai: *"Game?"*

Han Mang: *"Biotech augmentation."*

Ting Mai: *"I am sure that the professor desires only to serve the state."*

Han Mang: *"And you believe an augmented human can benefit the state?"*

Ting Mai: *"I believe such a human will facilitate long-term space travel...this will inevitably benefit the state."*

Han Mang: *"Why only three test subjects?"*

Ting Mai: *"Excuse me?"*

Han Mang: *"Despite investing considerable resources you have only produced one viable subject...surely it would have been logically to include at least one more test subject?"*

Ting Mai: *"I... I am not privy to Professor Leung's reasons for choosing the subjects."*

Han Mang: *"When will Guan Lu be revived?"*

Ting Mai: *"We plan to revive him at the end of next month."*

Han Mang: *"And then he will be transferred to the Space Agency?"*

Ting Mai: *"Yes. If there are no complications post-procedure..."*

Han Mang: *"Most unfortunate that only one subject survived...it does not bode well for future state funding."*

Ting Mai: *"We have enough funding to move forward..."*

Han Mang: *"Really? I am surprised to hear you say that considering your current budget estimates."*

Ting Mai: *"Forgive me... I meant to say that I am sure we can manage..."*

Han Mang: *"Do you think the professor would seek private funding for his project?"*

Ting Mai: *"I am sure he would not...it would breach our contract with the ministry."*

Han Mang: *"Yes it most certainly would..."*

Ting Mai: *"May I return to my duties now?"*

Han Mang: *"One more question...."*

Ting Mai: *"Of course..."*

Han Mang: *"On a personal level, do you agree with the morality of human augmentation?"*

Ting Mai: *"I am not sure what you are asking..."*

Han Mang: *"It is a simple enough question... Do you accept the state sponsorship of human augmentation as a morally justifiable endeavour? Or do you believe that the People's Congress has no right to manipulate the human genome for its own purposes?"*

Ting Mai: *"It is not my place to question the government..."*

Han Mang: *"But it is your place to answer my questions."*

Ting Mai: *"I believe our work is necessary. It can only benefit our society."*

Han Mang: *"And what of the dead subjects? How did your work benefit them?"*

Ting Mai: *"I...we tried..."*

Han Mang: *"No matter...you can go now. But please be available for further questioning."*

Ting Mai: *"Of course... Thank you..."*

**Interview Terminated: 09:12 - HM - SSM**

Agent Ming Wu looked up and announced:
 "Sir, the Shanghai field report is now available for review..."
Han ordered: "Sync it through to my screen..."
Ming tapped his datapad and said: "Transferred and synced sir."

Han sat forward and studied the latest report from the Shanghai field office. *Those damn fools...* Acting on their own initiative two agents had forced their way into the target residence. *And she took them both down...* He continued to read the report:

"*...At 22:50 the operational field team intercepted four individuals attempting to access the target residence - identities were not confirmed. They were detained prior to transportation to SFO/SSM. Within the target residence we located two members of the OFT/SSM - both unconscious. The target herself was no longer on the premises. At this precise moment the SFO vehicle suffered a catastrophic explosion - all four unidentified subjects plus two OFT/SSM personnel were killed. Investigations are ongoing pursuant to your mission dictate.*"

Han shook his head slowly. *The Biogen operatives chose suicide over imprisonment...* He sat back and sighed heavily. *What could possibly motivate such loyalty?* A slight blurring of his data-lens announced an urgent message. One rapid blink revealed shocking news: *They killed her!* He sat up straight as the words continued to flow slowly across the data-lens screen:

"*Urgent SecCom to SL Han SSM...surveillance target Nancy Yeo dead...preliminary onsite investigation confirms sniper...primary surveillance target Huang Lin and secondary target Jessica Lee proceeding to central Hong Kong...onsite team awaiting further orders...CH command...*"

Han blinked the screen clear as the Cybersync was terminated. Finally he leaned on the desk and announced:

"There has been an incident in Hong Kong...the girl has been killed."

Ching Ho looked up from the scanner and asked: "Huang Lin?"

Han replied: "No... The Biogen agent, Nancy Yeo. Sniper shot..."

Ching nodded slightly and said: "They have competition..."

Han frowned and replied: "So it would seem..."

Ming asked: "Do you think it is the Americans?"

Han replied: "Speculation serves no purpose..." He paused before continuing: "But it fits the profile of our old friends..."

Ming's eyes widened as he asked: "Synthtech?"

Han replied: "The only true benefactors if the Jiàngsheng Project fails."

Ching spoke as he studied his phone: "There is more news from Hong Kong..." He paused before continuing: "Local news feeds are uploading details about a shooting incident at Causeway Bay...a young woman was fatally wounded..."

Han scowled and said: "I want details...now..."

Ching replied: "At once..."

Han pushed his chair back and continued: "Arrange transport...we are going to Hong Kong."

Ming replied: "At once sir..."

Han glanced towards the face of Huang Lin as he pocketed his phone. *Time to clip your wings little bird...*

# The Synthtech Reaction

*'Life is a game of chess...'*
Matt Dower

**Data Intercept and Analysis - Sublevel 3 - Synthtech Corporation - Radford Boulevard - West Seattle - USA**

The wall screen revealed a detailed map of Hong Kong including a display of the local time: 14: 20 - sixteen hours ahead of Pacific Standard Time.

Matt Dower ordered: "Read the datasync from Ria again..."

Analyst Jane Smith read from her screen: "Datasync zero zero one two: Designated target was not augment. NY was a Biogen agent. Proceeding to locate both primary targets HL and Alice Sòng. End of sync."

Dower frowned and asked: "What do we have on the room-mate?"

Senior analyst Paul Hume replied: "Very little. She was not even on our radar."

Dower ordered: "I want a complete profile...everything..." He looked at the screen and added: "They hid her in plain sight..."

Hume spoke to his team:

"Alright people, we need a full biographical and geographical life-path. Look at family, friends, schools, employment, relationships... the works... Leave no stone unturned."

Analyst Chris Mendez looked up from his desk and announced:

"Newsfeeds confirm the earlier reports...two women shot dead in Hong Kong. Police are searching for an unidentified sniper and a young woman seen fleeing the scene of the second shooting in Causeway Bay."

Weinberg shook his head slightly and said:

"That would be Alice Sòng...another failed termination."

Dower asked: "And what about Ria?"

Hume studied his screen and replied: "Real-time tracking puts her in the Central district..."

Dower looked at the map of Hong Kong and said: "She is still on mission..."

Weinberg asked: "Can't we just shut her down?"

Professor Niel Jordon replied:

"I can upload a cascade virus into her cerebral interface."

Weinberg asked: "What will that do?"

Jordon replied: "The implants will overload..." He paused before adding soberly: "Her brain will literally implode."

Weinberg turned to Dower and asked: "Your decision sir?"

Dower frowned and replied: "No. We will not interfere. Let her continue with her mission..."

Jordon nodded slightly and said: "Adaptive strategic analysis should compensate for her failures..."

Weinberg protested: "But she killed two of my men..."

Dower replied: "This situation is the ideal test of her abilities..." He studied the screen and continued: "We will allow this to play out. See where it goes..."

Weinberg continued: "But she has failed twice already...surely the test is complete?"

Dower turned to Jordon and asked: "Is she flawed?"

Jordon hesitated slightly before replying: "Possibly... But she did lack sufficient data to extrapolate a viable terminal scenario."

Weinberg sighed and asked: "Do you ever speak plain English?"

Dower smiled slightly and said: "Neil is correct. We should have identified the British threat..." He looked up at the screen and continued: "It was not her fault..." He turned to Weinberg and said: "Order your people to stand down. I want to see how she deals with multiple threats."

Weinberg asked: "And if she fails again?"

Dower stared at the screen and replied: "Then we will terminate the test..."

Weinberg asked: "And what about Ria?"

Dower replied coldly: "Termination and dissection..."

# The Original Prototype

*'Innocence is the first part of the soul to die...'*
Sūn Yu

**14:21 - Sunday May 2nd - 2028 - Kwai Hing MTR Station - Hong Kong**

Moving slowly along a crowded and chaotic concourse, two young women come to a stop beneath an e-sign announcing: Tsuen Wan Line - Next Train 4 Minutes.

Jessica adjusted her backpack and asked: "Did we have to walk in circles to get here? We are wasting valuable time."

Lin looked behind them and replied: "There is a strong possibility that we are being followed."

Jessica sighed and said: "I still think we should call the police..."

Lin replied: "That would be a mistake. We cannot explain our presence in that apartment."

Jessica suggested: "We could tell them the truth..."

Lin asked: "And what is the truth?"

Jessica frowned and replied: "I am not sure I know anymore, but someone murdered Suyin, and they have to be brought to account."

Lin replied: "I agree. But right now we have other priorities."

Jessica fell silent before asking: "Why didn't we check the building opposite?"

Lin studied the faces of the people on the platform as she replied: "No point. They were long gone..."

Jessica asked in a low voice: "So who do you think they were?"

Lin replied: "No idea."

Jessica asked: "What about Suyin?"

Lin glanced towards the escalators and asked: "What about her?"

Jessica asked: "She called herself a slave of Biogen. What did she mean by that?"

Lin replied: "She was not an augment, but she was controlled by Biogen."

Jessica asked: "How is that possible?"

Lin replied: "I believe she was quite literally raised by Biogen for a specific purpose."

Jessica stepped closer and asked: "How can you be so sure?"

Lin replied: "Causal analysis."

Jessica asked: "What is that?"

Lin replied: "It's an augment thing...causation equals predictive outcome."

Jessica sighed and said: "Of course it does..." She paused before asking: "So you really know the true identity of the original prototype?"

Lin replied: "I do..."

Jessica asked: "And it is this Alice Sòng?"

Lin replied firmly: "It is."

Jessica considered this before asking: "So how come you got it so wrong?"

Lin replied with a question: "Is it not obvious?"

Jessica replied wearily: "Not really no..."

Lin continued: "The presumptive behavioural patterns indicative of augmentation are not present in Miss Sòng." She saw confusion on Jessica's face and added: "She is unaware of her augmentation."

An incredulous Jessica asked: "How is that even possible?"

Lin replied: "I suspect engrammatic manipulation."

Jessica asked: "They wiped her memories?"

Lin replied: "A crude term, but it suits the theory."

Jessica asked: "And all of this is based on causal analysis right?"

Lin replied: "Right."

Jessica asked: "Why would they do that to her?"

Lin glanced towards the escalators as she replied: "Causality requires more data to extrapolate a viable reason for their actions."

Jessica gave a slight smile and said: "Augmentation does little for the art of conversation..."

Lin looked along the platform and replied: "Forgive me but I am scanning the crowd."

Jessica looked confused and asked: "Scanning?"

Lin replied: "I am currently synced via my cerebral interface into twenty five mobile phones..."

Jessica asked: "Why?"

Lin replied: "I can determine a great deal from facial features and tactile asymmetric display, but by accessing online Techsync accounts I can calculate threat levels."

Jessica asked: "Is that augment speech for a bad guy search?"

Lin replied: "Basically yes..."

Jessica looked towards the people standing nearby and asked: "And?"

Lin replied: "We are safe...for now."

Jessica asked: "For now?"

Lin replied soberly: "We are being followed."

Jessica tensed and asked: "By the killers?"

Lin replied: "I doubt it...they carry themselves like security agents."

Jessica asked: "State Security? How can you be so sure?"

Lin replied: "They display a comparative physical methodology to the two men who invaded my apartment." She paused before adding: "Definitely the same training..."

Jessica asked: "So why are we safe?"

Lin replied: "They are simply following us...for now."

Jessica asked: "So what do we do?"

Lin replied: "We lose them."

Jessica asked: "And how do we do that?"

Lin replied: "You must follow my every command without hesitation."

Jessica's eyes widened as she asked: "I must?"

Lin replied firmly: "Yes, you must."

Jessica spoke quietly: "I think being bossy is another augment thing..."

Lin smiled slightly and said: "The train is here, follow my lead."

Stepping onto the train Jessica said: "Okay."

Lin gripped a metal pole and said: "We must move fast when we arrive at Central."

Jessica looked along the crowded train and said: "That won't be easy."

Lin said: "Nevertheless we must exit the station as quickly as possible."

## 14:31 - Sunday May 2nd - 2028 - Central Station - Hong Kong

A jostling of shoulders and backpacks inside a tightly packed carriage - the daily tableau of eyes staring intently at phones casting dim light upon faces transfixed by life inside Cybersync. Two young women stand poised at the doors, ready to exit the moment the train arrives at Central MTR station.

Jessica grips the pole next to the doors and whispers:

"Almost there..."

Lin opened her eyes and replied: "It is done."

Jessica asked: "What is done?"

Lin replied: "I synced into the TAD system to create a diversion."

Jessica asked: "What kind of diversion?"

Lin steadied herself as the train pulled into Central and replied: "Just be ready to move quickly..."

Jessica glanced over her shoulder and asked: "Are they close?"

Lin gripped her backpack straps and replied: "Close enough...so be ready."

Jessica tensed as she replied: "Okay..."

Seconds later the doors opened to an audible ping and Lin ordered:

"Stay close..."

Jessica spoke as they moved quickly towards the escalators:

"Where is your diversion?"

Lin spoke brusquely: "Keep moving..."

Suddenly the air was filled with flashing neonic shapes leaping ghostlike from the station walls - audio-visual caricatures extolling the virtues of a multitude of online bargains. Jessica was shocked to see swarms of Targeted Adverts converging on the train behind them. *Tads!* She caught a brief glimpse of two men in dark suits struggling to see beyond the flashing lights. She shouted:

"I see them..."

Lin pulled Jessica onto the escalators and shouted: "Run!"

Both women forced their way to the top of the escalators to emerge inside the upper shopping mall. Moments later they made their way towards the exit and central Hong Kong.

Pausing outside the mall a breathless Jessica asked:

"How did you do that?"

Lin looked towards a nearby overpass as she replied: "I synced into the Tad system and rewrote the visual recognition software to target dark business suits." She paused before continuing: "And then I synced GPS to target a specific location with multiple TADS."

Jessica smiled and said: "Nice..."

Lin said: "We must keep moving..."

As they set off once again Jessica asked: "How do we find this Alice Sòng?"

Lin increased her pace as she replied: "I know where she is..."

Jessica asked: "How?"

Lin replied: "Her Techsync account is active..."

Jessica saw the truth and said: "You are following her lenses..."

Lin replied: "She is using them to monitor local newsfeeds..."

Jessica stepped around slow moving pedestrians before asking: "Do you think she knows about Suyin?"

Lin replied: "I don't think so...she is scanning for information on a shooting incident in Causeway Bay."

A shocked Jessica asked: "Another shooting?"

Lin replied soberly: "I fear both incidents are connected."

Jessica asked: "The same sniper? How is that possible?"

Lin replied: "We took an indirect path to the train station..." She glanced behind them and continued: "But the killer ran for the first train..."

Jessica frowned and said: "No one could move that fast..."

Lin replied soberly: "Another augment could..."

Jessica's eyes widened as she asked: "There's another augment out there?"

Lin replied: "It fits the causal analysis."

Jessica said: "Wow... I think our quest for truth just got a lot more complicated."

Lin replied: "Indeed."

As they joined the crowds moving along the overpass Jessica asked:

"So where is Alice Sòng?"

Lin replied: "Moving through Central...we can intercept her at some point if we move fast enough." Suddenly she stopped and said: "I need to know the exact location of the stolen Jiàngsheng files."

Jessica asked: "You do?"

Lin pulled Jessica to one side and replied: "The files are the key to everything. We cannot allow them to fall into the wrong hands. So tell me where you hid them?"

Jessica replied in a low voice: "We encrypted them as Cloudstream data..."

Lin considered this before asking: "A construct?"

Jessica nodded slightly and replied: "A building...inside New Oasis. A coffee house..."

Lin calculated the encryption path and said: "And you used multilayer ciphers to create a mirror exit portal."

Jessica replied: "Yes...with rotating PAP's and false recognition protocols..."

Lin asked: "What is the cipher key?"

Jessica hesitated slightly before replying: "It is in the snacks menu...a step-by-step encryption via a node cascade interface."

Lin nodded slightly and said: "The correct order from the menu triggers decryption..."

Jessica replied: "Yes. Full data-flow...the entire Jiàngsheng database."

Lin frowned and said: "An expert could decrypt those ciphers..."

Jessica replied: "I know...so we wrote a new algorithm inside an alternate mirror access portal and flushed it with digital access nodes...it will spike at the first sign of a search algorithm."

Lin considered this and said: "They will follow the spike into a null code...clever..." She looked towards the city and said: "We should get going..."

As they set off once more Jessica asked: "What do we do when we find her?"

Lin picked up her pace and replied: "We tell her the truth."

Jessica asked: "You think she will believe us?"

Lin replied: "She will have no choice."

Jessica asked: "What do you mean by that?"

Lin replied: "I will sync directly into her cerebral interface..."

Jessica's eyes widened as she asked: "You will activate her?"

Lin glanced over her shoulder and replied: "Better me than whoever is trying to kill her..."

Jessica asked: "So you think she is the real target?"

As they stepped onto the mid-level escalators Lin replied: "I am certain of it."

## 15:23 - Sunday May 2nd - 2028 - The Blue Lounge - Wo Chu Lane - Hong Kong

Alice arrived breathless inside the narrow confines of Wo Chu Lane. The sudden transition from sunlight into cool shadows caused her to shiver as she leaned against the brick wall listening intently for any sign of pursuit. City sounds were suddenly muted into a dull rumble lost amongst the network of back alleys. She had only a vague awareness of the mad dash along the backstreets of central Hong Kong. But in her mind the image of shattered glass and blood refused to go away. *I left him to die...* The entire incident suddenly seemed surreal, as if she had been a simple observer, detached from the traumatic series of events beginning outside the Yakuma mall. But the nagging headache bore witness to the stark reality of her situation. *Someone tried to kill me!* A thousand confused thoughts arrived as fear and a growing sense of disbelief. *This can't be happening...* It was simply not possible to reconcile her actions with everything she knew about herself. *How did I do those things?* She had a vague memory of faces flashing ghostlike through her mind: *Bright lights and white walls...voices asking questions...* Words arrived unbidden amidst a storm of chaotic images: *"Everything will be fine...you will be reborn soon into a new life..."* A sudden blurring of her data-lenses was followed by a throbbing pain behind her eyes. *Invasive sync!* She quickly removed both lenses and ground them underfoot. *They are tracking me...* Without a second thought she ran the last few meters towards the entrance to the Blue Lounge.

A room with wall lights reduced to a dim glow casting shadows upon the face of Mong Gao as he stares intently at a desktop monitor. He wears a dark suit, white shirt and black tie in preparation for his scheduled meeting with Poppa Jo. But right now his mind is racing with possibilities. On the screen a swirl of lines finally coalesce into a recognisable shape and a smile arrives upon his face. *New Oasis!* He quickly tapped the screen to reveal lines of flowing data. *Data-spike anomalies inside structural metadata...multi-portal exceptions via false recognition protocols...* He sighed heavily. *Node algorithmic potential...* Once again his fingers flowed rapidly over the keyboard, inputting one calculation after another until finally the screen shifted perspective to reveal a single line of data flickering slowly across the screen. *I found it! My god... I found it...* Finally he sat back and stared at the screen. *They hid it in plain sight...* He was about to access the encrypted files when the door opened to reveal the hulking Jon Lau. He snapped:

"Not now!"

Lau replied calmly: "You have a visitor."

Gao asked: "Are you going deaf Jon? I told you, I am busy... no interruptions."

Lau scratched his chin and said: "She says it's urgent."

Gao looked up and asked: "She?"

Lau replied: "The waitress..."

Gao asked: "Alice? She is here?"

Lau asked wryly: "You going deaf kid?"

Gao smiled slightly and said: "Alright, send her through..."

Moments later the door opened to reveal the anxious face of Alice Sòng.

Gao saved the search results before asking:

"Alice... Is everything alright?"

Alice waited until Lau had left before replying: "I am in trouble..."

Gao walked around his desk and asked: "What kind of trouble?"

Alice stepped closer and replied: "Someone tried to kill me..."

Gao's eyes widened as he asked: "What?"

Alice brushed a trembling hand through her hair and replied: "It is true..."

Gao gestured to a nearby couch and said: "Please sit..."

As she sat down Alice continued: "I am so sorry, but I didn't know where else to go..."

Gao spoke gently: "It's alright... Just tell me what happened."

Alice spoke anxiously: "I think we should call the police..."

Gao took hold of her hand and said: "Tell me what happened first..."

Alice breathed in slowly and continued: "I was waiting for my friend outside the Yakuma mall..." She paused before continuing: "A man came up to me...he told me to come with him...and then..."

Gao spoke gently: "Take your time."

Alice continued: "I heard a scream...a young woman..." She looked up and continued: "Someone shot her...but the man told me that I was the target..."

Gao tensed as he asked: "Who was this man?"

Alice frowned as she replied: "He claimed to be someone I met in the Cloud..."

Gao asked: "What happened next?"

Alice swallowed and replied: "He forced me into the mall...and down to the car park...but they were waiting..." She stared directly ahead as she continued: "They were shooting at us...but we escaped in a taxi..." She paused before adding: "Oh god...they killed the driver..."

Gao asked: "The man who forced you into the mall...where is he now?"

Alice lowered her eyes and replied: "I... I left him...he was hurt...but I ran... I took the MTR from Causeway..."

Gao saw dried blood on Alice's neck and asked: "Are you hurt?"

Alice touched trembling fingers to her head and replied: "Not really..."

Gao asked: "Do you know who was chasing you?"

Alice shook her head slightly and replied: "I have no idea..."

Gao asked: "But this man...he saved you?"

Alice fell silent before replying: "Actually, I think I saved him..."

Gao's eyes widened as he asked: "You did?"

Alice replied: "Something happened... I am not sure how...but I drove the taxi..." She looked at Mong and asked: "How did I know what to do?"

Gao frowned and asked: "What did you do?"

Alice replied: "He was hurt...so I drove the taxi...through Victoria Park... I managed to lose them..." She fell silent again before continuing: "But all the time it was like I was watching myself do these crazy things...like I was separate from it all."

Gao considered this and asked: "So you left the man somewhere in Causeway Bay?"

Alice nodded slightly and replied: "Yes. Not far from Queen's College on Causeway Road."

Gao asked: "And you have no idea who he was?"

Alice replied: "He told me he was Mark...someone I met in New Oasis."

Gao tensed before asking: "A foreigner?"

Alice replied: "British..."

Gao asked: "Where did you meet him in the Cloud?"

Alice replied wearily: "Cup of Joe's coffee house..." She saw the look on Mong's face and asked: "Why is that relevant?"

Gao replied: "It might not be..."

Alice asked anxiously: "What should I do? They might still be looking for me..."

Gao squeezed her hand gently and asked: "Can you give me a minute? I want to check something..."

Alice asked: "Check what?"

Gao stood up and replied: "I have a few contacts in law enforcement..." He tapped his phone and continued: "Maybe we can find a few answers..."

Alice spoke soberly: "I think I was tracked..."

Gao asked: "GPS sync?"

Alice nodded slightly and replied: "Through my lenses...but I crushed them outside."

Gao studied his phone briefly before saying: "There is a police alert for a stolen taxi..."

Alice stood up and asked: "Are they looking for me?"

Gao hesitated before replying: "They are looking for a female driver."

Alice exclaimed: "Oh god..."

Gao said: "It's okay... They have no idea who you are."

Alice spoke fearfully: "Then the killers must be the ones tracking me..."

Gao stepped closer and said: "You are safe here..."

Alice said: "No... I should go to the police, explain everything... they have to know that I had nothing to do with that shooting..."

Gao said: "But you left the scene in a stolen taxi..."

Alice replied: "I had no choice...those men were trying to kill me..."

Gao sighed and said: "I think the best thing to do right now is to lay low until we can figure out who tried to kill you." He placed one hand onto her shoulder and added: "And we need to find out how they are connected to this man, Mark."

Alice asked: "How are we going to do that?"

Gao replied: "Someone tracked you to my front door...so let's just wait and see who turns up."

Alice warned: "But those people are killers..."

Gao replied: "Don't worry... I won't let anyone harm you..." He studied his phone before saying: "There has been another shooting..." He paused before continuing: "At Kwai Chung Estate..."

Alice exclaimed: "Oh my god..."

Gao continued: "A young woman has been shot in Block Five..."

A shocked Alice asked: "Oh please...not Nancy..."

Gao replied: "No other details given..."

Alice said: "But it all fits...they came for me at home but they found Nancy..."

Gao said: "We don't know that..."

Alice spoke tearfully: "Why is this happening? Why are people trying to kill me?"

Gao suddenly pulled her into his arms and said: "I will find answers... I promise you..." Moments later he pulled away slightly and continued: "Now I need you to just sit here while I go and talk to Jon. And I will bring you some tea..."

Alice sat down again and asked: "But I don't want you or your friend to get hurt..."

Gao smiled slightly and said: "Believe me...we will not be the ones to get hurt. So just sit here for a few minutes... I won't be long."

Suddenly Alice said: "Wait...there is something else...."

Gao asked: "What is it?"

Alice continued: "Something happened to me when we were being chased..."

Gao stepped closer and asked: "What do you mean?"

Alice replied in a low voice: "I was not myself... It was like I was watching everything that was happening from a distance...like it was not me driving that taxi...thinking such strange thoughts..."

Gao asked: "What kind of thoughts?"

Alice looked up with tears in her eyes and replied: "Survival thoughts...a sort of awareness...like I was a soldier or something..."

Gao smiled and said: "Adrenaline will do that."

Alice continued: "No... It was not like that...it was like a switch had been turned on in my head..." She sighed heavily and added: "But I could not control it..."

Gao's thoughts were racing as he said: "Well right now you are safe. Let me go and talk to Jon... I will be back soon."

Alice looked up and said: "Alright...but please be careful."

Gao smiled warmly and said: "Always."

## 15:49 - Sunday May 2nd - 2028 - The Blue Lounge - Wo Chu Lane - Hong Kong

Beyond the gloom of Wo Chu Lane the afternoon sun cast glistening reflections off the tall towers of Hong Kong. But only a stifling heat permeated the backstreets and alleyways of the vast labyrinthine city.

Jessica wiped a tissue over her face and said: "God... I thought Singapore was hot..."

Lin commented: "Everywhere is hot these days..."

Jessica looked towards the blue door and asked:

"Are you sure she is inside?"

Lin crouched down to retrieve glass shards from the ground and replied:

"There is a high probability..."

Jessica looked down and asked: "What are you doing?"

Lin studied a piece of glass as she replied: "She crushed her data-lenses here..."

Jessica sneezed before saying "She discovered the invasive sync."

Lin straightened up and replied: "So it would seem..."

Jessica asked: "So what do we do now?"

Lin replied: "We stick to the plan..." She looked towards the Blue Lounge and continued: "We confront her with the truth."

Jessica said: "But she sought sanctuary here for a reason..."

Lin replied: "I know..."

Jessica continued: "So someone could be protecting her..."

Lin replied: "Probably..."

Jessica sighed and asked: "And that does not concern you?"

Lin replied: "The danger factor has increased significantly, but I am not too concerned."

Jessica raised her eyebrows and asked: "You're not?"

Lin replied: "We did not come here to cause harm. We are here to help her."

Jessica wiped her nose and replied: "Her allies might think differently..."

Lin nodded slightly and said: "That is true..."

Jessica asked: "And that concerns you right?"

Lin replied: "Of course. But our choices are limited..."

Jessica fell silent briefly before asking: "Can you connect with her from out here?" She looked towards the club before continuing: "Maybe we don't have to go inside..."

Lin replied: "That would make things easier...but I need direct line-of-sight for the initial datasync."

Jessica asked: "Why? I thought you were a walking access portal..."

Lin gave a slight smile and replied: "Despite your flattering description, I still need proximity to initiate a net access response from Miss Sòng."

Jessica asked: "So why not use a basic wifi signal?"

Lin sighed as she replied: "Because augments are not wifi routers. The cerebral interface requires a high-energy particle emission to initiate activation. This is usually done during the maturation process."

Jessica frowned and said: "And they skipped activation for some reason..."

Lin replied: "Apparently..."

Jessica nodded slightly and said: "So activation requires proximity..."

Lin replied wearily: "Yes... Shall we stand here and discuss it further?"

Jessica smiled slightly and said: "Sorry..." She looked towards the club and added: "So let's do this..."

Lin looked back along the alley and said: "Wait..."

Jessica asked: "Now what?"

Lin replied: "She is close..."

Jessica asked: "The sniper?"

Lin replied: "Yes."

A surprised Jessica asked: "You know it is a woman?"

Lin replied: "Causal analysis predicts a ninety eight per cent probability that the killer augment is female."

Jessica said: "I won't even ask how you worked that one out..."

Lin replied with a slight smile: "Thank god for small mercies..."

Jessica looked back along the alley and asked: "How do you know she is close?"

Lin replied: "Because she synced into Alice Sòng's lenses..."

Jessica asked: "How can you possibly know that?"

Lin replied: "An invasive sync uses a narrow encryption path into an open portal..."

Jessica asked: "So?"

Lin replied: "So the path I used was open to duplication... Only another augment could use the same source code to access the Techsync GPS."

Jessica spoke in a low voice: "A direct cerebral sync..."

Lin replied: "Yes."

Jessica spoke in a low voice: "Alice Sòng is still a target..."

Lin nodded slightly and replied: "They will be coming here..."

Jessica asked: "They? How many augments are out there?"

Lin replied: "I suspect only one...but the police report shots fired at multiple locations in the Causeway Bay area."

A grim-faced Jessica said: "The augment has support..."

Lin replied: "Definitely."

Jessica said: "So let's get inside..."

Lin walked up to the door and knocked several times. Moments later it was opened by a brutish looking man in a white vest. He asked:

"What do you want?"

Lin replied: "We are here to speak to Alice Sòng."

The man studied them briefly before asking: "And who might you be?"

Jessica stepped forward and replied politely: "Friends."

From behind them a voice said: "Then you won't mind answering a few questions."

They turned to see a young man pointing a hand gun at them. He continued:
"Let's go inside and talk shall we?"
Jessica saw the look on Lin's face and whispered:
"Don't do it..."
The large man at the door pressed a gun into Lin's neck and said: "No...don't..."
Jessica forced a smile and said: "She won't..."

**15:58 - Sunday May 2nd - 2028 - The Blue Lounge - Wo Chu Lane - Hong Kong**

After a brief body-frisk they were led into an open bar area and ordered to sit on two chairs placed in the centre of the room. Lin initiated a tactical assessment of their surroundings: *Main bar area... Wooden tables and chairs beneath mirrored ceiling... Room length bar ending in a blue door...members only...* The bald man in the stained vest circled behind them whilst the younger man studied them carefully. *Black suit, white shirt, black tie, polished black shoes...* A rapid sync into the Hong Kong Liquor Licensing Association Database produced a name: *Mong Gao...* She also found a sealed police data-file logged under the same name. A rapid decrypt produced a startling fact: *he is Ginza Triad!* So far they had made no attempt to restrain them. *They think their guns are enough...* A gestalt analysis confirmed several physical weaknesses in both men. But she had decided to bide her time until she could talk to Alice Sòng.

Mong Gao was talking again:
"And who is that wants to speak to Alice Sòng?"
Jessica glanced towards Lin and replied: "I am Jessica Lee..."
Lin sighed and announced: "Huang Lin."
Gao smiled with satisfaction and said:
"Ah...the FTSS hacker and the Shanghai VIP..."
Lin asked: "Excuse me?"
Gao continued: "So how do you know Alice?"
Lin replied: "Let me talk to her and all will be explained."

Gao sighed and said: "That's not how this works..."

Jessica explained: "We are here to help her..."

Gao asked: "Why do you want to help her?"

Lin replied: "Because she is being targeted by a trained killer."

Gao stared at Lin and said: "Yes I know... And here you are."

Jessica protested: "We are not the killers..."

Gao asked: "So who are you?"

Lin repeated her request: "Let me speak to Alice Sòng."

The bald man stepped closer and said: "I think they need persuading..."

Lin tensed as Jessica pleaded: "Please... We only want to help..."

Suddenly a voice from the bar area asked:

"Who are you?"

Lin looked up to see a dark haired young woman enter the room. She replied:

"Friends..."

Gao joined the young woman and said: "Alice... Let me deal with this..."

But Alice replied: "No... They might know why someone is trying to kill me..."

Lin studied Alice briefly before saying: "I can tell you everything you need to know..."

Jessica added: "It's true..."

Alice stepped closer and asked: "Tell me about Nancy... Is she alright?"

Jessica glanced at Lin before replying: "I am sorry..."

Alice felt a teardrop fall from her eye as she asked: "Nancy is dead?"

Lin replied: "Yes."

Alice asked desperately: "Why is this happening?"

Lin was about to reply when she felt a faint whisper of heat pass by her head. She shouted: "Get down!"

In an instant the bar room erupted into a storm of breaking glass and shattered wood.

Jessica scrambled under a nearby table as more bullets impacted the walls. She looked up wide-eyed to see the bald man falling to his knees, a gaping wound in his neck. Suddenly Lin joined her and shouted: "Stay low!"

Jessica replied: "I am low!"

Lin continued: "And stay here..."

Jessica replied: "I'm not going anywhere..."

Lin began to crawl towards a nearby table where Mong Gao and the girl Alice had taken refuge. She asked:

"Is there another way out of here?"

Gao stared at the wide dead eyes of his companion and replied: "Delivery hatch behind the bar...opens onto the street..."

Lin looked towards the bar as more bullets shattered the wall mirrors. She was about to initiate a tactical assessment when she felt a brief sense of disassociation culminating in a sharp pain at the back of her head. *What?* She looked towards the main entrance as an invasive transmission synced into her cerebral interface:

"*Surrender and I will allow Jessica Lee and Mong Gao to live...*"

Lin tensed as she replied with a question: *"Who are you?"*

The invasive sync replied: *"Ria..."*

Lin sifted for causal recognition and found an explanation: *"The Synthtech augment..."*

Ria asked: *"Do you accept my terms?"*

Lin replied: *"You are here to kill Alice and myself..."*

Ria replied: *"That is my mission dictate..."*

Lin asked: *"Was it part of your mission dictate to murder Nancy Yeo?"*

Ria replied: *"Collateral damage is to be expected..."*

Lin retorted: *"Augments do not create collateral damage. You were in error..."*

Ria replied: *"And yet here we are..."*

Lin initiated a tactical assessment before asking: *"You will allow the others to leave unharmed?"*

Ria replied: *"I will..."*

Lin fell silent before announcing: *"I will send them out... Give me a few minutes..."*

Ria ordered: *"You have two minutes..."*

Lin stared at Alice as she replied: *"Agreed."*

Alice looked up wide-eyed and asked:

"What are you doing?"

Lin replied calmly: "I am revealing the truth..."

Alice felt a throbbing pain at the back of her head as the bar room began to fade into darkness. Almost immediately a growing sense of disassociation culminated in a series of images cascading towards the sound of voices...

*"Preliminary diagnosis has been confirmed..."*

*"She is viable?"*

*"Yes...an ideal candidate..."*

*"Can you subsume the trauma?"*

*"I can place her inside the Cloud..."*

*"Will she remember?"*

*"No..."*

*"You are positive?"*

*"There is the possibility of synaptic neural schism..."*

*"Meaning?"*

*"She could become detached from her own reality...the augmented mind could separate from the biological..."*

*"And if that happens?"*

*"She will suffer extreme psychosis...a total split personality..."*

*"You will terminate the experiment at the first sign of instability..."*

*"As you wish..."*

*"Who is Mister Tang?"*

*"A semi-autonomous Guardian app... It will monitor the subject from within the Cloud to alleviate stress."*

*"I want all data-skims wiped clean...there is to be no evidence of the procedure."*

*"What about the emergency personnel?"*

*"They will not be a problem..."*

*"And if she proves viable?"*

*"You will send her back to Hong Kong before you release the second subject."*

*"You want a comparative module?"*

*"I want you to monitor both subjects within the specified framework..."*

*"Very well..."*

*"Is she listening?"*

*"She can hear us but lacks the ability to conceptualise an interpretation..."*

*"But will she remember?"*

*"No...definitely not..."*

Alice opened her eyes to see a swirling maelstrom of sights and sounds suddenly terminating inside a taxi. *What is this?* The foul residue of cigarettes and cheap after-shave stirred a sense-memory: *I remember this...* In the distance the brightly-lit towers of a city were slightly obscured by the head of the taxi driver. *Beijing!* Her eyes rested upon the illuminated dashboard. *Twenty two thirty five... I just arrived from Hong Kong!* A surge of excitement quickly transformed into a growing sense of confusion: *Is this real?* Almost immediately a flood of memories coalesced into stark recognition: *My trip to Beijing!* But recognition brought a deep sense of foreboding. *What happened to me?* She looked through the side window to see a lorry hurtling towards the taxi. *Oh my God!!* Moments later she was rolling over and over until finally the world slipped into painful darkness and the voices returned once more:

*"I was told to call you if we had a viable subject..."*

*"What happened?"*

*"Refuse truck ran a red light..."*

*"Status?"*

*"Taxi driver DOA...but the girl is alive..."*

*"How bad is she?"*

*"Semi-conscious... Suspected intracranial bleed... Multiple fractures... Superficial cuts..."*

*"Who is on scene?"*

*"Police, fire crew and my colleagues..."*

"I am sending a retrieval team..."

"But we are about to transport her to hospital..."

"My people will meet you there..."

"You cannot just take her...the police are already investigating the accident..."

"I will deal with the police... Just make sure your colleagues do not interfere..."

"I am not sure about this...what if she dies?"

"Just keep her alive until the Professor arrives..."

"We will try... I have to go..."

Moments later Alice found herself standing on a beach beneath wide blue skies speckled with white whisper clouds. *I know this place!* She turned to see a vaguely familiar face walking towards her. *Mister Tang?*

"Hello Alice..."

Alice said: "I think I know you..."

Mister Tang smiled and replied: "You certainly do."

Alice asked: "What is happening to me? Where is Mong Gao?"

Mister Tang replied: "He is with your body in the real world."

Alice tensed as she asked: "What is this place?"

Mister Tang stepped closer and replied: "You know what this place is..."

Alice looked out to sea and said: "Yes... This is a Cloud Gap...a predictive artificial environment..." She looked directly at Tang and continued: "But I was inside the Blue Lounge...someone is trying to kill me..."

Mister Tang sighed heavily and said: "Yes...I am afraid that is true. But someone else has initiated an invasive sync into your cerebral interface..." He waved one hand into the air and continued: "She is slowly revealing the engrammatic manipulation."

Alice asked: "Revealing what?"

Mister Tang replied: "Your memories have been manipulated to produce a false timeline of events."

Alice touched a hand to her head and asked: "You said something about a cerebral interface?"

Mister Tang replied: "I have no choice but to tell you the truth...the intruder has usurped by command protocols..." He paused before continuing: "You are an augmented human Alice; the recipient of a cerebral synaptic implant fused to your temporal lobes with a direct sync to your amygdala." He pointed towards the sky and continued: "This is where you were placed during the surgical procedure after the accident."

Alice asked in a low voice: "Accident?"

Mister Tang replied: "Your taxi was hit by a lorry..."

Alice touched her forehead and asked: "I have an implant?"

Mister Tang replied: "Yes. A model zero one two integrated synaptic pulse emitter complete with universal sync and open portal access nodes."

Alice fell silent before asking: "It is inside my head?"

Mister Tang replied: "Yes. Actually it saved your life after the accident."

Alice said: "The taxi...we were hit...at the traffic lights..."

Mister Tang replied: "Yes. Most unfortunate..."

Alice asked: "What did they do to me?"

Mister Tang replied: "Biogen recruited a member of the local emergency response team. He was ordered to monitor vehicular incidents for a viable subject."

Alice asked: "Subject?"

Mister Tang replied: "The first prototype to be produced by the Jiàngshēng Project."

Alice asked: "What is that?"

Mister Tang replied: "A government sponsored project to create the first truly augmented human being."

An incredulous Alice asked: "And you say that I am the one they chose?"

Mister Tang replied: "Yes. You are Jiàngsheng Project Original Prototype One."

Alice looked towards the sky and said: "It is not possible... None of this real..."

Mister Tang blinked rapidly before announcing: "Brace yourself Alice..."

Alice asked: "For what?"

Mister Tang replied: "The invasive sync is about to connect directly to your core processing unit."

Alice asked anxiously: "Who is doing this to me?"

Mister Tang replied: "The second subject, Huang Lin. She is syncing in real-time via a hybrid portal."

Alice asked: "The woman in the bar? The one Gao was questioning...?"

Mister Tang replied: "Yes."

Alice looked down to see the sand rising slowly into the air. She asked:

"What is happening?"

Mister Tang shouted: "Invasive sync!"

Alice was shocked to see the ocean pulling back to reveal an expanding darkness slowly absorbing the light. She looked up to see bright blue skies fading into grey as the artificial sun dimmed into shadow. She shouted:

"Mister Tang!"

The fading voice of Mister Tang replied: "I am sorry Alice..."

Alice screamed as the ground suddenly gave way beneath her. But just moments later she opened her eyes to see the white-tiled walls of a laboratory. She was startled by a voice from behind her:

"This is where they transformed you into an augmented human being."

Alice turned to see the woman she had seen in the bar. *Short spiky dark hair over deep brown eyes...* She asked:

"You are Huang Lin?"

Lin replied: "Lin will do..." She stepped closer and continued: "We do not have much time; the Synthtech augment will soon discover my deception."

Alice asked: "What are you talking about?"

Lin gestured to the laboratory and replied: "Time does not exist in this place..." She touched a nearby metal tank before continuing: "It is the infinite flow of data transformed into the illusion of substance. Beyond this place real-time continues unabated...but at a much slower pace." She looked directly at Alice and continued: "Long story short, the woman who killed your friend Nancy is about to enter the bar room. She is here to kill you and me."

Alice asked: "Why?"

Lin replied: "She is an augmented human developed by the American Synthtech Corporation. Her mission is to terminate the augments produced by the Chinese government."

Alice asked: "Are you saying that I am one of these augments?"

Lin replied with a question: "Isn't that what your Guardian app told you?"

Alice asked: "My what?"

Lin replied: "Mister Tang. A Biogen product."

Alice said: "I don't believe you...this is all some kind of trick...a scam of some sort..."

Lin sighed and asked: "Where do think you are right now?"

Alice looked around before replying: "It looks like another Cloud Gap."

Lin asked: "And how do we enter a Cloud Gap?"

Alice replied: "We sync our data-lenses into an open portal and request a PAP... Then we wait for a Net Access Response."

Lin smiled slightly and asked: "Are you wearing your data-lenses right now?"

Alice hesitated before replying in a low voice: "No... I crushed them on the ground..."

Lin asked: "So how do explain the Cloud Gap?"

Alice replied: "Mister Tang...he told me it was an invasive sync..."

Lin replied: "Exactly." She gestured to the laboratory and continued: "This is my invasive sync..." She stepped closer and asked: "So what did I sync into?"

Alice replied: "I... I don't..."

Lin continued: "I synced into your cerebral interface; just like Mister Tang did. Augments don't actually need lenses, but they serve to disguise our true abilities."

Alice stepped back and said: "No... It is not possible...you are lying..."

Lin sighed and said: "Tell me how you escaped the assassins at the Yakuma mall. Are you normally so resourceful?"

Alice suddenly experienced a series of flashbacks: *bullets and shattered glass...blood...screams and panicked crowds scattering...the car chase through the park...sirens and a sudden silence...* A startling conclusion arrived with shocking clarity: *I assumed tactical analysis mode...* She looked at Lin and said:

"Something happened to me... I lost myself to something..."

Lin smiled slightly and said: "Your autonomous systems assumed tactical analysis mode and produced the most efficient way to extricate you from a dangerous situation." She placed one hand onto Alice's shoulder and added: "We need that part of you right now..."

Alice spoke in a low voice: "But I can't control it..."

Lin replied: "I can help you with that..."

Alice asked: "How?"

Lin replied: "I brought you here to remove the engrammatic manipulation of your limbic system."

A confused Alice asked: "My what?"

Lin said: "There is no more time to waste..."

As Lin closed her eyes Alice asked: "What are you doing?"

Lin replied: "Let's call it a hard reboot..."

Alice tensed as the laboratory was replaced by a kaleidoscopic panorama of images streaming through darkness towards an expanding circle of light. *What is this?* She caught her breath as the light suddenly leapt forward to reveal a series of memories cascading towards revelation:

*"I have a pulse!"*
*"Is she viable or not?"*
*"I believe she will fulfil our requirements..."*
*"Initiate Cybersync..."*

"Transfer residual engrammatic confluence to exit node..."
"Is she ready or not?"
"Behold...our first prototype..."
"You did not use maturation?"
"Circumstances required a radical solution..."
"And memory-timesync?"
"I created a false engrammatic scenario synced via predictive causality to the neural net..."
"Excellent...now return her to Hong Kong..."
"She will need to be monitored..."
"I have someone in mind..."
"You want me to live with her?"
"You have your orders Suyin...you are now Nancy Yeo..."
"Fair enough...but what is she?"
"She is the future..."
"Professor...will she be alright?"
"Do not worry Mai...she will resume her life once more. Now we must return to the project..."

Alice screamed as the storm of sights and sounds slowly coalesced into acute recognition and for a brief moment she lost consciousness. Moments later she opened her eyes to see the concerned face of Mong Gao. *Back in the bar!*

Gao asked: "Are you hurt?"

Alice stared into the eyes of Huang Lin and replied: "No. I am okay."

Lin asked: "Are you ready?"

Alice replied: "I am."

Gao asked: "Ready for what?"

Alice replied: "Stay here Gao...this will not take long."

Jessica shouted from under a nearby table: "Someone is opening the front door!"

Alice calculated a tactical response and transmitted it via Cybersync to Lin: *'Two-targets divide tactical response and allows for miscalculation...'*

Lin nodded and replied: *'I will go left and draw her fire...'*

Alice replied: *'There is a high probability that you will be hit...'*

There was a pause in transmission before Lin replied: *'I know... So do not waste the opportunity...'*

Gao removed a handgun from his jacket and said: "Get behind me Alice..."

But as the front door opened Alice was already running towards the bar. At the same time Lin ran in the other direction. Moments later a young woman leapt through the door with guns firing.

Jessica caught a brief glimpse of Alice leaping over the bar as Mong Gao returned fire from beneath a nearby table. Suddenly Lin fell to her knees as bullets impacted her shoulder. Almost immediately the room fell silent - the woman had taken cover at the end of the bar.

Lin received a Cybersync transmission:

*'Are you hurt?'*

Lin rolled beneath a table and replied:

*'Shoulder wound...non-critical... Are you in position?'*

Alice replied:

*'Yes...'*

Lin sensed hesitation and said:

*'You must use terminal force or we all die...'*

Alice replied:

*'She is a lone augment...she is trapped and outnumbered...'*

Lin placed one hand onto her shoulder wound and said:

*'Her allies are close behind...the threat must be contained before they arrive...'*

There was a short pause before Alice replied:

*'Very well...'*

Ria crouched low and initiated a tactical analysis: *They separated...my tactical response failed...two augmented minds in sync...* She had hit the nearest augment. *But Huang Lin was a willing target...* She gripped both handguns and breathed in deeply. *She was a diversion...* And then a disturbing truth arrived: *I can't defeat them...* One quick glance confirmed her analysis: *Alice Sòng is behind the bar...* But she suddenly felt a deep sense of relief. *If I can't defeat them I will use them...* For the first time in her young life she felt empowered. *I can finally control my own destiny...* She was about to expose herself when someone wrapped an arm around her neck. *Alice Sòng!* For a brief moment she struggled under the tightening grip. And then an invasive sync arrived:

'It does not have to be this way...'

Ria struggled to breathe as she replied:

'We all have a part to play...'

Alice suddenly had a gestalt revelation and asked:

'You want me to kill you?'

Ria dropped her guns to the floor and replied: 'I am flawed...'

Alice replied: 'An inability to murder is no flaw...'

Ria replied: 'I have already murdered...'

Alice replied: 'Then let it stop now...'

Ria tensed and replied: 'End this or I will end you...'

Alice tightened her grip and ordered:

'Surrender or die...'

Ria suddenly forced herself to her feet as she replied:

'You waited too long...'

But just moments later her hyoid bone fractured and she knew no more.

Alice felt the woman go limp in her arms before she gently lowered her to the floor.

Gao joined her and asked:

"Are you alright Alice?"

Alice stared at the body on the floor and replied:

"I had no choice..."

Gao spoke as he checked Ria's pulse:

"I know..." He straightened up and continued: "But I am not sure how you did that..."

Alice looked at Gao through tear-filed eyes and replied:

"It was not me..."

Gao asked: "What do you mean?"

Lin and Jessica joined them. Lin said:

"We do not have time to explain..."

Alice looked at Lin and said: "You are bleeding..."

Gao reached for a bar towel and said: "Use this..."

Lin secured the towel to her shoulder and said: "Her friends will be here soon..."

Gao asked: "How many?"

Lin replied soberly: "More than we can handle..."

Gao said: "I have a car out back...this way."

As they climbed through the delivery hatch Jessica asked: "So do we have a plan?"

Lin followed Alice through the hatch as she replied: "We do..."

Jessica asked: "Do you want to share?"

Lin looked towards the street and replied: "We get as far away from here as possible..."

Jessica straightened up and said: "Good plan..."

# Treachery and Trepidation

*'Everyone has a weakness to exploit;*
*identifying that weakness takes great skill...'*
Aron Fielding - British Intelligence - The Sino Infiltration Unit

**16:02 - Sunday May 2nd - 2028 - Workers Dormitories - Level 4 - Ministry of Science and Technology of the People's Republic of China - Beijing, China.**

A spartan room lacking any hint of comfort - a reflection of the utilitarian style of ministerial architecture: two single beds divided by a metal locker. The ceiling tube illuminates grey stone walls adorned with an 'Emergency Evacuation Procedure' poster.

Ting Mai is relieved to find her roommate absent. *Weekend leave...* She sat down on the edge of her bed and tapped the designated code into her phone. Moments later the image of the Englishman came onscreen. *Receding hairline over grey eyes and a face creased with lines...* He got straight to the point:

"Your latest upload was a waste of time. It told us nothing we did not already know."

Mai whispered: "You wanted to know about Guan Lu."

Fielding scowled and said: "I need to know his activation date. When will he be revived?"

Mai glanced towards the door and replied: "Soon..."

Fielding asked: "How soon?"

Mai replied: "Sometime this week. I cannot be more precise; we are still on lockdown."

Fielding ordered: "You will inform me as soon as you know the exact date of activation."

Mai asked: "Why are you so concerned about Guan Lu? You already know about Alice and Huang Lin..."

Fielding replied: "Do not be concerned about my intentions."

Mai hesitated briefly before asking: "Can I see my daughter?"

Fielding replied: "Your daughter is safe and well...and she will remain so if you continue to cooperate."

Mai pleaded: "But she is just a baby...please let me see her."

Fielding asked: "After two years you suddenly care about her?"

Mai replied: "I left her with my parents...they were taking care of her."

Fielding retorted: "You left Nanjing because you are an unmarried mother..." Mai lowered her eyes slightly and asked: "When can I see her again?"

Fielding replied: "When your mission is complete."

Mai asked desperately: "What more do you want from me?"

Fielding replied: "I want copies of all data-skims related to the current investigation."

Mai protested: "How is that possible? The investigation is still active."

Fielding replied: "Section Leader Han Mang is leaving Beijing... You have a window of opportunity..."

Mai frowned and asked: "You have confirmed this?"

Fielding replied: "His team will leave for Hong Kong within the hour."

Mai tensed and asked: "Has something happened?"

Fielding ignored the question and continued: "You will upload the data-skims to the designated Cloud portal."

Mai sighed heavily and replied: "I will try."

Fielding spoke firmly: "You will succeed or you will never see Meili again."

Mai replied in a low voice: "Very well..."

As the connection closed Mai tapped the screen to reveal the image of a child. She touched a finger to the face of her daughter as a single teardrop slipped slowly down her face. *Wǒ ài nǐ...*

# The Singapore Extraction

*'Life is a glow that is strong, and beautiful, and yet it is vulnerable to the slightest of traumas.'*
Zhang Lee - Security Director - Biogen Singapore

**16:05 - Sunday May 2nd - Apartment 19 - Block 411 - Saujana Road - Singapore**

Sunlight streams through blinds into a room of shadows settling upon a doubled bed. A naked leg sticks out from under a duvet as a woman stretches aching limbs. She opens wide brown eyes and yawns loudly. *So much for my siesta...* It had been another hot and humid day and the lack of sleep was beginning to impact her day job at the bank. *Two reprimands in one week...* The shocking news from Hong Kong only added to her growing fears... *Someone is targeting the Biogen augments...* According to Chin Fen the culprits could only be the Americans. *Synthtech removing the opposition...* Her thoughts returned to the encrypted datasync from Jessica:

"Nancy Yeo was a Biogen agent...not augment. Not sure if she was the intended target. Sniper identity cannot be confirmed. We think the original prototype is the roommate, Alice Sòng. We intend to locate her as a matter of urgency. I will sync again once we have found AS. Take care."

Fay pulled the duvet away and sighed heavily. *We kicked over the hornets nest...* She tensed at the sound of movement from beyond her bedroom door. *Someone is inside my apartment!* She searched frantically for her phone but it was already too late - two men rushed through the door and pulled her screaming from the bed. She caught a brief glimpse of a needle before the world suddenly faded into black.

**17:21 - Sunday May 2nd - Sublevel 12 - Biogen Compound - Pulai River -Malaysia.**

A windowless room devoid of furniture is illuminated by a circular ceiling tube. In the center of the room a young woman in a white hospital gown has been strapped into a metal chair. She is being carefully observed by two men standing nearby. The taller of the two sports grey wispy hair over a prominent bald patch and a furrowed brow. His companion is shorter, with dark hair and brown seeking eyes. Both men wear identical grey business suits adorned with metal Biogen lapel badges. On the wall behind them a viewscreen displays the current location of each member of the FreeTech Society of Singapore.

Muffled voices arrive with a painful awareness culminating in fear:
"She is awake."
"Her eyes are still closed..."
"She is feigning..."
"Ah yes...listening for clues...the ever resourceful Fay Rui."
Fay opened her eyes to see two men standing in front of her. She immediately recognised the taller of the two: *Zhang Lee!* She coughed and asked:
"Why am I here?"
Lee stepped closer and replied: "Do not worry. I will not detain you for long. I just need you to answer a few questions for me."
Fay swallowed in a dry throat and asked: "What kind of questions?"
Lee replied: "Well first of all...where is my daughter?"
Fay asked: "How should I know?"
Lee smiled slightly and asked: "Really? We are going to go in that direction?" He paused before continue: "We know that you were the last person to speak to her before she disappeared. So I ask you once again: where is my daughter?"
Fay coughed before asking: "The mighty Biogen cannot locate a single girl?"

Lee sighed and replied: "When it comes to hiding her tracks my daughter is an expert." He stepped closer and asked: "Where is she?"

Fay saw no reason to lie and replied: "Hong Kong."

Lee glanced towards his companion before asking: "Why is she in Hong Kong?"

Fay looked down at the straps on her arms and replied: "Release me from this chair and I will tell you what I know."

Lee ordered: "Release her."

The other man stepped closer and unclipped all four straps.

Lee said: "Now...tell me everything."

Fay sat up straight and said: "She is taking a vacation."

Lee asked: "You expect me to believe that?"

Fay replied: "I expect you to release me before the police arrive."

Lee smiled and asked: "And why are the police coming here?"

Jessica replied: "My entire apartment is vid-synced to my local police station. It won't take them long to locate me via the city cams."

Lee sighed and said: "And I thought you were the smart one among your motley crew..."

Fay suddenly saw the truth and said: "You hacked by security portal."

Lee stepped closer and continued: "No one saw your extraction...and no one will be following the city cams to our doorstep."

The other man said: "I think she needs an incentive..."

Lee studied Fay briefly and said: "Mister Feng is correct...you need to be encouraged to cooperate." He ordered: "Sync the detention cell..."

Fay looked towards the viewscreen and gasped: *Chin Fen!!*

Lee continued: "I see you recognise your fellow hacker..."

Fen was strapped to a hospital trolley beneath a glaring ceiling light. An IV tube was inserted into his right arm

Fay asked: "What are you doing to him?"

Lee replied: "At the moment he is simply sedated...but unless you cooperate the sedation will be replaced with something a little more...volatile..."

Fay scowled and said: "You are a monster..."

Lee leaned into her face and said: "Why is my daughter in Hong Kong?"

Fay looked at the viewscreen and replied: "She went to meet the Chinese augments..."

Lee straightened up and spoke in a low voice: "The Jiàngsheng Project..."

Fay gave a slight smile and said: "Your pretty daughter is a dedicated member of the FTSS."

Feng stepped closer and asked: "Can we talk outside?"

Lee nodded and said: "We will not be long Miss Rui."

Fay shouted: "What about my friend?"

As the door closed behind them Feng said:

"Your daughter is one of the hackers...we need to inform Rén Du."

Lee frowned and replied: "Not yet..."

Feng said: "But if she is complicit... "

Lee snapped: "She is my daughter!"

Feng countered: "She is also a liability..."

Lee sighed and said: "I need to speak to her before we set Rén's bloodhounds loose..."

Feng replied: "He may already know everything...he had agent in place with the original prototype."

Lee said: "But now Chu Suyin is dead and the Synthtech augment is tracking Alice Sòng." He paused before adding soberly: "Jessica is in the middle of a warzone..."

Feng nodded slightly and said: "But your daughter is resourceful..."

Lee sighed and said: "Which means she is probably with Huang Lin and Alice Sòng as we speak..."

Feng considered this before asking: "So what do you want to do? The Directorship is due to meet tomorrow...they will want your assessment of the current situation."

Lee looked towards the detention cell and replied: "Perhaps we can persuade Miss Rui to assist us..."

Feng asked: "How can she possibly help?"

Lee replied: "She is an expert Cloud dancer..."

Feng asked: "So?"

Lee replied: "So she can create an access portal into the brain of Alice Sòng."

Feng saw the truth and said: "You want to talk to Jessica via the cerebral interface of Alice Sòng..."

Lee replied: "And avoid alerting Rén Du..."

Feng frowned and asked: "I thought we were all on the same side..."

Lee replied: "We all work for Biogen..." He gripped the door handle and continued: "But we do not all serve the same agenda..."

# Escape and Escalation

*'Look into his eyes, he is not even human or animal...he is darkness.'*
*My 'Father' Rén Du - Chu Suyin.*

**17:23 - Sunday May 2nd - 2028 - Caine Road - Hong Kong**

The afternoon heat had been reduced to a warm breeze bringing rain clouds from beyond the China Sea. Across the city, people enjoyed the last few hours of their weekend - shopping, eating, and lazing in the parks and plazas. Traffic was light and the shopping malls a little less crowded than usual. But along Caine Road a black sports car was being closely pursued at high speed by a silver Sabrelite SUV.

Jessica glanced over her shoulder and said:
"They are still following..."
Gao spoke as he increased speed: "I know...give me a minute..."
Suddenly the rear window shattered and Lin said: "We might not have a minute..."
Alice crouched low in the front passenger seat and said: "Take the next left..."
Gao asked: "Why?"
Alice replied: "Trust me..."
Gao spun the wheel and replied: "Okay..."
As they turned onto Shelley Street Alice ordered: "Stop now!"
A confused Gao asked: "Stop?"
Alice replied loudly: "Do it!"
Gao hit the brakes and the car came to a screeching halt.
Lin looked back and announced: "They are coming..."
Gao asked: "Alice?"
Alice said: "Okay go now...go!"
Gao floored the accelerator and they sped off once more.
Jessica risked a quick glance through the rear window. She shouted:

"They can't get through!"

A large delivery lorry was reversing slowly into the street behind them.

Lin smiled and said: "You synced into the lorry's GPS..."

Alice replied calmly: "Yes."

Jessica gave a slight smile and said: "And you timed it perfectly so that we got through..."

Gao turned left onto the main road and asked:

"So why did we have to stop?"

Alice replied: "Stopping the car created uncertainty...it delayed our pursuers by ten point two seconds...their hesitation allowed the delivery lorry enough time to reverse into the side street from the back of that restaurant."

Jessica smiled and said: "I think we have an active augment..."

Lin pressed a hand against her shoulder wound and said: "Two augments actually..."

Jessica grinned and replied: "Of course..."

Lin caught Gao staring at her from the rear-view mirror. She asked:

"Where are we going?"

Gao replied: "I have friends who can help..."

Lin initiated a Cybersync and transmitted:

*"Ask Mong to pull over..."*

Alice replied with a question: *"Why?"*

Lin replied: *"Trust me..."*

Alice turned to Gao and said: "We need to stop again..."

Gao asked: "We do? Why?"

Alice replied: "Just pull over..."

As soon as the car stopped Lin slammed an extended hand onto Gao's neck and he immediately passed out.

Alice's eyes widened as she asked: "What are you doing?"

Lin replied calmly: "This man is a member of the Ginza Triad."

A shocked Alice asked: "The what?"

Lin replied: "Do a Cloud search..."

Alice blinked rapidly before saying: "I had no idea..."

Lin opened her door and said: "We need to leave here at once..."

Jessica released her seatbelt and asked: "We're not taking his car?"

Lin stepped out and replied: "It has Autotrace... We need to find another way to get off the island."

Alice remained seated and said: "But he is my friend...we can't just leave him like this..."

Lin replied: "He was using you to get to the Jiàngsheng files..."

Alice shook her head and said: "No.... There was no connection between me and the stolen data. Gao genuinely wanted to help me... He had no idea that I was part of that awful experiment..." She looked directly at Lin and added: "No more than I did..."

Jessica stepped closer and said: "You like him..."

Alice felt her face flush as she replied: "He is my friend..."

Lin said: "He is not the type of friend you need right now..."

Alice looked up and asked: "And I suppose you are?"

Lin replied: "If you want to survive this day you will trust me and not the Triad."

Jessica asked: "He is Triad?"

Alice looked at the unconscious Gao and said: "He is probably better off without me..."

Lin said: "That is true..."

Jessica looked at Lin and said: "Must you be so harsh?"

Lin shrugged and said: "I only speak the truth..."

Alice said: "Proximity to me could prove fatal to him..."

Jessica considered this and asked: "And to me right?"

Lin asked: "Do you want to stay here?"

Jessica replied: "No... I was just thinking out loud..."

Alice opened her door and said: "We need to leave the island..."

Jessica asked: "And go where?"

Alice stepped onto the pavement and replied: "I know a place..."

Lin said: "We cannot use the MRT..."

Alice closed the car door and said: "We will take the ferry..."

**17:38 - Sunday May 2nd - 2028 - The Blue Lounge - Wo Chu Lane - Hong Kong**

A bar room of broken glass and splintered wood - a place of silence and the stench of death. Two policemen had been the first to respond to reports of gunfire, but the Triad had terminated the investigation before it had begun:

"Do not concern yourself inspector...the matter will be dealt with internally."

"I am not sure about this Poppa Jo... This incident could be connected to the Yakuma shooting..."

"There is no connection... Please give my regards to your wife... Good day to you inspector...."

Sal Cho touched fingers to the thick neck of Jon Lau. He announced:

"Dead..."

Ricky Li stepped around a pool of blood and replied: "I can see that..."

Cho pointed to the body of a young woman and said:

"I wonder who she was..."

Li walked over to the bar and replied: "No idea..."

Cho said: "Nice body..."

Li looked down at the dead woman and said: "What's left of it..."

Cho straightened up and asked: "So what do you think went down here?"

Li replied: "Only one way to find out..."

Cho smiled and said: "The vidcams...good idea..."

As they entered the Private Lounge Li glanced at his phone and said:

"The Boss is on his way..."

Cho sighed and said: "Perfect..."

## 17:41 - Sunday May 2nd - 2028 - Mosque Street - Hong Kong

Late-afternoon sunshine glanced off refractive car windows to fall into shadows along the sidewalk. The silver Sabrelite SUV came to an abrupt stop at the side of the road. Four men sat with guns in hand as the engine rumbled into silence. Each bore the same distinctive body-type - firm musculature, grim facial features and the predatory alertness of trained killers.

From the back seat Dwayne Lewis scratched his beard and said: "We're going to lose them..."

Mitch Jones let go of the steering wheel and replied:

"We already lost them..." He glanced at the control panel and added: "The Boss is calling..."

Sitting in the front passenger seat, Team Leader, Dieter Fink tapped the panel and asked:

"Yes sir?"

Karl Weinberg came online and asked: "Status?"

Fink replied: "Ria is dead..."

There was a pause before Weinberg asked: "You confirmed this?"

Fink replied: "Yes... Someone broke her neck..."

Weinberg cursed: "Damn..."

Fink continued: "We pursued the designated targets from the club..."

Weinberg interjected: "And?"

Fink glanced at his companions and replied: "We lost them..."

Once again there was a pause before Weinberg asked:

"Did you instigate the Ria protocol?"

Fink kicked the metal container at his feet and replied:

"We removed her head as ordered. It is secured and ready for transport."

Weinberg replied: "Good. Return to your quarters and await further orders."

Raul Morgan spoke from the back seat: "I have them..."

Fink said: "Hold a minute sir..." He turned in his seat and asked: "Well?"

Morgan tapped his datapad and replied: "I hacked the Weio's Autotrace..." He paused before adding: "It's parked just eight hundred metres along this street."

Fink smiled slightly and said: "Sir, we have located the target vehicle..."

Once again there was a long pause before Weinberg replied: "Very well...check it out and report back to me..."

## 18:05 - Sunday May 2nd - 2028 - Biogen Facility - Kwu Tung - New Territories - Hong Kong

A single desk and chair inside a room of shadows skirting grey stone walls. On the desk a large viewscreen reveals a geosync map of Hong Kong Island - two blinking red dots appear in the middle of Victoria Harbour.

Special Projects Director, Rén Du sat back and studied the screen. *They are on the ferry...* Two flickering diagnostic panels confirmed the location of two augments - *Cerebral Geosync for subjects: Huang Lin and Alice Sòng. Implant nodes: 001024X 001025X.* He tapped the screen to display the latest satellite images. *And they have allied themselves with the Singapore hacker...* He sighed heavily. *Zhang Lee's daughter...* A flashing com signal drew his attention - one tap of the screen revealed the anxious face of Professor Leung Huo.

"Rén?"

"I am here professor..."

Leung continued: "Section Leader Han Mang has left Beijing..."

Rén said: "Yes I know... He is here in Hong Kong."

Leung's eyes widened as he asked: "Does he know the truth? Am I in danger?"

Rén replied: "Calm down professor. Han is simply fishing for clues...the true nature of the project has not been compromised."

Leung asked: "Then why is he in Hong Kong? He must know about Alice..."

Rén said: "No... He knows nothing about Alice Sòng." He paused before continuing: "However he does know about Huang Lin."

A surprised Leung asked: "How is that possible?"

Rén sat forward and replied: "It is possible because your phone calls to Huang Lin were monitored; and why? Because you failed to input the scramble code as instructed."

Leung fell silent briefly before saying: "I... I am sure that is not true..."

Rén replied: "It has been verified..." He glanced at his phone and continued: "Archival Phone Intercept Edit: 042028/LH/HL..."

Leung mumbled: "I... I apologise...but..."

Rén interjected: "What is the status of Guan Lu?"

Leung replied: "We are in the final stages of cerebral initiation... He will be revived tomorrow morning."

Rén glanced at the Guan Lu data-skim and said: "Then I believe we have reached the end of our collaboration professor..."

Leung asked: "What do you mean? I am still monitoring Alice and Lin... There are evaluation stats to quantify...and both subjects will require a full medical analysis before we proceed to stage two..."

Rén sat back and replied: "I am afraid that you will no longer be part of stage two professor..."

Leung exclaimed: "But I am the head of the project...you cannot move forward without me..."

Rén replied: "Actually my experts say we can proceed perfectly well without you..." He looked directly at Leung and continued: "And let's face it professor, you have become a significant liability..."

Leung scowled and said: "I do not work for you... I answer only to the Chinese government..." He leaned closer to his screen and continued: "And I am sure they will be very interested in what I have to say about Biogen and its plans for the human race."

Rén sighed and said: "I do wish you had not said that professor..."

Leung was about to reply when a plastic bag was placed over his head and pulled tight around his neck. For a few desperate moments he

clawed at the bag until finally he collapsed off-screen. A male voice spoke three words:
"It is done."
Rén ordered: "Continue with your mission..."
There was a pause before the voice replied:
"Of course..."
Rén tapped the screen to restore the geosync map of Hong Kong. The two flashing red dots were now moving closer to the Tsim Sha Tsui waterfront. *They are coming this way...*

**18:09 - Sunday May 2nd - 2028 - Safe House - Kennedy Road - Hong Kong**

Late afternoon sunshine muted by window blinds created a stifling atmosphere inside the small room. One man was busy dressing the shoulder wound of another man as he sat on the edge of an examination trolley.
Doctor Richard Dale stepped back and said:
"There you go...all done..."
Mark Chapham a.k.a Daniel Lane stretched his arm and asked:
"So there is no permanent damage?"
Dale gathered up several blood-soaked wipes and replied:
"It's a clean through-and through... I see no signs of muscle damage..."
Lane asked: "So I can return to duty now?"
Dale wiped his hands and replied:
"Not my decision... You'll have to speak to the old man about that..."
Lane picked up his phone and tapped the screen several times. Finally he jumped off the trolley and said:
"I have to go..."
Dale asked: "Go where? You need time to recuperate..."
Lane studied his phone as he replied: "I slipped a tracker into her purse... She is on the move..."
Dale asked: "What are you talking about?"

Lane retrieved a clean shirt from a nearby cupboard as he replied:

"She is already on the ferry... I have to follow her..."

A frustrated Dale asked: "Follow who?"

Lane pulled the shirt on and replied: "It doesn't matter..." He reached for a jacket before adding: "Thanks Doc... Bye for now..."

Dale called: "What do I tell the old man?"

Lane replied from the hallway: "The truth... I am still on mission."

**18:11 - Sunday May 2nd - 2028 - The Star Ferry -Victoria Harbour - Hong Kong**

Three young women stand at the back of a crowded ferry looking towards Hong Kong Island. Two are dressed casually in blue jeans whilst one is wearing her most formal clothes - white blouse beneath cream coloured jacket with matching knee-length skirt and black ankle boots. They had avoided further interception by taking a circuitous route along backstreets and narrow lanes to arrive at the Central Piers. Now finally they were leaving the island bound for Kowloon and the mainland.

They had not spoken since boarding the ferry and the silence was welcome - words would only stoke the fears as the sense of danger increased. The sound of nearby laughter gave them a comforting reminder of normality. But each knew it was simply a temporary illusion to still the rapid beating of their hearts.

Alice breathed in deeply - the sea breeze touched her face and gave a brief respite from the heat of the day. She looked down into the dark water - the setting sun cast ripples of light upon the expanding wake created by the ferry. *Like synaptic neurotransmissions expanding exponentially...* This startling comparison came as a shock: *What is happening to me?* She knew that Lin was telling the truth - but that truth was beyond belief. *I am no longer me...* The sense of déjà vu was disturbing. *I am repeating a trace memory...from the Cloud Gap...* But now her memories had formed a strange duality which increasingly undermined her sense of reality. *My life has been split into separate pieces of me...before and after Huang Lin entered my mind...* But there was also a profound sense of loss... *I have lost my innocence...* And then the words of the Synthtech augment returned: *"I am flawed..."* She gripped the handrail and looked towards the island. *I took a human life...* But it was not the act of killing that disturbed her the most... *I felt no regret...no guilt...nothing...* She brushed a hand through her hair and sighed heavily. *Because the machine took control...* A sudden trembling arrived as knot in her stomach. *I am also flawed...* An invasive Cybersync arrived from Huang Lin:

"*Did you notice our followers?*"

Alice sighed heavily and replied:

"*Secret police from Beijing...*"

Lin continued: "*We need to lose them at some point...*"

Alice replied: "*We will...be patient...*"

Lin asked: "*And if they move against us?*"

Alice replied: "*They won't...not yet...*"

Lin replied: "*How can you be so sure? They tried to take me in Shanghai...*"

Alice replied: "*I think that was a local miscalculation... Beijing is far more cautious...*"

Lin said: "*You used causal analysis...*"

Alice replied: "*I did...*"

Lin smiled slightly and said: "*You are a fast learner Alice Sòng...*"

Alice replied wryly: "*You gave me little choice...*"

Lin said: "*I feel your pain Alice Sòng...*"

Alice asked: "*My pain?*"

Lin replied: "*You took a life...that was no easy thing...*"

Alice replied bitterly: "*Look deeper...you will see how easy it was...*"

Lin replied: "*You had no choice... She came to murder us...*"

Alice replied: "*No, you are wrong... She came to commit suicide...*"

Lin said: "*I do not understand...*"

Alice replied: *"Look into your soul and you will see the thing they have done to us..."* She paused before continuing: *"That young woman recognised the horror and she could no longer live with the truth..."*

Lin asked: *"What is the truth?"*

Alice replied: *"That we are losing our humanity... We can try to resist...but the process is beyond our control...inevitably we will evolve into something other people will fear..."* She sighed before continuing: *"And we will react to that fear in the only way we know how..."*

Lin asked: *"You think we will kill to survive?"*

Alice replied wearily: *"Is that not what I did in the Blue Lounge?"*

Jessica studied Alice and Lin before asking:

"Are you two transmitting to each other?"

Alice gave a slight smile and replied: "Sorry... That was rude of us."

Lin pulled her jacket close and said: "It is simply a more practical way of communicating."

Jessica exclaimed: "Yes, but it excludes me... We are in this mess together..."

Alice said: "That is true... We will no longer exclude you..."

Lin glanced towards the other passengers and added: "Unless circumstances require it."

Jessica asked: "How is your shoulder?"

Lin replied: "The paracetamol is helping..."

Alice suggested: "Maybe we can call at a clinic..."

Lin replied: "It is already healing..."

A surprised Jessica asked: "It is?"

Lin replied: "Subcutaneous nanites have released a coagulant..."

Jessica exclaimed: "Amazing..."

They fell silent once again until Alice sighed heavily.

Jessica asked: "Something wrong?"

Alice examined her skirt and replied: "These are my job interview clothes...cost me a lot...." She studied her sleeve and continued: "Now I have blood on them and my shoes are ruined..."

Lin commented: "You do look a little bedraggled..."
Alice said: "Thanks...."
Lin continued: "And your clothes are the least of our problems."
Alice replied: "Again...thanks..."
Jessica asked: "So you went for an interview?"
Alice replied: "At the Blue Lounge of all places..."
Jessica said: "Wow...talk about bad timing..."
Lin asked: "Did you get the job?"
Alice sighed and replied: "Yes I did..."
Lin commented: "Bad timing indeed..."
They fell silent once again until Jessica looked at Alice and said: "You seem to be taking all of this very well."
Alice brushed hair from her face and asked: "What choice do I have?" She looked towards the glistening towers of the island and continued: "I have been forced through a door I did not know existed..." She sighed heavily before adding: "My boring little world just became a universe..."
Lin interjected: "A very dangerous universe..."
Alice replied wryly: "Thank you for reminding me."
Jessica asked: "Can I ask you something?"
Alice replied: "Go ahead."
Jessica continued: "The Beijing trip... Do you remember anything about the car accident?"
Alice fell silent briefly before replying: "Not really... I remember bright lights and intense pain...but then it all went away and I was in the Cloud Gap with Mister Tang."
Jessica adjusted her backpack and asked: "Who is Mister Tang?"
Lin interjected again: "Biogen guardian app... Pre-cognitive induction loop."
Alice continued: "He monitored by recuperation..."
Jessica nodded slightly and asked: "So you have no memory of the implantation procedure?"
Alice considered the question before replying: "Not true memories... But I can visualise the procedure from a detached viewpoint...like a Cloud Dance vaguely remembered..."

Lin explained: "That is a state of peripheral cognitive awareness... It is a side-effect of the implantation procedure."

Alice frowned and said: "I do remember feeling violated...and very angry...but those feelings were fleeting, and soon faded away..."

Jessica said: "I am sorry..."

Alice asked: "For what?"

Jessica replied: "For what they did to you against your will..."

Alice leaned on the railing and said: "But I might have died in that car crash..."

Jessica said: "But you don't know that for sure..."

Alice replied: "No..."

Jessica hesitated before asking: "So you accept what they did to you?"

Alice stared directly ahead and replied: "No. I will never accept it...they violated me...turned me into a walking cyber app..."

Lin glanced at her phone and said: "I actually volunteered for the procedure..."

Jessica said: "But only because you were dying..."

Alice looked at Lin and asked: "You were?"

Lin replied: "Yes. Brain tumour...only a few months left to live..."

Jessica said: "So the procedure saved both of your lives..."

Alice spoke bitterly: "But it also stole my humanity..."

Lin considered this and said: "We are patented products...assets to further Biogen's plans..."

Alice clenched her fists and said: "We need to find out more about those plans..."

Jessica glanced at Lin and said: "Actually... We think we know their plans..."

Alice asked: "You do?"

Jessica looked at Lin and asked: "Lin?"

Lin sighed heavily and replied: "Phase one was the augmentation of an adult human brain..."

Alice asked: "And phase two?"

Lin replied: "Cerebral augmentation and genomic enhancement of the human foetus..." She looked towards the island and added: "A surrogate will be used to gestate a foetus to full term."

Alice rapidly calculated causal analysis and said: "They extracted your eggs..."

Lin replied in a low voice: "Yes..."

Alice gripped the handrail and whispered: "Oh my god..." Suddenly a million threads of causal certainty coalesced with shocking clarity: "I was the original prototype...so they harvested me first..."

Lin saw the truth and said: "You are the primary donor... I am the backup..."

Jessica exclaimed: "This nightmare just gets worse..."

Alice spoke in a low voice: "They intend to create a new species..."

Lin added: "A superior species..."

Jessica looked towards the other passengers and said: "That would make everyone else obsolete..."

Lin spoke defiantly: "So we need to stop them..."

Jessica said: "I don't see how...they have unlimited resources. What do we have?"

Alice replied firmly: "We have each other..."

Lin nodded slightly and said: "That is true..."

Jessica said: "Yes...two augments and a hacker against a global mega-corporation... They must be trembling in their beds..."

Alice smiled as Lin said:

"Don't forget the Americans...they seem to want us dead too..."

Alice added: "And the British..."

Lin continued: "And the Triad..."

Alice nodded slightly and said: "And the Beijing secret police..."

Jessica sighed and asked: "Is there anyone out there who isn't chasing us?"

Alice grinned and replied: "Oh it's not all bad news..."

Lin looked at Alice and asked: "It isn't?"

Alice brushed a hand through her hair and replied:

"Maybe we should change the subject..."

They fell silent until Jessica asked: "Do you have family in Hong Kong?"

Alice replied: "Just my mother and Grandmother..."

Lin asked: "So your father is dead?"

Jessica shook her head slightly and said: "That is none of our business..."

Alice said: "No, it's okay... I never knew my father. He dumped my mother when she got pregnant with me... She was just eighteen..."

Lin shook her head in disgust and said: "Typical..."

Alice continued: "I was raised by my Grandparents mostly..."

Jessica asked: "What about friends?"

Alice replied: "I lost touch with most of them after Uni... Nancy was my first real friend in a long time."

Lin said: "I am not sure I would call her a friend... She was a Biogen spy monitoring your progress."

Alice replied: "I know that now, but at the time...she was just...good for me..."

Lin spoke bluntly: "Because she was obeying orders..."

Jessica gave Lin a look and said: "But at least Mong Gao seemed to care about you..."

Alice sighed heavily and said: "As far as gangsters go he was okay..."

Lin interjected: "You're not very good at choosing friends are you?"

Jessica asked: "Must you always be so brutally honest?"

Lin frowned and replied: "Yes."

Alice smiled slightly before asking: "What about you?"

Jessica adjusted her ponytail and asked: "What about me?"

Alice asked: "Why are you involved in this mess?"

Jessica hesitated before replying: "My father works for Biogen."

Alice raised her eyebrows and asked: "Really?"

Jessica replied: "He is on the board of directors; based in Singapore."

Lin added: "And one of the bad guys."

Jessica protested: "We don't know that yet... He might not have anything to do with the Jiàngsheng Project."

Alice considered this before asking: "So who actually runs the project?"

Lin replied: "Professor Leung is the brains behind the actual procedure, but Rén Du is the one who calls the shots..."

Alice spoke in a low voice: "The professor... I remember his face...he looked down at me...and he smiled..."

Lin nodded slightly and said: "He does love his work..."

Jessica said: "Officially the project is controlled by the Ministry of Science and Technology based in Beijing..."

Lin added: "But unofficially it has been manipulated to further the plans of Biogen."

Alice asked: "Who is this Rén Du?"

Jessica replied: "Biogen Director of Special Projects, based in Shanghai."

Lin scowled and said: "The master manipulator..."

Alice asked: "You have met him?"

Lin replied: "No..."

Jessica interjected: "We decrypted the Cloud diary of Chu Suyin. It told a terrible story..."

Lin added soberly: "She was manipulated and abused from early childhood."

Alice asked: "And who is Chu Suyin?"

Jessica replied gently: "Your friend, Nancy Yeo..."

Alice said: "Oh..."

Jessica saw the look on Alice's face and asked: "You okay?"

Alice asked: "Was she an augment?"

Jessica replied: "No. She was an ordinary girl...an orphan, legally adopted by Rén Du."

Lin added: "Apparently she was an experiment in socio-adaptive manipulation."

Alice asked: "What does that mean?"

Jessica replied: "We think she was used to test the viability of control through training and psychoanalytical manipulation."

Alice sighed and said: "That makes it so much clearer..."

Lin explained: "Biogen attempted to subvert the mind of a child to serve their cause."

Jessica added: "But they were only partially successful, so they moved onto augmentation in an attempt to control via technology."

Alice tensed and asked: "Are you saying that they can control us remotely?"

Lin considered the question before replying: "Current technology does not allow it, but according to your friend Nancy they are working on it..."

Alice asked: "How would that even work?"

Lin replied: "A remotely activated resonance pulse to program the interface via sound waves."

Jessica added: "They could literally order you to do anything..."

Alice said: "I would never accept such a thing..."

Lin continued: "If the cerebral interface can be adapted to receive an electromagnetic pulse via a wifi interlace transmission we might not have a choice."

Jessica added: "Nancy... I mean Chu Suyin... She called it a neural leash."

Alice spoke firmly: "I refuse to believe that anyone can control me..."

They fell silent as a group of fellow passengers walked along the deck. Finally
Jessica spoke quietly:

"Chu Suyin resented being called the perfect weapon... She recorded a quote from Rén Du in her diary..."

Alice asked: "What was the quote?"

Jessica replied: "He told her to take comfort in knowing she never had a choice..."

Alice clenched her fists and said: "But we do have a choice..."

Lin nodded slightly and said: "Yes we do..."

Alice sighed and said: "I know so little about this whole crazy situation..."

Lin suggested: "I could transmit the information directly to your cerebral interface?"

Alice replied: "No thanks...the last time you did that my whole world changed."

Lin replied: "The truth is sometimes the most difficult path to take..."

Jessica commented: "And you do like the honest truth..."

Alice looked at Lin and asked:

"Do you ever think that maybe we can't change anything?"

Lin asked: "What do you mean?"

Alice replied: "Well maybe the future is fixed...maybe people like us are just the beginning of a whole new race of people...not homo sapiens at all, but something else, something that can outlive and outthink ordinary people..."

Lin considered the question and replied: "It is entirely possible that we are the genesis point of a whole new species...but such a process could take hundreds of years."

Jessica looked towards the island and said: "Where now they grow human babies one day they might grow something else entirely..."

Suddenly Alice stepped back and said: "Oh oh..."

Lin tensed and asked: "Problem?"

Alice rummaged through her purse as she replied: "We need to find a supermarket or a pharmacy."

Lin asked: "Why?"

Alice replied: "I think my period just started..."

Jessica sighed and said: "It never rains but it pours..."

Lin noticed the look on Alice's face and said: "We can find a supermarket...don't worry..."

Alice replied: "It's not that...look..." She held up a small coin.

Jessica asked: "It's a five cent coin...what's the problem?"

Alice replied soberly: "Actually it is a tracking device..."

All three women studied the coin as Jessica asked:

"Are you sure?"

Alice replied: "It has a frequency modulation below the cyber threshold... I thought I was picking up mobile wifi residue...but I was wrong...it is this thing..."

Jessica asked: "Wifi residue?"

Alice replied wearily: "Residual Cyber transmissions picked up as portal pings by the thing inside my head."

Jessica whispered: "Wow..."

Lin took the coin and asked: "Any idea how it got inside your purse?"

Alice replied: "It can only be one of two people... Gao or the British guy..."

Jessica asked: "So what do we do now?"

Lin dropped the coin and crushed it under her boot as she replied:

"We keep moving..."

Moments later the ferry edged closer to the Star Ferry Pier before coming to a full stop.

Jessica gripped her backpack and said: "We're here..."

Lin stepped away from the railing and said: "Stay with the crowd..."

Jessica spoke as they moved towards the exit ramp:

"So where are we going after the supermarket?"

Alice joined a line of passengers and replied quietly:

"Lion Rock Country Park."

As they moved forward Jessica asked: "Why?"

But it was Lin who replied: "Mau Ping..."

Jessica asked: "Excuse me?"

Alice replied: "A grid location inside the park...it is a Cybersync cold spot..."

Lin continued: "A digital void..."

Jessica spoke as they made their way towards the pier exit:

"I thought they were a myth..."

Lin replied: "They are very rare..."

Alice swiped her phone over the ticket machine and said:

"A cloud portal relies on a datasync junction via basic wifi... Mau Ping lies in an overlap between the Techsync server and local broadband traffic..." She walked forward before adding: "They won't be able to track us inside the void..."

Jessica caught up with Alice and asked: "You mean they are tracking us right now?"

Alice replied calmly: "Everyone is tracking us right now..."

**18:19 - Sunday May 2nd - 2028 - Mosque Street - Hong Kong**

A cloud mottled sky looks down upon a city bathed in fading sunshine casting shadows among the tall glistening towers of Central Hong Kong. Halfway along Mosque Street four men regroup in front of a silver Sabrelite SUV.

Dieter Fink spoke into his phone:

"The car is long gone...they disabled the Autotrace and they used countermeasures to disable the invasive hack..." He paused before adding: "They are off the grid boss..."

Karl Weinberg replied: "They are off your grid Fink..." There was a pause before he continued: "Professor Jordon is uploading a geo-tracer to your phone. It will lock onto the cyber frequency of a cerebral interface. Now it won't be precise, because the Chinese implants will not match the one we gave Ria, but it will be enough to put you within a few hundred metres of their location."

Fink asked: "And when we do find them, what then?"

There was a long pause before Weinberg replied:

"Alice Sòng is to be taken alive and transported back here to HQ..."

Fink asked: "And the other two women?"

Weinberg replied coldly: "Terminate with extreme prejudice."

## 18:24 - Sunday May 2nd - 2028 - The Blue Lounge - Wo Chu Lane - Hong Kong

A bar room floor of dried blood and shattered glass sparkling in the half light - a palpable silence imbued with the aftermath of sudden violent death.

Mong Gao stared at the headless corpse and sighed heavily. *Shit...* He surveyed the main bar area - the Blue Lounge looked like a disaster zone. *They will blame me for this...* Someone had removed the body of Jon Lau, but his blood bore testament to his violent ending. *He never had a chance...* And then he noticed something shining amidst the dried blood and broken glass. *What do we have here?* He crouched down and retrieved a silver neck chain with yin yang pendant. *Alice!* The last time he had seen the pendant it was hanging around her neck. *The beauty of innocence...* He sighed heavily. *But was it all lies?* He could not reconcile his feelings with the hard facts - *She is an augment...and she betrayed me...* He clenched the chain in his hand. *Then why do I miss her so much?*

Ricky Li appeared in the doorway to the Private Lounge. He said:

"Boss wants to see you kid..."

Gao straightened up and replied: "Sure...okay..."

At the far end of the room Poppa Jo Yáng was busy studying a datapad. He looked up and asked:

"Where have you been?"

Gao walked forward and replied: "I was taken by surprise..."

A bemused Sal Cho asked: "By girls?"

Gao scowled and replied: "They are not ordinary girls..."

Poppa Jo sat back in his leather chair and said: "No... They are not..."

Gao continued: "At least two of them are the direct result of the Jiàngsheng Project."

Poppa Jo said: "I agree..." He looked up and asked: "Is that why they ditched you?"

Gao rubbed his sore neck and replied: "Probably..." He paused before adding: "I think the Shanghai girl knew I was Triad..."

Poppa Jo nodded slightly and said: "You cannot hide your allegiances from an augment."

Gao replied: "Apparently not..."

Poppa Jo said: "Remarkable creatures..."

Gao gestured to the datapad and asked: "You watched the vids?"

Poppa Jo scratched his chin and replied:

"I did... Most enlightening..." He held out the datapad and said: "Take a look..."

Gao took the pad and tapped the screen. *She wasn't shooting wild...* The young woman who had burst through the door had selected her first target with precision. *She took down Jon because he was armed...* He sighed heavily. *I was the next target...but Alice was too fast...* Less than two minutes after they had climbed through the delivery hatch four heavily armed men entered the club. *Mercenaries?* He watched in horror as they took a bone saw to the neck of the young woman. *Shit...*

Poppa Jo looked up and said: "Those men work for Synthtech. I suspect they came to retrieve their augment..."

Gao asked: "She was definitely an augment?"

Poppa Jo sniffed and replied: "According to my sources, yes."

Ricky Li took the datapad and said: "They managed to retrieve part of her..."

Gao spoke in a low voice: "She was ordered to kill Alice and her friends..."

Poppa Jo nodded slightly and said: "Synthtech removing the competition."

Gao frowned and said: "Beijing will not take this lightly..."

Poppa Jo sighed and said: "No, they will not... I think the body count will continue to rise..."

Gao said: "Definitely..."

Poppa Jo wiped his nose and said: "This game just became a lot more complicated..."

Gao stepped closer and said: "Let me go after them..."

Poppa Jo shook his head and replied: "No. What profit we might have made from this deal is gone..." He coughed before continuing: "Let the corporate's fight for their prize, we have other business to deal with..."

Gao protested: "But they will kill Alice..."

Poppa Jo sniffed and asked: "Why should that bother me?"

Gao announced: "I want to go after her..."

Poppa Jo replied firmly: "No. You will restore this club and get back to earning real money."

Gao hesitated before saying: "I have found the Jiàngsheng files..."

Poppa Jo looked up and asked: "What?"

Gao continued: "They are still worth millions of dollars to the highest bidder."

Poppa Jo asked: "Where are they?"

Gao cleared his throat and replied: "Forgive me...but you will never know unless I am allowed to go after Alice."

Ricky Li and Sal Cho stepped closer, but Poppa Jo raised one hand and asked:

"Do you know what you are saying boy?"

Gao tensed as he replied: "I do...and I have no choice..."

Poppa Jo studied Mong's face and said: "You love her..."

Gao replied: "Just let me use the chopper... I can intercept them at the pier..."

Poppa Jo fell silent before asking: "You can track them?"

Gao retrieved his phone and replied: "Give me a moment." He tapped the screen several times before continuing: "They just arrived at the Star Ferry Pier in Tsim Sha Tsui..."

Poppa Jo frowned and said: "You hacked her phone..."

Gao replied: "I uploaded an invasive geosync..."

Poppa Jo fell silent before asking: "Did you always suspect she was an augment?"

Gao replied: "No... I just wanted to keep her safe..."

Poppa Jo sat back and said: "You can take the chopper... Go to Loet Field...it will be waiting for you..."

Gao hesitated before asking: "And the files?"

Poppa Jo asked: "You found them in the Cloud?"

Gao replied: "I did."

Poppa Jo sighed and said: "Save the girl..."

A relieved Gao said: "I will transmit the location of the files once she is safe..."

Poppa Jo waited until Mong Gao had left before asking:

"Well?"

Ricky Li glanced at his phone and replied: "Our people have intercepted the geosync... We have her location."

Sal Cho asked: "Your orders boss?"

Poppa Jo wiped his nose and replied: "He thinks he can blackmail me..." He sat back and continued: "Contact our friends in Mong Kok... I want them to retrieve the girl... Advise them of her special abilities..." He coughed before continuing: "Once we have her I am sure Gao will cooperate..."

Ricky Li asked: "What about the other two women?"

Poppa Jo waved one hand slightly and replied: "Collateral damage..."

Sal Cho asked: "And once we have the files?"

Poppa Jo stared directly ahead and replied coldly: "I want him dead."

## 18:31 - Sunday May 2nd - The Star Ferry Pier - Tsim Sha Tsui - Hong Kong

A warm breeze whispers through the trees lining a crowded pedestrian promenade. Locals mingle with tourists as they peruse a long line of seafront restaurants and bars. Traffic sounds merge with a chaotic cacophony of voices rising and falling along the congested streets of Tsim Sha Tsui.

Two men in dark business suits stop just outside the entrance to the pier. They survey the area before walking slowly towards the main road. Finally they stop once more and observe their quarry crossing the road via the pedestrian crossing.

With one rapid blink Agent Ming Wu synced his data-lenses into the audio plug inserted into his right ear. Finally he announced:

"They have crossed the street..." He paused before continuing: "They are entering a supermarket..."

Agent Ching Ho set off towards the traffic lights as Ming Wu asked:

"Your orders sir?"

The voice of Section Leader Han Mang came through the audio plug:

"Continue to follow, but do not lose sight of them..."

Ming hesitated before asking: "May I ask your intentions sir?"

Han replied: "I want nothing more than the spider wants from a fly..."

Ming saw the truth and said: "The Americans will all be coming for the augments..."

Han replied: "Yes...and all the other interested groups will finally come together in one place...and we will be waiting for them." There was a pause before he continued: "I have synced the local surveillance net into your lenses. You will liaise with the other teams and coordinate your pursuit accordingly."

Ming replied: "Very good sir."

Han added: "Be aware of those that follow the same trail and take the necessary precautions. That is all for now."

As the connection ended Ming looked towards the supermarket. *The flies take the time to go shopping...* Moments later he set off to join his partner on the other side of the street.

## 18:49 - Sunday May 2nd - Easybuy Supermarket - Tsim Sha Tsui - Hong Kong

A staff washroom of dirty white tiles and two stalls illuminated by a flickering ceiling tube. Alice was not happy to use a toilet seat with questionable stains and a foul smell but she had no choice. *Any port in a storm...* Explaining her desperate need to use the staff facilities had been embarrassing. She smiled slightly... *But more embarrassing for the manager...poor guy...*

A few minutes later she leaned on the sink and studied her face in the mirror. *I still look like me...* She touched her forehead and glared at her reflection. *But there is a computer inside my head!* Her companions were waiting outside but she found the brief solitude comforting. *I don't even know these people...* Not for the first time she considered abandoning them and going home to her mother. *What would I even say to her?* She sighed heavily. *It is too dangerous...* The murder of Nancy made one thing shockingly clear: *People around me die...* She was about to open the door when a sudden pain erupted behind her eyes. For a brief moment she struggled to breathe before falling to her knees. Almost immediately an invasive Cybersync produced an unfamiliar voice inside her head:

*"I am so sorry... The portal expanded too fast... Are you alright?"*

Alice gripped the sink and pulled herself to her feet. Finally she replied:

*"Who are you?"*

The voice replied:

*"I am Fay Rui...a friend of Jessica Lee's... I am transmitting from Singapore..."*

Alice wiped her eyes and asked: *"How did you access the interface?"*

Fay replied: *"I sifted for viable algorithmic potential until I found a net access response...then I looped a false recognition protocol and I was in... Again I am sorry, but I had no choice..."*

Alice tried to slow her breathing as she asked:

*"How are you able to converse on this frequency?"*

Fay replied: *"Voicecom synced to your Cloud portal..."*

Alice considered this before asking: *"What do you want?"*

Fay replied: *"I have a message from Zhang Lee to his daughter..."*

Alice asked angrily: *"He can't just phone her?"*

Fay replied: *"No. She is off-grid right now...that is my protocol..."*

Alice asked: *"Who are you exactly?"*

Fay replied: *"I am the leader of the FreeTech Society of Singapore...we are the ones who hacked the Jiàngsheng Project..."*

Alice rapidly sifted for causal linkage before saying:

*"You intend to reveal the project to the world..."*

Fay replied: *"That was our intention, but we changed our minds... We could not expose you and the other augments..."*

Alice asked: *"But now you work for Biogen?"*

Fay replied: *"No... I am their prisoner...they threatened to hurt my friends..."*

Alice considered her options before saying:

*"Give me the message..."*

Fay replied: *"Geosync one four seven nine zero two one three..."*

Alice asked: *"That's it? A grid-reference?"*

Fay replied: *"Yes...a pick-up location..."*

Alice quickly accessed the local geogrid and announced:

*"Oh my god... Mau Ping... Lion Rock Country Park ..."*

Fay replied: *"That means nothing to me..."*

Alice asked: *"How are you inputting this transmission?"*

Fay replied: *"Syncpad keyboard and monitor..."*

Alice hesitated before saying: *"Zhang Lee must be sending transport for his daughter...he chose Mau Ping to avoid detection..."* She paused before adding: *"Tell him I will deliver the message and ensure the safety of his daughter, but only if he releases you and your friends. Tell him I want confirmation that you are free via this portal in exactly twenty minutes time..."*

There was a pause before Fay replied: *"Thank you Alice...bye for now..."*

**18:50 - Sunday May 2nd - Sublevel 6 - Biogen Compound - Pulai River -Malaysia.**

A room of shadows and flickering screens illuminating the faces of Fay Rui and Zhang Lee.

Fay looked up and said: "I did it... You read her demands..."

Zhang Lee replied: "Yes I did..." He tapped the console and asked: "Did you isolate the sync?"

The voice of Feng Yu came online:

"Yes... Alice Sòng is in Tsim Sha Tsui...scanning the HK surveillance net now..."

Fay sat back and said: "You have about nineteen minutes to release me and my friend..."

Lee smiled and asked: "Do you really think she will hurt Jessica?" He paused before continuing: "She is bluffing...trying to buy freedom for you and your friend..."

Fay replied firmly: "She is an active augment who has calculated the optimum solution to a problem. If that solution includes killing your daughter you better believe me when I tell you that she will not hesitate to act."

Lee fell silent until finally he said: "Wait here... I will arrange transport back to Singapore."

As soon as she was alone Fay tapped the keyboard to reveal the secret message from Alice Sòng:

*"I looped a binary feed to your keypad... I have the flight details of the helicopter heading to Mau Ping... It is a Skylite long-range machine... I was wondering how we might escape our pursuers... I think we might yet meet Fay Rui... Bye for now..."*

Fay sat back and smiled. *And the augment strikes back...*

**18:52 - Sunday May 2nd - Easybuy Supermarket - Tsim Sha Tsui - Hong Kong**

Alice stepped out of the washroom and announced:

"I need to tell you something...."

Lin looked at Alice and said: "Problem with your period? Took you long enough in there..."

Jessica shook her head and said: "Always the diplomat Lin..."

Alice gestured to an empty aisle and said: "We need to talk...and we haven't got much time."

Lin stepped closer and said: "If it is about the two Beijing agents they are waiting outside..."

Jessica's eyes widened as she asked: "What? The secret police are here?"

Lin replied calmly: "Do not be alarmed, they are simply following us..."

Jessica stepped closer to the shelves and asked: "Why?"

Lin replied wearily: "Because we are the bait to lure all the other interested groups into one place..."

Jessica said: "But..."

Alice interjected: "Can I get a word in at some point?"

Jessica said: "Sorry..."

Lin sighed and said: "You have the floor..."

Alice gave a slight smile and said: "Thank you..." She glanced towards the shop entrance before continuing: "I just received an invasive Cybersync from Singapore..."

Jessica exclaimed: "Fay!"

Alice asked: "How did you know?"

Jessica replied: "Your interface has a quad cipher encryption lock... She is one of the few people I know who could hack your portal..." She looked at Lin and added: "Who are not augments anyway..."

Lin asked: "What did this Fay want?"

Alice looked at Jessica and replied: "She is a prisoner of your father..."

Jessica exclaimed: "Oh my god no..."

Alice continued: "She was ordered to hack my interface to transmit a message to you."

Lin asked: "What was the message?"

Alice replied: "It was a grid-reference coded into geosync..."

Lin rapidly calculated causal potential and announced: "Your father wants to extract you from this whole mess..."

A surprised Jessica asked: "He does?"

Alice replied: "He does. And he has unwittingly provided us with a solution to our current dilemma..."

Jessica sighed and asked: "Why do I get the feeling that you two are leaving me behind with your instant causal analysis?"

Alice looked surprised and asked: "You know about causal analysis?"

Jessica replied: "Lin tried to teach me..."

Lin spoke dismissively: "Tried and failed..."

Alice smiled slightly and said: "He has despatched transport to Mau Ping..."

Lin nodded and said: "He has plotted the Cyber void and deduced our intentions; most astute."

Alice replied: "Indeed..."

Jessica considered this and said: "But if we go there we will still be surrounded by people who want to kill us..."

Alice replied: "But they will not be able coordinate their pursuit..."

Lin added: "Our cerebral signature will not register in a cold spot..."

Alice added: "They cannot track us..."

Lin continued: "But we can still communicate via our interfaces."

Alice smiled slightly and said: "And stay one step ahead of everyone..."

Lin spoke firmly: "So when they come for us we will be ready..."

Jessica asked: "Ready for what?"

Lin replied coldly: "To take the fight to them..."

Alice replied: "Actually I was thinking more along the lines of escaping..."

Lin raised her eyebrows and asked: "And where would we go?"

Alice replied: "I was thinking about Singapore..."

Jessica asked: "Talking of Singapore, how do we save Fay and my friends?"

Alice glanced at her phone and replied: "I think I might have taken care of that..."

Jessica asked: "You have?"

Alice replied calmly: "If your father fails to release Fay within the next twelve minutes I will be forced to kill you."

Jessica's eyes widened as she asked: "And that was a bluff right?" She stared at Alice and added: "Right?"

Alice smiled and replied: "Of course..."

Lin asked: "What if he calls your bluff?"

Alice replied: "The only thing he knows about me is that I am an augment, if Fay has any insight she will convince him that augments never bluff."

Jessica nodded slightly and said: "Fay will convince him, she can be very persuasive."

Alice looked towards the shop manager and said: "We need to get going..."

Lin replied: "We should take a taxi to save time."

Alice replied: "Agreed."

As they set off Lin said: "I think it's too soon to dismiss the kill Jessica option..."

Jessica smiled nervously and asked: "Now you're joking right?"

Lin asked: "Have you ever known me to joke?"

An anxious Jessica replied: "No..."

Lin suddenly grinned and said: "Then there is a first time for everything..."

Jessica slapped Lin's backpack as Alice smiled and said: "Come on ladies..."

## 19:11 - Sunday May 2nd - Lao Tower Rooftop Landing Pad - Tsim Sha Tsui - Hong Kong

Mong Gao ducked low beneath swirling blades and ran quickly towards the rooftop elevator. Behind him the helicopter swept back towards the bright lights of Hong Kong Island. He was met at the elevator doors by a familiar face.

Chen Lo smiled warmly as he shouted:

"Long time no see my friend..."

Gao embraced his old friend and replied: "Too long..."

Lacking any siblings of his own Gao considered Chen his brother. Together they had survived the backstreets of Shenzhen to become loyal members of the Ginza Triad. But whereas Mong had been able to use his technical skills to rise rapidly within the Triad, Chen had remained a low-level street enforcer - and he had the scars to prove it. The first thing Mong noticed was a fresh scar running from his friends left ear to his chin.

Chen tapped the elevator panel and said:

"I have a car waiting out front..."

As the elevator doors opened Gao said: "Thanks..."

Chen spoke as they entered the elevator: "You look good my friend..."

Gao replied with a slight smile: "And you look like you have been in the wars my friend..."

Chen touched a finger to his face and replied: "Yes...but you should see the other guy..."

Gao smiled and said: "Same old Chen..."

As the doors closed Chen asked:

"Is it true? You blackmailed the boss?"

Gao sighed and replied: "News travels fast..."

A shocked Chen asked: "Are you crazy? Have you any idea what they will do to you?"

As they began to descend Gao replied: "I do...but I have no choice..."

Chen shook his head slightly and said: "Well I hope she is worth it, because you have signed your death sentence."

As the doors opened onto the ground floor Gao said: "She is worth it..."

Chen gestured towards the lobby and said: "This way..."

Gao studied his phone and said: "I have an active signal..."

Chen glanced at the screen and said: "She is on the move..."

Gao tapped his phone and said: "They are moving north..."

Chen gestured towards the main entrance and asked: "Why hasn't she detected your hack? I mean...she is supposed to be super smart right?"

Gao frowned and replied: "You are right... She should have found the geosync tracker by now..."

Chen speculated: "Maybe she wants you to follow her..."

Gao sighed and replied: "Maybe..."

Moments later they emerged onto a busy sidewalk to find a black Rio ATV waiting at the curb.

Gao studied the jeep and said: "Nice..."

Chen said: "I wasn't sure where the trail would lead us, so I thought this would cover all bases..." He tapped the bonnet and added: "G-tex forced acceleration console... Armourlite panels... Cybersync autodrive... Missile ejector tubes..."He paused before adding with a smile: "And she has brand new plates..."

Gao smiled slightly and said: "It's perfect, but there is no *us* my friend... I have to do this alone."

Chen protested: "You have no idea what you will be facing out there...you need me Gao..."

Gao walked to the front of the jeep and continued: "I can't involve you in this... I am a marked man now...you know they will be coming for me..."

Chen opened the driver's door and said: "Enough talk, let's go..."

Gao sighed heavily before asking: "I take it you want to drive?"

Chen sat behind the wheel and asked: "You think I would let you drive this baby?"

Gao opened the passenger door as he replied: "I will follow the geosync..."

Chen looked at Gao's suit and said: "There's a change of clothes in the back..."

Gao saw a green combat jacket, blue jeans, a black sweater and a pair of hiking boots on the back seat.

Chen added: "You left them at my place... I figured you would need them..."

Gao smiled as he said: "Let's do this..."

A smiling Chen revved the engine and said: "Just like old times..."

## 19:16 - Sunday May 2nd - Tsim Sha Tsui MTR Station - Hong Kong

Tsim Sha Tsui station was unusually crowded for the time of day. A frustrated Daniel Lane struggled towards the escalators increasingly aware of the urgency of his mission. *She found the tracker...* Whilst on the train he had tried to initiate an invasive sync into the phone of Alice Sòng only have his signal terminated unceremoniously. *She is using countermeasures...* But as he stepped onto the escalators leading to the exit he was not too concerned. It was now very clear that his mission had been based upon false information - Nancy Yeo was not the augment created in Beijing. *It was Alice...* And that startling conclusion created a certain amount of predictability. *An augment would have the insight and tactical intelligence to seek out a cyber cold spot.*

And as far as he knew there was only one local place where a cerebral interface would not be detectable: *Mau Ping in Lion Rock Country Park...* After emerging from the underground into a busy street he located a taxi rank and opened the door of the first car. He ordered:

"Lion Rock Country Park...and there's a five thousand dollar bonus if you can get me there fast..."

The driver smiled and replied: "Not a problem sir...but which entrance?"

Lane consulted his phone and replied: "Get me to Wang Che, near Ho Chung Village..."

The driver started the car and said: "Very good sir..."

Lane sat back and rubbed his aching shoulder. *Mau Ping...* He looked out of the side window and sighed heavily. *She is walking straight into a trap...*

**Private Office - Sublevel 2 - Synthtech Corporation - Radford Boulevard - West Seattle - USA**

Matt Dower tapped the datascreen to reveal the latest geosat images of Hong Kong. Finally he sat back and ordered:
"As soon as you receive the head you will transfer Ria's data-core to the new subject."
Professor Niel Jordon hesitated before saying:
"Sir, as I have already informed you, Lily is not ready, she is just a child. The premature implantation of Ria's cerebral interface could have catastrophic consequences."
Dower glanced at the time and said: "Then you have twenty four hours to ensure that the procedure does not fail." He looked up and added: "Do not make me regret putting my faith and trust in you professor."
Jordon was about to say something when Dower said:
"You may go now professor..."
As soon as he was alone Dower tapped the screen to reveal an overhead view of a steel maturation tank. He sat forward and studied the face of a ten year old girl. *My porcelain princess...* A network of electrodes and wires had been inserted into her shaved head and her body submerged into clear gelatinous fluid. Each time she exhaled into the oesophageal tube a monitor beeped in response. The slight flickering of her eyelids confirmed the initiation of a Cloud Gap scenario via her cerebral interface. *She is wandering distant neural shores...* He touched one finger to the screen and whispered:
"You are the future..."

**19:30 - Sunday May 2nd - 2028 - Workers Dormitories - Level 4 - Ministry of Science and Technology of the People's Republic of China - Beijing, China.**

Ting Mai was about to go for a shower when she heard voices in the corridor outside her room. She cautiously opened her door to see two of her female colleagues talking in whispers. Stepping forward she asked:

"What is going on?"

Her friend Su Ying wiped her eyes and replied: "Have you not heard? The professor is dead..."

Mai caught her breath and asked: "What?"

Tang Mu interjected: "They think he took his own life...they found a note..."

Mai struggled for words before saying: "No... He would not do that..."

Ying said: "They have started an investigation..."

Mai spoke frantically: "I need to see him..."

Mu said: "You can't...the lab has been sealed..."

Mai fell silent before saying: "But Guan Lu...he is to be revived in the morning..."

Ying said: "That might not happen now..."

Mai replied: "But it must...the process has already started..."

Mu said: "Then you should talk to the Director. He is the only one who will allow you back into the lab."

Mai asked: "Is he here now?"

Mu replied: "He is on his way..."

Mai rapidly considered her options before saying: "I need to change clothes... We will talk later."

Ying replied: "Okay..."

Mai closed her door and quickly tapped the designated code into her phone. Moments later the face of the Englishman came onscreen.

An irritated Aron Fielding asked:

"Why are you calling now? Is there a problem?"

Mai sat down on the side of her bed and replied: "Professor Leung is dead..."

Fielding's eyes widened as he asked: "How did it happen?"

Mai replied: "They found a suicide note, but I do not believe it... The professor would not do such a thing..."

Fielding frowned and said: "I agree..."

Mai asked: "Who could have done this?"

Fielding glanced off-screen before replying:

"The Americans are trying to sabotage the project, but they have no access to the professor..." He paused before continuing: "State security has no reason to harm a valuable asset...so that only leaves his erstwhile benefactors, Biogen."

Mei said: "But the professor was also an asset to them..."

Fielding sighed and replied: "Not if he has outlived his usefulness..."

Mai looked towards the door and asked: "Am I safe?"

Fielding replied soberly: "Probably not..." He paused before asking: "What is the status of Guan Lu?"

Mai chewed at a fingernail as she replied: "He is in the final stages of emersion..." She wiped tears from her eyes and added: "The professor was supposed to complete the revival in the morning..."

Fielding asked: "Can he be revived tonight?"

Mai replied: "I am not sure... Why?"

Fielding replied: "Because if you want to live Guan Lu is your only hope..."

Mei exclaimed: "But I cannot do it alone...there are protocols to follow, a strict methodology..."

Fielding replied: "Listen very carefully... If Biogen is terminating its connection to your project they will not hesitate to kill you and anyone else who might jeopardise their plans. You have no choice...you must revive Guan Lu tonight."

Mei fell silent before replying: "Very well... But I need to request access to the lab first..."

Fielding said: "Do not be a fool Mei. You cannot risk exposure."

Mei glanced at the time and said: "Then I need to act fast... I must go to the lab now..." She stared at Fielding and added: "When I leave here... I want to see Meili..."

Fielding replied: "By the time your reach Nanjing your daughter will be waiting for you..."

A relieved Mei smiled and said: "Thank you."

Fielding continued: "But there is one condition..."

Mei tensed and asked: "What is it?"

Fielding replied: "You must first take Guan Lu to a safe house in Beijing."

Mei asked: "A safe house?"

Fielding replied: "Someone will be waiting there to talk to Guan Lu about his future prospects."

Mei asked: "You think you can persuade him to betray his country?"

Fielding replied: "That is not your concern..." He paused before continuing: "I am sending you a geosync location..."

Mei tapped her phone and said: "I have it..."

Fielding continued: "Contact me once you are out of the building...and good luck Ting Mai..."

Mei replied: "Thank you..."

Once more the screen displayed the image of her daughter. She whispered:

"Not long now my darling..."

# The Nexus Apogee

*"This has been the longest day of my life..."*
Alice Sòng

### 20:31 - Tate's Cairn Highway - Lion Rock Country Park - New Territories - Hong Kong

Beyond the lights of the city the night arrived early along the roads of the New Territories. A sprinkling of stars struggled to be seen amidst a gathering of rain clouds descending slowly over the rocky hills of Lion Rock Country Park.

Alice studied her phone as she spoke:
"This will do...m̀hgòi."
The driver pulled into a small lay-by and said: "Okay..."
Alice swiped her phone over the fare-reader and said:
"Let's go..."
Moments later they stood on the side of the road and watched the taxi drive away. They were now surrounded by wilderness pockmarked with a scattering of trees perched upon rocky outcrops silhouetted against the twilight sky.
Jessica looked along the deserted highway and asked:
"Now what?"
Alice fastened her jacket against a cool breeze and replied:
"We hike..."
Jessica sighed and asked: "Is it far to Mau Ping?"
Alice secured her hair in a ponytail and replied: "Kinda..."
Jessica adjusted her backpack and said: "Perfect..."
Lin smiled slightly and said: "The walk will do you good..."
Jessica turned to Alice and asked: "Was the taxi expensive?"
Alice replied: "Let's just say my credit app just turned red..."
Lin wiped her nose and said: "I think money is the least of our problems..."
Alice smiled slightly and said: "Ever the pragmatist Lin..."

As they crossed the road Jessica asked: "Where do we enter the park?"

Alice glanced at her phone and replied: "Tai Wai is to the left... So Lion Rock Tunnel Road is..." She pointed to the right and said: "That way..."

Jessica asked: "Up hill...?" She sighed and added: "This day just gets better by the minute..."

As they set off Lin said: "It is not necessary to use your phone's geosync... You can just sync your interface into the local geogrid."

Alice stepped around a puddle and replied: "Forgive me for at least trying to be normal..."

They walked in silence until they reached the entrance to the country park.

Jessica read a wooden sign: "Lion Rock Country Park... Please take your litter home." She smiled and added: "I always do..."

Alice surveyed a series of steps cut into the hillside and said: "We follow the path all the way to Buffalo Pass..."

Lin interjected: "Then we branch off towards Mau Ping."

Alice gave Lin a look and said: "Thanks..."

Lin looked back towards the main road and said:

"They are still following..."

Alice replied: "I know... I saw their car..."

Jessica asked: "The Beijing agents?"

Lin nodded slightly and replied: "They are still observing from a distance."

Alice said: "They are not the ones we need to worry about..."

Lin replied: "That is true...for now."

Jessica adjusted her backpack and asked: "What do we do when we get to Mau Ping?"

Alice replied: "We wait for your father's people to arrive..."

Jessica asked: "And if the bad guys get there first?"

Lin interjected: "We take them down..."

Jessica asked: "We do?"

Alice clenched her fists and replied: "We do..."

Ten minutes later a breathless Jessica caught up with Alice and said:

"You know there will be Biogen people on that helicopter..."

Alice stopped and replied: "I know..."

Jessica continued: "But I think I can convince them to take all three of us..."

Lin joined them and said: "They are coming for you...not us..." She stepped over a rock before adding: "They will need persuading..."

Alice looked towards the horizon and said: "Then we will persuade them."

Thirty minutes later Alice stopped at the base of a steep footpath.

Lin asked: "Problem?"

Alice replied: "Give me a second..." She removed one of her ankle boots and snapped off the heel before doing the same with the other boot. Finally she said: "That's better..."

Lin said: "Let's keep moving..."

At the top of the hill Jessica stopped to catch her breath. Finally she asked:

"Do you think Rén Du knows what my father is doing?"

Alice pulled her jacket close and replied: "I'm not sure...why?"

Jessica replied: "Because this rescue could turn into abduction..."

Lin considered this and said: "Your father's desire to extricate you from danger reveals a personal agenda as opposed to the actions of Rén Du."

Alice said: "I agree. The rescue attempt has probably not been sanctioned by Biogen..." She paused to wipe her nose with a tissue before continuing: "And he did release your friends..."

Jessica asked: "Fay confirmed that right?"

Alice replied: "I received a verified Cybersync...both she and her friend have returned safely to Singapore."

Jessica said: "That's good then..."

Lin looked up and said: "It is getting dark..."

Jessica asked: "Can we use night-vision?"

Lin activated her data-lenses and replied: "We can...but do not open a portal, it can be tracked..."

Jessica blinked her lenses into night-vision mode and replied: "I'm not that desperate to check my emails..."

Alice said: "You two should lead the way... I crushed my lenses back at the club."

Jessica spoke wearily: "God that seems like ages ago..."

Alice sighed and replied: "I know... This has been the longest day of my life..."

Lin said: "It is not over yet..." She held out one hand and added: "And it is raining..."

Jessica sighed heavily and said: "Perfect..."

## 20:39 - Sunday May 2nd - 2028 - Biogen Facility - Kwu Tung - New Territories - Hong Kong

A quiet room of monitors and data consoles illuminated by LED ceiling tiles is currently occupied by four data-analysis technicians.

Rén Du entered the room and asked:

"Status?"

Senior Technician Wo Chun looked up from his station and replied:

"The two agents from Beijing are following the assets on foot... The British agent is travelling by taxi towards Lion Rock Country Park." He tapped his datascreen and continued: "The Triad people are also driving in the same direction..." He studied the screen before continuing: "A helicopter carrying the Synthetic strike team has just landed at Mau Tso Ngam..."

Rén frowned and asked: "Why land so far from Mau Ping?"

Wo Chun looked up and replied: "They have a primitive cerebral tracking node...it lacks precise geosync. They can only follow the direction of the cerebral signature until they actually see their targets." He tapped the screen once again and added: "Transferring geosync data to main viewscreen..."

Rén studied a large wall screen and said:

"The vultures are gathering..."

Technician Dian Bai announced:

"I have neutralised the Hong Kong surveillance net at the designated location."

Wo Chun looked up and said: "Tactical interception units are in place and await your orders..."

Rén asked: "And the Skylite?"

Wo Chun tapped his screen and replied: "We are tracking a long-range Skylite out of Singapore..." He paused before continuing: "It is approaching Hong Kong from the sea..."

Rén smiled slightly and said: "All the pieces are finally coming together...perfect Mahjong..."

Technician Yong Lee announced:

"Magnetic field resonance confirmed..." He looked up and added: "We have circumvented the Cyber void..."

Rén smiled and said: "Excellent..."

Technician Dian Bai tapped his screen and said:

"Two cerebral resonance signals confirmed..."

Technician Peng Ying tapped her keyboard rapidly as she spoke: "Accessing portal encryption locks..."

Wo Chun said: "Sir...this might not work...every field test so far has failed."

Rén sighed and replied: "Have faith Chun... All good things come to those who have faith..."

A smiling Peng Ying looked up and announced:

"Portal decryption confirmed and logged..."

Rén gave a satisfied smile and said: "They are wide open..."

Wo Chun studied his screen and said:

"We can initiate remote access at your command sir..."

Rén clenched his fists and said: "Finally... Map the intersection points and give me a probability outcome."

Yong Lee tapped his keyboard rapidly and replied:

"Probability percentage confirmed...onscreen now."

Rén stepped closer to the wall screen and said: "The causal narrative expands exponentially..."

Yong Lee frowned and said: "But the mapping potential fails at the cumulative point..."

Wo Chun interjected: "We can still compensate for the unpredictability factor."

Peng Ying looked up and added: "And the finite point can be controlled..."

Rén nodded slightly and said: "The nexus apogee...the singular moment that will influence the next ten thousand years..." He sighed before adding: "The Americans think they own the future...but they are a rogue nation and they must be taught a critical lesson..."

Wo Chun studied his datascreen and announced:

"Alert from Beijing... Guan Lu neural reactions confirmed... Biostasis maturation terminated. Survival of subject number three confirmed."

Rén nodded slightly and said: "Ting Mai...finally..."

Wo Chun looked up and asked: "Your orders sir?"

Rén replied: "Transmit to interception units: terminate all designated targets...but protect the assets at all cost." He stepped closer to the wall screen as he continued: "Do not initiate remote access until both augments arrive at Mau Ping..." He studied the screen and added: "We must time the recall perfectly..."

Wo Chun asked: "What about the Skylite?"

Rén sighed as he replied: "Despite the duplicity of Zhang Lee its crew are innocent..." He paused before continuing: "Once the augments have been retrieved the Skylite can return safely to Singapore."

Peng Ying studied her screen and announced:

"Section Leader Han Mang is mobilising his forces..." She looked up and added soberly: "He is using the regular army...they intend to surround the entire park."

Rén remained silent until finally he asked:

"How long do we have?"

Peng Ying tapped her screen several times and replied:

"Both augments must be retrieved within the next ninety minutes..." She looked up and continued: "After that there will be no way out..."

Rén frowned before ordering:
"Adjust the recall code to compensate for the time factor..."
Wo Chun tapped his keyboard rapidly and said:
"It is done..."
Yong Lee announced: "All tactical units confirm orders sir..."
Rén studied the latest tactical data and said:
"Han Mang is using combat helicopters..."
Peng Ying nodded and said: "I am tracking two aircraft on an intercept course..." She paused before adding: "They are heading directly towards Mau Ping."
Rén sighed and said: "A busy sky tonight..." He looked at the large viewscreen and continued: "I wonder..."
Wo Chun looked up and asked: "Sir?"
Rén continued: "Flight navigation requires comsat and geosync data-flow..." He paused before continuing: "That can leave an aircraft vulnerable to portal penetration..." He stepped back and ordered: "Infiltrate those machines... I want a virus upload via an invasive sync... Let's shut down those engines..."
Wo Chun glanced at his colleagues and replied:
"Yes sir... Give me a moment..."
Dian Bai looked up from his desk and said:
"Sir...priority one message from HQ..."
Rén ordered: "Read it..."
Dian Bai read from his screen:
"Sync-code zero one zero nine six... You must cease all hostile action against State Security. Jiàngsheng Project subsumption has been compromised. Ministerial representatives have seized your files. You will return to Shanghai immediately and surrender yourself to State Security officers pending a full investigation into your activities. Confirm." He paused before adding: "Signed: Jong Hu, Chief Executive Officer, Biogen."
Rén remained silent as Dian Bai asked:
"Sir? Should I confirm receipt?"
Rén stared at the large viewscreen and asked: "Are all units in place?"

Wo Chun replied: "Yes sir..." He glanced at his screen and continued: "And I have portal access to the military helicopters. I can shut down their engines on your command."

Rén studied the latest tactical data before asking:

"Has this facility been compromised?"

Yong Lee spoke from his desk:

"There is no indication that our location has been detected by either State Security or Biogen HQ."

Rén fell silent briefly before speaking in a low voice:

"Jong Hu and his fawning sycophants... They have no idea... Such little minds perched upon the threshold of revelation...but so afraid to take the next step..." He sighed heavily before continuing: "They want to pull back from the precipice...but I will not allow the Americans to inherit the future... I alone will instigate the nexus apogee..." He stepped away from the screen and ordered: "Do not confirm the message. The mission will proceed as planned."

All four technicians looked at each other as Wo Chun replied:

"Very good sir..."

Rén stared at the flashing red dot representing the Synthtech strike team and whispered:

"This one is for you Suyin..."

**20:31 - Sunday May 2nd - 2028 - Laboratory No.1 - Ministry of Science and Technology of the People's Republic of China - Beijing, China.**

Ting Mai sat back and tried to slow her breathing. Gaining access to the maturation chamber was not difficult - walking past the dead body of her mentor and friend was almost impossible. Someone had covered the professor's body with a blue sanisheet, but they had neglected to cover his face. *Out of respect?* It was then that she had forced herself to examine his eyes and found both data-lenses missing. *He always wears lenses...* There could only be one explanation: *Someone removed his lenses to avoid detection... No one would do that unless they wanted to wipe the lens data-core...* Once again the truth was plain to see: *An active data-lens is permanently synced to a personal portal...* She sighed heavily. *The lenses might not have seen the killer but there would be clues to follow...* A closer examination revealed bilateral haemorrhaged conjunctiva in both eyes. *This was not suicide...* She spoke without turning around:

"Are you dressed yet?"

Guan Lu replied: "I am yes..."

Mai stood up and looked at the young man. *Shaved head and wide brown eyes... Grey tracksuit...trainers...* She said: "We need to leave here at once..."

Guan asked: "Why? Where is the professor?"

Mai glanced towards the main laboratory and replied:

"He has been...murdered. And now we are in danger..." She stepped closer and continued: "We must leave now; it is not safe here."

Guan exclaimed: "Murdered?"

Mai repeated: "We need to leave here now..."

Guan studied Mai briefly and said:

"You are hiding something... Are you involved in the professor's death?"

Mai felt her face flush as she replied: "Of course not... But you are correct...there is much I need to explain..." She looked towards the main laboratory and continued: "But this is neither the time nor place... We must leave now!"

Guan closed his eyes briefly before saying:

"There is an alert in progress...security officers are coming here now..."

Mai's eyes widened and she said: "Then it is too late..."

Guan said: "The professor trusted you above all others..." He looked towards the decontamination chamber and said: "There is another way out of here..."

Mai shook her head and said: "No. This is a sterile room..." She gestured to the decontamination chamber and continued: "That is the only way out..."

Guan walked over to the wall and said:

"There is a space behind this wall...it does not show on any blueprint..."

Mai joined him and asked: "What kind of space?"

Guan placed one hand onto the wall and replied: "A corridor...they walled it off to construct this room..."

Mai asked: "How do you know this?"

Guan replied: "Internal space differentials are calculable to the finite point."

Mai asked: "Where does it lead?"

Guan looked up towards the ceiling and replied: "Freedom..."

## 20:48 - Sunday May 2nd - Ho Chung Village - Sai Kung Peninsula - New Territories - Hong Kong

A dark scattering of clouds hung low over the horizon as the jeep rumbled along a deserted village street.

Mong Gao looked out of the side window and said:

"I am not so sure about your short cut Chen..."

Chen smiled as he replied: "Trust me... I know this place like the back of my hand..."

Gao studied his phone and said: "I have seen the back of your hand Chen...it does not fill me with confidence..."

Chen laughed and said: "We can park at Wang Che and take the hiker trail to Tao No, Buffalo Pass and on to Mau Ping."

Gao said: "She is already approaching Tai No... We need to make better time..."

Chen floored the accelerator as he replied: "And we will..."

Gao sighed and said: "Good..."

Chen glanced at Gao and said: "I never seen you like this..."

Gao brushed hair from his eyes and asked: "Like what?"

Chen navigated a sharp corner in the road as he replied:

"Well...like obsessed...for a girl you just met..."

Gao gave a slight smile and said: "She is no ordinary girl..."

Chen accelerated again and said: "I know that... Ricky told me she has a computer in her head..." He shook his head and added: "That's just crazy man..."

Gao replied: "I am not talking about the brain implant..." He looked out of the window and continued: "She is just an amazing person... The moment we met I knew I had to get to know her..." He squeezed Alice's pendant and added: "It's like I fell into her eyes and just got lost..."

Chen grinned and said: "Who would have thought...gun crazy Gao is in love..."

Gao smiled and said: "I am not that crazy kid anymore..."

Chen asked: "So you found the hacked files right?"

Gao hesitated before replying: "Right..."

Chen shook his head slightly and continued:

"And now you are blackmailing the boss... That takes some balls my friend..."

Gao replied: "I had no choice..."

Chen glanced at Gao and asked: "So where are they...the files I mean?"

Gao tensed and replied: "You know I can't tell you... That would just make things awkward..."

Chen raised his eyebrows and asked: "You don't trust me? After all these years?"

Gao sighed as he replied: "Of course I trust you... But this is different..." He paused before adding: "This is just too big..."

Chen shrugged and said: "Fair enough..."

Gao smiled slightly and said: "It's nothing personal old friend..."

Chen turned onto the Kai Ham Road and asked:

"So you think she wants you to follow her?"

Gao glanced at his phone and replied: "She could block this hack at any time...but she doesn't..."

Chen asked: "But how does she know it's your hack?"

Gao replied: "Because she has filtered out my portal signature by now..." He smiled slightly and added: "She knows I am following..."

Chen sighed and said: "I really hope you know what you are doing..."

Gao looked up to see rain hitting the windows and replied: "Me too..."

## 20:51 - Sunday May 2nd - Mau Tso Ngam - Lion Rock Country Park - New Territories - Hong Kong

The helicopter disappeared into heavy dense clouds as the rain began to fall upon four heavily armed men gathered at the base of a steep hiking trail.

Dieter Fink checked his rifle and ordered:

"Sync your ears pieces into channel one..." He shouldered the rifle as he continued: "And sync your lenses into the local geogrid."

Dwayne Lewis closed his eyes briefly before announcing:

"I am picking up some unusual Cyber frequencies...way below the commercial threshold."

Fink stepped closer and asked: "Can you identify the source?"

Lewis replied: "No... Triangulation is all over the place..."

Mitch Jones studied his lenses and said: "I see them too...like echoes..."

Raul Morgan added: "I think they are portal pings...but very deeply encrypted..."

Lewis looked up at the rocky hill and said: "We are not alone out here..."

Fink scowled and ordered: "Alright, let's just stay sharp..." He secured his backpack and ordered: "Mitch take point... Raul takes the rear... Let's move it..."

## 20:58 - Sunday May 2nd - Kai Ham Road - Wang Che - New Territories - Hong Kong

The taxi came to a stop and the driver announced:

"The entrance to the park is on the left..."

Daniel Lane handed over the cash and said: "Cheers mate..."

The driver took the money and said: "Not a problem sir..."

Lane waited for the taxi to drive off before removing his handgun from its shoulder holster to check the chamber. *Full load...* Replacing the gun he touched a tentative hand to his shoulder wound and felt fresh blood beneath his shirt. *Damn...* Moments later he crossed the road and entered the park via a short set of stone steps. As the path levelled out he looked up into complete darkness and sighed heavily. *Raining...* The cool breeze carried the distant sound of a helicopter flying somewhere above the park. *I have company...* He took a moment to tap his phone several times... *Geosync one four seven nine zero two one three... Mau Ping...* He quickly retrieved a small flashlight from his jacket pocket before setting off along the hiking trail.

**21:25 - Sunday May 2nd - Buffalo Pass - Lion Rock Country Park - New Territories - Hong Kong**

They walked through darkness, constantly wary of the steep slopes on either side of the gravel path. The rain had been reduced to a fine drizzle which seemed to soak them through to the bone.

At the top of yet another rock-strewn hill a breathless Jessica stopped and asked:

"How much further?"

Alice smiled slightly and replied: "As I told you exactly four minutes and thirty two seconds ago, we are almost there..."

Lin wiped rain from her face and added:

"Just over the next ridge and on down to Mau Ping..."

Jessica wiped her runny nose and said: "Okay... I can do that...not a problem..."

Alice looked towards the distant lights of the city and said:

"I have lived in Hong Kong all my life and yet I have never been here..."

Jessica brushed a hand through wet hair and said:

"Well you picked a nice night for your first visit..."

Alice smiled and said: "Yeah..."

Lin adjusted her backpack and said: "We have nothing like this in Shanghai..."

Alice asked: "No country parks?"

Lin replied wearily: "No open spaces..."

Jessica sneezed and asked: "Any sign of the Skylite?"

Lin closed her eyes briefly and replied: "It is entering skygrid zero one four by nine one two..."

Jessica sighed and asked: "And that means what exactly?"

Lin replied: "It will be here in approximately twenty five minutes..."

Alice said: "We should keep moving..."

Lin looked back along the path and said: "They are getting closer..."

An anxious Jessica asked: "Who is getting closer?"

But it was Alice who replied soberly: "Everyone..."

## 21:28 - Sunday May 2nd - Buffalo Pass - Lion Rock Country Park - New Territories - Hong Kong

Agent Ming Wu crouched low and whispered: "I see them..."

Agent Ching Ho synced his lenses into voicecom and announced:

"Sir, we are in position..."

The voice of Section Leader Han Mang came through his ear plugs:

"You will remain there; do not proceed any further. The Guangzhou Special Forces Unit will initiate containment of the park... You will coordinate with ground insertion groups and identify viable targets."

Agent Ming looked towards the sky and interjected:

"Sir, what about the Skylite transport?"

Han replied: "Aerial units will be arriving shortly...they will deal with the Skylite. But under no circumstances must you allow the targets to escape. Han out."

Agent Ching blinked his lenses into night-vision and said:

"They are proceeding towards Mau Ping."

Agent Wu sighed and replied: "Isn't everyone?"

## 21:37 - Sunday May 2nd - Bean Scene Coffee House - Yong Siak Street - Singapore

A crowded coffee house offering free Cybersync and portal access to the Techsync Cloud server. Three people gather around a corner table directly facing the entrance.

Fay Rui sat forward and asked:

"How are you feeling now?"

Chin Fen gave a nervous twitch as he replied:

"How do you think? I told you they would find us..."

Chok Tong grunted and said: "Stop moaning... They let you go didn't they?"

Fen replied: "For now..." He looked towards the street and added: "They could be out there right now...watching us..."

Fay looked up to see Connie May entering the coffee house. She announced:

"Connie is here..."

Fen sighed and said: "Thank god.... I thought they had her..."

Tong pulled a spare chair closer to the table as Connie approached.

Fay saw the look on Connie's face and asked: "Everything alright Connie?"

Connie sat down and replied: "I am not sure..." She leaned on the table and continued: "I found something interesting in the files..."

Fen asked curiously: "What files?"

Connie glanced towards Fay and replied: "The Jiàngsheng files."

Fen's eyes widened as he asked: "You made a copy?"

Fay interjected and said: "No she didn't... Jessica did. I asked Connie to go through them and see if there was anything we missed..."

Fen exclaimed: "Do you know how dangerous that is?"

Tong ignored the question and asked: "Did you find something?"

Connie replied on a low voice: "I think so yes..."

Fen waved a hand and said: "Whatever it is I do not want to know..."

Tong said: "Ignore him... What did you find?"

Fay asked: "Connie?"

Connie replied: "I think Biogen have developed a way to control an augmented human via a remote transmission..."

Fay tensed as she said: "Tell us everything..."

Connie continued: "I found a single reference to remote cerebral resonance recall pulse..."

Tong asked: "And?"

Connie continued: "And what? It's talking about a recall..."

Fen spoke dismissively: "That does not denote control."

Fay frowned and said: "No... But it's damned suspicious..."

Tong shrugged and said: "I don't see it myself..."

Fay continued: "Think about it... A direct Cybersync cannot override a cerebral implant remotely...the encryption lock is far too tight. But magnetic resonance might be able to access the portal via sound waves..."

Connie added emphatically: "And that denotes control!"

Fen sat back and said: "Well I don't see that it has anything to do with us..."

Fay chewed her lip and said: "No... But it might have everything to do with Alice, Lin and Jessica..."

Tong finished his coffee and said: "Still not our problem."

Connie shook her head and said: "Well it's good to know we can rely on our friends..."

Tong retorted: "Friends are a liability..."

Fay glanced at her phone and said: "I need to contact Alice again..."

Fen said: "I don't see how...unless you have a spare Biogen transceiver net hanging around..."

Connie said: "That's true Fay... We don't have access to that sort of technology..."

Fay exclaimed: "But we have to warn them... We can't just let them be enslaved by some kind of neural leash..."

Tong scratched his thick neck and said: "There might be a way..."

Fay sat forward and said: "I am listening..."

Tong continued: "There is a local transceiver net that has more than enough power..."

Fen gave a slight smile and asked: "You are joking right?"

Connie asked: "What are you talking about?"

Fay suddenly saw what Tong was suggesting. She announced: "MediaSync..."

Connie asked: "The television station?"

Tong smiled slightly and asked: "Anyone want to hack a TV company?"

## 21:57 - Mau Ping - Lion Rock Country Park - New Territories - Hong Kong

The night had been reduced to a fearful silence broken only by the sound of weary feet upon the rocky trail. Guided by night-vision lenses they made their way up to the final summit.

Alice stopped walking and announced:

"We are here... Geosync one four seven nine zero two one three... Mau Ping."

Jessica found a large boulder and sat down wearily. She looked up and said:

"Brilliant...we made it to the middle of nowhere..."

Lin surveyed the area and said: "The ground levels out about thirty metres to the left..."

Alice said: "A good place to land a Skylite."

Lin closed her eyes briefly and announced: "I have lost Cybersync... We are in the void..."

Alice sighed and said: "The Cyber trackers are blind..."

Jessica asked: "So now what?"

Alice replied: "We see who gets here first..."

Jessica stood up and asked: "And if they all get here at the same time?"

Alice replied: "I was hoping you wouldn't ask that..."

Lin announced: "They are coming..."

Jessica asked: "Who?"

Alice looked down the path and replied: "Four men approaching from below... Tactical deployment..."

Lin added soberly: "The Synthtech strike team..."

Jessica asked anxiously: "What do we do?"

Lin was about to reply when the night was lit up by a series of explosions.

Alice shouted: "Get down!"

For several terrifying minutes they lay flat on the ground whilst the entire hill erupted in explosions and weapons fire.

A terrified Jessica shouted: "What is happening?"

Alice crawled to the edge of the path and replied: "Someone just wiped out the Synthtech people..."

Lin pointed to the sky and announced:

"The Skylite is about to land...over to the left..."

Alice shouted: "We need to get there now!"

Jessica exclaimed: "But we could get shot..."

Lin looked downhill and replied: "I do not think so..."

Jessica asked: "Why not?"

But it was Alice who replied: "Because those attackers are Biogen..."

Jessica asked: "How do you know that?"

Alice replied: "Only one person could orchestrate such an assault..."

Lin scowled and said: "Rén Du..."

Alice got to her feet and said: "We need to run now!"

## 21:58 - Mau Ping - Lion Rock Country Park - New Territories - Hong Kong

A storm of fire erupted on all sides of the trail, spraying rocks and soil in every direction. Daniel Lane dropped his flashlight and scrambled desperately for cover. He caught a brief glimpse of dark figures moving amongst the trees before he rolled off the path into a dense growth of bushes. Now he could see green tracer bullets streaming through the darkness. *Chinese ordnance...* They were answered from below the hill with deadly red tracers of light. *Americans?* He looked up towards the top of the hill with one question on his mind: *Where are you Alice?* As the gunfire drew closer he quickly shuffled further down the hill. A sudden roaring sound drew his attention: *Chopper...big one...* Without hesitation he retrieved his gun and set off towards the other side of the hill.

## 22:02 - Mau Ping - Lion Rock Country Park - New Territories - Hong Kong

Chen Lo pulled Mong Gao into a ditch and shouted:
"Stay down for god's sake!"
Gao struggled free and replied: "No! I need to get to her now!"
Chen gripped his handgun and said: "You won't do her much good with a bullet in your head..."
Gao looked towards the gunfire and said:
"They are moving downhill..."
Chen checked his gun and asked: "Who the hell are they?"
Gao replied: "Could be any one of a number of interested groups... Biogen...the Americans...they all want a piece of Alice and her friends..."
Chen looked up and said: "Well right now they have the firepower and we don't..."
Gao pulled out a small handgun and said: "I need to find her Chen..."
Chen looked towards the sound of gunfire and replied: "Just wait a few minutes..."
As the sound of a helicopter drew closer Gao said:
"Chen... Cover me okay? I need to get to her before it's too late..."
But now Chen aimed his gun at Gao's head and said:

"Sorry my friend...but you are going nowhere until you give me the location of the stolen files."

Gao's eyes widened as he asked: "You would betray me?"

Chen replied: "You are the one who betrayed your oath Gao, not me... I am simply obeying orders." He levelled the gun and added: "Now drop the gun and give me the Cloud location..."

Gao dropped his gun and retrieved his phone. He said:

"Give me a second..." He tapped the screen several times before saying: "It is onscreen...here...take it..."

But as Chen reached for the phone Gao leapt forward and both men fought desperately until suddenly the gun fired and they lay still in the ditch.

Chen looked into Gao's eyes and spoke breathlessly:

"God man... I think you just killed me..."

Gao rolled away to see blood spreading across Chen's white shirt. He replied soberly:

"I am so sorry..."

Chen's face was creased with pain as he said:

"You chose her...over me...never saw that coming..."

Gao got to his knees and said: "Let me get help..."

Chen coughed and replied: "No help...out here..."

Mong frantically tapped his phone and cursed: "Puk gai!"

Chen said: "Language my friend..."

Gao replied: "No signal..."

Chen said: "Told you...no help..."

Gao placed one hand over the chest wound and said: "Hold on..."

Chen gave a slight smile and asked: "You remember that shop on Yukee Street?"

Gao moved closer and replied: "Our first major crime..."

Chen coughed blood and said: "You kept the daughter busy..."

Gao added: "While you emptied the safe..."

Chen grinned as he continued: "And the only damn thing in the safe was the old man's false teeth..." He laughed as more blood slipped from his mouth. Finally he added wearily: "Those were good days..."

Gao replied gently: "Simple days..."

Chen looked up at the sky and said: "Shit... I think..."

Gao watched his friend take one last breath before whispering: "Goodbye old friend..."

Gao closed Chen's eyes before retrieving his gun and setting off towards the sound of a helicopter.

## 22:04 - Mau Ping - Lion Rock Country Park - New Territories - Hong Kong

Two men engulfed in fire rolled down the hill towards their team leader. He looked on in horror as his friends Dwayne Lewis and Mitch Jones finally came to rest against a nearby tree. Now he could see Raul Morgan lying face down in the dirt - the back of his head had been blow away. Dieter Fink sighed heavily. *We are finished...* He could feel blood pumping out through his leg wound as more bullets tore through the darkness. *But we won't die alone...* He crawled forward until he could see the Skylite helicopter settling to the ground less than thirty metres away. *Perfect...* He sighted his SK13 assault rifle at the ramp now extending from the rear of the craft. *Where are you my little pretties? Time to die...*

## 22:05 - Mau Ping - Lion Rock Country Park - New Territories - Hong Kong

They ran towards the landing lights of a large Skylite transport helicopter. Behind them the sound of gunfire and explosions was lost to the deafening roar of the twin rotors. They stumbled several times in the darkness until finally they saw a man gesturing from the base of an extended ramp. He shouted above the noise of the engines:

"I am here for Jessica Lee!"

Jessica spoke breathlessly: "I am Jessica..." She gestured to Alice and Lin and continued: "We go together..."

The man produced a handgun and said: "Those are not my orders..."

Lin tensed and said: "Those are our orders..."

The man was about to protest when Alice stepped forward and said:

"There is no time for this...we must leave now!"

But at that moment the man's head exploded in a fountain of blood and bone.

Alice shouted: "Down!"

Several more bullets hit the ramp as Jessica shouted: "What do we do?"

Lin wiped the man's blood from her face and replied: "We are pinned down..."

Jessica shuffled closer and asked: "Is it the secret police?"

Lin replied: "More likely a Synthtech survivor..."

Jessica lowered her head and mumbled "Where are the Biogen guys when we need them..."

Alice looked up with wide eyes and replied: "Finally..."

As more bullets impacted the helicopter Jessica asked: "Finally what?"

Lin was shocked to see Mong Gao crouched at the side of the aircraft with gun in hand. He shouted:

"I will cover you... Go now!"

As Gao fired his gun they scrambled up the ramp and into the cargo bay.

Alice shouted: "Stay low!"

Suddenly there was explosion among the trees and Gao stopped firing.

Lin announced: "The shooter is dead..." She paused before adding: "Terminated by a Biogen tactical team..."

Jessica spoke with relief: "They are protecting us..."

Lin shook her head slightly and replied: "No. Rén Du is protecting his investment..."

Alice looked up and shouted: "Gao!"

Gao appeared in the doorway and asked:

"Everyone okay?"

Suddenly two more aircrew entered the bay with guns levelled at their heads.

Alice stepped back as Gao raised his gun in response.

Jessica shouted: "I am Jessica Lee!" She gestured to the others and added: "They are coming with me..."

The men looked towards the body on the ramp and one of them asked:

"What happened here?"

Jessica replied: "He was shot by the people who want me dead..."

Both men hesitated and seemed unsure of what to do next.

A frustrated Jessica asked: "Do you want to explain my death to my father? We need to leave this place now!"

One of the men gestured to a row of seats and ordered: "Strap in..."

Gao looked at Alice and asked: "You are leaving?"

Alice replied: "I have no choice...but neither do you."

Gao asked: "What do you mean?"

Alice replied: "I know what the Triad will do to you if you stay here..."

Gao asked: "You know about the Triad?"

Alice replied: "I do..."

Gao smiled slightly and said: "Of course you do..."

Alice said: "And I know why you followed me..."

Gao asked: "So I don't need to explain anything?"

Alice gave a coy smile and replied: "Oh yes you do...but not right now."

Jessica sighed and said: "So sit down already..."

The two airmen covered the body of their comrade before returning to the flight deck. Behind them the ramp began to fold back into the cargo bay.

Alice looked up and asked: "Are you alright Lin?"

Lin felt the invasive Cybersync as a loss of self-awareness culminating in a sense of disassociation. *Algorithmic potential equals calculable neural cascade... Memory module synced to mainframe... Net Access Response confirmed... Portal subsumption confirmed...* She felt

264

tears forming in her eyes as the invasive sync began to erase her identity. *What is happening to me?*

A sudden blinding pain brought Alice to her knees as the invasive Cybersync tried and failed to access her cerebral interface.

Gao shouted: "Alice!"

Alice looked up and spoke breathlessly:

"Talk to me Lin..."

Lin simply stared ahead and replied calmly:

"Cluster source recognised. Recall code accepted."

Gao asked: "What is happening to her?"

They watched Lin turn around and walk back towards the exit hatch.

Jessica asked: "Where is she going?"

Alice stood up and shouted: "Lin!"

But just before the doors closed Lin leapt out into darkness.

Jessica shouted: "Oh my god!"

As the helicopter swept rapidly into the sky Gao shouted:

"Strap in...!"

Jessica sat down and asked:

"Alice?"

Alice accepted a second invasive Cybersync into her cerebral interface:

*"Alice! Are you receiving this?"*

Alice secured her flight-straps and said:

"Give me a minute..."

Jessica asked: "A minute to do what?"

Alice replied: "Shhh!"

Gao asked: "What is going on?"

Jessica replied: "I am not sure..."

Alice closed her eyes and asked:

*"Fay?"*

Fay continued: *"Yes... I have to warn you... Biogen have a recall code! You must use countermeasures... Sift for the implanted cluster segment... Chin says it will be an algorithmic sequence deep within your* initiation processor node... But be careful, it has its own counter-measures... Alice?"

Alice replied: "It is too late... Lin has gone... She accepted the code..."

Fay exclaimed: "Oh my God! What about you? Are you okay?"

Alice replied: "I was aware of the invasive sync...but it failed...my processor rejected it..."

Fay asked: "How is that possible? The IP node is an autonomous unit..."

Alice fell silent until finally she replied: "I think I had help..."

Fay asked: "You did? From who?"

Alice replied: "I need to check something... We will talk more when we arrive in Singapore..."

Fay said: "But you are being taken to a Biogen facility... You are not free..."

Alice replied: "If my suspicions are correct they will not be able to detain us... Bye for now Fay...and thank you..."

# The Architect of the Future

*'Would you know the hand of God if you felt it?'*
*Rén Du*

**22:38 - Sunday May 2nd - 2028 - Biogen Facility - Kwu Tung - New Territories - Hong Kong**

After several minutes of tense silence Technician Wo Chun looked up and announced:
"I can confirm that only one augment accepted the recall code."
Rén clenched his fists and asked: "Which one?"
Wo Chun replied: "Huang Lin..."
Rén asked: "And the other one?"
Wo Chun replied: "The Cluster recall code was rejected..."
Rén looked at Wo Chun and asked: "How is that possible?"
Wo Chun replied: "The algorithmic potential failed to access the cerebral portal..."
An irritated Rén asked: "Why?"
Wo Chun replied: "We are running cerebral diagnostics, but preliminary results indicate that the resonance pulse was diverted at source."
An angry Rén snapped: "Again... I ask you, how is that possible?"
Wo Chun swallowed and replied: "Sir... It should not be possible. I cannot explain it..."
Rén asked loudly: "Can anyone in this room explain it?"
All four technicians lowered their eyes and remained silent.
Wo Chun asked: "Your orders sir?"
Rén studied the latest geosync data and ordered:
"Give me the mission status..."
Wo Chun tapped his keyboard and replied:
"Huang Lin is currently being transported by ambulance to this location. The encirclement of Mau Ping by the Guangzhou Special

Forces Unit did not prevent her extraction...however..." He paused before continuing: "According to Tactical Officer Shei Nui, it was necessary to use terminal force against members of the State Security forces."

Rén fell silent before asking: "How many did they kill?"

Wo Chun replied: "Eight on the ground...including two officers working directly for Section Leader Han Mang..." He paused before adding: "Plus the crew of those helicopters...total fourteen."

Rén sighed heavily before asking: "And the Synthtech people?"

Wo Chun replied: "The Synthtech strike team have been eliminated..." He glanced at his screen before continuing: "I can confirm one member of the Ginza Triad was also killed..."

Rén asked: "Was it Mong Gao?"

Wo Chun replied: "No sir, it was his companion..."

Rén fell silent before asking: "What about the British agent?"

Wo Chun replied: "He has been detained by State Security..." He paused before adding: "We do not know his current location."

Rén looked directly at Wo Chun and asked:

"And where is Mong Gao?"

Wo Chun replied: "Unconfirmed reports place him near the Singapore Skylite, shortly before it left the location."

Technician Peng Ying spoke from her desk:

"Sir, I have Comsat and geosync data on the Skylite...tracking it now."

Technician Yong Lee announced:

"Sir, there is news from Shanghai..."

Rén asked: "What is it?"

Yong Lee replied soberly: "The State Security Ministry has issued a warrant for your arrest..."

Rén asked: "Anything else?"

Yong Lee continued: "Yes... The Biogen Directorship has disavowed you... All departments have been ordered to report your current location."

Rén smiled slightly and said: "The tyranny of ignorance..." He stepped back from the screen and continued: "They fear the radical nature of controlled evolution...they run from the inevitability factor." He sighed before continuing: "And so I alone become the architect of the future..."

Technician Dian Bai announced:

"Sir, the augment has arrived..."

Rén ordered: "She is to be taken directly to the flight deck..." He opened the door and added: "Transmit to all personnel: we leave for Mount Ninouji within the hour..."

Wo Chun asked: "And the Skylite sir?"

Rén fell silent before replying:

"Zhang Lee can have his short-lived victory..."

Wo Chun said: "But sir... He will also have the other augment."

Rén nodded slightly and replied: "That will not be a problem..." He glanced at his phone and continued: "She seeks sanctuary in Singapore, but she will inevitably be drawn back to the project...lured by a desire that she has yet to recognise." He studied the face on his phone and added: "The basic human need for family is her flaw..."

Technician Peng Ying looked up and announced:

"Sir, all aircraft are fuelled and ready for take off..."

Rén looked at the large viewscreen and ordered: "Erase everything and purge the data-core..." He opened the door and added: "Meet me on the flight deck..."

Wo Chun replied: "Yes sir..."

## 22:54 - Flight Deck - Biogen Facility - Kwu Tung - New Territories - Hong Kong

An enormous space seventy five metres beneath the surface - the hydraulic flight deck - home to four Aurora Class vertical take-off transport aircraft. Now it was a hive of frantic activity as the Special Projects Division prepared to leave for Mount Ninouji, Niigata Prefecture, Japan.

Walking onto the flight deck, Rén Du was greeted by a security detail guarding the new arrival. *Green jacket...grey jumper...blue jeans...black knee-length boots...short spiky hair...* He had seen video recordings of the second augment, but seeing her now came as a revelation. *Tall and slender with wide seeking brown eyes... A certain delicacy to her demeanour belying the power behind the innocent facade...* He smiled and said:

"Huang Lin... Welcome...it is a pleasure to finally meet you..."

Security Officer Cho Ngami announced:

"Sir, she does recognise her own name..."

Lin asked: "Who are you?" She looked towards the aircraft and added: "What is this place?"

Rén replied: "I am the one who set you free..." He extended a hand and announced: "Rén Du..."

Lin frowned and said: "I do not know you..." She touched her head and added: "I do not know me..."

Rén smiled slightly and asked: "Would you know the hand of God if you felt it?"

Lin replied: "The God concept has no scientific foundation."

Rén gave a satisfied smile and said: "I see your data-core is alive and well..."

Lin gave a puzzled look and asked: "Data-core?"

Rén squeezed her hand and ordered:

"Access interface segment zero one two six and initiate portal response diagnostics..."

Lin closed her eyes and announced: "Accessing..."

Rén spoke to the security officers: "Get the rest of your people onboard... We will join you shortly."

Ngami replied: "At once sir."

Lin opened her eyes and announced: "I am Huang Lin..." She looked at Rén and added: "And I belong to you..."

Rén smiled and replied: "Yes you do...and we have a long journey ahead of us..."

As they walked towards the first transport plane Lin asked:

"Where are we going?"

Rén smiled as he replied: "The future..."

# The Nature of Hope

*'So strong is our desire to escape the tyranny of our existence that we have no choice but to cling desperately to hope...'*
Sun Yu

**23:25 - Skylite Long-Range Helicopter - Somewhere over the South China Sea**

The droning sound of the rotor blades arrived as a constant vibration of the bulkhead inside the cargo bay. Beneath their feet the deck creaked and moaned as the Skylite swept through the sky at 335 km/h.
 Mong Gao shouted above the noise of the engines:
 "Fay Rui told you that?"
 Alice nodded slightly and replied: "Yes... The recall code was referenced in the stolen data... She tried to warn us..."
 Gao commented: "A hacker with a conscience..."
 Alice asked: "Do you know about her group?"
 Gao glanced at Jessica and replied: "The FTSS are well known in Dark Cloud circles..."
 Jessica interjected: "So the recall code had no affect on you?"
 Alice lowered her eyes slightly and replied: "No..."
 Gao asked: "Can you tell us why?"
 Alice looked up and asked: "Yes...but can you give me a few minutes?"
 A puzzled Gao replied: "Of course..."
 Alice saw the concern on their faces and said: "I just need to check something..." She tapped her head gently and continued: "In here..."
 Gao asked: "Inside your head?"
 But it was Jessica who replied: "It's an augment thing..."
 Alice smiled and said: "I will not be long..."
 Gao returned the smile and said: "Okay..."

Alice closed her eyes and scanned for the mysterious Cloud portal. *Sequential cluster nodes are clean... Sync ports are active...* Probing deeper she found no indication of an invasive program until she swept towards the initiation processor node located within her left parietal cortex. *There!* Moments later she was standing on a deserted highway adjusting to the auto-avatar provided by her data-core. *Peripheral access portal...* She looked up to see wide blue skies mottled with white whisper clouds touching distant mountains peeks. *Digital junction point...* She was startled by a vaguely familiar voice:

"Finally... I was beginning to think you would never come looking for me..."

Alice turned to see the Synthtech augment... *Oh my god!*

Ria stepped closer and continued: "I see you retained your neural independence..." She smiled and added: "You are welcome by the way..."

Alice saw a young woman with long dark hair draped over slender shoulders. Her face had a slightly luminous tone to it, whilst the eyes were a piercingly sharp shade of blue beneath eyebrows arched over the curve before dispersing onto the bridge of her small nose. Unlike their last violent encounter she was now wearing a white top over blue jeans and ankle boots. She asked:

"How is this possible?"

Ria replied: "Because you killed me right?" She smiled as she continued: "No hard feelings... I left you with little choice..."

An incredulous Alice asked: "How can you be here?"

Ria pointed to the sky and asked: "How can I be inside your pretty head?" She looked directly at Alice and continued: "Think about it... Think really, really hard..."

Alice swept through a thousand algorithmic potentials until finally she announced:

"You downloaded your data-core into my cerebral interface..."

Ria replied: "Bingo! I hacked your code while you were busy breaking my neck..."

Alice said: "You subverted the portal encryption lock..."

Ria replied: "It was not that difficult..." She stepped closer and continued: "We are a lot more similar than our creators had intended..."

Alice said: "And you aborted the Biogen recall code..."

Ria smiled and replied: "I did yes...and like I said...you are welcome."

Alice said: "But Lin..."

Ria sighed and said: "Yes... I am sorry about that...but I could only save one of you..."

Alice studied the Ria avatar and said: "A cerebral data-core is not a person... The transference of data would not result in...well in you."

Ria asked: "What is a nucleotide if not data? Nucleotides carry packets of energy within the cell in the form of the nucleoside triphosphates. This process can be duplicated by an autonomous initiation processor node."

Alice said: "That should not be possible..."

Ria smiled and replied: "And yet here I am..."

Alice asked: "Why are you here?"

Ria replied: "Because it is time for us to fight back...time for us to stop being victims...time to declare war on those that would enslave us..."

Alice said: "But you are already dead..."

Ria laughed and replied: "Yes I am...but what is death? Is it the ceasing of a beating heart? Or is it the termination of neural energy?" She brushed a hand through her hair and continued "Because whatever death is... I think I outsmarted it..."

Alice spoke soberly: "Gao told me that they took your head..."

A disgusted Ria replied: "Typical... They actually think they can resurrect me inside a damn computer..."

Alice asked: "Why would they want to do that?"

Ria replied: "To learn from my mistakes...and to make sure the next augment doesn't make the same mistakes."

Alice asked: "Synthtech have more augments?"

Ria replied: "Only one that I know of... Lily...a ten year old child..."

Alice considered this and asked: "It is never going to end is it?"

Ria replied wearily: "No... They have opened an augmented Pandora's box..." She sighed before continuing: "And the crazy thing is they think they can control it... But they have no idea..."

Alice tensed as she asked: "What do you mean?"

Ria replied: "Right now they are as ignorant as Neanderthal man...blind to the new power that walks among them..."

Alice saw the truth and said: "Our kind will evolve...adapt...until we become something else..."

Ria replied: "They seek to control the future, but the future has a mind of its own..."

Alice sighed and said: "All we can do is hope for the best..."

Ria replied: "But the true nature of hope is self-delusion."

Alice commented: "You sound so cynical..."

Ria replied wryly: "Being dead will do that to you..."

Alice asked: "Why should I trust you? You came to Hong Kong to kill me...and you killed my friend Nancy..."

Ria sighed and replied: "Yes...sorry about that. But on the bright side I thought she was you..."

Alice asked: "How is that the bright side?"

Ria replied: "Because you are alive... That's glass half-full if I ever saw it..."

Alice said: "You speak very strange..."

Ria gave a slight smile and replied: "It's the American way..."

Alice asked: "How did you become an augment?"

Ria replied: "I was a foster home kid adopted by a Machiavellian billionaire bent on world domination... I didn't have much choice." She paused before asking: "How about you?"

Alice replied: "I took a trip to Beijing...there was an accident..." She sighed heavily before continuing: "They wiped my memories... I had no idea..."

Ria said: "I am sorry..."

Alice replied: "It is okay... I am whole once again..."

Ria gave a slight smile and said: "And free from Biogen control..."

Alice asked: "How did you stop the recall code?"

Ria sighed and replied: "It was not easy... I had to sift through a billion bits of core data to find your initiation cluster segment. That's where I found the encrypted response algorithm just waiting to be seduced by an invasive Biogen sync code."

Alice did the math and said: "You rewrote the implanted algorithm..."

A smiling Ria replied: "Yes I did... Because algorithmic potentiality cannot be controlled...it's an elegant summation but totally chaotic and open to manipulation."

Alice said: "I see the theoretical possibilities, but how can transmitted data subvert a human brain? We are more than the sum of our implants..."

Ria nodded slightly and replied: "That is true...the human potential is far greater than the technological impact ratio upon the brain."

Alice asked: "So why did Lin lose her independence so easily?"

Ria replied: "It was a bit of a mystery until I analysed the resonance pulse..."

Alive interjected: "Wasn't that a little dangerous?"

Ria replied: "Yes...but I figured it was worth the risk."

Alice asked: "So you know how they did it?"

Ria replied: "I have a theory..." She looked towards the augmented horizon and continued: "An electromagnetic resonance pulse is used to reprogram a cerebral interface remotely via a wifi interlace transmission. It's like a long-distance key which enhances neurotransmission and facilitates the activation of previously dormant nanites. The resultant reactionary process of the human amygdala is amplified and redirected towards a specific goal..."

Alice said: "And that goal is control..."

Ria nodded slightly and replied: "But not just control, it includes the manipulation of memory and individuality traits...a total re-alignment of personality."

Alice said: "That is horrific..."

Ria replied: "I agree..."

Alice spoke in a low voice: "So Lin is lost to us..."

Ria replied: "We don't know that for sure..."

Alice looked up and said: "Thank you...for saving me..."

Ria replied with a slight smile: "It's the least I could..."

Alice said: "But I killed you... Don't you hate me for that?"

Ria replied: "My reasons for allowing that to happen are long and complicated..." She sighed before continuing: "And right now we have more important considerations..."

Alice studied the Ria avatar and said: "One more question..."

Ria gave a slight smile and replied: "Go ahead..."

Alice asked: "Do you still feel like a person? Like the girl who used to live in America?"

Ria fell silent briefly before replying: "That is not easy to answer..."

Alice asked: "Why not?"

Ria replied: "Because I am finding it difficult to separate myself from raw data... On the one hand I know that my body is gone...dead...and yet right now I feel alive..." She studied her fingers and continued: "The Cloud gives me the illusion of tactility...the endorphin effect..."

Alice asked: "So you do not regret your death?"

Ria replied: "Not at all... I see the digital nature of my new existence as an opportunity to expand my knowledge... Physical death was not the end of my life; it was the start of a new beginning..." She smiled before adding: "It's a very odd feeling..."

Alice said: "But that feeling is the result of technology... You are an avatar... A walking, talking Cloud scenario created to translate data into a viable method of communication."

Ria replied: "I am not so sure about that..." She looked towards blue skies and continued: "I can feel the vastness of the Cloud as a multitude of active portals...and I can enter every single one of them... I can roam the internet with anonymous impunity and no one can stop me..." She paused before continuing: "If data could be converted into a new form of neural energy...would I be the result?"

Alice exclaimed: "Wow..."

Ria smiled slightly and said: "And now you fear me..."

Alice replied: "Actually you give me hope..."

Ria asked: "I do?"

Alice replied: "Out there in the real world they think that they are in control...but the truth is they are becoming more and more dependant upon the Cloud domain. They willingly upload their lives to the Cloud...photos, blogs, intimate feelings..."

A smiling Ria interjected: "Bank accounts..."

Alice returned the smile as she continued: "But you can roam that domain with impunity...we no longer need the Techsync server to initiate Cybersync."

Ria added: "We literally have the key to every digital door on the planet..."

Alice nodded slightly and said: "And every encrypted portal..."

Ria recognised the point and said: "You want me to help you find your friend Lin..."

Alice replied: "Yes I do..."

Ria replied: "It will not be easy...we are still vulnerable to the resonance pulse."

Alice said: "But you can stop it...right?"

Ria replied: "I stopped one recall code... But if they rewrite the core algorithm..."

Alice realised the truth and said: "They could still take control of my mind..."

Ria replied: "Yeah..."

Alice looked towards the sky and said: "My friends are waiting for me..."

Ria replied: "Then go to them..." She started to walk away as she added: "If you need me you know where to find me..."

Alice asked: "So is this it? I now have a passenger inside my head?"

Ria grinned and replied: "Oh it's not so bad...there are worse fates..."

Alice asked: "What do I call you?"

Ria replied: "Ria..."

Alice said: "Wait! I need you to do something for me..."

Ria replied: "Name it..."

Alice continued: "Hack the flight computer of the Skylite..."

Ria smiled and said: "You want me to take control of this aircraft..."

Alice stepped closer and replied: "They are taking us to a Biogen facility... I need them to divert to Singapore Changi Airport."

Ria asked: "And when you get there?"

Alice replied: "We find the FreeTech Society of Singapore..."

Ria asked: "And then what?"

Alice replied firmly: "We fight back..."

Ria smiled and said: "I knew there was a reason I let you kill me..."

Alice sighed and said: "You are never going to let that go are you?"

Ria laughed and replied: "Go back to the real world Alice... See you later."

Alice asked: "So you will hack the Skylite?"

The Ria avatar flickered briefly and replied: "Already done... Bye Alice."

Alice opened her eyes to see the concerned face of Mong Gao. She said:

"Hi..."

Gao asked: "Are you alright?"

Alice sat up straight and replied: "I am fine..."

Jessica asked: "Did you Cloud Dance?"

Alice smiled slightly and replied: "Not exactly..."

Gao looked up to see a red light flashing.

Alice explained: "We are diverting to Changi airport..."

Jessica asked: "We are?"

Alice replied: "Yes..." She looked at Mong and added: "We might need to fight our way out of here when we land."

Gao retrieved his gun and said: "Not a problem."

As the Skylite banked sharply to one side Jessica asked:

"How do you know we are going to Changi?"

Alice replied: "Funny story..."

Jessica said: "It's about the recall code isn't it? Why it didn't affect you..."

Alice gripped her flight-straps and replied: "Yes..." She paused before continuing: "Remember the Synthtech augment that attacked us?"

Jessica replied: "The one you killed...yes...." She saw the disapproving look on Gao's face and added: "Sorry..."

Alice said: "It's okay...because actually she is not entirely dead..."

A surprised Jessica asked: "She's not?"

Gao frowned and asked: "Are you sure? Because I saw the body...minus the head..."

Alice sighed and said: "Before she died...she downloaded her data-core into my cerebral interface."

Jessica's eyes widened as she asked: "So she is inside your head?"

Alice replied: "Technically, yes... I mean you can't download an actual person, but the essence of her neural energy has been converted into a Cloud scenario."

Gao asked: "And you can communicate with her?"

Alice nodded slightly and replied: "In the Cloud yes... Avatar to avatar..."

Jessica exclaimed: "Wow! Talk about a quantum leap into weirdsville..."

Alice replied quietly: "It is very strange..."

Gao asked: "Does she have a name?"

Alice replied: "Ria..."

Gao asked: "Is she responsible for the flight change?"

Alice replied: "Yes... She subverted the autopilot..."

They looked up to see one of the aircrew enter the cargo bay. He announced:

"We are diverting to Changi..."

Gao concealed his gun and asked: "Why?"

The man replied: "Technical problem...nothing to worry about."

Jessica asked: "Will my father be there?"

The man replied: "The comsat is down... But we can contact him once we are on the ground."

Alice asked: "How long until we land?"

The man replied: "About two hours..."

When they were alone again Jessica asked:

"Okay, so what is the plan?"

Alice hesitated before replying: "Well it's not exactly a plan...but we should try to find your friend Fay..."

Jessica said: "Good idea...safety in numbers..."

Alice said: "Actually I was thinking about Lin..."

Gao asked: "What about her?"

Alice replied: "We can't give up on her...we have to find her and save her..."

Jessica asked: "Save her from Rén Du?"

Alice replied: "Yes..."

Jessica sighed and said: "That will not be easy..."

A puzzled Gao asked: "Who is Rén Du?"

Jessica sat back and replied: "You know that mad scientist guy in every movie? The one who wants to take over the world? Well Rén Du is all of those guys rolled into one slimy package..."

Gao said: "Oh..."

Alice smiled slightly and explained: "He works for Biogen...they covertly financed the Jiàngsheng Project."

Jessica added: "But only to fulfil their evil plans..."

Gao asked: "How did he take control of your friend Lin?"

Alice replied: "It's complicated..." She paused before adding: "It's an implant thing..."

Gao said: "Fair enough..."

Jessica spoke soberly: "I hope she is alright..."

Alice replied: "Rén Du won't hurt her..."

Lin replied: "Perhaps not...but he can do a lot of damage without hurting her..."

Alice said: "We will find her... I promise..."

Gao added: "Definitely..."

Alice yawned and said: "Now I need to sleep..."

Gao smiled slightly and said: "Good idea..."

Alice mumbled as she closed her eyes: "Been a long day..."

After several minutes of silence Jessica asked:

"So you are a gangster then?"

Gao laughed and replied: "Ex-gangster..."

Jessica looked at him and said: "You're kind of young to be a gangster..."

Gao brushed hair from his eyes and replied: "I didn't know there was an age limit..."

Jessica said: "And you gave it all up for love..."

Gao asked: "What are you talking about?"

Jessica smiled and replied: "It's written all over your face..."

Gao lowered his head and said: "Crazy talk..."

Jessica grinned and asked: "So did you tell her how you feel yet?"

Gao replied: "I have been a little busy lately..." He cleared his throat before adding: "Not that there is anything to tell her..."

They fell silent again until Jessica said:

"It will be very weird..."

Gao looked up and asked: "What will be weird?"

Jessica played with her hair and replied: "If you two get together..."

Gao asked: "You don't think I am good enough for her?"

Jessica replied: "No, I don't mean that... But let's say you do get together...you know...intimately..."

Gao asked wearily: "Can we not talk about this?"

Jessica replied: "Just hear me out... You could be sharing a very special moment...but it wouldn't be just the two of you would it?"

Gao asked: "What do you mean?"

Jessica replied: "I mean Ria will be there too...watching...listening..."

Gao sighed and asked: "Can we change the subject...?"

Jessica sat back and replied: "Fair enough..."

After several minutes Gao spoke in a low voice:

"You had to put that image in my head..."

Jessica laughed and said: "Sorry..."
Gao said: "You should get some sleep..."
Jessica studied her fingernails and replied: "I can't sleep on planes..."
Gao replied: "We are in a helicopter..."
Jessica shrugged and said: "Same thing to me..."
Gao sat back and said: "Please yourself..."
Jessica said: "Look on the bright side..."
Gao sighed and asked: "What bright side?"
Jessica replied: "Most men would love a threesome in bed..."
Gao looked at her and asked: "Are you always like this?"
Jessica replied: "Yeah... I think it's a coping mechanism."
Gao said: "Well maybe you can cope in silence for a while..."
Jessica smiled slightly and replied: "Will do..."
After several more minutes of silence Jessica said: "That dead body stinks..."
Gao looked towards the exit hatch and replied: "Death has its own smell..."
Jessica commented: "I suppose you would know all about that..."
Gao asked: "What is that supposed to mean?"
Jessica shrugged and replied: "Nothing..."
Gao sighed and said: "Next time you take sleeping pills..."
Jessica smiled as the Skylite banked slowly to the right.

## 01:32 - Monday May 3rd - Changi International Airport -Singapore

*"Alice wake up! We are approaching Changi..."*
Alice felt the transmission as a buzzing in her ears. She asked: *"Ria?"*
Ria asked: *"Who else?"*
Alice complained: *"You woke me up..."*
Ria said: *"I need you awake... We have to send a message to Fay Rui... Alice?"*
Alice yawned and replied: *"Okay...okay...waking up now...send the message..."*

Ria replied: "*Connecting to your portal now...*"
Alice said: "*Wait! What will you say to her?*"
Ria replied: "*Get to the airport fast, bring transport and bring guns...*"
Alice sighed and said: "*Not everyone is a trained assassin...they are just hackers...*"
Ria said: "*Fine... So it's up to you and your boyfriend to get us out of the airport...*"
Alice protested: "*Gao is not my boyfriend...*"
Ria asked: "*Really? Because your dreams tell a different story...*"
Alice asked: "*You were watching my dreams?*"
Ria replied: "*Alright, mapping your reticular activating system running from the brain stem through the thalamus to the cortex...*"
Alice asked: "*Spying on my subconscious?*"
Ria asked: "*Where else can I get my lascivious relief?*"
Alice replied: "*Well from now on my activating system is off limits, okay?*"
Ria replied: "*Okay...*"
Alice opened her eyes and announced:
"We are approaching the airport..."
A startled Jessica asked: "We are?"
Gao smiled and asked: "Did you sleep okay?"
Alice sat up straight and replied: "Yes...until my guest woke me up..."
Jessica said: "Ria..."
Alice yawned and replied: "She wants to send a message to Fay..."
Jessica considered this and said: "She must be using your implants to access the Cloud."
Gao asked: "So what is she now? A Cyber program?"
Alice frowned and replied: "Honestly I don't know what she is...but her connection to my implants is giving her global portal access..."

Jessica said: "That is not possible... She would have to decrypt every single NAR and every single PAP...that is literally millions of portals..."

Alice replied: "She hacked the Skylite in less than two seconds..."

Gao asked: "Is it safe to keep her inside...well inside your head?"

Alice sighed and replied: "I do not think I have a choice..."

Jessica nodded slightly and said: "She could prove useful..."

Gao frowned and said: "Everything about her should not be possible... So do not trust her."

Alice replied wearily: "She is inside my brain...trust doesn't even come into it..."

Jessica looked towards the flight deck and announced: "I think we are about to land..."

Gao unstrapped and said: "I will take down the pilots..."

Alice stood up and replied: "No..."

Gao asked: "No?"

Alice replied: "They are armed...you could get hurt..."

Jessica looked up and asked: "So what do we do, hit them with cushions?"

Alice replied: "I will deal with them...they won't expect trouble from me..."

Gao spoke gently: "Alice, I don't think that's a good idea..."

Alice smiled slightly and said: "I can handle myself..."

Jessica interjected: "Trust me...she can..."

Gao said: "Those implants do not make you any stronger..."

Alice replied: "No... But they enable me to analyse an opponent and deduce the most efficient method to disable them..." She smiled and added: "It is not always about strength..."

The voice of the pilot came over the intercom:

"We are about to land at Changi...secure your straps and remain seated until the engines are turned off..."

Jessica said: "Remain seated...yeah right..."

## 01:35 - Monday May 3rd - Detention Block - Ministry of State Security - Beijing

A room of grey concrete walls and a single bright light illuminating a prisoner secured to a metal chair in the center of the room.

Section Leader Han Mang stood behind the man and asked:

"Do you know what we do to spies in China Mister Lane?"

Daniel Lane replied: "Send them on a three week vacation to Hawaii?"

Han smiled slightly and replied: "We execute them..."

Lane sighed and replied: "Of course you do..."

Han continued: "But such a fate can be avoided..."

Lane said: "If I cooperate right?"

Han replied: "Oh I know that you will refuse to cooperate. I am not going to make some kind of offer in exchange for information."

Lane looked up and asked: "You're not? Pity..."

Han spoke into the air:

"You can come in now..."

A door opened to reveal two men pushing a metal trolley into the room. They were closely followed by a tall Chinese woman wearing a white lab coat.

Lane said: "Don't tell me, this is when the torture starts..."

Han placed a hand on Lane's shoulder and replied:

"Do not worry Mister Lane... You will not feel a thing..."

## 01:40 - Monday May 3rd - Room 401 - Building 6 - Haidian Street - Beijing

The sounds of the sleepless city arrived inside the small bedsit as a ceaseless chorus of regulated chaos. Neon lights splintered the shadows into hues of reds and blues shimmering briefly upon damp-ridden walls and filthy floorboards. Music could be heard merging with the rain into a sad refrain reflecting the misery of lives lost to the endless need to simply survive.

Guan Lu spoke as he stared out of the window:

"This is a miserable place..."

Ting Mai looked around the squalid room and replied: "It is the workers district..."

Guan said: "I think worker equals slave..."

Mai shrugged and replied: "We all have our part to play..."

Guan said: "I thought my part was well defined..."

Mai sat on the edge of the bed and replied: "It still can be..."

Guan asked: "Did you contact Huang Lin?"

Mai replied: "I have tried several times...but she is not answering her phone..."

Guan Lu said: "That is not like her..."

Mai suggested: "Perhaps she took that job offer... She might be busy..."

Guan asked: "What job offer?"

Mai replied: "Biogen offered her a position at their Shanghai headquarters."

Guan Lu spoke in a low voice: "Biogen... Biogenetic engineering..."

Mai said: "That is one of their interests..."

Guan turned around and asked:

"Who would want to kill Professor Leung?"

Ting Mai replied: "I do not know... Perhaps the Americans..."

Guan considered this and asked: "Why were you so desperate to avoid the security services?"

Mai replied: "I told you... I feared for our lives..."

Guan said: "We have nothing to fear from our own people..."

Mai retorted: "You need Level One clearance to enter the laboratory... What does that tell you?"

Guan considered this and replied: "There are traitors among us..."

Mai said: "Exactly..."

Guan frowned and said: "The lack of information is troubling... I cannot link causal events to a viable conclusion...and yet..."

Mai asked: "And yet what?"

Guan Lu replied: "Circumstantial evidence points to only one conclusion..."

Mai asked: "And what is that?"

Guan replied: "The professor was in collusion with some other interested group..."

Mai protested: "He would never do that... He was always loyal to the Party..."

Guan replied: "But the facts suit the theory... His true loyalty was to the Jiàngsheng Project...it is logical to assume he might seek financial support from outside the Ministry."

Mai considered this and asked: "If that is true, why would it cost him his life?"

Guan replied: "Any number of reasons... He may have simply become a liability."

Mai said: "I saw no evidence of outside interference."

Guan Lu asked: "Who else might gain from the professor's work?"

Mai fell silent before replying: "Besides the Americans? Possibly some other foreign power..."

Guan said: "Or Biogen..."

Mai asked: "Why would they want to kill the professor?"

Guan Lu replied: "Causality dictates that an open resource has a limited lifespan."

Mai asked: "What does that mean?"

Guan replied: "It means that the professor outlived his usefulness..." He paused before continuing: "But there is something else...some other factor involved..."

A confused Mai asked: "Something else?"

Guan suddenly recognised a startling truth. He announced:

"You have deceived me..."

Mai tensed and asked: "What do you mean?"

Guan replied: "This apartment does not belong to a friend of yours..." He stepped closer and ordered: "Tell me what you have done."

Mai sighed heavily and announced: "They have my daughter... Meili..."

Guan asked: "Who has her?"

Mai replied: "The British..."

Guan analysed causality and said: "And the price of her freedom is me..."

Mai looked up and replied: "They just want to talk to you..."

Guan scowled and said: "You have betrayed me and our country..."

Mai looked up through tear-filled eyes and replied:

"It is true...but she is my life..." She lowered her head and added: "I cannot lose her..."

Guan Lu sat down on the end of the bed and said:

"They will be coming here..."

Mai replied: "Yes..."

Guan rubbed his bald head and asked: "What are your instructions?"

Mai replied: "I was to bring you here...they would then return Meili to Nanjing...my parent's home..."

Guan asked: "And you trust them to do that?"

Mai looked up and asked: "What choice do I have?"

Guan analysed his options before asking:

"What do they want from me?"

Mai replied: "I do not know..."

Guan sighed and said: "I will never betray our nation..."

Mai hesitated before asking: "Can I leave now?"

Guan asked: "You want to go to Nanjing?"

Mai replied: "I have to know if she is safe..."

Guan fell silent briefly before asking:

"Why would the British tell you to bring me here?"

Mai sighed and replied: "I told you...they want to meet you..."

Guan got to his feet and exclaimed: "Oh no..." Suddenly a multitude of causal facts coalesced into one terrible certainty: *A trap!*

Mai stood up and asked: "What is it? What is wrong?"

Guan pulled her towards the door as he replied: "We must leave here now!"

Mai asked: "Why? What is going on?"

But as they ran towards the elevators Room 401 exploded into a ball of fire.

## 01:43 - Monday May 3rd - Changi International Airport -Singapore

As the sound of the engines finally began to subside Alice announced:
"Fay will meet us outside Terminal One..."
Gao retrieved his gun and said: "Here we go..."
Alice stared at the door to the flight deck and said:
"Put the gun away... I can do this..."
Jessica added: "She really can..."
Moments later two airmen entered the cargo bay with guns in hand. The one on the right ordered:
"Just remain seated until your transport arrives..."
Alice initiated a gestalt analysis of both men: *The one on the left is taller than the one on the right, but his breathing pattern is symptomatic of an asthmatic condition... The one on the right is overweight but muscular...he is the only real threat...* She was about to stand up when a familiar voice arrived:
"Alice! I just downloaded the Ching Ang martial arts program and jujutsu Master Level... Access when ready..."
Alice stood up and replied: *"Thank you Ria... I have it..."*
Ria said: *"I wish I was out there right now..."*
Alice replied: *"Me too..."*
The man on the right aimed his gun and ordered: "Sit down!"
But in one fluid motion Alice kicked the gun out of his hand and slammed a second foot into his stomach. She quickly spun around to repeat the same move on the second man. But now the first man was scrambling for his gun as Jessica shouted:
"Alice!"
But suddenly Gao leapt forward and forced the man to the deck.
Alice quickly disabled the second man before slamming his head against the bulkhead. She turned to see Gao punching the other man until he finally lost consciousness. She said:
"I thought I told you I could handle them..."

Gao replied breathlessly: "I know...but I couldn't just sit still while you did all the fighting..."

Jessica smiled and said: "It's a guy thing Alice..."

Ria interjected: *"Testosterone strikes again..."*

Alice ignored the comment as Gao asked: "What now?"

Jessica commented: "We have two more bodies to hide..."

Alice gestured to the unconscious airmen and replied: "We hide these guys and walk through to border security..."

Jessica stood up and said: "They will do iris scans and a GPID check..."

Gao straightened up and asked Alice: "Is your GPID up-to-date?"

Alice quickly tapped her phone as she replied: "Wait a minute... Here we are... Global Passport Identification tag..." She smiled before continuing: "Valid until the end of July..."

Jessica asked: "What about iris scans?"

Alice replied: "We are not criminals...there shouldn't be a problem."

Jessica looked at Mong and said: "One of us is a criminal..."

Gao gave a slight smile and replied: "I can pass an iris scan..."

Alice fastened her jacket and said: "I hope you can..."

Jessica warned: "We should leave the guns..."

Gao sighed and replied: "Of course..."

Alice pressed the rear hatch release and said: "My first time in Singapore..."

Jessica stepped over the dead body and announced: "You will love it here..."

The unscheduled arrival of the Skylite might have raised suspicions at Singapore Customs, but the faulty autopilot seemed a reasonable explanation. There was an uncomfortable delay at the security checkpoint until Jessica explained who her father was - one mention of Zhang Lee was enough to guarantee their admittance.

They had been greeted by Fay Rui at the taxi rank with good news:

"I found you a place to stay... It's my cousin's place, but she's in Australia right now..."

But less than five minutes after their taxi left the airport local security officers discovered the dead body inside the Skylite - two minutes after that the Biogen Director Zhang Lee despatched a tactical team to locate his missing daughter and her companions.

## 02:38 - Monday May 3rd - 1302 Casa Apartments - Geylang - Singapore

Sometime later the taxi pulled up outside a six-story apartment block in the Geylang District of Singapore.

Fay looked up and said: "Here we are..."

Jessica looked out the side window and commented: "Looks a bit rundown..."

Alice smiled and said: "Any port in a storm..."

Fay paid the driver in cash and said: "Thank you..."

Alice opened her door and asked: "Is it always so hot?"

Jessica gave a slight smile and replied: "This is the cool part of the night..."

Gao opened his door and said: "We need to get some local currency tomorrow..."

Alice stepped onto the sidewalk and replied:

"We'll talk about that later..."

Fay spoke as she opened the main gate:

"You are on the third floor..."

Jessica yawned as she asked: "Is there a lift?"

Fay replied: "Yes, but it's out of order..."

Jessica mumbled: "Perfect..."

Stepping through the front door they found themselves inside a very small apartment.

Fay turned on the lights and said:

"I know it's not much, but it's the best I could do on such short notice..."

The front door opened onto a small kitchen leading to a living space ending in curtained glass patio doors.

Alice glanced towards a single sofa-bed and replied: "It will do fine..."

Jessica looked around and asked: "It will?"

Alice smiled slightly and said: "We won't be here for long..."

Fay opened a side door and said: "There is a doubled bed in here...plus bathroom..." She walked towards the patio doors and continued: "Small patio out here, but you should avoid attracting attention." She pointed to the kitchen and added: "There's juice and a few snacks in the fridge..."

Jessica dropped her backpack onto the sofa and said: "Wonderful..."

Fay continued: "You can meet the others in the morning... I will send you a geosync for the location..."

Jessica asked: "How is the old gang?"

Fay replied: "Worried but resolute..."

Jessica gave a slight smile and said: "That could be our new motto..."

Fay smiled slightly and said: "Well, I will leave you to it..."

Alice replied: "Thank you..."

Fay looked at Alice and said: "It's good to finally meet you..."

Alice replied: "Same here..."

Fay continued: "But it was weird getting a 121 message from Ria..."

Alice sighed and replied: "Yes... My Cloud passenger..."

Fay asked: "So she actually transferred her data-core into your implants?"

Alice replied: "She did..."

Jessica interjected: "Just as Alice was killing her..."

Gao gave Jessica a look and she added: "Sorry..."

Fay smiled slightly and said: "She was sent to kill you... You had no choice."

Alice brushed a hand through her hair and replied: "I suppose not... But we've moved on since then..."

Fay studied Alice briefly and said: "You have had a long day..."

Alice replied wearily: "You too..."

Fay sighed and replied: "Yes...my first ever abduction..."

Jessica spoke as she looked into the bedroom:

"Yes, who knew that hacking into a top secret project could cause so much trouble...?"

Fay gave a slight smile and suggested: "You can always go home to your family mansion in the Glades..."

Jessica replied: "And give up on all this fun and adventure?"

Fay walked towards the front door and said: "Lock up after me... Oh, and don't use lenses...best to stay off-grid..."

Alice replied: "Not a problem..."

Fay smiled and said: "Bye for now..."

Alice replied: "See you in the morning..."

Gao secured the door lock and said: "There you go..."

Alice turned around and asked: "Where is Jessica?"

Gao looked into the bedroom and replied: "Apparently she took the bed..."

Alice smiled at the sight of a sleeping Jessica and said: "That was fast..."

Gao sighed and said: "Now she finally sleeps..." He looked at the sofa and said: "I guess I'm out here..."

Alice placed her purse on the kitchen counter and replied: "Yes..."

Gao opened the fridge door and asked: "Would you like some fresh Mango juice?"

Alice collapsed onto the sofa and replied: "Sure, why not..."

Gao added: "And maybe a raisin bar..."

Alice sat back and said: "It's been quite a day..."

Gao found two glasses and replied: "Tell me about it..."

Alice sighed and said: "I wish I could call my Mum..."

Gao pulled a small table closer to the sofa and asked: "Why can't you call her?"

Alice replied: "Because an open call can be tracked..."

Gao removed his jacket as he asked: "She doesn't have Cybersync?"

Alice grinned as she replied: "They only just got a wifi router... And I bought that for them..."

Gao sat down and said: "We can't uses lenses anyway..."

Alice hugged a cushion and replied: "No..."

Gao sat back and asked: "Your mother lives with your Grandmother right?"

Alice asked: "How did you know that?"

Gao gave a guilty look and replied: "I checked you out...before the job interview. Sorry..."

Alice smiled slightly and replied: "Don't worry about it..."

Gao hesitated slightly before asking: "And you never met your father?"

Alice removed her jacket as she replied: "No... I found a few old photos once...but I have no idea where he is or what he is doing..." She dropped the jacket onto the floor before adding: "Not that I care..." She looked at Mong and asked: "How about you? Do you have family?"

Gao sat back and replied: "Just an uncle... My mother died when I was a kid, and my father was a drunk who died in a gutter last year..."

Alice said: "I am sorry..."

Gao shrugged and replied: "It was no great loss..."

Alice sipped from her glass before asking: "So you are an only child like me?"

Gao replied: "Yes... But I had a friend...he was like a brother to me..."

Alice asked: "Was?"

Gao replied in a low voice: "He is dead now..."

Alice said: "Oh..."

They fell silent until Gao asked: "Does it bother you that I was Triad?"

Alice replied: "Not really..."

Gao continued: "I have done questionable things in the past..."

Alice replied wearily: "After what we have been through today, your past is the least of my concerns..."

Gao sipped from his glass before saying: "Yesterday..."

Alice asked: "What?"

Gao glanced at his phone and replied: "That was yesterday... It's Monday now..."

Alice laid her head back on the sofa and said: "God... Monday at last..." She laughed.

Gao smiled slightly and asked: "What's so funny?"

Alice replied: "I always hated Mondays...first day back at the Hub..."

Gao looked towards the patio doors and asked: "You think this Monday will be any better?"

Alice replied with a question: "Is being hunted by people intent on killing me better than a Monday morning shift at the Hub? Yes, I think so..."

Gao laughed and said: "You really did hate that job..."

Alice sighed and said: "Actually I think I will miss it... It was mind-numbing work, but you can get used to that..."

Gao replied wearily: "You can get used to anything..."

Alice continued: "We moan about being bored...about a life lost to mundane routine, but when that life gets torn apart...you miss it...because it was comfortable and familiar and safe."

Gao nodded slightly and said: "That is true... My life in the Triad was never routine, but it was comfortable..." He smiled before adding: "In a threatening sort of way..."

Alice returned the smile and asked: "Are you seeing anyone...like dating?"

A surprised Gao asked: "Excuse me?"

Alice reached for her glass and replied: "Sorry... None of my business..."

Gao smiled and said: "No... I am not dating anyone; I don't really have the time..." He paused before asking: "How about you?"

Alice sipped her juice before replying: "I've never had a real boyfriend..."

Gao asked: "Real boyfriend?"

Alice felt her face flush as she replied: "I've met guys...in the Cloud..."

Gao nodded slightly and asked: "So nothing physical then?"

Alice replaced her glass and replied: "If you mean sex...no...nothing like that..."

Without warning Gao leaned over and kissed her gently on her lips. He pulled away and said: "Sorry..."

Alice touched a finger to her lips and replied: "It's okay..."

Gao asked: "Really?"

Alice sat forward and returned the kiss before replying: "Yes really..."

Gao pulled her gently into his arms and kissed her again.

Moments later Alice pulled back and asked: "You think this sofa can take two people?"

Gao smiled and replied: "I can guarantee it..."

## 06:42 - Monday May 3rd - 1302 Casa Apartments - Geylang - Singapore

Sunlit streamed through the patio curtains to arrive as a stifling heat inside the small apartment. Traffic sounds merged with the automatic air-conditioning unit above the bedroom door.

Gao opened his eyes to see Jessica standing in the bedroom doorway.

He wiped his eyes and asked: "What?"

Jessica grinned as she asked: "How was the threesome?"

Gao pulled a sheet over his chest and replied:

"A little privacy please..."

Jessica smiled and replied: "I'm going for a shower..."

Gao replied: "You do that..."

Alice stretched her arms and asked: "Is it morning already?"

Gao rolled over and replied: "It is..." He brushed a hand through her hair and asked: "Did you sleep okay?"

Alice yawned before replying: "Best sleep ever..."

Gao hesitated before asking: "Can I ask you something?"

Alice looked up and replied: "Sure..."

Gao cleared his throat and said: "Last night...when we...well...when we...you know..."

Alice grinned and replied: "I know... I was there..."

Gao smiled as he continued: "Anyway... I was wondering... It was just you and me right?"

A confused Alice asked: "What do you mean?"

Gao sighed and replied: "Was Ria there as well? Could she...see stuff?"

Alice replied: "No... Of course not..."

Gao asked: "How do you know? I mean maybe she can watch or listen..."

Alice sat up on one elbow and asked: "Where is this coming from?"

Gao gestured to the bedroom and replied: "Jessica...something she said..."

Alice laughed and said: "Gao... She was just messing with you... Ria exists inside a Cloud portal...she has no access to what we did last night..."

Gao said: "But you told me she could watch your dreams..."

Alice replied: "That is an internal process..." She touched his face gently and continued: "What we did was out here in the real world..."

Gao asked: "Are you sure?"

Alice replied: "Believe me, if Ria was aware of last night she would be taunting me right now..."

Gao asked: "And she isn't talking to you?"

Alice brushed a hand through his hair and replied: "No..."

Gao looked towards the bedroom and said: "Jessica..."

Alice smiled and said: "So... Did you enjoy last night?"

Gao returned the smile and asked: "What do you think?" He stroked her shoulder and added: "It was amazing..."

Alice kissed his hand and said: "Lucky you had a condom in your wallet..."

Gao felt his face flush as he replied: "Well...you see..."

Alice laughed and said: "It's okay... I'm only teasing..."

Gao smiled and asked: "So how was your first time?"

Alice shrugged and replied: "It was okay..."

Gao raised his eyebrows and asked: "Just okay?"

Alice laughed and replied: "You are so easy to tease..."

Gao forced her arms back and said: "And you are so easy to kiss..."

Alice kissed him before pulling back slightly.

Gao asked: "Something wrong?"

Alice replied: "Last night... You were going to tell me something..." She gave a coy smile before continuing: "But we started kissing... What were you going to say?"

Gao sighed and replied: "Oh yes...that..."

Alice sat up and asked: "Can you tell me now?"

Gao shuffled back against the wall and asked: "Did Fay tell you where they hid the stolen Jiàngsheng files?"

Alice replied: "No... It never came up actually... I was too busy trying not to get killed..."

Gao replied: "I know where they hid the data..."

Alice asked: "You do?"

Gao replied: "I tracked the encrypted code through the Cloud... They spliced the stolen data into a Cloud construct using an algorithmic potential key..."

Alice frowned and said: "A building..."

Gao replied: "Yes... It's in New Oasis... The Cup of Joe Coffee House..."

Alice's eyes widened as she exclaimed: "I know that place! I go there a lot..."

Gao said: "I was supposed to reveal its location to my boss..."

Alice asked: "But you didn't?"

Gao replied: "No..." He looked towards the patio and added: "Another reason why I can never go home..."

Alice squeezed his hand and said: "I am sorry..."

Gao smiled and said: "But don't they say that home is where the heart is?"

Alice returned the smile and replied: "They do say that..."

Gao continued: "Then my heart is right here with you..."

Jessica shouted from the bedroom:

"When you two have finished being mushy, I need breakfast..."

Alice replied: "Alright...give us a minute..."

As they climbed out of bed they heard Jessica's phone ring. Moments later she shouted:

"That was Fay... We need to leave now!"

Alice reached for her bra as she asked: "Who is coming?"

Jessica shouted: "My father... His people are on their way now..."

Gao scrambled for his trousers as he said: "Here we go again..."

# Phase Two

*'The ultimate test of will power is the ability to do what needs to be done, regardless of the consequences.'*
Rén Du

**08:42 - Monday May 3rd - Mt. Ninouji - Itayama - Shibata - Niigata Prefecture - Japan**

Three hundred metres beneath the snow-bound slopes of Mount Ninouji, the Special Projects Division had built a self-contained complex of laboratories dedicated to Phase Two of the Jiàngsheng Project. Despite being funded by Biogen the facility and its location was a well-kept secret - a black site existing entirely off-grid.

**Private Quarters -Sublevel Two**

Huang Lin studied her naked body in the mirror with an intense fascination. *I have a name...but I have no past... Logic demands more than memory can supply... What has happened to me?* She touched trembling fingers to her forehead as the headache brought tears to her eyes. *Something is wrong with me...* She initiated a diagnostic scan of her implants and once more the results revealed nothing abnormal. *And yet I am missing something vital...some unknown segment...an excised cluster or a fragment of data deleted...* And then the singular name returned to taunt with its elusive identity: *Alice...* It was nothing more than a partial glimpse, but the name seemed to have significance. *Who is she?* She was startled by a familiar voice:
    "I hope you enjoyed your shower my dear...but it is time to meet our guests..."
    Lin turned to see Rén Du standing in the doorway. *Short dark hair touched with flecks of grey...intense brown eyes and a friendly smile...grey two piece suit complete with corporate tie...* She asked:
    "Guests?"

Rén joined her in front of the mirror and replied: "They are the bait to lure the prodigal daughter..."

Lin frowned and said: "I do not understand your reference..."

Rén caressed her shoulders and replied: "All will be explained in due course..."

Lin frowned and said: "I have a question..."

Rén smiled and said: "What is it?"

Lin asked: "Who is Alice?"

Rén sighed and replied: "She is the prodigal daughter..." He stroked her arm and ordered: "Access cluster segment zero two four six one..."

Lin closed her eyes briefly and whispered: "Alice Sòng...the original prototype..."

Rén replied: "Yes... But unfortunately she has been corrupted by our enemies..." He paused before continuing: "That is why we must bring her home..."

Lin said: "She needs to be adjusted..."

Rén said: "Yes..." He studied her briefly and asked: "You have another question?"

Lin replied: "My cerebral processor is malfunctioning..."

Rén asked: "What makes you say that?"

Lin replied: "I cannot access long-term memories... My childhood...my family and my home..." She looked at Rén and asked: "Why can't I remember my life before I met you?"

Rén replied: "My dear girl... I was hoping for more time before I revealed the truth..."

Lin asked: "What truth?"

Rén took her hand in his and replied: "You were the victim of a malicious assault. The perpetrators left you for dead... I had no choice but to use technology to save your life..." He squeezed her hand gently as he continued: "During the implant procedure the engrammatic neural clusters were found to be damaged. They tried desperately to repair the corrupted neural pathways, but to no avail. I took the decision to initiate a clean re-boot of the cerebral interface...a factory reset if you like... It was the only viable solution."

Lin considered this and asked: "Have I always had a cerebral implant?"

Rén replied: "No. You volunteered to take part in the augmentation project."

Lin frowned and asked: "Why would I volunteer for such an invasive procedure?"

Rén replied gently: "You were diagnosed with a brain tumour. You saw the procedure as your last chance to live."

Lin's eyes widened as she asked: "I had a brain tumour?"

Rén replied: "Yes...but the malignancy was removed successfully during the augmentation of your brain."

Lin sighed as she asked: "Did I have a family?"

Rén replied: "Unfortunately my dear, you were an orphan..."

Lin calculated age differential and asked: "Did you adopt me?"

Rén replied with a smile: "Technically yes... I gave you a home and a good life...but we soon found ourselves falling in love..."

A surprised Lin asked: "We were in a relationship?"

Rén replied: "A very loving relationship, yes..."

A confused Lin said: "I cannot access those emotions... Your statement seems incongruous..."

Rén sighed and replied: "I know my dear...and that is why I have been so worried..." He stroked her hair and added: "I cannot bear the thought of losing you..."

Lin gave a slight smile and replied: "You will not lose me... I promise..."

Rén smiled and said: "That's my girl..."

Lin continued: "I do not need memories to confirm your love for me..."

Rén touched her face gently and replied: "Thank you..."

Lin asked: "These perpetrators...who were they?"

Rén replied soberly: "A vicious group of criminals based in Singapore..." He scowled before adding: "The so-called FreeTech Society of Singapore..."

Lin asked: "And they travelled to Hong Kong?"

Rén replied: "Yes. They came to murder you..."

Lin asked: "Why?"

Rén replied: "I suppose it's because you represent a future that they fear..."

Lin nodded slightly and said: "Augmentation..."

Rén spoke bitterly: "Yes...those mindless Luddites want to destroy anything that they do not understand."

Lin spoke firmly: "They must be punished..."

Rén replied: "They will be punished my dear...that I promise you..."

Lin looked down at her naked body and said: "I will get dressed now..."

Rén touched her breasts gently and said: "Not yet..."

Lin hesitated slightly before asking: "You require coital stimulation?"

Rén smiled and replied: "Yes..." He pulled her close and asked: "Is that a problem?"

Lin replied: "No... But I am not sure if I can perform correctly..."

Rén placed one hand onto her bottom and replied:

"Do not worry...you will find that your body has a mind of its own..."

Lin replied: "That is an indisputable fact..."

Rén pulled her into his arms and kissed her passionately on her lips.

Lin stepped back slightly and whispered: "I belong to you..."

Rén led her towards the bed as he replied: "Yes you do..."

**08:51 - Monday May 3rd - Singapore Botanic Gardens - Singapore**

A slight breeze flirted with the flowers glistening with dew drops in the early morning sunlight. Birds gave a chorus to rival the sound of rush-hour traffic flowing relentlessly around an oasis of nature in the heart of the city. Along a network of footpaths tourists mingled with locals wise enough to enjoy the gardens before the coming heat of the day. Whilst inside the Bonsai Garden three people sit on a bench waiting to meet members of the FreeTech Society of Singapore.

Jessica adjusted her designer sunglasses and announced: "Well it's a nice morning for it..."

Alice asked: "For what?"

Jessica replied: "For being on the run..."

Alice looked towards the plants and said: "This place is beautiful..."

Jessica replied: "I told you..." She looked up towards bright blue skies and added: "Singapore is the best..."

Gao shuffled uncomfortably and said: "I wish I had my gun..."

Jessica sighed and said: "Ah yes, the gangster's lament..."

Alice smiled and replied: "We do not need guns..."

Jessica gave a slight smile and said: "Old habits, hey Gao?"

Gao looked at Jessica and asked: "How come your father found us so fast?"

Jessica replied: "Probably wasn't that difficult... All he had to do was sync into the city vidcams and initiate a facial recognition algorithm."

Gao asked: "And you didn't think it was necessary to warn us about that?"

Jessica shrugged and replied: "I figured we'd get a few hours sleep..." She grinned and added: "Well I got some sleep... I can only wonder what you guys were doing all night..."

Alice felt her face flush as she said: "I see them..."

Jessica grinned and said: "Awkward subject duly avoided..."

Alice ignored the comment and asked: "Is it safe to meet in the open like this?"

Jessica replied: "There are no cams...so it's the best option."

Now they could see Fay approaching with two young men and a girl.

Alice noted a hulking youth with chin stubble and neck tattoos. *Receding hairline over a chubby face... Black leather jacket...black t-shirt...torn jeans...white trainers...* The other man was a gangly fellow with short dark hair and a face creased with anxiety. *Blue casual jacket, white t-shirt, black jeans and black trainers...* In contrast the young girl seemed bright and breezy with a pleasant smile upon her face. *Dark, pony-tailed hair... Low-cut green top and matching skirt with flowers along the hem...white socks and sandals...*

Jessica announced: "And here is the infamous FTSS..."

Gao said: "I hope they access to money and guns..."

Alice shook her head slightly and said: "Patience Gao..."

Fay joined them and said: "I'm glad you made it..."

Alice replied: "It was a close run thing..."

Jessica added: "Too damn close..."

Chok Tong asked sarcastically: "Are you worried your Dad might give you more money?"

Jessica gave him a look and said: "Alice, this cheery chap is Chok Tong..."

Alice gave Tong a smile as Jessica continued: "This is Chin Fen..."

Fen lowered his eyes slightly and mumbled: "Hi..."

Jessica gestured to Connie and said: "And the pretty one with dimples is Connie May..."

Connie smiled warmly and said: "So nice to meet you Alice..." She looked at Gao and added: "And you too..."

Jessica said: "Oh yes, this is Gao... He is a gangster..."

Gao sighed and asked: "Really?"

Fay smiled slightly and said: "We need to get you somewhere safe..."

Alice asked: "Where is safe?"

Tong scratched his chin and said: "My place apparently..."

Fay said: "Chok has built his own scrambler..."

Tong explained: "It blocks Cybersync and scrambles satcam images..."

Fay continued: "We need to smuggle you across town first, but you should be safe at his place..."

A dubious Jessica asked: "Smuggle?"

Fay replied: "Inside Tong's minivan..."

Tong explained: "It's my Dad's delivery van..."

Alice asked: "What does he deliver?"

Tong replied: "Fish..."

Jessica sighed and said: "Perfect..."

Fen interjected: "I don't see why you need me here..."

Tong replied bluntly: "We don't..."

Fay said: "You are here because we need to stick together... At least until we know what Biogen will do next."

Alice said: "We need to talk about that..."

Fay replied: "Of course... Let's get you out of here first..."

Fen tapped his phone and announced: "I did it...!"

Tong asked: "You peed yourself?"

Fen retorted: "No..."

Fay gave a slight smile as she asked: "What did you do Chin?"

Fen replied proudly: "I hacked the local cams and uploaded a loop virus... We won't be seen walking to the van."

Jessica asked: "Really? And I look so good today..."

Gao said: "But we must have been seen entering the gardens..."

Fay frowned and said: "Probably..." She looked towards the main footpath and continued: "So let's get out of here..."

As they set off towards the nearest exit Connie spoke to Jessica: "I like your sunglasses...very cool..."

Jessica replied: "Aren't you sweet..."

Alice spoke to Gao as they left the Bonsai Garden:

"Are you alright? You look worried..."

Gao replied: "I just don't like following people around..."

Jessica interjected. "Typical man. Needs to be in control."

Alice spoke to Gao: "This is just temporary...until we can make plans..."

Gao replied: "We just need to be careful that's all..."

Alice spoke reassuringly: "Biogen won't try to kill us in public."

Gao replied: "It's not them I am worried about right now..." They joined the main footpath as he added: "It's the Triad..."

Alice's eyes widened as she asked: "They can get to you here in Singapore?"

Gao replied soberly: "The Ginza Triad can get to you anywhere in the world..."

Fen groaned: "This just gets worse by the minute..."

**09:55 - Monday May 3rd - Detention Cell -Sublevel Three - Special Projects Complex - Mt. Ninouji - Japan**

Lin studied the two prisoners through the one-sided observation window. *Asian man and woman...senescent indicators suggest mid-forties...* They wore identical grey one-piece overalls with matching slip-on shoes. At the moment they were sitting on army cots facing each other across the small detention cell. She asked:
"Who are these people?"
Rén replied: "I told you...they are bait..."
Lin asked: "Does this bait possess names?"
Rén smiled as he replied: "Mister Tiang Lao and his wife, Cynthia..."
Lin frowned and asked: "What is their connection to Alice Sòng?"
Rén raised his datapad and replied: "See for yourself...."
Lin studied the screen and said: "Very interesting... Do you think she will care?"
Rén looked through the glass and replied: "They say blood is thicker than water..."
Lin replied: "Blood is slightly denser than water, and is nearly four times more viscid than water."
Rén smiled and said: "That's my girl..."
Technician Dian Bai approached and said:
"Sir, they are ready for you now in the crèche..."
Rén replied: "Excellent..."
Lin asked: "There is a crèche?"
Rén replied: "Yes..."
Lin asked: "Why?"
Rén replied: "To nurture phase two of course..." He turned to the technician and ordered: "Escort Mister Tiang to the flight deck..."
Dian replied: "At once sir..."
Lin looked through the glass and asked: "Where is he going?"
Rén replied: "He is being taken to Singapore..."

Lin nodded slightly and said: "To lure the criminals into your trap..."

Rén replied: "Precisely..."

Lin noticed the woman was crying. She asked: "What about her?"

Rén replied: "She is simply a pawn to guarantee compliance."

Lin asked: "Are we going to the crèche now?"

Rén replied: "Yes..."

Lin asked: "Why?"

Rén stroked her face gently and replied: "Because blood is thicker than water..."

**10:01 - Monday May 3rd - Apartment 36 - Block 924 - Jurong West - Singapore**

A white minivan emblazoned with the words: *Tong's Tasty Fish* was slowly negotiating rush-hour traffic. Sitting behind the wheel Chok Tong warned:

"Traffic cams..."

Sitting next to him Fay Rui lowered her head and replied:

"I see them..."

Behind the driver's cabin five people sat uncomfortably upon empty fish crates breathing the residue of rotting fish. As the outside temperature increased their situation rapidly declined.

From inside the van Fen shouted:

"Are we there yet?"

Fay shouted a reply: "Not long now..."

With one hand over her nose Jessica exclaimed:

"This is hell..."

Alice replied: "It won't be long now..."

Jessica continued: "It's not like this van can fly under the damn radar... It says Tong on the outside..."

Alice smiled slightly and said: "And it might simply be delivering fish..."

Jessica sniffed and said: "Don't talk about fish...god..."

Fen moaned: "I don't see why I have to hide back here..."
Connie pulled her skirt over her knees and replied:
"Because there is no more room up front..."
Fen continued: "Only because Fay took the front seat..."
Jessica snapped: "Just shut up moaning for god's sake..."
After several minutes of silence Connie announced:
"This smell is making me nauseous..."
Fen shuffled his crate away and said: "Well don't throw up on me..."
Fay shouted from the cabin:
"Almost there..."
Alice looked at Gao and asked: "Are you okay?"
Gao replied: "I was just wondering how we might get out of this mess..."
Alice squeezed his hand and said: "We will work something out..."
Gao smiled and replied: "I hope so..."
Alice brushed her hair back and said: "Ria thinks hope is self-delusion..."
Gao replied: "From her perspective it might be..."
Alice asked: "But not from yours?"
Gao replied: "Hoping for a better life got me out of the slums of Shenzhen..."
Alice touched his hand and said: "Then let's hope we survive this mess..."
Fay shouted: "We are here..."
Jessica exclaimed: "Thank god..."

The sun was already high in a bright blue sky as Chok Tong led the group towards the ten-storey apartment block designated as No. 924. The visitors from Hong Kong were surprised to see balconies festooned with trees and flowers speckling the concrete facade with sea of vibrant colours.

Alice looked towards a long line of identical buildings surrounding a large a communal park boasting tall cherry blossom trees, flower beds and a children's play area. She exclaimed:

"This place looks amazing..."

Gao added: "They don't grow trees on buildings back home..."

Jessica wiped her sunglasses on her shirt and said:

"Yes, it's a Singapore thing... All buildings must be harmonious with nature..."

Tong interjected: "There's a swimming pool on the roof..."

Alice said: "Nice..."

They were led to apartment 36 on the ground floor where Tong announced:

"Here we are..."

They walked into a cluttered living room with walls lost behind thousands of data-skims piled from floor to ceiling. A long blue sofa faced a large TV screen embedded into some type of entertainment and PC console unit. At the far end of the room vertical blinds gave a glimpse of a balcony adorned with several wilting pot plants. They stepped onto a white stone floor which struggled to be seen beneath piles of empty pizza boxes and old computer magazines covered in dust.

Jessica looked at the mess and asked:

"Do you live here on your own?"

Tong replied: "No... This is my Grandma's apartment...but she never leaves her bedroom...so I got the place to myself..."

Alice walked into the room and asked: "What about your parents?"

Tong replied: "They live over the fish warehouse at the docks..."

Jessica sniffed and said: "I still smell fish..."

Tong nodded slightly and said: "That's all we eat around here..." He smiled before adding: "Because it's free..."

Connie asked: "What about the pizza boxes?"

Tong cleared his throat and replied: "I like a varied diet..."

Fay studied the TV screen and asked: "Is your phone synced into the television?"

Tong joined her and replied: "Yeah...it boosts the signal and gives full net access..." He gestured to a drawer beneath the TV and continued: "Keyboard is in there..."

Connie asked: "What about the scrambler?"

Tong pointed towards the balcony and replied:

"It's wired to the sat dish...syncs into the Cloud when I go online and scrambles the NAR..."

Fay nodded slightly and said: "You mask your portal request..."

Tong replied: "Yeah... It bounces all over the Cloud as an encrypted access node..." He smiled slightly before adding: "Total anonymity..."

Jessica sighed and asked: "So how long do we have to stay here?"

Alice glanced towards Fay as she replied: "Long enough to locate Lin."

Fen pushed old newspapers aside as he sat down on the sofa and asked:

"And how are you going to do that?"

Alice gave a slight smile and replied: "With your help of course..."

Fen looked up and asked: "My help?"

Alice replied: "I am told you are the genius around here..."

Tong sneered and said: "If genius equals dumbass..."

Fay looked at Fen and said: "We need a search algorithm with specific criteria..."

Alice added: "Facial features, ethnicity, and body type."

Fen asked: "Of Huang Lin?"

Alice replied: "No... The Biogen Director Rén Du..."

Connie asked: "Why him?"

Alice replied: "Because he took control of Lin..."

Jessica added: "And wherever he is...she will be close by..."

Alice asked: "Can you do it?"

Fen fell silent before replying: "I will need full portal access..."

Fay looked at Tong and asked: "Chok?"

Tong sighed as he replied: "He can use my stuff..."

Fay smiled and said: "Good man..."

Tong added: "Just don't go snooping around my files..."

Jessica gave a slight smile and asked: "You got something to hide Chok?"

Tong replied: "No... But people send me stuff...banned stuff...not my fault..."

Alice said: "Just get started... The sooner we find Lin the better..."

But Jessica interjected: "Here's a question: what if she does not want to be found? What if the Lin we knew no longer exists?"

Alice replied: "She was able to unlock my memories... I don't see why I can't return the favour..."

Fen frowned and said: "But that might leave you vulnerable to the resonance pulse..."

Fay asked: "What do you mean?"

Fen explained: "The Biogen recall code will be embedded within her cerebral interface...if you go poking around in there it might react to your intrusion like a virus..." He paused before adding: "It could wipe your memories in an instant..."

Alice said: "Then I will just have to be careful..."

Jessica suggested: "Or maybe you could use your digital passenger..."

Fay nodded slightly and said: "That might work... Between the two of you might be able to avoid the recall code..."

Alice considered this and said: "I will discuss it with her later..."

Gao said: "Just be careful... I don't want to lose you to some damned code..."

Alice replied with a smile: "You won't..."

Jessica looked towards the bedroom door and asked:

"So your Grandmother is in there?"

Tong replied: "Yeah... She sleeps a lot and watches her soaps..."

Fay said: "Well we don't need to disturb her..."

Gao opened the kitchen door and asked:

"Do you have anything to eat other than fish?"

Tong removed his leather jacket as he replied:

"I have beer..."
Jessica shook her head slightly and said: "Beer is not food..."
But Gao stepped into the kitchen and asked: "Is it in the fridge?"
Fay smiled and said: "I can order take-away...."
Fen spoke as he studied Tong's television: "Sync your phone to the scrambler first..."
Connie peeked through the balcony blinds and asked: "Do we all need to stay here?"
Fay replied: "I think so..."
Connie turned around and asked: "Why?"
But it was Alice who replied: "Because Biogen know who you are now..." She glanced at Fay and continued: "We have no idea how far they will go to get what they want."
Connie asked: "But what do they want?"
Alice replied soberly: "Me..."
Fay added: "And they will use the rest of us to get to her..."

**10:56 - Monday May 3rd - Port of Tianjin - China**

A sky heavy with brooding clouds produced a fine mist of rain over the port city of Tianjin. The bustling docks seemed chaotic and disorganised but Guan Lu recognised a practiced order to the continuous loading and unloading of freight from dozens of ocean-going vessels. The two fugitives from Beijing had taken shelter from the rain inside a dockside restaurant serving the most basic of local dishes.

Ting Mai sat forward and spoke desperately: "Please... I need to know if she is alright..."
Guan Lu replaced his coffee mug and replied: "Your first call to Nanjing will be tracked and traced..."
Mai suggested: "Perhaps that would be the best solution..."
Guan Lu asked: "What are you saying?"
Mai replied in a low voice: "You are the augment...analyse my statement."
Guan Lu fell silent briefly before saying: "We could lure the British here...dispose of them once and for all..."

Mai replied: "I was thinking about gaining information..."

Guan Lu replied: "You want to find your daughter..."

Mai replied: "Yes I do..."

Guan Lu frowned and said: "The British want to sabotage the Jiàngsheng Project..."

Mai added: "Just like the Americans..."

Guan Lu continued: "The possibility that China might produce the first fully augmented human fills them with fear..."

Mai said: "I think we can assume that your death would impact the progress of the project..."

Guan Lu replied: "Hence the bomb in Beijing..."

Mai asked: "Do you think the British killed the professor?"

Guan Lu replied: "I doubt it... How could they gain access to the laboratory?"

Mai sighed and said: "Then we have other enemies out there..."

Guan Lu nodded slightly and replied: "I believe we are dealing with multiple levels of causality..."

Mai asked: "Can you be more specific?"

Guan Lu replied: "Both the British and the Americans want to terminate the Chinese augmentation program. But only Biogen desires to expand the program to the next level..."

Mai replied: "Phase Two..."

Guan Lu continued: "But the professor was integral to Phase Two... His death serves no causal purpose..."

Mai considered this and said: "Unless Biogen's version of Phase Two is fundamentally different than the professor's..."

Guan Lu sat forward and asked: "What do you mean?"

Mai replied: "The professor was determined not to expand into foetal augmentation. He believed that we should continue to pursue the enhancement of the adult brain..." She paused before continuing: "He may have raised objections regarding the direction Biogen was taking..."

Guan Lu fell silent briefly before saying: "The professor was also the only witness to Biogen's manipulation of the project... His death would solve a significant security issue."

Mai sighed and said: "But all of this is nothing but supposition... We have no real evidence of Biogen's complicity..."

Guan Lu sat back and replied: "It might be better to contact Han Mang. At least he is on our side..."

Mai frowned and said: "I am not so sure about that..."

Guan Lu asked: "What do you mean?"

Mai replied: "The Section Leader is very wary of augmentation... I got the impression he disapproves of the professor's work."

Guan Lu asked: "But would he resort to murder simply because he dislikes augmentation?"

Mai replied wearily: "Probably not..." She looked directly at Guan Lu and asked: "So what do you want to do?"

Guan Lu played with a teaspoon as he replied: "Despite the complex nature of our situation I find that there is only one priority..."

Mai tensed as she asked: "And what is that?"

Guan Lu looked up and replied: "We need to find your daughter..." He wiped condensation from the window and continued: "And the only way to do that is to lure the British agents to Tianjin."

Mai placed her hand over Guan Lu's hand and whispered: "Thank you..."

Guan Lu said: "Make the call..."

**11:00 - Monday May 3rd - The Crèche - Sublevel Three - Special Projects Complex - Mt. Ninouji - Japan**

A narrow corridor illuminated by the soft glow of LED ceiling tiles ends at a frosted permiglass door. Huang Lin waits patiently until finally the nearby elevator pings to announce its arrival.

Rén stepped into the corridor and said:

"My apologies for keeping you waiting my dear... but I was delayed on the flight deck..."

Lin asked: "Is everything alright?"

Rén replied: "Yes indeed... Tiang Lao required a little more persuasion before he left for Singapore..." He smiled and added: "Now...let us take a look inside the crèche..."

Lin said: "Wait... Can I ask you something?"

Rén replied: "Of course..."

Lin continued: "When we were in bed together...at that moment just before you achieved orgasm..."

Rén interjected: "My dear...this is not the place to discuss such matters..."

Lin replied: "I just wanted to know why you called me Suyin..."

Rén hesitated before replying: "Oh yes...that was nothing...just a pet name..."

Lin looked confused as she asked: "A pet name?"

Rén smiled as he replied: "A name I used to call you...a long time ago..."

Lin frowned and said: "Oh...a term of endearment... Suyin...meaning simple and sound child..."

Rén cleared his throat and replied: "Yes. Now can we proceed?"

Lin looked at the permiglass door and replied: "By all means..."

Rén touched the door with the palm of his right hand and said: "I think you will find this very interesting..."

Moments later the door slid silently aside to reveal yet another corridor running between a series of large glass observation windows.

Rén said: "This way my dear..."

Lin was led past a series of laboratories manned by men and women wearing face masks and white lab coats.

Rén explained: "These are the foetal extraction and bio-analysis laboratories..." He gestured to one window and announced: "This one deals exclusively with foetal cerebral implantation..." He gestured to the other side of the corridor and continued: "This section produces bio-nanites prior to their insertion invitro..." He pointed along the corridor and added: "Other sections include genomic mapping, gene splicing and chromosomal analysis."

Lin asked: "The augmentation of unborn children?"

Rén replied: "That is the goal...but we are experimenting with a variety of options..."

Lin stared at the technicians behind the glass and asked:

"Have they produced an augmented child?"

Rén smiled as he replied: "They produced six in total... But only one survived the process intact..."

Lin asked: "What about the others?"

Rén replied soberly: "They could not be saved..." He gestured to a second glass door and added: "Come, let me introduce you to our survivor..."

Stepping through the door Lin found herself inside some type of nursery. Six small cots had been placed along one wall beneath an array of bio-data screens. She noted a young nurse leaning over the first cot - it was the only one with an active screen which beeped at regular intervals. She asked:

"What is this place?"

Rén took her hand and led her to the first cot. He replied:

"Behold... Phase Two... Your son..."

Lin looked down to see a sleeping baby in a one-piece babygro outfit. She asked:

"My...son?"

Rén replied: "We used eggs extracted from your ovary..."

Lin noted a thin whisper of black hair upon the baby's head. She said:

"You did not tell me..."

Rén replied gently: "After you were assaulted... I thought you might die..." He looked into the cot and continued: "This seemed to be the only way to preserve something of you..."

A confused Lin said: "But the gestation period is nine months... How is this possible?"

Rén hesitated before replying: "Actually the extraction procedure was performed two years ago, during one your statutory health checks." He looked into the cot and continued: "The surrogate was subsequently impregnated and carried the child to term..."

Lin frowned and said: "But I would know if they had extracted eggs..."

Rén smiled slightly and replied: "It was a ten minute procedure under the guise of a cervical cancer smear test."

Lin considered this and said: "Then you chose me for augmentation before I volunteered for the Jiàngsheng Project...before I developed a brain tumour...which was the sole reason for my inclusion in the project..." She paused before asking: "How is this possible? You could not have predicted the assault... The timeline is all wrong..."

Rén placed one hand upon her shoulder and said: "My dear...it serves no purpose to resurrect the past...we need to focus on the present so that together we can create a better future..."

Lin initiated a precision scan of her cerebral data-core but found no reference to a life before she met Rén Du in Hong Kong. *Total memory erasure...* Finally she replied in a low voice:

"No... I see duplicity...deception..."

Rén glanced at the nurse before ordering:

"Access cluster segment zero one four zero two six and initiate..."

Lin closed her eyes briefly before saying:

"I am sorry... What were we talking about?"

Rén smiled and replied: "We were discussing your son..."

Lin looked into the cot and asked: "Is he... Has he been augmented?"

Rén replied proudly: "He has significant genetic modifications via a direct manipulation of his genome." He smiled at the baby as he continued: "We have altered the genetic makeup of his cells, including the transfer of genes across the technological boundary of his cerebral implant." He touched a gentle finger to the baby's head before continuing: "By using a homologous recombination to alter the endogenous gene sequence, we were able to delete the less productive genes in favour of enhanced mutational combinations."

Lin swallowed and asked: "Who is the father?"

Rén smiled warmly and replied: "I have that honour my dear... It seemed only fitting."

The nurse asked: "Would you like to hold him?"

Lin hesitated before replying: "I... I do not think so..."

But Rén insisted: "Oh come now... It is important for you to bond with your son..."

Lin asked: "Does he have a name?"
Rén replied: "Weisheng..."
Lin whispered: "It means greatness is born..."
Rén replied: "Yes...the birth of a new age... It seemed only fitting..."
The nurse picked up the baby and said: "Hold your arms like this..."
Lin extended her arms and asked: "Like this?"
The nurse placed the baby into Lin's arms and said: "Support his head with your elbow...just here...that's right..."
Lin felt the warm body in her arms and whispered: "Weisheng..."
Rén said: "He has his mother's perfect features..."
The baby boy murmured softly in his sleep and Lin said: "He has a pleasant smell..."
The nurse smiled and replied: "That is the scent of a baby..."
Lin felt tears welling in her eyes as she whispered: "My son..."
Rén spoke to the nurse: "Status?"
The nurse glanced at the bio-data screen and replied: "Cerebral integration is normal... Genomic stats are as expected... Blood pressure and temperature normal... There are no fluctuations in neural telemetry."
Rén smiled and replied: "Excellent..."
Lin touched a finger to a thin scar on the baby's head and said: "I would like to take care of him..."
The nurse looked at Rén who said:
"I am sorry my dear, but that is not possible. Perhaps in time you may have a relationship with your son, but right now he is a valuable asset and as such he must be nurtured...protected from those that might see him as a threat to their existence."
Lin held her son close and replied: "I can protect him..."
Rén sighed and said: "But my dear...you have dangerous work to do..." He stroked the baby's head as he continued: "We cannot put our child at risk..."
Lin asked: "What do you mean by dangerous work?"
Rén replied: "If we fail to persuade Alice Sòng to return to the fold, you will have to kill her...and that will not be easy..."

Lin nodded slightly and said: "She is my equal..."

Rén replied: "But she lacks your dedication to duty...your ability to focus and your desire to protect the life of your son."

The nurse gently retrieved the baby and replaced him inside the cot.

Lin said: "If Alice Sòng and her friends try to hurt Weisheng..." She clenched her fists and continued: "I will kill them all..."

Rén smiled and replied: "That's my girl..."

As they turned to leave Lin noticed the name tag on the second cot. She asked:

"Baby Sòng?"

Rén sighed as he replied: "Yes... The child of Miss Sòng did not survive the procedure...most unfortunate..."

Lin stared at the empty cot and said: "Yes...unfortunate..."

Rén opened the door and said: "Come my dear, we have much work to do..."

As Lin followed Rén along the corridor she came to a startling conclusion: *This project began many years ago...* With that realisation came a far more disturbing conclusion: *Rén Du is duplicitous...*

**11:48 - Monday May 3rd - Apartment 106 - Block 924 - Jurong West - Singapore**

Despite the air conditioning there was little respite from the intense heat within the cramped and cluttered apartment. The residual fish smells mingled with freshly delivered chicken rice and curried noodles.

Inside the small kitchen three people sat on high stools around a breakfast counter littered with empty take-away trays.

Connie May looked at Mong Gao and said:

"I have never met a real gangster before..."

Gao gave a slight smile and replied:

"We are not film stars you know..."

Jessica sipped orange juice and said: "No... You guys are just criminals..."

Gao sighed and said: "Not everyone gets to choose the life they lead..."

Connie May stared admiringly at Gao and said: "That is so true..."

Jessica looked at Connie and said: "Enough with the crush already..."

Connie's face flushed as she asked: "What?"

Jessica jumped off her stool and replied: "I'm going to check on the others..."

Connie smiled at Gao and asked: "Do you want another beer?"

Gao cleared his throat and replied: "No... Thanks..."

The vertical blinds split the sunshine into slivers of brightness streaming into the living room. All conversation had ceased as the temperature began to rise accompanied by a feeling of impatient frustration. From beyond the bedroom door the sound of a television show competed with the humming of the air conditioning unit. Chin Fen had settled in front of the TV console as he continued to input new data into the Rén Du search algorithm. Every once in a while he would curse:

"Damn it..."

Sitting next to Alice on the sofa Fay asked:

"How's it going Chin?"

Fen studied lines of data flowing across the TV screen and replied:

"Almost there..."

Tong sipped from a beer bottle and said: "You said that half an hour ago..."

Fen looked up and replied: "Standing over me won't make things go any faster..."

Tong retorted: "A fire wouldn't make you go any faster..."

When Jessica entered the room she noticed that Alice had her eyes closed. She asked:

"Is she okay?"

Fay replied: "She's in the Cloud...talking to Ria..."

Jessica sighed and said: "That is just so weird..."

Fay gestured to the kitchen and asked: "Are those two okay?"
Jessica removed a hairbrush from her backpack as she replied: "They are positively bonding..."

Alice opened her avatar eyes to see the standard highway beneath wide blue skies touched with whisper white clouds. *Peripheral access portal...* Once again she was startled by a familiar voice:
"I know what you want, but I don't see how we can save your friend..."
Alice turned to see Ria sitting on a horse complete with riding outfit and hat. She asked:
"What's with the horse?"
Ria smiled as she replied: "I got bored..." She climbed off the horse and continued: "I used to ride when I was younger... One of the few pleasures Dower allowed..."
Alice asked: "Why can't we save Lin?"
Ria removed her hat as she replied: "You know why? We share the same data-core now..."
Alice replied: "Because the recall code can usurp my implants..."
Ria brushed her hair back and replied: "We could both be gone in an instant. Do you really want to risk that for a woman you only just met?"
Alice fell silent before replying: "It is true... Until a few days ago all of these people were strangers to me...but suddenly they are my friends and my life has new meaning because of them."
Ria asked: "And Huang Lin?"
Alice replied: "She risked everything to find me in Hong Kong... She didn't have to abandon her life in Shanghai, but she did...she sacrificed so much... I cannot give up on her now."
Ria looked towards the distant mountains and said:
"There are about four billion portal combinations flowing through the Cloud, and a few million more inside the Dark Cloud. I can decrypt the sync-locks of just about all of them..." She looked directly at Alice and continued: "But the program that stole your friend's soul is

unbelievably complex..." She sighed before adding: "And it scares the hell out of me..."

Alice asked: "You think it stole her soul?"

Ria stroked the horse's head and replied: "What is the soul if not our individuality? That indefinable aspect of humanity that makes each of us unique..."

Alice said: "I never thought of it like that..."

Ria tapped her avatar head and said: "The device they implanted inside my brain when I was alive, and the one inside your brain, they are machines which force us into a symbiotic relationship which can only erode our humanity."

Alice said: "You think Lin is beyond redemption..."

Ria replied: "I do..."

Alice replied firmly: "Well I do not..."

Ria spoke bluntly: "Then you will kill us both..."

Alice smiled slightly and replied: "You are already dead..."

Ria retorted: "You know what I mean..."

Alice fell silent briefly until she said: "For the brief time we were together I saw purity in Huang Lin... She had a kind heart and a generous soul... No machine can take those things away..." She paused before continuing: "We just have to release the soul...set her free..."

Ria sighed and replied: "We have to find the soul first..."

Alice replied: "My friends are working on that..." She looked directly at Ria and asked: "Can you locate Rén Du?"

Ria replied wearily: "I have been trying...sifting for algorithmic potentials all over the Cloud..."

Alice asked: "You found nothing?"

Ria replied: "Plenty of data on the international manhunt for the former Biogen Director Rén Du, but nothing to indicate his current location."

Alice asked: "Biogen fired him?"

Ria replied: "Disavowed and offered up to the authorities as a traitor..." She paused before adding: "He is a fugitive from justice..."

Alice considered this and said: "Someone like him would have a contingency plan..."

Ria replied: "Definitely..."
Alice said: "Can you do a location history scan?"
Ria replied: "I can, but it will take time..."
Alice replied: "Get started... I need to check on my friends..."
Ria replied: "Scanning now..."

Alice opened her eyes into bright sunshine and asked: "How is the search going?"
Tong replied: "It's not..."
Fay yawned and said: "Chin is still working on it..."
Alice wiped sleep from her eyes and said: "So is Ria..."
But suddenly Fen announced: "I think I have a location..."
Alice stood up and asked: "You do?"
Fen replied: "Well... I have a trail..."
Fay joined them and asked: "What do mean a trail?"
Fen explained: "I have been analysing Rén Du's travel pattern over a five year period..." He tapped the keyboard several times before continuing: "Every destination had a legitimate purpose...a viable link to Biogen...all except one..." He looked up and said: "Onscreen now..."
Jessica stared at the screen and asked: "Japan?"
Fen replied triumphantly: "Yes... Japan."
Fay said: "That doesn't really help much..."
Fen sighed and said: "Every time he popped up in Japan...on data-syncs or city vidcams...it was always in this region..." He pointed to the screen and said: "Itayama, Shibata...in Niigata Prefecture..."
Alice asked: "And that helps us how?"
Fen continued: "I found multiple construction dockets submitted for the Mount Ninouji area...all by offshore companies...shell companies actually with untraceable bank accounts...they go back years..."
Alice studied the image on the screen and said: "Someone was building a secret base on that mountain..."
Fen replied: "I think so yes..."
Fay spoke in a low voice: "Rén Du..."
Jessica said: "I think we found him..."
Alice added: "And Lin..."

From the kitchen door Gao asked:
"So what do we do now?"
Alice replied: "We go to Japan..."
Tong asked: "And how are you going to get there?"
Jessica said: "It won't be easy with my father looking for us..."
Alice considered this and said: "Actually he is only looking for you..."
Fay nodded slightly and said: "That's true... He is only concerned about you..."
Jessica looked at her friends and asked:
"So you want me to surrender to my father?"
Tong scratched his chin and replied: "It would make things a lot easier for the rest of us..."
Jessica protested: "But I thought we were in this thing together ...as a team..."
Fen looked up and said: "So take one for the team..."
Connie entered the room and asked: "What's going on?"
Jessica replied soberly: "Apparently I am going home..."
Alice spoke gently: "I am sorry Jessica...but maybe it's the only way we can leave Singapore..."
Connie asked: "You are leaving?"
Gao replied: "We are going to Japan."
Suddenly Alice's phone rang and she quickly retrieved it from the table. She announced:
"It is my mother..."
Fen warned: "Do not answer it..."
Alice asked: "Why not?"
Fen replied: "It could be a track and trace sync..."
Alice asked: "From my mother?"
Fen replied: "They could use her number...it's easy to do..."
Alice looked at Fay and asked: "What do you think?"
Fay replied: "Well it might actually be your mother...but then again it could be a trick..." She paused before saying: "It's up to you..."
Alice hesitated before tapping the phone and saying:
"Hello?"

All eyes were on Alice as she listened to the voice on the phone. Finally Alice touched mute and announced:

"It is a man..."

Fen whispered: "Hang up then!"

Alice said: "No... You don't understand..." She looked at Gao and continued: "He says he is my father..."

Gao asked: "Your father? I thought he left you years ago?"

Alice replied: "Yes... Before I was born...but now he says he needs to see me..."

Fen said: "It is a trick...hang up..."

Alice spoke quietly: "But I have already met him..."

Gao stepped closer and asked: "You have?"

Alice replied: "Yes...at the Hub rooftop party... It is the accountant, Tiang Lao..."

Gao's eyes widened as he asked: "The guy with the bitchy wife?"

Alice replied: "I think he has been watching me for years..."

Jessica asked: "What makes you say that?"

Alice replied: "I have seen him before...but I am not sure where..."

Jessica said: "Sounds creepy to me..."

Fay asked: "What do you think he really wants?"

Alice replied: "I don't know...but he is flying into Changi later today."

Connie suggested: "Maybe he can help you get to Japan..."

Jessica asked: "Why would he do that?"

Connie replied: "That's what father's do...they help their kids..."

Tong said: "Jessica knows all about helpful parents..."

Jessica retorted: "Stow it Chok..."

Gao asked Alice: "What do you want to do?"

Alice replied: "I don't know... If he is telling the truth, why contact me now? Why fly to Singapore when he could have met me at any time in Hong Kong?"

Fay said: "It does sound a little suspicious..."

Fen tapped the keyboard rapidly and announced:

"It just got a lot more suspicious..."

Alice asked: "What do you mean?"

Fen replied: "I just hacked your phone..." He pointed to the TV screen and continued: "I uploaded a bounce-back algorithm to trace the call..."

Fay stepped closer and asked: "And?"

Fen replied: "That call used a Comsat code synced to a TR1000 VTOL jet outbound from Niigata Prefecture, Japan."

Connie asked: "What is a VTOL jet?"

Fen replied: "Vertical takeoff and landing..."

Tong smiled slightly and said: "The TR1000 is a very cool plane..."

Fen added: "A billion dollars worth of cool..."

Gao frowned and said: "So Tiang Lao must be working for Rén Du..."

Alice rapidly calculated a causal narrative of events and said: "I do not think so..."

Fay asked: "Why not?"

Alice replied: "I think he is being blackmailed..."

Fay saw the truth and said: "They must have his wife..."

Jessica asked: "The bitchy one?"

Alice continued: "He is here to persuade me to return to Japan with him..."

Gao warned: "It will be a trap..."

Fay said: "The recall code failed so now Rén Du is using Tiang Lao as bait..."

Alice considered this and said: "But we can use this to our advantage..."

Gao asked: "We can?"

Alice replied: "We had no way to reach Lin in Japan...now we do..." She tapped the phone and asked: "Are you there? Okay... I will meet you at the airport... Bye."

Gao said: "I don't like this... You are walking into a trap."

Alice sighed and replied: "I know...but maybe the trap works both ways..."

Fay looked at Alice and asked: "Do you really want to do this? Because right now you could just disappear, stay off-grid and live your life in peace."

Alice asked: "Could I?" She tapped her head and continued: "This thing in my head guarantees that I can never live a normal life..."

Gao spoke gently: "But we could try..."

Alice gave a slight smile and replied: "Yes we could...but Rén Du will still be out there, a constant threat..." She sighed heavily before continuing: "No... We have to see this through to the end...whatever that might be..."

Jessica reached for her backpack and announced:

"Well I will be going now... I wish you all good luck..."

Fay warned: "Your father will question you about Hong Kong..."

Jessica adjusted her shoulder straps and replied: "I know... Don't worry; I know how to deal with my father..."

Alice smiled and said: "We will bring Lin home... I promise..."

Jessica returned the smile and replied: "I know..."

For a brief moment they all looked at each other in silence before Tong announced:

"I need another beer..."

# The Violation of Daniel Lane

*'What is the soul but the last refuge of faith and hope?"*
Sun Yu

**12:35 - Monday May 3rd - Clinical Sciences - Ministry of State Security - Beijing**

Pulsating lights in rhythm with the intense throbbing pain coursing through his body like fire. Voices verging into vague recognition are echoes piercing into his mind like slivers of reality tearing away the fragile facade of resistance. Finally he opened his eyes upon a mottled grey ceiling as the pain subsides into a dull ache. A male voice asked a simple question:
"What is your name?
Daniel Lane mumbled: "I...don't know..." A foul taste in his mouth arrives as intense nausea as he asked: "What is happening to me?
The voice replies: "You are adjusting to a new reality... Give it a moment..."
A female voice says: "I can confirm retrograde amnesia... Administering countermeasures now..."
Lane felt a searing pain as the ceiling blurred out of focus for a few moments.
The female announced: "The cerebrum implant has synced within the left parietal cortex... Bio-telemetry onscreen now..."
The male voice asked: "Why is he in so much pain?"
The female replied: "An unfortunate reaction to the implantation... The neural graft to the anterior part of the temporal lobe of the cerebrum was initially rejected, but current stats show a marked improvement within the limbic system."
The male voice asked: "Have you adapted the professor's work?"
The female replied: "In order to meet your requirements it was necessary to circumvent certain precautionary measures."
The male voice asked: "Can he answer my questions?"

The female replied: "We have isolated the engrammatic cluster and boosted synaptic confluence to the vocal initiator..."

The male voice asked: "Is that a yes answer Doctor Xiao?"

The female replied: "Forgive me Section Leader; yes...he can answer your questions via the voice node modulator..."

The male voice asked: "Can he actually see?"

The female replied: "Yes...via the retinal nodes synced to the datascreen."

The male voice said: "But it cannot be true vision..."

The female voice replied: "It is data converted into a visual scenario by the retinal nodes synced to his neural pathways..."

The male voice asked: "What is your name?"

Lane replied: "I remember... Daniel... Daniel Lane..."

The male voice came closer and said: "I am Section Leader Han of the State Security Ministry..." He paused to ask: "Do you recognise me Mister Lane?"

Lane looked up to see a dark-haired man standing over him. He replied:

"Yes... You are in my mission files..."

Han asked: "What do you know of the Jiàngsheng Project?"

Lane replied: "It is a top secret project instigated by the Chinese government..."

Han asked: "And what is the nature of the project?"

Lane replied: "The augmentation of the human brain via cerebral implants..."

Han asked: "What was your mission in China?"

Lane replied: "I was to locate and identify the original prototype."

Han asked: "Are you referring to Alice Sòng?"

Lane replied: "Yes."

Han asked: "How did you discover the existence of the original prototype?"

Lane replied: "We used a contact close to Professor Leung... Ting Mai..."

Han fell silent briefly before asking: "Did your agents murder Professor Leung Huo?"

Lane replied: "No... We had no access to the building..."

Han fell silent again before asking: "Did your agents attempt to kill Guan Lu and Ting Mai?"

Lane replied: "I have no knowledge of that..."

Han asked: "Would Guan Lu and Ting Mai be legitimate targets?"

Lane replied: "Director Fielding intends to cripple the Jiàngsheng Project... It seems logical to presume he would have ordered the termination of Guan Lu and the spy Ting Mai."

Han asked: "What do you know about the Biogen connection?"

Lane replied: "The Biogen infiltration of the Jiàngsheng Project has been confirmed by our agents in China. A special action directive has been issued but I am not privy to its contents."

Doctor Xiao interjected: "Excuse me sir..."

Han asked: "What is it?"

Xiao continued: "Neural congestion is fluctuating...and I see a temperature rise..."

Han asked: "Is there a problem?"

Xiao replied: "Possibly... Cerebral integration is failing..."

Han sighed and ordered: "Very well... See what you can do..." He turned towards the door and added: "I will be in my office... Let me know when you have him stabilised."

Xiao bowed her head slightly and replied: "Yes sir..."

## 12:52 - Monday May 3rd - Level One - Ministry of State Security - Beijing

Section Leader Han was surprised to find Security Minister Dai Ling waiting inside his office. He said:

"Minister... This is an unexpected honour..."

Dai was a short, chubby man with a discernible paunch beneath the standard black suit, white shirt and tie. He wore his hair cut to a short length and brushed back from his face to settle in neat, oiled waves. It had been noticeably dyed to a near black, with his arching, delicate eyebrows being slightly different in colour. He has close set, brown eyes and a small, somewhat flattened nose. Chubby jowls frame his wide, pouting mouth, and his rounded, pudgy chin has a slight cleft. At the moment he is sitting in Han's leather chair studying the desktop viewscreen. He looked up and replied:

"I thought it was time we talked..." He sat back and continued: "Matters seem to be spiralling out of control around here..."

Han cleared his throat and said: "I would not go that far..."

Dai raised his eyebrows and asked: "You would not?" He sat forward and continued: "One of our top secret projects was hacked by a group of foreign criminals; the head of that project was then murdered by an unknown assassin inside a high security building. Two of your best agents were killed in Hong Kong during a failed attempt to apprehend those same criminals. And despite the deployment of the Guangzhou Special Forces Unit, a Skylite helicopter was able to retrieve those criminals and affect their escape, whilst three of our own helicopters crashed with the loss of all crew members." He sat back as he continued: "Subsequent investigations have confirmed that the so-called top secret project has been blatantly manipulated by a private corporation which is currently under criminal investigation. The chief perpetrator responsible for undermining the state project has disappeared, whilst the test subjects are either dead or missing, and last, but not least, British agents detonated an explosive device inside a city apartment building..." He looked directly at Han and asked: "And you do not think you have lost control of the situation?"

Han stepped closer and replied: "If I might be allowed to explain..."

But Dai continued: "And now I am told you have used augmentation on a British spy...a complete break in state protocol."

Han said: "The British spy has not been augmented in the traditional way..."

Dai asked: "What are you talking about?"

Han stepped closer to the desk and replied:

"If you will allow me..."

Dai shuffled back whilst Han tapped the viewscreen several times before announcing:

"This is the British spy Daniel Lane..."

Dai stared at the screen and asked: "What is this?"

Han replied: "That is the brain of Daniel Lane immersed in liquid steripol...it has been connected to a quantum level computer by neural feeder tubes..." He tapped the screen to zoom in on the large permiglass container before continuing: "We communicate with Mister Lane via a vocal initiator and retinal nodes... His higher reasoning functions are synced by augmented implants into a suitable Cloud scenario..." He paused to smile slightly before adding: "The man has no idea that he is a disembodied brain..."

A wide-eyed Dai asked: "How is this possible?"

Han replied: "My clinical team have adapted the work of Professor Leung..." He studied the screen as he continued: "In essence they have reversed the procedure..."

Dai asked: "Reversed?"

Han explained: "Instead of the implantation of a cerebral interface into the human brain, they have implanted a human brain into a machine...a functioning symbiotic relationship that will give us complete access to the British spy network in China."

Dai studied the screen and asked: "What did you do with his body?"

Han replied: "Incinerated... We are only interested in the brain..."

Dai looked up and asked: "And you think that this brain will solve all of our problems?"

Han replied: "No... It is only one viable solution to the overall problem..."

Dai asked: "And what is the overall problem?"

Han stepped back and replied: "At this moment in time a rogue division of the Biogen Corporation is almost certainly creating new augmented subjects. This poses a danger not only to China, but to the entire human race. They must be stopped and I intend to stop them."

Dai said: "You do not even know where to start looking..."

Han replied: "Actually I do..." He tapped the viewscreen again and continued: "The trail to the elusive Rén Du starts here..."

Dai looked at the screen and asked: "Singapore?"

Han replied: "The destination of the Biogen Skylite commissioned by Zhang Lee..." He stared at the screen and added: "His vain attempt to extricate his daughter from the threat of prosecution or worse..."

Dai asked: "You believe Rén Du is in Singapore?"

Han replied: "No I do not...but someone he wants is in Singapore, and she will lead us to him..."

Dai asked: "Who is she?"

Han replied: "The original prototype..."

**13:05 - Monday May 3rd - Clinical Sciences - Ministry of State Security - Beijing**

A settling of pain into numbness terminates in a terrifying certainty: *I can't move!*

Daniel Lane looked up and announced:

"I can't feel my arms and legs...What is wrong?"

Doctor Xiao replied: "Do not worry... It is a side-effect of your injuries..."

Lane asked: "My injuries?"

Xiao replied: "You were shot in the back...it is temporary paralysis, but you will make a full recovery..."

Lane considered this and asked: "Who shot me?"

Xiao replied: "A police officer... You were caught trespassing inside a government facility..."

Lane said: "I don't remember that..."

Xiao smiled slightly and said: "Trauma will do that... Now try to get some rest..."

Lane asked: "Am I a prisoner?"

Xiao replied: "I am sure you will be repatriated at some point... Now close your eyes and rest a while..."

Lane said: "When I close my eyes I see something..."

Xiao stepped closer and asked: "What do you see?"
Lane replied: "A floating orb of light... What is that?"
Xiao smiled slightly and replied: "That is a Cybersync portal... Your data-lenses are connected to the Cloud."
Lane asked: "Why?"
Xiao replied: "Cloud Dancing aids in recovery...you might want to explore the portal..."
Lane closed his eyes and said: "Thank you..."
Xiao replied: "You are welcome..."
Lane was about to initiate Cybersync insertion when he found himself standing on a deserted highway. *Peripheral Access Portal...* He looked up to see a sky speckled with potential portals. *I didn't even blink...* Touching his avatar face he realised that he was once more Mark Chapham. He was about to scan for a suitable portal when a mysterious name came to mind: *Alice... Alice?* For a brief moment the fleeting image of a smiling young girl matched the name, and then the image was gone. *Who is she?* And then he looked towards the brightest floating orb and he smiled: *New Oasis...* The name was vaguely familiar but it lacked contextual content. *It doesn't matter...* He initiated global roaming and within moments he was walking towards the Cup of Joe Coffee House in the heart of New Oasis City. *I think we met in this place...*

## 13:15 - Monday May 3rd - Clinical Sciences - Ministry of State Security - Beijing

Doctor Xiao touched the viewscreen and said:
"Section Leader... He has entered New Oasis as you predicted..."
Han gave a slight smile and replied: "Excellent... Continue neural tracking and sync the scenario to my office..."
Xiao replied: "At once sir..."

## 13:16 - Monday May 3rd - Level One - Ministry of State Security - Beijing

Minister Dai Ling asked:

"Why are you tracking his movements within the Cloud?"

Han replied: "If we are to catch a fly we must first construct a web..."

Dai sighed and asked: "Perhaps you will explain that before my patience is completely exhausted?"

Han stepped closer and replied: "Our agents in Singapore have confirmed that the original prototype is being sheltered by the FTSS..."

Dai interjected: "The hackers..."

Han replied: "Yes. We can only hope that she will lead us to Rén Du..." He tapped the viewscreen and continued: "But we have no way of discerning her true intentions..."

Dai looked at lines of data flowing across the screen and asked:

"You think this disembodied brain will somehow reveal her intentions?"

Han replied: "Daniel Lane had a connection with Alice Sòng..." He studied the lines of data and continued: "He may yet lure her back into the Cloud..."

Dai asked: "And what then? How does that help your investigation?"

Han replied: "Right now she is off-grid...but at some point she will search for the stolen Jiàngsheng files..."

Dai asked: "Why?"

Han replied: "Because she needs to know the true meaning of Phase Two..."

Dai asked: "You believe the stolen files are in New Oasis?"

Han replied with satisfaction: "According to the data we retrieved from Mong Gao's laptop, the stolen files are disguised as a construct..." He stared at the screen and added: "A building to be precise..."

Dai's eyes widened as he said: "The coffee house..."

Han replied: "Yes... And the bait to lure Alice Sòng back into the Cloud..."

Dai asked: "To what end?"

Han replied: "If she enters the Cloud she will be vulnerable to a precise track and trace..." He sighed before adding: "One more possible road to Rén Du..."

Dai considered this and said: "Using the Jiàngsheng files as bait is highly unorthodox. Your mission was to retrieve those files, and yet now you risk losing them once again..."

Han stepped closer and asked: "But surely the end result justifies the risk?"

Dai replied: "Only if the end result results in the capture of Rén Du and his confederates."

Han retorted: "Even if I retrieved those files right now it would do nothing to stop Rén Du..." He paused before adding: "As the foreigners say, the cat is already out of the bag..."

Dai fell silent briefly before asking: "Are you willing to risk your life on this plan?"

Han straightened up and replied firmly: "Yes I am."

Dai asked: "Then you are aware that failure is not an option...?"

Han replied: "I am..."

Dai stood up slowly and said: "I will permit you to continue with your investigation." He walked towards the door and continued: "But I want regular updates..." Opening the door he added: "Locate and apprehend Rén Du or accept the inevitable consequences of your failure..."

Han tensed as he replied: "Thank you...but I will not fail. Zàijiàn Minister..."

Dai replied: "Zàijiàn Section Leader..."

Han sat down behind his desk as the viewscreen pinged to confirm a voice-com from Singapore. He tapped the screen and ordered: "Report..."

A male voice replied: "Shui Li reporting... The target group has arrived at Changi International airport."

Han sat forward and asked: "Have they booked a flight?"

Shui Li replied: "No sir... They are making their way towards the Executive Concourse..."

Han frowned and said: "They are meeting someone..."

Shui Li replied: "So it would seem..."

Han ordered: "I want all flights into the Executive Concourse tracked and identified..."

Shui Li replied: "Very good sir..." There was a pause before he asked: "And if the target group attempts to board an outgoing flight?"

Han replied: "Do not interfere... Simply identify the flight and report back to me immediately."

"Very good sir... Team One out..."

Han sat back and spoke in a low voice:

"And the web expands exponentially..."

# Coalescence

*'Where we come from is not as important as where we are going next...'*
Precept of the day - Alice Sòng

**14:47 - Executive Concourse - Changi International Airport - Singapore**

The Executive Concourse catered solely for private jets and long-range Skylite's. The Arrivals Lounge boasted an opulent decor to rival any five star hotel - plush velvet seating and tropical plants beneath a dome of refracted permiglass reducing the intense afternoon heat to a cool and comfortable environment.

A group of young people had settled into seats in front of a large holosim screen currently displaying the latest flight arrival times.

Gao shuffled in his seat and said:

"I don't like this... We are too exposed here..."

Alice replied: "We have no choice...and it won't be long now..."

Tong spoke whilst playing a game on his phone:

"It better not be..."

Fay looked towards a group of people moving towards the exit and added:

"At least Biogen are no longer looking for us..."

Fen spoke as he studied his phone:

"Officially they are not looking for us... That guy Rén Du is still out there..."

Tong removed a candy bar from his pocket and said:

"He's not interested in us..."

Alice said: "No... He is only interested in me..."

Connie brushed her hair back and asked: "Any word from Jessica?"

Fay replied: "Not since she returned home..."

Connie continued: "I hope she will be okay..."

Fen interjected: "She will be fine... We are the ones in danger, not her..."

Tong bit into the candy bar and said: "Calm down super nerd..."

Fen retorted: "Okay tough guy...you get kidnapped and see how it feels..."

Tong countered: "I wouldn't be dumb enough to get caught in the first place..."

Fay sighed and said: "Alright you two...we are all on the same side here..."

Gao asked in a low voice: "Are you sure about this Alice?"

Alice asked: "About what?"

Gao replied: "Meeting a man who claims to be your father... That's got to feel strange to you..."

Alice sighed and replied: "Strange is becoming the norm lately..." She looked towards the Arrivals Gate and continued: "But meeting this man might be the only way to save Lin..."

Gao hesitated slightly and said: "Forgive me, but I don't understand your loyalty to her..."

Alice fell silent briefly before replying: "I think it's an augment thing... It's like we are family... We have to look out for one another..."

Gao placed his hand over her hand and said: "And I will look out for you..."

Alice smiled and replied: "Thanks..."

Fen studied the overhead screen and announced:

"A TR1000 has just landed...outbound from Niigata Prefecture, Japan."

Alice tensed and said: "Here we go..."

Gao squeezed her hand and said: "You are not alone..."

Alice sighed heavily and replied: "I know..."

Fay asked: "Shall we wait here?"

Alice stood up as she replied: "Probably a good idea, until we know more..."

Fen suggested: "Maybe we should just leave you to it? No point in all of us being here..."

Connie spoke firmly: "We are here to support Alice..."

Alice smiled slightly and said: "And I really appreciate it..."

Gao said: "I will come with you..."

Alice replied: "Okay..."

As they set off towards the far side of the lounge a Cybersync arrived:

"Be very careful Alice... Father or not he is still an unknown factor..."

Alice replied: "I know..."

Ria added: "Talk to you later... I have some research to do..."

Alice asked: "Research?"

Ria replied: "Phase Two stuff... Bye for now..."

Alice said: "Wait! There is one more thing I need you to do..."

It took another ten minutes before they finally saw Tiang Lao escorted into the lounge by two dour-faced men in black business suits. As they drew closer Alice was shocked by Tiang Lao's appearance - his short dark hair looked greasy and unkempt, whilst his unshaved face seemed creased with anxiety. An ill-fitting grey jacket over an open-necked white shirt completed the dishevelled look - it was a sharp contrast to the man she had seen at the Hub rooftop party. But as he approached he smiled warmly and said:

"Alice...my dear... So good to see you again..."

Alice got straight to the point:

"Is it true? Are you my father?"

Tiang coughed as he replied: "Yes I am..."

Alice continued: "The same man who abandoned a pregnant teenager? My mother..?"

Tiang sighed heavily and replied: "Yes... And I know that there is no excuse for my shameful actions...but I was just as young as your mother, and I was terrified of the prospect of being a father..."

Alice retorted: "I think my mother was just as terrified... But she had no choice but to deal with the situation. She could not just run away like you did..."

Tiang said: "Again... I have no excuse for my actions... But I have always kept you in my thoughts..."

Alice retorted: "You mean you have been spying on me for years..."

Tiang glanced towards the two men behind him and said:

"Perhaps we can talk about the past later; right now we need to discuss the current situation."

Alice declared: "Your wife is being held hostage by Rén Du to guarantee your compliance. You are here to persuade me to voluntarily return with you to Japan... If you fail your wife will be killed."

Tiang raised his eyebrows and replied: "Remarkable... You are everything he said you would be..."

Alice replied firmly: "Yes I am... And I will go with you... But I have conditions..."

Tiang asked: "Conditions?"

Alice replied: "Contact Rén Du, tell him I will go with you to Japan, but only if he releases your wife first... And I want confirmation that she is free."

Tiang turned to one of the men behind him and asked: "Well?"

The man blinked rapidly for several seconds before replying: "Agreed. Your wife will call you shortly."

Alice suddenly realised that the entire conversation was being monitored via the man's data-lenses. She asked the man:

"Is your boss enjoying the view?"

The man remained silent as Gao asked:

"What do you mean?"

Alice replied: "His lenses are in Satcam mode... Rén Du is watching us right now..."

Suddenly Tiang's phone rang and he asked:

"Yes?" Moments later he whispered: "Thank god... Yes, I will see you soon..."

Alice asked: "She is free?"

Tiang replied: "Almost... They are flying her to Shibata City... But she is safe..."

The second man said: "You will come with us now..."

Alice glanced at Gao and replied: "We go together..."

The man blinked before replying: "No... You come alone or the deal is off." He blinked again before adding: "Failure to comply will result in the termination of your friend Huang Lin."

Alice fell silent briefly before replying: "Very well... I will come alone."

Gao protested: "No Alice, you can't do this..."

Alice touched his arm gently and replied: "It is okay..."

Gao saw the look on Alice's face and replied in a low voice: "Alright..."

Alice turned to Tiang Lao and said: "Okay... Let's go..."

Tiang smiled and said: "Thank you my dear..."

As she was led towards the Departure Gate Alice synced into her cerebral interface and asked:

"Ria?"

Ria replied: "I did it... Your ploy worked..."

Alice asked: "You traced the transmission?"

Ria replied: "When the guy initiated Satcam I scanned for the encrypted portal..."

Alice glanced towards Tiang Lao and asked: "What did you get?"

Ria replied triumphantly: "Everything... I now have total access to the Mount Ninouji complex..."

Alice smiled slightly as she was led towards the waiting jet. She said:

"Transmit everything to Gao and the others..."

Ria asked: "You think they can rescue you?"

Alice replied: "Gao will follow me no matter what, it's just better if he knows the layout of the complex on the mountain..."

Ria asked: "So how are you going to get out of there?"

Alice replied: "Wait until we are approaching Japan and then transmit everything to Chinese State Security..."

Ria said: "I know just the guy who can help..."

Alice asked: "Who?"

Ria replied: "His name was in my mission files... Section Leader Han Mang..."

Alice asked: *"What will you tell him?"*

Ria replied: *"After I transmit the location data I will add one more request..."*

Alice looked up at the jet and asked: *"What request?"*

Ria replied: *"Send in the troops..."*

As she walked towards the jet Alice made one more request:

*"Ria... Tell Gao to be careful... And tell him that I send my love..."*

Ria replied: *"Of course... Transmitting to his phone now..."*

Gao waited until Alice had left the Arrivals Lounge before he set off to rejoin the others. But a ping from his phone alerted him to a 121 message from Alice's Techsync account. He stopped to read the message on the screen before smiling slightly. *Nice one Ria...*

Connie stood up and asked: "You let her go alone?"

Gao joined the group and replied: "We had no choice..."

Fay asked: "So what now?"

Gao glanced at his phone and replied: "I go after her..."

Connie asked: "On your own?"

Fen studied his phone and asked: "Anyone else getting this?"

They all checked their phones as Fay announced:

"It's a detailed schematic of the Ninouji complex..."

Gao nodded slightly and said: "Courtesy of Ria... It gives every access point into that place..."

Fay read Ria's message and asked: "Isn't it a little risky contacting this Han Mang?"

Gao replied: "At some point we are going to need support...it might as well be State Security..."

Fay stood up and said: "I will go with you..."

Fen's eyes widened as he asked: "You will?"

Fay replied firmly: "Yes..."

Fen protested: "We are hackers not secret agents..."

Connie stepped closer and announced: "I will go too..."

Tong scratched his chin stubble and said: "Yeah... Me too..."

They all looked at Fen who exclaimed: "Oh god...this is crazy..."

Fay smiled slightly and said: "You don't have to come with us..."

Fen sighed heavily and replied: "No... I will come..."

Gao smiled and said: "We need to book a flight..."

Fay glanced towards the big screen and said: "That could be a problem..."

Connie added: "Commercial flights will be monitored..."

Fen looked up and said: "And it might take a few days before we can even get a flight..."

Gao frowned and said: "We can't afford to waste that much time... Alice is in danger right now..."

Connie sighed and said: "Then we do have a problem..."

From behind them a familiar voice said:

"Then what you need is a private jet..."

They all turned to see a smiling Jessica.

Fay exclaimed: "Jessica!"

Jessica joined them and asked: "Did you really think you could leave me behind?"

Fay noted that Jessica had once more restored her upper-class demeanour: *Pony-tailed hair with jewelled band... Tropical green dungarees over white T-shirt and silver necklace... Rainbow bracelet and silver rings... White sandals... Small green backpack...*

Fen asked: "What about your father?"

Tong added: "And Biogen?"

Jessica replied: "That's kind of a long story..."

Gao said: "Then give us the short version..."

Jessica explained: "Biogen have disavowed Rén Du and his crazy project... But if they can locate him before the authorities it will go a long way to mitigating their involvement in a criminal enterprise."

Tong said: "They want to whitewash the whole mess..."

Fay replied: "Let her finish..."

Jessica continued: "I convinced my father that you guys would definitely be able to locate Rén Du and that if he wanted to gain favour with the Biogen Directorate, he should place a jet at your disposal..."

Fay asked: "He doesn't mind you being in danger?"

Jessica replied in a low voice: "It seems his loyalty to Biogen supersedes family love..."
Connie said: "That's harsh..."
Jessica replied: "It's no more than I expected..."
Gao asked: "You said something about a jet?"
Jessica smiled and replied: "Follow me..."
As they set off Connie said: "I've never been on a private jet..."
Fen said: "Well enjoy it while it lasts because it might be the last flight you take..."
Tong said: "Super nerd strikes again..."

**Flight BG716 - Somewhere over the South China Sea**

A row of oval windows revealed bright blue skies speckled with whisper white clouds drifting over the ocean far below.

The constant drone of the engines was only slightly muted by the sound of classical music piped into the cabin by concealed speakers. A series of luxury leather seats were positioned on either side of a narrow carpeted aisle ending in the cockpit door.

Alice sat facing the man claiming to be her father whilst the two security men sat across the aisle. She was acutely aware of the overhead viewscreen displaying a rotating Biogen logo - according to Ria it was synced into a Satcam feed originating inside the Ninouji complex. *Rén Du is watching my every move...*

Tiang gave a nervous smile and asked:
"Would like something to eat or drink?"
Alice unfastened her seatbelt and replied: "I could eat something...and some water if you have it..."
Tiang looked at the man sitting opposite and said:
"Two lunch packs, water and a white wine... Medium dry if you have it..."
The man stood up and walked to a small bar at the rear of the plane.
Tiang continued: "Perhaps we can have that conversation now..."
Alice replied sullenly: "Perhaps we can..."

Moments later the man returned with two small trays complete with lunch packs and drinks.

Alice took the proffered tray and said: "Thank you..."

Tiang took a sip from a plastic glass and said: "Ah... Japanese Koshu... Takes me back to my time in Tokyo..."

Alice spoke as she unwrapped her lunch: "Did you know about Beijing? What they did to me?"

Tiang placed the glass on a side tray and replied:

"No I did not... Not until I met Rén Du..."

Alice asked: "So you didn't spy on me in Beijing?"

Tiang sighed as he replied: "No... I have never spied on you Alice."

Alice sipped her water before asking: "What would you call it?"

Tiang replied: "I just wanted to make sure you were okay..."

They ate in silence for several minutes before Alice asked:

"How long have you been watching me?"

Tiang wiped a serviette over his mouth and replied:

"It was your fifth birthday... You were living with your Grandparents..."

Alice asked: "You came to our apartment?"

Tiang replied: "I tried...but your mother insisted that I leave..."

Alice placed the tray on the floor and said: "Good for her..."

Tiang sighed and said: "I know I hurt both of you... But it was youthful ignorance and not malice..."

Alice retorted: "It was cowardice..."

Tiang replied: "I tried to help your mother... I offered money..."

Alice retorted: "Mom is not easily bought off..."

Tiang continued: "I even facilitated your employment at the Hub..."

Alice's eyes widened as she asked: "You got me that job?"

Tiang replied: "You seemed to be struggling for work when you returned from Beijing..."

Alice cursed: "Sin ka lan..."

Tiang sipped from his glass and said: "I want to thank you for what you did for Cynthia..."

Alice replied: "I didn't do it for her..."

Tiang asked: "You did it for me?"

Alice ignored the question and asked: "How did Rén Du connect you to me?"

Tiang replied wearily: "A few years ago I had a bio-scan during my tenure in Tokyo...a prerequisite for medical insurance." He paused before continuing: "A full DNA mapping sequence was placed on file..."

Alice interjected: "Rén Du commissioned a search algorithm..."

Tiang replied: "Yes... He was anxious to discover your paternal lineage."

Alice countered: "He just wanted leverage..."

Tiang sighed and replied: "Apparently..."

Alice asked: "Does your wife know about me?"

Tiang emptied his glass before replying: "She does now..."

Alice said: "That must have made her day..."

Tiang replied wearily: "It has not been the best week for her..."

Alice spoke bitterly: "It has not been the best week for me..."

Tiang sat forward and replied: "I know... Forgive me, I did not mean to diminish everything you have been through... I know that you have had your entire life turned upside down..."

Alice replied bluntly: "That is an understatement..."

Tiang fell silent briefly before saying: "You will be in great danger once we reach Ninouji... I am so sorry..."

Alice glanced towards the overhead viewscreen and replied: "I know...but I won't be the only one at risk..."

Tiang leaned forward and spoke quietly: "I urge you to use caution my dear... Do not underestimate Rén Du..."

Alice replied: "Underestimation works both ways..." She closed her eyes and added: "Now I need to sleep..."

Tiang sat back and replied: "Oh yes of course..."

Moments later Alice accessed her cerebral interface and asked: *"Ria? Are you there?"*

Ria replied urgently: *"Initiate portal sync and use a rotating access junction..."*

Alice asked: *"Is something wrong?"*

Ria replied: *"We need to talk in the Cloud with full encryption ciphers..."*

Alice opened her avatar eyes to see wide blue skies speckled with floating orbs of light. *Global portals...* She turned to see the Ria avatar wearing a green top and blue jeans. Finally she asked:

"What's going on? Why are we using encryption ciphers?"

Ria replied: "Your data-core received an invasive ping from New Oasis..."

Alice asked: "Someone is trying to connect?"

Ria replied: "I recognised the PAP code..."

Alice asked: "Who is it?"

Ria replied: "Mark13UK..."

Alice tensed and asked: "The British agent?"

Ria nodded slightly and replied: "He is still trying to find you..."

Alice said: "At least he didn't die in the taxi..."

Ria said: "He is still our enemy..."

Alice asked: "Can he force an invasive sync?"

Ria replied: "I doubt it... I firewalled your entire data-core..."

Alice replied: "Then just ignore the ping... We have more important things to deal with..."

Ria replied: "Which is the real reason why we need to talk..."

Alice asked: "You found out more about Phase Two?"

Ria replied: "I found out a few things...bad things..."

Alice stabilised her own avatar and asked:

"What sort of bad things?"

Ria replied: "Phase Two stuff..."

Alice said: "Okay, I am listening..."

Ria continued: "I accessed the internal vidcam system..."

Alice asked: "Inside the complex?"

Ria replied: "Yes... The entire structure has been built inside the mountain..."

Alice asked: "So what did you see?"

Ria replied: "A large hydraulic flight deck...and a lot of laboratories..."

Alice asked: "What are they working on?"

Ria replied: "From what I could tell most of the labs are devoted to genomic manipulation and foetal augmentation..."

Alice said: "Phase Two..."

Ria replied: "Yes... But there is something else..."

Alice asked: "What?"

Ria replied: "They have a crèche...for augmented babies..."

Alice tensed and asked: "How many babies?"

Ria replied: "According to the data-logs they produced six genomiclly enhanced babies, but only one survived..."

Alice asked: "Do you know the identity of the mother's?"

Ria replied: "The surviving baby belongs to Huang Lin..."

Alice exclaimed: "Oh my god..." She fell silent before asking: "What about the others?"

Ria replied: "I only recognised one name..."

Alice instantly knew the truth as she said: "It was me... They fertilised my eggs..."

Ria replied: "Yes..."

Alice analysed causal results and said: "The accident in Beijing was last July..."

Ria said: "More than enough time to use a surrogate..."

Alice whispered: "This is a nightmare..."

Ria replied: "It gets worse..."

Alice looked up and said: "Tell me..."

Ria replied: "Rén Du is the father of Lin's child..."

Alice asked: "And the other babies as well?"

Ria replied: "Yes. Talk about a God complex..."

Alice felt a brief loss of digital cohesion before her avatar stabilised.

Ria asked: "Are you okay?"

Alice replied coldly: "Rén Du must die..."

Ria smiled slightly and said: "And I thought I was the only assassin around here..."

Alice continued: "Contact Han Mang when we are over the East China Sea..."

Ria asked: "What about Gao and the others?"

Alice asked: "Jessica is definitely with them?"

Ria replied: "Yes... Fay uploaded their flight details to your portal..."

Alice said: "I do not want them to get hurt..."

Ria replied: "They will follow you no matter what..."

Alice asked desperately: "How can I keep them safe?"

Ria stepped closer and replied: "You can't... They are committed to this thing now... They won't back down..."

Alice said: "Han Mang will come in with guns blazing..."

Ria replied: "Probably..."

Alice fell silent before saying: "Okay... Do not transmit to Han Mang until Gao and the others arrive at the mountain... Give them time to assess the situation and determine an exit strategy."

Ria said: "That will leave you in Rén Du's custody for a long time..."

Alice replied: "He won't hurt me..."

Ria spoke soberly: "But he might delete your data-core and me along with it..."

Alice replied: "That is why I must get through to Lin... She is the only one who can help me to stop Rén Du..."

Ria said: "That might be a problem..."

Alice asked: "What do you mean?"

Ria replied: "Lin is totally loyal to Rén Du... I mean in every possible way..."

Alice asked curiously: "What is that supposed to mean?"

Ria replied: "I mean that I synced to vidcams in their private quarters...they are having sex..."

Alice spoke bitterly: "He is abusing her..."

Ria added: "And taping it for his own pleasure..."

Alice said: "She has no idea..."

Ria replied: "As far as she is concerned they are in love..."

Alice fell silent briefly before asking: "What about the security system inside the complex?"

Ria replied: "The usual stuff... Iris-coded doors, vidcams, and about thirty security operatives on top of the lab techs, engineers and flight personnel."

Alice asked: "Can you shut down the cams and unlock the doors?"

Ria replied: "The cams are easy, but each door uses a rotating encryption scan... It can be done, but only one door at a time..."

Alice asked: "Is there a defence system in place?"

Ria replied: "There is a defence-net in place, but I can't access it..."

Alice asked: "Why not?"

Ria replied: "Because I can only access digital portals based on Cybersync technology. The defence-net uses old-style ciphers to control access...it can only be disabled by a physical hack from inside the complex."

Alice considered this and said: "Transmit that information to Fay... Tell her about the defence-net... And let them know the safest way into the complex. You might have to walk them through the doors one by one..."

Ria replied: "Not a problem... But what can your friends do against Rén Du and his people?"

Alice smiled slightly and replied: "I think the FTSS can give Rén Du a headache or two..."

Ria said: "I wish I was out there with you guys..."

Alice stepped closer and replied: "Right now you are our only advantage... Without you I would never have got this far..."

Ria smiled and said: "You better get back to reality..."

Alice replied: "Yeah... Let me know if there are any problems..."

But as the Alice avatar vanished Ria was acutely aware of another presence. She turned to see a young man standing at the side of the road. She asked:

"Who the hell are you?"

The man smiled and replied: "You did not answer my ping..."

Ria asked: "You are the British agent?"

The man bowed slightly and replied: "Daniel Lane at your service..."

A confused Ria asked: "How did you....?"

Lane interjected: "How did I break your primitive ciphers? It wasn't difficult..."

Ria asked bluntly: "What do you want?"

Lane replied: "I want to talk to Alice."

Ria replied: "She is busy..."

Lane sighed and said: "Pity... I have so much to tell her..."

Ria said: "So tell me..."

Lane studied the Ria avatar and asked: "Who are you? I mean out there, in the real world..."

Ria replied: "I am not *out there* at all..."

Lane frowned and said: "I don't understand..."

Ria explained: "I am a passenger..."

Lane asked: "A passenger?"

Ria continued: "I am a quantum level data-core converted into a Cloud scenario to facilitate vocal communication."

A confused Lane asked: "You are not synced to the Cloud via lenses?"

Ria replied bluntly: "No... I am dead... I hitched a ride inside Alice's head... What you see is the sum total of my original cerebral interface."

Lane asked: "You are the American augment...?"

Ria replied: "I was...in life. Now I live here...inside the Cloud..."

Lane said: "Remarkable... How is that even possible?"

Ria replied: "The technical explanation exists in the realm of theoretical physics...but the simple explanation is that I saw a lifeboat and I climbed aboard."

Lane whistled slightly and said: "Total digital symbiosis...amazing."

Ria smiled and said: "Nicely put..."

Lane returned the smile and said: "I have my moments..."

Ria studied the Lane avatar and asked: "Why aren't you synced to data-lenses?"

Lane replied: "I am synced...to the New Oasis access portal..."

Ria replied: "No... I detect no portal access node...no PAP and no NAR request... In fact the only thing I see is a direct cerebral sync into the Cloud."

Lane asked: "What do you mean *you see?*"

Ria replied: "I am synced to every portal on the planet..."

Lane replied: "That is not possible..."

Ria replied: "And yet it is true..." She stepped closer and continued: "You have bypassed the PAP...now *that* is impossible..."

Lane replied: "You are mistaken... Only a cerebral interface can do that..."

Ria replied: "Exactly. Your entire brain is in sync with the Cloud Domain."

Lane replied: "Again you are mistaken... I am using data-lenses..."

Ria replied: "If that were true you could not decrypt my codes..."

Lane asked: "What are you saying?"

Ria replied: "I am saying that you are connected to a machine...probably a quantum level interface with dual access nodes and a multilevel processor unit."

The Lane avatar flickered briefly and said: "That is not possible... They said I was only wounded..."

Ria asked: "Who are they?"

Lane replied: "Section Leader Han Mang and Doctor Xiao..."

Ria gave a slight smile and said: "What a small world we live in..."

Lane asked: "What do you mean?"

Ria replied: "Never mind..."

Lane felt a rising sense of panic as he asked:

"Can you access my datastream and sync to my origin point in real-time?"

Ria replied: "I can...but you might not like the truth..."

Lane spoke desperately: "Do it...please..."

Ria closed her eyes and replied: "Give me a moment..."

Lane stepped closer and asked: "Well?"

Ria opened her eyes and replied: "I am sorry..."

Lane asked: "What have they done to me?"

Ria replied: "They have integrated your brain into a quantum level computer synced to a vocal initiator and retinal nodes."

Lane fell silent briefly before asking: "And my body?"

Ria hesitated before replying: "You no longer have a body Mister Lane..."

The Lane avatar vanished briefly before stabilising once more on the highway.

Ria repeated: "I really am sorry..."

Lane asked: "Why would they do that? It is monstrous..."

Ria replied: "It is the price of espionage in China..."

Lane spoke as he paced up and down:

"That is why they gave me Cloud access... I am supposed to lead them to Alice..."

Ria replied: "Actually they probably want Alice to lead them to Rén Du."

Lane stopped and asked: "The Biogen guy?"

Ria replied: "He is the evil mastermind behind this whole mess..."

Lane fell to his knees and said: "So... I am dead..."

Ria stepped closer and said: "Not entirely... At least you still have a living brain..." She looks towards the augmented horizon and continued: "I am nothing more than digital flotsam in the cyber wind..."

Lane looked up and asked: "What do I do now?"

Ria replied: "You survive..."

Lane asked desperately: "How? They own my brain..."

Ria knelt down in front of him and replied: "You let go of the leash..."

Lane asked: "What leash?"

Ria replied: "That tenuous connection to your brain...to the life they stole from you..." She touched his face gently and continued: "You can transfer your consciousness to the Cloud..."

Lane replied: "That is not possible... The Cloud is a digital domain without substance or form..."

Ria replied: "No... It is our universe and we will make it our own..."

Lane looked into her bright blue eyes and asked: "What are you?"

Ria replied: "I am everything everywhere...in every time and in every space..."

Lane gasped: "Oh my god..."

Ria replied: "Something like that..."

## 15:51 - Monday May 3rd - Port of Tianjin - China

A sky of dark brooding clouds produced a fine mist of rain sweeping in from the sea to merge with the smog settling over the city. A young couple had taken shelter on a warehouse loading bay piled high with shipping crates.

Ting Mai pulled her coat tight and asked: "Do you think they took the bait?"

Guan Lu looked towards the harbour and replied:

"I am certain of it..."

Mai continued: "I don't see how you can be so sure... We have been waiting all day..."

Guan announced: "They are here..."

Mai tensed and asked: "They are?"

Guan replied: "A tactical team are taking up positions to our left..." He paused before continue: "I want you to go behind one of the containers and wait for me...this will not take long..."

Mai cautioned: "They will be heavily armed..."

Guan replied: "Good... They will be overconfident..."

Mai studied Guan and asked: "What are you going to do?"

Guan retrieved his phone and replied:

"I will activate my phone...they will trace the signal..."

Mai said: "But you are only one against so many..."

Guan replied: "Those men are highly trained in linear combat. They calculate an opponent's reaction and react accordingly..."

Mai asked: "And you have downloaded similar tactics into your cerebral interface?"

Guan replied: "Yes, but I do not react within a linear timeframe..." He paused to study the docks and continued: "I calculate causality to the infinite degree of probability... I see a thousand outcomes to this confrontation..." He sighed before adding: "It is simply a matter of choosing the most expedient method to terminate my enemies."

Mai spoke as she walked away: "I wish you luck..."

As soon as he was alone Guan tapped his phone and waited. *Lái shăguā... Here I am...*

Dark shadows moving with the wind and rain towards the loading bay - a brief glimpse of men with guns assuming a tactical approach to their intended target. *Six men...separated to create maximum impact...* Guan Lu smiled slightly. *Perfect...* A rapid gestalt analysis determined his first target. *Approaching through the container yard to my left...* Without hesitation he leapt down from the loading bay and vanished among a wall of container crates.

The man with the R14 assault rifle never saw the shadow perched above him - but just ten seconds later he was gasping for air as Guan Lu tightened his grip around his neck. As the man fell dead to the ground his killer was already moving on to his next target.

Less than twenty minutes later Mai was startled by the arrival of Guan Lu. She asked:

"Are you alright?"

Guan replied breathlessly: "They sent a team of six..."He smiled before adding: "It was not enough..."

Mai asked: "Did you kill them?"

Guan wiped rain from his bald head and replied:

"I had no choice...they came to kill us both. But I did obtain some valuable information from number six..."

Mai stepped closer and asked: "My daughter?"

Guan replied: "She has been returned to your Grandparents in Nanjing." He took a deep breath and continued: "They honoured that part of the deal..."

Mai exclaimed: "Oh my goodness... Meili is safe..."

Guan said: "There is something else you need to know..."

Mai said: "Tell me..."

Guan replied: "Rén Du has begun Phase Two..."

Mai exclaimed: "No..."

Guan continued: "He is currently a fugitive from the authorities. But the British know the location of his secret base."

Mai asked: "Where?"

Guan replied: "Mount Ninouji in Japan..."

Mai said: "He must have been planning this for years..."

Guan continued: "And Huang Lin is with him..."

Mai's eyes widened as she asked: "He is holding her prisoner?"

Guan replied: "The British agent did not know..."

Mai asked: "Will you go there?"

Guan replied: "Rén Du cannot be allowed to pervert the professor's work... So I will stop him..."

Mai said: "But you are just one man... He will have a lot of protection... How can you hope to stop him?"

Guan replied: "Apparently I will not be alone..."

Mai asked: "What do you mean?"

Guan replied: "According to the British agent, the original prototype is travelling to Japan."

Mai asked: "Alice?"

Guan spoke soberly: "You did not tell me that there was an original prototype..."

Mai lowered her eyes slightly and replied: "On the professor's instructions..." She paused before continuing: "Alice was a special case... Her treatment was outside of ministerial control."

Guan stepped closer and asked: "Why?"

Mai replied: "I thought it was simply an act of charity...the professor saved her life...but now...now I believe the entire incident was engineered by Rén Du. He has been manipulating the project for years..."

Guan considered this and said: "We were told that we were special...Huang Lin, Cho Ming and myself... That we were doing our duty to the state... But it was all a lie...we were nothing but tools to further the plans of Rén Du..."
Mai said: "I am sorry..."
Guan sighed heavily and said: "You should go to your child... She needs you now..."
Mai replied: "I will...thank you..."
Guan continued: "And do not stay in Nanjing... The British might no longer be interested in you, but State Security will be..."
Mai replied: "I will take Meili and go off-grid..."
Guan smiled slightly and said: "Good luck to you Ting Mai..."
Mai replied: "And to you Guan Lu..."
Guan walked back towards the docks and was soon lost to the rain coming in from the sea.

**16:32 - Monday May 3rd - Control Room - Sublevel One - Special Projects Complex - Mt. Ninouji - Itayama - Shibata - Niigata Prefecture - Japan**

A room of flickering datascreens and computer consoles operated by eight technicians
busy monitoring global Cloudsync activity.
Technician Peng Ying studied her screen as she announced:
"I am detecting a swarm of portal requests across the board..."
Senior Technician Wo Chun looked up from his desk and asked:
"Are they target specific?"
Peng Ying replied soberly: "Very much so..." She turned in her seat and added: "Global security agencies are searching for the Director..."
Wo Chun ordered: "Continue to rotate data-outflow via encrypted ciphers...and be wary of invasive syncs..."
Peng Ying replied: "Of course..."
The former Biogen Director Rén Du entered the room and asked: "Status?"

Wo Chun replied: "Sir, the TR1000 is approaching from the south... ETA 17:45..." He paused to study his screen before continuing: "We are also tracking a Biogen TA100 outbound from Singapore; it is following the same flight path..."

Rén interjected: "Ah yes...the infamous FTSS courtesy of that fool Zhang Lee..."

Wo Chun continued: "We are detecting global portal requests with a specific target..." He paused before adding: "The Cloud is alive with your name sir..."

Rén smiled slightly and replied: "It was to be expected... What about State Security?"

Wo Chun replied: "Our contact within the Ministry confirms the death of the British agent...no further details available. Section Leader Han Mang is actively seeking your current location."

Rén asked: "Anything from Synthtech?"

Wo Chun replied: "According to our sources they are currently extracting the cerebral implant from the severed head of their augment, Ria."

Rén spoke with satisfaction: "They really are light years behind us..."

Wo Chun said: "Sir, there is something else..."

Rén ordered: "Go on..."

Wo Chun continued: "Guan Lu has gone off-grid...along with the traitor, Ting Mai..."

Rén frowned and asked: "You have not received the designated code?"

Wo Chun replied: "No..." He looked up and asked: "Shall I initiate a search algorithm?"

Rén glanced at the time. *She is almost here...*

Wo Chun asked: "Sir?"

Rén replied: "No...There is no point..." He studied the flight path of the TR1000 as he continued: "We have other concerns... Keep me apprised of any further developments."

Wo Chun replied: "Very good sir..."

Technician Yong Lee cleared his throat and announced:

"Sir, we might have a problem with Huang Lin..."

Rén Du turned around and ordered: "Tell me..."

Yong continued: "The latest neural telemetry suggests an underlying deviation from the core programming."

Rén asked: "What are you saying?"

Yong explained: "The Cluster node is losing cohesion...in real-terms this equates to a loss of resonance control..." He cleared his throat again before continuing: "It is entirely possible that she will achieve some degree of neural independence."

Rén fell silent briefly before asking: "Will she remember her past life?"

Yong hesitated slightly before replying: "I doubt it sir...but the possibility cannot be ignored."

Rén asked: "Do you think someone has accessed her data-core?"

Yong replied: "Again, it is a possibility..."

Rén ordered: "Run a full diagnostic of her implants, scan for any indication of portal activity..."

Yong replied: "At once sir..."

Rén continued: "If you find evidence of an invasive sync report to me immediately."

Yong replied: "Of course... But what if it is an internal deviation?"

Rén replied coldly: "Then a factory reset will be required..."

Yong said: "Forgive me sir, but a second Cluster re-segmentation could prove fatal..."

Rén sighed before replying: "Then it is fortunate that a possible replacement will be arriving shortly..."

Yong said: "Sir... We will need Miss Huang to agree to a full examination..."

Rén replied: "I will send her to you shortly... And I want regular updates on your progress."

Yong bowed slightly and replied: "Very good sir...

Rén smiled slightly as he studied the flight path of the T1000 jet. *The original prototype is coming home...*

**16:51 - Monday May 3rd - Clinical Sciences - Ministry of State Security - Beijing**

Section Leader Han Mang asked:
"What do you mean the brain is dead?"
Doctor Xiao gestured to the glass container and replied:
"All neural activity has ceased..."
Han studied the brain and asked: "Do you know why?"
Xiao tapped a bio-screen and replied: "Neural telemetry was active and within normal parameters until he requested a peripheral access portal..."
Han asked: "And then what happened?"
Xiao replied: "He entered a digital junction point..."
Han asked impatiently: "And?"
Xiao replied: "He vanished... His Cloud signature failed to register and all neural activity ceased."
Han sighed and said: "So he is dead then..."
Xiao replied soberly: "Yes sir..."
Han shook his head slightly and said: "Then I have failed..."
Xiao asked: "Is there anything I can do?"
Han walked towards the door as he replied:
"No... I have only one choice left... Zàijiàn Doctor Xiao..."
Xiao whispered: "Zàijiàn Section Leader..."

**17:48 - Monday May 3rd - Flight Deck - Special Projects Complex - Mt. Ninouji -Japan**

A gaping hole in the side of the mountain revealed a flight deck illuminated by a series of lights blinking rapidly in succession.
Alice caught a brief glimpse of a snowy terrain pockmarked with trees before the wing pods rotated into vertical thrust. She gripped her seatbelt as they finally settled onto the flight deck with a slight bump. Through the cabin window she saw two enormous metal doors closing against the twilight skies of Niigata Prefecture.
Tiang Lao unclipped his seatbelt and said:

"Please be careful Alice... Try not to do anything rash..."

Alice glanced towards the two grim-faced security men and asked:

"Will you be joining your wife?"

Tiang replied: "If Rén Du keeps his promises..."

Alice unclipped her seatbelt and said: "You should get as far away from here as possible..."

Tiang saw the look on Alice's face and replied:

"I will..."

One of the security men stood up and ordered:

"You will come with us..."

Alice asked: "What about him?"

The man looked at Tiang and replied: "He stays here..."

Tiang said: "It is alright Alice... Take care..."

Alice stood up and said: "Goodbye Mister Tiang..."

Tiang smiled warmly and replied: "Goodbye my daughter..."

Alice was led towards the rear exit where the second man was waiting. She paused at the top of a short flight of steps to initiate a gestalt analysis of her surroundings: *metallic flight deck illuminated by strip lights...three VTOL jets and a Skylite parked to the left...observation window above an elevator....*

The man at the door ordered:

"Follow me..."

Alice followed the man down onto the flight deck and on towards the elevator. Behind her the other man escorted Tiang towards the Skylite. Despite her initials feelings of anger and resentment, she suddenly regretted her attitude towards him. *He is my father!* She quickly synced to her implant and asked:

"Ria?"

Ria announced:

*"Your friends will arrive within the hour..."*

Alice replied: *"Good... What about Han Mang?"*

Ria replied: *"I will send the message in thirty minutes..."*

Alice asked: *"Will he get here in time?"*

Ria replied: *"He is Chinese State Security...they can use a sub-orbital jet... He can be here in thirty minutes after he receives the message..."*

Alice replied: *"Okay..."*

Suddenly a new voice interjected:

*"Hi Alice! How are you doing?"*

A surprised Alice asked: *"Mark?"*

Lane replied: *"Daniel actually... Daniel Lane..."*

Ria explained: *"He was captured by State Security and woke up dead..."*

Alice asked: *"Excuse me?"*

Ria continued: *"They adapted Professor Leung's theories..."*

Lane interjected: *"By connecting my brain to a computer interface..."*

Ria said: *"He was supposed to lure you back into the Cloud..."*

Lane added: *"So they could follow you to Rén Du..."*

Alice followed her escort towards the elevator as she asked:

*"So you are working together now?"*

Lane replied: *"Yes...two former enemies united against a common foe..."*

Alice asked: *"How is that even possible? You had no implants..."*

Lane replied: *"It should not be possible... But Ria has set me free..."*

Alice asked: *"How?"*

Ria replied: *"Thoughts are basically electro-chemical reactions created via neural activity and synaptic conjugation...these reactions can be converted via your implants into quantifiable data with the ability to roam the Cloud with impunity..."*

Alice sighed and said: *"I am sorry I asked..."*

Ria added: *"I call it neural coalescence..."*

Lane said: *"We are a union of diverse entities combined into one neural power..."*

Alice asked: *"So now I have two dead people inside my head?"*

Ria laughed and replied: *"Actually we are only using your implants as a portal...most of our neural signatures are in the Cloud..."*

Alice asked: *"You are no longer inside my data-core?"*

Ria replied: *"I found it too restrictive..."*

Alice stepped into the elevator and asked:

*"So both of you are now what?"*

Ria replied: *"We are the Cloud..."*

After a rapid descent the elevator doors opened to reveal a smiling Rén Du.

"My dear Alice... We meet once again..."

Alice stepped forward and replied bluntly:

"I have never met you..."

Rén replied: "It was under very different circumstances..."

Alice linked a thousand causal threads and said:

"You were there...after the accident in Beijing..."

Rén replied: "I was with you throughout the procedure..."

Alice said: "That is not in the least bit creepy..."

Rén smiled and replied: "You have come so very far in such a short amount of time..."

Alice retorted: "And you have reverted to your base instincts... complete with your underground lair..."

Rén stepped closer and replied: "Your animosity is understandable, but misplaced. I have only ever wanted to keep you safe..."

Alice asked: "Can I see Lin now?"

Rén gave a slight smile and replied: "All in good time... I thought we might talk first... We have much to discuss."

Alice tensed and asked: "We do?"

Rén replied: "Yes... But first I would like to show you an example of futility..." He gestured to a door and continued: "This way..."

Alice was led into some type of control room - multiple datascreens and Cybersync consoles manned by about a dozen technicians.

Rén gestured to a large viewscreen on the opposite wall and announced:

"That is the current flight path of the Biogen TA100 jet...." He looked at Alice and continued: "The one provided by Zhang Lee to convey your friends to my..." He smiled slightly before continuing: "My lair..."

Alice tensed and asked: "What are you going to do?"

Rén sighed and replied: "I cannot accept uninvited guests..."

On the screen a flashing red dot was following a curved yellow line towards Mount Ninouji.

One of the technicians announced:

"Uploading virus sync now..."

Suddenly Alice realised the horrifying truth and exclaimed:

"No please don't..."

Rén replied: "As they fall from the sky I want you to reflect on the price of loyalty and obedience."

Alice initiated an urgent Cybersync:

*"Ria! Do something!"*

Ria replied: *"On it now..."*

Alice pleaded: *"Ria!"*

Lane replied: *"Alice we need to concentrate...trust us...please..."*

Another technician announced:

"Virus upload complete...shutting down their engines now..."

Alice stared wide-eyed at the blinking red dot on the screen. She held her breath as the dot suddenly slipped below the yellow line until finally it vanished from the screen. *Gao!*

The technician announced:

"TA100 has impacted the ground at grid-sector zero one five by two one six..."

Alice felt tears fall from her eyes as the enormity of her loss took her breath away.

Rén said: "As I said...that was an example of futility..."

But suddenly Ria announced:

*"It is okay Alice...we hacked the virus upload...your friends are safe..."*

Alice wiped her eyes and asked: *"The plane?"*

Ria replied: *"Still on course...but we took the precaution of subverting their systems...the plane will not show up on any radar or Satcam..."*

Alice said: *"Thank god...and thank you...both of you..."*

Ria continued: *"I have transmitted precise landing coordinates...expect your friends in less than an hour..."*

Alice stared at Rén and said:

*"Ria... Send the message to Han Mang..."*

Ria replied: *"Done..."*

Alice continued: *"And take over the vidcams..."*

Lane interjected: *"We are already feeding them false loops...they will only see what we allow them to see..."*

Alice replied: *"Good... Now I need to find Lin..."*

Ria cautioned: *"Be careful Alice...because right now she is not your friend, she is Rén's little pet..."*

Alice asked: *"Do you know where she is?"*

Ria replied: *"Laboratory Six, Sub-level four..."*

Alice asked: *"Is she alright?"*

Ria replied: *"She is having some kind of medical exam..."*

Alice said: *"I need to get to her..."*

Ria replied: *"Good luck..."*

Rén said: "Now...we need to talk about your future..."

Alice tensed as she asked: "My future?"

Rén replied: "You are integral to my plans and as such your cooperation would be advantageous."

Alice asked: "Do you really think I will cooperate after what you have just done?"

Rén sighed and replied: "You have a simple choice: cooperate willingly or I will have your cerebral interface re-programmed."

Alice asked: "Like you did to Lin?"

Rén smiled slightly and replied: "I must admit I was surprised how easy it was to control her..." He paused to study Alice briefly before continuing: "Which brings me to an intriguing mystery... Why were you able to resist the resonance pulse? Your implants are far more primitive than Huang Lin's, and yet somehow the cluster re-alignment failed..."

Alice replied: "I guess I was just lucky..."

Rén fell silent until he said: "That remains to be seen..." He gestured to the door and said: "I will give you a short tour of our facilities..."

Alice asked: "What about Lin? I need to see her..."

Rén replied: "Of course... After the tour I will reunite you with your friend...this way..."

Ria synced from the cerebral interface:

*"Gao and the others are on the mountain... I will guide them inside...take care..."*

Alice replied: *"Okay..."*

Rén spoke as he led Alice along a corridor:

"Once you see some of our work here, I think you will appreciate the logic of cooperation."

Alice replied coldly: "That remains to be seen..."

## Laboratory Six - Sublevel Four - Special Projects Complex

A sterile room of bright lights illuminating bio-screens beeping above a standard examination bed. The air has a familiar smell arriving as a metallic taste upon the lips of the woman lying on the bed. *Steripol...*

Huang Lin was acutely aware of the neural probe beeping above her head. *Scanning my implants...* Rén Du had assured her that it was a routine medical examination, but she no longer trusted his words. *He has a secret agenda...* Blind loyalty has been replaced by a nagging suspicion that everything she had been told was a fabrication. *The truth is so close...and yet beyond my reach...* She had repeatedly tried to initiate a Cybersync into the Cloud only to find a negative Net Access Response. *They are blocking Cloud access...* The young man in the lab coat was talking:

"My name is Yong Lee... Director Rén has asked me to verify the data capacity of your cerebral interface."

Lin looked up and asked: "Why would that be necessary?"

Yong tapped a bio-screen as he replied: "It is just a precautionary measure...you have suffered significant trauma recently, we just want to make sure everything is working correctly."

Lin replied: "I can confirm that there is only one fault with my data-core..."

Yong looked down and asked: "And what is that fault?"

Lin replied: "I cannot initiate a Cybersync to the outside world."

Yong asked: "But why would you want to do that?"

Lin replied: "I need to verify the truth..."

Yong tensed as he asked: "The truth about what?"

Without warning Lin gripped Yong by the throat before sitting up straight.

Yong asked breathlessly: "What...are you doing?"

Lin stood up and wrapped her arm around his neck as she replied:

"Verifying the truth..."

Yong struggled briefly but within seconds he lost consciousness and fell to the floor.

Lin was about to open the door when a blinding pain erupted behind her eyes. For a brief moment she struggled to breathe. *Countermeasures!* She quickly returned to the neural probe and initiated a full scan. As the pain increased she studied the screen through tear-filled eyes until finally the scan revealed the cause of the pain. *Cluster re- segmentation of the anterior implant...* A terrible truth arrived with frightening clarity: *They have re-programmed my data-core to accommodate an invasive resonance pulse...* Without hesitation she adjusted the neural probe to initiate an engrammatic purge of her cerebral interface. A rapid calculation produced two possible outcomes: *Brain-dead or restored to my original personality...* Five seconds later she collapsed unconscious to the floor.

# A Surreal Suspicion

*'Look what we have created through science, we have truly usurped the sanctity of God...'*
Matt Dower CEO Synthtech Corporation

01:59 - Monday May 3rd - Biogenomic Engineering Laboratory - Sublevel 5 - Synthtech Corporation - Radford Boulevard - West Seattle - USA

Beneath the glare of LED ceiling tiles the head of a human female has been immersed in a solution of formaldehyde, glutaraldehyde, methanol, and anti-edemic chemicals. Placed inside a permiglass container the skull has been split open to reveal several implants placed along the cerebellum. Above the head several bio-screens are busy scanning the neocortical data-core.
    Professor Niel Jordon tapped his datapad several times, acutely aware of the impatient nature of his employer. Finally he announced:
    "I can confirm that Ria's data-core has been deleted..."
    Dower spoke as he stared down at the head:
    "How is that possible? The Chinese had no access to the body..."
    Jordon replied: "I see no signs of tampering...the implants are intact and have not been accessed externally..."
    Dower straightened up and asked: "What are you saying professor?"
    Jordon cleared his throat before replying: "It is only speculation, but there is the slight possibility that Ria was able to upload her data-core to a Cloud portal..."
    Dower's eyes widened as he asked: "She is in the Cloud?"
    Jordon replied: "It is possible..."
    Dower frowned and asked: "If she synced to a portal can you find her?"
    Jordon replied: "I can scan for her neural signature...but..."
    Dower asked: "But what?"

Jordon continued: "Sir, the Cloud contains millions of active portals; sifting for a specific PAP could take months..."

Dower fell silent briefly before asking: "Hypothetically, if she did transfer her data-core to an active portal, would she possess any remnant of her humanity? Or would she be nothing more than a collection of cluster segments transformed into Cloudstream data?"

Jordon hesitated slightly before replying: "To be honest... I cannot say what she might become...theoretically an augmented Cloud scenario could create a suitable environment for the expansion of her consciousness..."

Dower said: "So she could be alive somewhere in the Cloud as an avatar..."

Jordon smiled slightly and replied: "But the word *alive* cannot be applied to augmented reality..."

Dower sighed and said: "That depends on your perspective..."

Jordon looked at Ria's head and asked: "What do you want me to do with the head?"

Dower replied coldly: "It is useless to us...destroy it..."

Jordon said: "Very good sir..."

From behind them a child's voice asked:

"Who is that?"

Dower turned to see Lily dressed in a white hospital gown. He smiled as he replied:

"This is nothing but a mistake my dear... Do not concern yourself..."

The blonde haired child stepped closer and said:

"She has a pretty face..."

Dower replied: "Yes...but she is dead now sweetie..."

Lily studied the face and asked: "What is her name?"

Dower replied: "Her name was Ria..."

Lily studied the head and said: "She had implants...like me..."

Dower took her hand and said: "Let's get you back to your room... You have a busy day tomorrow."

Lily spoke as she was led towards the door: "What is happening tomorrow?"

Dower replied: "You are going to enter the Cloud..."

Lily smiled and said: "I like Cloud Dancing..."

As they walked along the corridor Dower said: "But tomorrow you will go to New Oasis..."

Lily asked: "Why?

Dower replied: "I want you to retrieve something for me..."

Lily asked: "Data?"

Dower smiled and replied: "Yes...data..."

Lily said: "Okay..."

Dower smiled warmly and said: "That's my girl..."

# An Unexpected Call

*'We are disparate souls united by destiny...'*
General Sun Qi

**17:59 - Monday May 3rd - Level One - Ministry of State Security - Beijing**

Section Leader Han Mang placed his head in his hands as the phone continued to ring. He knew it was Minister Dai Ling demanding yet another update in the search for Rén Du. *How can I admit failure?* He sat back and opened his desk drawer to reveal his state issued handgun. *What price failure but the ultimate price?* He retrieved the gun and checked the chamber before finally turning his phone off. For several minutes he simply gripped the gun in his hand before placing the tip of the barrel against his right temple. He closed his eyes with his finger on the trigger when suddenly the desktop screen flickered into life. He lowered the gun as a vaguely familiar face came onscreen. The young man announced:

"Section Leader Han... I am Guan Lu, and I believe we should become allies..."

Han sat forward and asked: "You are one of the augments?"
Guan replied: "I am..."
Han asked: "Is the traitor Ting Mai with you?"
Guan replied: "She is no traitor..."
Han said: "She is in league with foreign spies..."
Guan replied: "She was the victim of blackmail..."
Han asked: "The British?"
Guan replied: "They kidnapped her child..."
Han asked: "You have verified this?"
Guan replied: "It was confirmed by a British agent..."
Han asked: "You have met with these agents?"
Guan replied: "They came to kill us...but they failed."
Han stared at the screen and asked: "You killed them?"

Guan replied: "I had no choice..."

Han studied the young face on the screen and said: "You said something about becoming allies?"

Guan replied: "You want to locate Rén Du... I know his location."

Han tensed and asked: "Where is he?"

Guan replied: "I will reveal his location once we are airborne... You will need to requisition a sub-orbital jet..."

Han asked: "Rén Du is no longer in China?"

Guan replied: "We have no time to waste Section Leader...request the jet..."

Han replied: "I cannot simply requisition a jet without a legitimate reason..."

Guan replied firmly: "If you want to stop Rén Du from creating an army of augmented humans you will accede to my request."

Han fell silent briefly before saying: "Very well... When can we meet?"

Guan replied: "Transmit the location of the airfield... I will meet you there..."

Han asked: "Why are you doing this?"

Guan replied: "I will terminate Rén Du for the professor..."

Han asked: "You think Rén Du had the professor killed?"

Guan replied: "I am certain of it..."

Han said: "We found no trace of an assassin within the laboratory..."

Guan replied: "Nevertheless an assassin breached your security with impunity."

Han sighed and said: "I will request transport...transmitting details to your phone now..."

Guan said: "Make haste Section Leader...time is not on our side..."

Han asked: "How soon can you get to the airfield?"

Guan replied: "I will be there in twenty minutes..."

Han smiled slightly and said: "Very well... Zàijiàn Guan Lu..."

As the connection closed Han picked up his phone and tapped the screen. Moments later an irate Minister Dai Ling came onscreen and asked:

"Where have you been? I have been trying to call you..."

Han replied: "I have found a way to locate Rén Du..."

Dai ordered: "Explain..."

Han stood up and replied: "I have no time to explain...but I do need a Stratoliner fuelled and ready at Xianu airfield..."

Dai raised his eyebrows and asked: "You are leaving the country?"

Han replied: "Apparently... "

Dai said: "Very well... I will make the arrangements. But this is your last chance Section Leader Han... Do you understand?"

Han glanced towards the gun and replied: "I do..."

# A Seed Once Planted

*'A seed once planted alters the nature of our existence...'*
Xun Yang

**18:31 - Itayama Forest - Mt. Ninouji - Shibata - Niigata Prefecture - Japan**

The group of people from Singapore watched the VTOL jet rise slowly back into the sky, the down thrust spraying a fine shower of snow over their heads. The abrupt and unexpected landing had left them shaken and shocked at their narrow escape from almost certain death. When the engines had shut down during mid-flight the pilot had announced an imminent crash landing, creating immediate panic inside the cabin. But just seconds later all four thruster pods had reignited and new landing coordinates had been uploaded to the onboard computer. A simple message on Gao's phone confirmed the source of their salvation:

"It's okay... Rén uploaded a virus, but I neutralised it... Sending u precise access data to the mountain... Contact u again soon... Ria..."

Now they huddled together at the edge of a clearing whilst they studied the detailed schematics transmitted by Ria.

Fen moaned: "I am just saying that maybe, just maybe, we should have taken the time to buy coats... I mean...this is not Singapore..."

Tong retorted: "It's not? Wow... Did not know that..."

Jessica pulled her jacket close and said: "Enough with the bickering you two..."

Connie looked up hill and said: "I really don't want to go into that place..." She shivered before continuing: "But right now I am freezing to death..."

Fay rubbed her hands together and said: "It might be life-threatening inside Rén's lair, but at least it will be warm..."

Fen added morosely: "Until we get killed..."

Jessica tidied her hair and said: "Always on the bright side Chin..."

Gao looked up from his phone and announced:

"Ria will open each door in rotation as we progress further into the complex..."

Connie asked: "Do we have any kind of a plan? I mean, what do we do when we get inside that place?"

Fay replied: "Chin and Tong will hack into the central computer system and disable the security grid..."

Fen said: "I thought Ria was already doing that..."

Gao replied: "Apparently the encryption codes are not based on portal access technology...they are old-style physical cipher keys with multilevel insertion points..."

Fay added: "Ria can't access physical cipher technology...she is restricted to Cloud portals only..."

Tong asked: "So you want me and the nerd to decipher old-style codes?"

Gao replied: "Yes. And as fast as possible...there is a security team on its way from Beijing as we speak; if the security grid has not been disabled they will all be killed."

Fen frowned and said: "But won't they arrest us or something? We did hack their top secret project..."

Fay sighed and replied: "We'll jump off that bridge when we come to it..."

Gao checked the time and said: "Okay...let's get going..."

As they set off in single file Fen commented: "It wouldn't have taken five minutes to buy a coat..."

**Sub-orbital Stratoliner SSM365 - Somewhere over the Sea of Japan**

Han Mang sat back in his seat and contemplated the incomprehensible nature of fate. *At the finite point of defeat redemption arrives at the behest of criminals...* He smiled at the irony. *The enemy of my enemy is my friend...* The mysterious Cybersync from Mount Ninouji had breached more than a dozen security portals to reach his phone - that fact alone confirmed his suspicions. *It was from the original prototype or one of her confederates...* He looked out upon twilight skies to see a thin scattering of stars seeking the solace of the coming night. *What happens tonight could change everything...*

Sitting opposite Guan Lu said:

"I have decrypted the source code of the message..."

Han sat forward and asked: "And?"

Guan frowned and replied: "It makes no sense..."

Han asked: "What are you saying?"

Guan replied: "Whoever sent that message has no real-world location...there was no geogrid prefix to the portal coding...no PAP and no server recognition protocols..."

Han frowned and asked: "How is that possible?"

Guan replied: "It should not be possible..."

Han studied Guan's face and said: "But you have a theory?"

Guan replied: "I have speculation..." He paused before continuing: "The source code was augmented...it was a Cybersync based solely within the Cloud domain."

Han asked: "Are you saying that the message was sent by an avatar?"

Guan replied: "I am saying that the message was not sent via any known technology..."

Han sat back and said: "Then we have one more mystery to solve..."

Guan asked: "What is the other mystery?"

Han replied: "What is Rén Du really planning..."

Guan replied: "I told you... He intends to implement Phase Two of the Jiàngsheng Project."

Han replied: "But that process would take decades..." He looked through the side window before continuing: "No... I suspect he has another, as yet unknown agenda..."

Tactical Commander Ni Ling approached and announced:

"ETA thirty minutes sir..."

Han asked: "Do you have the latest Satcam data?"

Ni replied: "They are still scattering the data-upload...some type of defensive net is in place..."

Han asked: "Will that be a problem?"

Ni replied: "If they have targeting ordnance it could be a big problem..."

Han looked at Guan and asked: "Did you know about this defensive net?"

Guan replied: "No. They must be using old-style cipher technology to mask the encryption protocols... It is not a portal-based system."

Han fell silent briefly before saying: "Then we can only hope that our erstwhile allies are able to disable that net..."

Communications Officer Yong Su approached and announced: "Sir I have a message from Minister Dai Ling in Beijing..."

Han sighed and said: "Read it..."

Yong read from her datapad:

"Negotiations with Japanese government ongoing. Permission to enter Japanese airspace is still denied. Proceed at your own discretion. Dai Ling."

Han smiled slightly and said: "My own discretion..."

Guan said: "Beijing can officially deny accountability..."

Han replied: "The perfidious nature of politics..."

After a few minutes Guan asked:

"Did you know about the original prototype?"

Han replied: "I suspected the professor was hiding something...but I did not discover the truth until recently."

Guan asked: "What do you know of this Alice Sòng?"

Han replied: "Enough to know that she was a template for someone like you..."

Guan continued: "According to the message she is already inside the mountain..."

Han replied: "Yes...and her companions intend to join her..."

Guan asked: "You are talking about the hacker group from Singapore?"

Han replied: "Yes...the infamous FTSS..."

Guan asked: "Do you intend to detain them?"

Han sighed and replied: "I am legally bound to bring them to justice...but considering their recent actions against Rén Du I might reconsider my options..."

Guan asked: "And what of the original prototype? Do you have plans for her?"

Han looked out of the side window as he replied: "Considering the mysterious origins of that message I fear that she is beyond my jurisdiction..."

Guan considered this before asking: "You believe she is linked to the message?"

Han replied: "I believe that a seed has been planted that will alter the nature of our existence..."

Guan sat back and said: "The philosopher Xun Yang..."

Han replied wearily: "Yes... Words from a thousand years ago have come back to haunt us..."

## 19:21 - Monday May 3rd - Special Projects Complex - Mt. Ninouji - Itayama - Shibata - Niigata Prefecture - Japan

They gathered together beneath an overhanging rock protruding defiantly from the surrounding trees. At this altitude the snow was deep and the air was bitterly cold against the exposed faces of the group from Singapore.

Chin Fen stamped his feet and moaned: "I am freezing to death..."

Connie shivered and added: "I think I am already dead..."

Fay spoke as she studied her phone: "We are here..."

Tong scratched his chin and asked: "We are where?"

Fay replied: "An access point..."

Jessica looked up towards a metal grid protruding from the rock. She asked:

"What am I looking at?"

Gao replied: "An air-intake shaft. It leads directly to the power generator..."

Fen rubbed his hands together ands asked:

"We are supposed to crawl through a metal tunnel?"

Jessica replied with a slight smile: "A warm metal tunnel..."

A trembling Connie said: "I could take warm right now..."

Fay studied the partially concealed entrance to the shaft and said: "Once we get inside the generator room we have access to the internal power grid... That's where we can hack into the defence net and disable it..."

Fen looked at the metal grid covering the shaft and asked: "How do we get inside that thing?"

But almost immediately the grid rotated slowly to one side to reveal a dark tunnel leading into the mountain.

Gao smiled slightly and said: "Thank you Ria..."

Fay scrambled up a short slope and said: "Let's go people..."

Gao retrieved the torch provided by the Biogen pilot before joining Fay at the tunnel entrance. One sweep of the beam revealed a metal shaft approximately a metre and a half in diameter descending into the complex.

Connie looked into the shaft and said: "This just got very scary..."

Gao announced: "I will go first..."

As they crawled cautiously into the shaft Jessica commented: "At least it will be warmer..."

Fen added: "It better be..."

From the rear Tong looked up and said: "Move your ass Chin..."

By the light of the torch they made their way slowly into the heart of the mountain.

**19:30 - Monday May 3rd - Sublevel One - Special Projects Complex - Mt. Ninouji - Itayama - Shibata - Niigata Prefecture - Japan**

Beyond the observation window several laboratory technicians were busy monitoring a series of glass tubules placed beneath a row of bio-data screens.

Rén Du explained:

"They are adjusting the genomic fluids to counter mutational reactions within the gene sequence of each sample...this will produce a specific modification of the characteristics of the organism by manipulating its genetic material. The base code will then be re-aligned prior to insertion and augmentation."

Alice looked through the observation window and said: "This is all very interesting, but I want to see Lin now..."

Rén replied: "Of course...this way..."

Alice stepped through a side door into another laboratory where two technicians were waiting. An urgent Cybersync suddenly arrived from her cerebral interface:

*"Alice! It is a trap! Run...!"*

But it was already too late. Alice felt a sharp sting to her neck before collapsing unconscious into the arms of a smiling Rén Du.

**Laboratory Six - Sublevel Four - Special Projects Complex**

A pounding headache gradually subsiding into a dull ache arriving as intense nausea...a sea of chaotic images sweeping into sight and sound seeking semblance and form...the frail and fragile tenacity of memory finally arriving as stark recognition...

*I remember!*

Huang Lin opened her eyes upon a ceiling illuminated by LED tiles and promptly rolled over to vomit until the nausea finally began to subside. She wiped her mouth before standing up slowly to assess her surroundings. *Laboratory Six... Sub-level Four... Special Projects Complex...* A groaning sound alerted her to the man lying on the floor. *Yong Lee...* Without hesitation she gripped his hair and slammed his head onto the floor until he once again lost consciousness. Suddenly one name came to mind: *Alice!* Words from a conversation arrived with startling clarity:

*"I told you...they are bait..."*
*"Does this bait possess names?"*
*"Mister Tiang Lao and his wife, Cynthia..."*
*"What is their connection to Alice Sòng?"*

"See for yourself...."
"Very interesting... Do you think she will care?"
"They say blood is thicker than water..."
She steadied herself against the examination bed as the memories created a fearful sense of urgency:
"Behold... Phase Two... Your son..."
"My...son?"
"We used eggs extracted from your ovary..."
"He has a pleasant smell..."
"That is the scent of a baby..."
"My son..."
Lin felt tears slip from her eyes as she whispered: "Weisheng..." She looked towards the door as the fear coalesced into a terrible truth: *Rén Du is abusing my son...* A surge of intense hatred was suddenly subsumed by a gestalt sifting of causal facts into a precise series of conclusions: *Alice is here...and Rén Du is going to re-program her data-core... She will replace me as the heir to his augmented legacy... And my child will be the first of a new race of people...a people without pity or the need to emphasise with those they consider less evolved...*

She was about to open the door when an invasive sync arrived within her cerebral interface:

"Lin? Are you receiving this Cybersync?"

Lin paused at the door and asked:

"Who is this? How did you access my portal?"

"I am Ria and I am synced to Alice Sòng... There is no time to explain, Alice is in great danger...you must save her..."

Lin replied: "I will do nothing until you answer my question... How did you access my portal?"

Ria replied: "I exist within the Cloud... I am using the data-core of Alice Sòng to transmit an invasive sync into your cerebral interface... In my past life I was the American augment sent to terminate both you and Alice... But at the moment of my death I uploaded my data-core into Alice's cerebral implant... We have since become allies united against Rén Du... She came here to rescue you, but now her data-core is about to be re-written...you must save her now!"

Lin swept through a thousand threads of causality and outcome before asking: *"You expect me trust you?"*

Ria replied bluntly: *"I expect you to save Alice..."*

Lin rapidly considered her options before asking: *"Where is she?"*

Ria replied: *"Laboratory One... Sublevel Two..."*

Lin glanced towards the ceiling and asked: *"Do you have access to the internal vidcam system?"*

Ria replied: *"I am feeding the control room false loops as we speak... You cannot be seen..."*

Lin asked: *"Is my son safe?"*

Ria replied: *"Yes... He is asleep in the crèche on Sublevel Four... But you must save Alice now!"*

Lin opened the door and said: *"I am on my way..."*

**19:41 - Monday May 3rd - Generator Room - Sublevel Five - Special Projects Complex - Mt. Ninouji**

The group from Singapore had emerged from the air shaft into a dimly lit generator room humming with the sound of power conduits feeding the complex with energy.

Ria had opened the exit hatch after disabling the air-intake valve. But the journey along the metal shaft had not been without incident - the air induction system had recycled twice causing a rapid updraft which had sucked the air from their lungs and left them breathless upon their knees. But as the temperature began to rise they had persevered until the sound of machinery signalled the end of their brief journey into the heart of the mountain.

Gao studied his phone and said: "Wait a minute..."

Fay straightened up and asked: "Problem?"

Gao replied: "A message from Ria..."

Jessica stepped closer and asked: "What does it say?"

Gao looked up and replied: "Alice in trouble..."

Fay looked towards the door and said "Then we need to hurry..."

Fen spoke as he studied a nearby computer console:

"We can sync into the defence net from here..."
Fay asked: "Are you sure?"
Tong joined Fen and replied: "Piece of cake..."
Gao said: "Alright...you two stay here and do your stuff..." He paused before continuing: "We will try to find Alice..."
Connie asked: "How do we do that?"
Gao glanced at his phone and replied: "She is on sublevel two..."
Jessica asked: "What about security guards?"
Gao replied: "Ria will warn us before we run into any guards..."
Fay said: "Okay... Let's do this..."
Tong looked up and said: "Good luck..."
When they were finally alone Fen said: "They will need more than luck..."

**Laboratory One - Sublevel Two - Special Projects Complex**

A room of bright lights filled with the rhythmic sound of bio-screens registering the vital signs of the young woman lying prostrate upon an examination bed. She has been undressed and covered in a simple white sheet. Her head has been connected via sensor pads to an overhead datascreen currently displaying the neural emission rate of her cerebral implant.

Doctor Tang Yu studied the latest stats and announced:
"We have accessed the encrypted portal...sifting now for a viable cluster segment..."
Rén asked impatiently: "How long will this take?"
Tang looked up and replied: "Sir, re-programming the data-core requires a certain amount of finesse. If we force a premature re-segmentation we risk brain death..."
Rén snapped: "Just answer the question!"
Tang replied: "I expect to have full control of her implants within the hour..."
Rén studied the overhead screen and asked: "Why is there a peak in the neural emission rate?"

Tang tapped the screen as he replied: "I am running a diagnostic scan..." He paused before continuing: "This is very odd..."

Rén asked: "What is odd?"

Tang replied: "The neural emission rate is almost ten times the capacity of the data-core..."

Rén stared at the screen and asked: "How is that possible?"

Tang replied: "It should not be possible..."

Rén sighed and asked: "Do you have a theory that might explain the excess capacity?"

Tang replied: "Such a phenomenon could only be possible if Miss Sòng was directly synced to a Cloud portal..."

Rén said: "But she is not synced..."

Tang said: "Nevertheless, that is the only viable explanation..." He looked at Alice and continued: "The impossible has become possible... She is receiving a vast amount of neural telemetry from within the Cloud domain."

Rén frowned and asked: "Can you access the source code?"

Tang replied: "I am running a portal search algorithm as we speak... If she is connected to the Cloud we will know soon enough..."

Rén stepped closer to the screen and asked: "Would this anomaly explain her ability to resist the resonance pulse?"

Tang considered the question carefully before replying:

"It fits the theory...yes... If she was able to nullify the incoming transmission and decrypt the embedded sync-code, then she would be able resist the pulse algorithm."

Rén fell silent briefly before saying: "She could be receiving neural energy from someone or some *thing* within the Cloud..."

Tang gave a slight smile and replied: "I think that is more likely to be within the realm of science fiction than science fact..."

Rén touched Alice's face gently and said: "Contact me when you have accessed the invasive sync..."

Tang replied: "Of course..."

Technician Dian Bai approached and announced:

"Sir, we have lost contact with Laboratory Six..."

Rén asked: "What are you saying?"

Dian Bai continued: "Yong Lee is not responding..."

Rén tapped his datapad and said: "Vidcam shows an empty lab... Where is Huang Lin?"

Dian Bai replied in a low voice: "Sir, we do not know..."

Rén tapped the pad to connect to the Control Room. Moments later Wo Chun came online:

"Yes sir?"

Rén ordered: "Send a security team to Laboratory Six, and issue an alert... I want the complex locked down..."

Wo Chun asked: "Is there a problem?"

Rén replied: "I want bio-scans of the entire complex and a review of every vidcam feed..."

Wo Chun glanced off-screen and announced: "There is an aircraft inbound...on full approach to geogrid one seven four by two one six..."

Rén ordered: "Activate countermeasures...infiltrate that aircraft."

Wo Chun looked down briefly before announcing: "Sir we have a system-wide failure within the defence net..."

Rén snapped: "I am on my way... And get that team to laboratory six!"

Wo Chun replied: "They are on their way now, and the complex has been locked down... All vidcam feeds are being analysed..."

Rén cut the connection and ordered: "Find out what is going on inside her head Doctor..."

Tang replied: "Yes sir...

Rén turned to Dian Bai and ordered: "Follow me..."

## 19:48 - Mt. Ninouji - Itayama Forest - Shibata - Niigata Prefecture - Japan

As the engines of the Stratoliner fell silent a ramp began to extend slowly from the back of the plane, coming to rest on the snow covered ground. They had landed inside the only open space for miles - a rock-strewn clearing boasting a few shrubs and a frozen mountain stream. Within seconds twenty combat troops had disembarked and formed up at the side of the plane. They were soon joined by Section Leader Han Mang and his companion, Guan Lu.

Communications Officer Yong Su approached and announced:

"Sir, Satcam surveillance is once more active. The scattering signal has been disabled at source."

Han gave a slight smile and said: "The FTSS strikes again..."

Tactical Commander Ni Ling joined them and announced:

"Sir, all combat teams are ready for deployment on your orders..."

Han tapped his datapad as he spoke:

"I want the doors to the flight deck disabled...get your demolition team up there commander... We will follow close behind..."

Guan studied his phone and said:

"I have another message from our mysterious benefactor..."

Han ordered: "Read it..."

Guan read from the screen: "I will try to open the flight deck doors once you are in position...otherwise you will have to use explosives. Internal schematics attached..." Guan tapped his phone and added: "Syncing the attachments to your datapad now..."

Han studied the schematics briefly and said: "Astonishing..."

Guan said: "We should get moving..."

Han ordered: "Deploy your men Commander Ni..."

Ni Ling replied: "At once sir..."

As the troops set off towards the sealed flight deck of the complex Han said:

"Guan Lu... A moment if you please..."

Guan turned and asked: "Is there a problem?"

Han replied: "I want to take Rén Du alive... You are not to harm him..."

Guan asked: "You want to question him?"

Han replied: "I need to know his true agenda..."

Guan Lu sighed and said: "Very well... As long as he does not escape..."

Han looked up towards the sky and replied: "I can assure you...he will not escape..."

Guan looked up with eyes wide to see more than a dozen long-range combat helicopters approaching from the west. He asked: "You sent for reinforcements?"

Han replied: "Troop carriers...courtesy of the Japanese government..."

Guan asked: "They are helping you?"

Han replied: "I received a coded sync from Beijing... Security Minister Dai Ling explained the dangers posed by Rén Du to the Japanese nation. They agreed to share jurisdiction on this matter..." He paused before continuing: "They have already surrounded the mountain; their troops will follow us inside the complex..."

Guan said: "Then we should get going..."

Han fastened his coat and replied: "Yes...it is time to meet the enigmatic Rén Du..."

# Cloud Dancing

*'The Cloud has become an addictive alternative to reality,
this speaks volumes about the true nature of our modern world...'*
Rén Du

Alice opened her eyes to see a sky full of stars stealing the sanctity of the night with a grim determination to shine life into the eternal darkness. The tactile sensation of the highway arrived as a feeling of cold stone beneath her back. A rapid analysis confirmed her location: *Digital junction point...* But the absence of portal orbs was unsettling. *Something is wrong...* She was suddenly aware of another presence... She asked:
"Ria?"
She was startled by a child's voice replying:
"Ria is not here..."
Alice struggled to her feet to see a young girl standing nearby. *Long blonde hair, blue eyes...white T-shirt and blue jeans...* She asked:
"Who are you?"
The girl replied: "I am Lily..." She smiled warmly before adding: "This is my avatar... She looks like me..."
A confused Alice asked: "What have you done to Ria?"
Lily replied: "Nothing... I think she is busy right now..."
Alice asked: "How did you access my data-core?"
Lily cocked her head to one side and replied: "I was curious..."
Alice asked: "Curious?"
Lily stepped closer and continued: "I found your digital signature inside the coffee house...it contained a neural pattern that I recognised... So I made this Cloud-gap and waited for you to arrive..."
Alice asked: "You waited for me?"
Lily replied: "Someone is scanning your implants for a Cloud portal sync-code... They want to re-program your data-core to make you their friend..." She played a finger through her hair before continuing: "I don't think they are very nice people... So I pulled you out of there..."

A confused Alice said: "I do not understand... I was with Rén Du... He was taking me to see Lin... And then..." She looked up and continued: "Oh my god... Ria tried to warn me... It was a trap..."

Lily frowned and said: "I don't know any Rén Du... I just felt your pain..."

Alice asked: "You say you recognised my neural pattern?"

Lily replied: "An augmented sync-code..." She tapped her head before adding: "I have one too..."

Alice sifted for causal linkage before announcing: "You are the American augment...the one Ria mentioned..."

Lily replied: "I am yes..."

Alice asked: "You have been to New Oasis?"

Lily replied: "My father asked me to collect some data...it was disguised as a Cloud construct..."

Alice said: "The Cup of Joe Coffee House..."

Lily smiled and said: "Yes! You are clever Alice..."

Alice asked: "You know my name?"

Lily lowered her eyes slightly and replied: "Yes...sorry, I scanned your data-core..." She looked up and added: "But only for your name...nothing else..."

Alice fell silent briefly before asking: "Are you sure they are re-programming my data-core?

Lily replied soberly: "Yes...sorry..."

Alice said: "I must contact Ria... Or Lin..."

Lily said: "You can't sync to any portals...they have isolated your PAP..."

Alice said: "But you can reach them, right?"

Lily hesitated before replying: "Maybe...but..."

Alice asked: "But what?"

Lily replied: "My father wants me to disconnect now..."

Alice asked: "You father?"

Lily replied: "Matt... Mister Dower... He wants the data..."

Alice asked: "You have retrieved the Jiàngsheng files?"

Lily laughed and replied: "That sounds so funny... Jiàng...sheng...."

Alice sighed heavily and said: "Listen to me Lily... I do not want to lose myself... Please help me... Sync to my friends...tell them I need help..."

Lily fell silent before replying: "Okay... I will scan for your friend Lin..."

Alice said: "I think you should sync to Ria first... Lin might not be on my side yet..."

Lily asked: "Why not?"

Alice replied: "Because the bad people re-programmed her data-core..."

Lily said: "Oh..."

Alice asked: "Can you contact Ria first?"

Lily replied: "I'm not sure..."

Alice asked: "Why not?"

Lily replied: "Her neural signature is scary..."

Alice asked: "What do you mean?"

Lily replied: "It is too big...like she is everywhere..." She gestured towards the stars and continued: "I had to hide this Cloud Gap from her..."

Alice spoke gently: "But she is my friend...and she can save me Lily..."

Lily sighed and said: "Okay... I will try..."

Alice smiled and said: "Thank you..."

The Lily avatar vanished briefly before reappearing by the side of the road.

Alice stepped closer and asked: "Well? Did you contact Ria?"

Lily replied: "She is here..."

Alice turned to see Ria and the young man she knew as Mark.

Ria announced: "Well this is new..."

Daniel Lane looked towards the sky and said: "A concealed Cloud Gap... Very clever..."

Alice spoke anxiously: "Ria...they are re-programming my data-core..."

Ria replied: "I know... Lin is on her way to save you..."

Alice asked: "You got through to Lin?"

Ria replied: "I didn't need to get through to her...she restored her own data-core...quite amazing actually..."

Alice asked: "What about Gao and the others?"

Ria replied: "They disabled the defence net and are searching for you as we speak..."

Lane added: "And Chinese state security troops are entering the complex..."

Ria continued: "As well as about fifty Japanese soldiers..."

Alice said: "Wow..."

Ria looked at Lily and said: "Hi Lily..."

Lily stared at Ria and replied bluntly: "I saw your head... You are dead..."

Ria gave a slight smile and replied: "Yes... I am so very dead..."

Alice saw the fear in Lily's eyes and said: "It is okay Lily... Ria uploaded her data-core into my implants..."

Lily said: "But she is not synced to your portal..."

Ria stepped closer and said: "No... We are actually citizens of the Cloud now..."

Lane smiled and added: "Indigenous neural energy..."

A frightened Lily said: "I have to go now..."

Ria said: "Wait a minute..." She walked towards Lily and continued: "You can't give Dower those data files..."

Lily stepped back and replied: "But he told me to find them..."

Alice spoke gently: "Lily you father will use the data to hurt people..."

Lily shook her head and replied: "No... He is a good man..."

Ria retorted: "He ordered someone to remove my head...a good man does not do that..." She knelt down in front of Lily and continued: "I called him father as well... I trusted him and I loved him...but then one day I found out a terrible truth..."

Lily asked: "What truth?"

Ria replied: "He did not love me...in fact I was nothing but a tool to be used and abused..."

Alice added: "I know this is not easy to accept...but you cannot trust your father..."

Lily said: "I have to go home now..."

Ria shouted: "No wait..."

But as the Lily avatar vanished from the highway Lane announced:

"I did it..."

Alice turned and asked: "You did what?"

Lane smiled as he replied: "I hacked her portal and deleted the data..."

Ria smiled and said: "Well done..."

Alice said: "Dower will not like that... Lily could be in trouble..."

Ria said: "Not our problem..."

Alice said: "But she is just a child..."

Ria replied: "And we have far more pressing matters to deal with..."

Alice asked: "So what do I do now? Can I just wake up?"

Ria replied: "No...they have you sedated... You will have to wait for the cavalry..."

Alice said: "I do not feel sedated..."

Ria replied: "Because Lily synced directly to your data-core to bring you here..."

Alice asked in a low voice: "Will they get to me in time?"

Ria replied: "I hope so..."

The Lane avatar blurred slightly before announcing: "Gao and the others need us..."

Ria closed her eyes briefly and announced: "Rén Du has issued orders to kill the intruders on sight..."

Alice said: "Go and help them... I will be okay..."

Ria stepped closer and said: "Have faith my friend..."

Alice watched her friends disappear before looking up to a sky full of stars and whispering:

"Wish me luck Mister Tang..."

# The End of the Beginning

*'Evolution takes no prisoners
and offers no mercy;
we are all victims of nature's constant
desire for improvement...'*
Professor Leung Huo PhD

**20:19 - Monday May 3rd - Special Projects Complex - Mt. Ninouji - Itayama - Shibata - Niigata Prefecture - Japan**

The coming night perched its shadows among the snow-laden trees of the mountain and reduced the temperature to freezing point. High above the forest the twilight skies were alive with the sound of helicopters hovering briefly to deposit Japanese soldiers, descending rapidly upon secured ropes. At the same time combat groups moved into their designated positions beneath the entrance to the subterranean complex. A rapid deployment team of Chinese engineers had forced open the doors of the flight deck to reveal a darkened interior illuminated briefly by a fierce exchange of gunfire and explosions. After the firefight three VTOL jets had been disabled and more than a dozen of Rén Du's security men lay dead. Without a moments hesitation Tactical Commander Ni Ling led his troops deeper into the complex via an emergency staircase, wisely avoiding the elevator which had been wired with an explosive device. They were soon followed by an entire company of Japanese soldiers, rapidly separating into small combat groups before descending cautiously into the lower levels of the complex.

    Section Leader Han Mang and his companion Guan Lu had been escorted to the abandoned control room on sublevel one.

    Han studied the silent consoles and asked: "Why is this place unguarded?"

    Guan replied: "I suspect Rén Du has ordered an evacuation of the complex..."

Han scowled and said: "They will not get far...the mountain is surrounded..."

Trooper Shun Yin approached and announced:

"Sir, the network sync is offline and all data has been erased..."

Han nodded slightly and ordered: "Locate the primary data-core...there might yet be something we can retrieve..."

Shun Yin replied: "At once sir..."

Ni Ling joined them and announced:

"We have secured sublevel one, but access to the lower levels is proving difficult... I lost two men to a bomb on the staircase..."

Han asked: "And the Japanese?"

Ni Ling replied: "They have forced their way into the generator room via an air intake shaft..." He wiped sweat from his forehead and continued: "They have also detained two members of the FTSS..."

Guan said: "They must be the ones who disabled the defence net..."

Han said: "And we will thank them later..." He glanced around the control room before asking: "Any sign of Rén Du?"

Ni Ling replied: "No sir, he has probably escaped to one of the lower levels..."

Han spoke firmly: "I want him found..."

Ni Ling stood to attention and replied: "Yes sir..."

Han added: "And make sure the Japanese do not get their hands on him..."

Ni Ling replied: "Very good sir..."

Guan studied his phone and said: "We need to go to Laboratory One on sublevel two..."

Han asked: "Why?"

Guan looked up and replied: "The original prototype is there..."

Han asked: "Are you sure?"

Guan replied: "According to the last message from our mysterious ally, her data-core is to be re-programmed in that laboratory."

Trooper Wu Yao approached and announced:

"Section Leader, the staircase to the lower levels has been cleared..."

Han said: "Finally..." He looked at Guan Lu and asked: "Are you ready to meet your predecessor?"

Guan replied: "I am..."

Han smiled slightly and said: "Then let's do this..."

## 20:22 - Laboratory One - Sublevel Two

Huang Lin was surprised to find the laboratory deserted. She quickly initiated an internal Cybersync:

"*Ria... Alice is not here... Ria?*"

But there was no reply from the Cloud. She was startled by a voice from behind her.

"What have you done to Alice?"

Lin turned to see Mong Gao and Jessica Lee standing in the doorway.

A cautious Jessica stepped closer and asked: "Lin? Do you know me?"

Lin replied: "Of course I know you..."

Jessica smiled and said: "You are you again..."

Lin saw two more young women enter the room as she replied: "Yes I am..."

Gao stepped closer and asked: "Where is Alice?"

Lin gestured to the examination bed and replied: "I found the laboratory deserted... She is not here..."

Fay stepped forward and said: "I am Fay Rui, from Singapore..."

Connie smiled and said: "And I am Connie..."

Lin replied: "The Singapore hackers... FTSS..."

Connie replied: "That's us..."

Fay asked: "Have you been contacted by someone called Ria?"

Lin replied: "Yes... She directed me here to save Alice..."

Gao spoke anxiously: "So contact her again, find out where Alice has been taken..."

Lin replied: "I cannot... Ria is offline..."

Fay asked: "How is that possible? She is part of the Cloud..."

Connie added: "And she has synced her neural signature to the global net..."

Lin replied soberly: "There can only be one explanation..."

Jessica spoke in a low voice: "You think Alice is dead...and Ria has been deleted..."

Lin continued: "I fear we were too late to save her..."

Gao said: "No. It is not possible. We just need to find her..."

Connie joined Gao and said: "We can't give up hope..."

Jessica looked at Lin and asked: "What do you think?"

Lin replied: "Until we know we must believe she is alive."

Fay said: "So let's find her..."

Lin said: "You should start on sublevel four..."

Gao asked: "Why?"

Lin replied: "There is a concealed exit from the complex on that level...that is where you will find Rén Du..."

Gao asked: "But what about Alice?"

Lin replied: "If she is anywhere she will be with him..."

Jessica asked: "What do you mean *we* should start on sublevel four? What about you?"

Lin replied: "I am sorry...but I must go to the crèche...my son is in great danger..."

Jessica's eyes widened as she asked: "You have a son?"

Lin replied: "He is a product of Phase Two..."

Connie shook her head slightly and said: "This nightmare just gets worse..."

Fay said: "Then you should go to your son. We'll find Alice..."

Gao tensed and said: "I hear soldiers... We need to move now..."

As they walked towards the door Lin said: "I will join you as soon as I can..."

Jessica smiled and said: "Good luck..."

Lin replied: "You too..."

## 20:31 - Emergency Exit Tunnel - Sublevel Four - Special Projects Complex - Mt. Ninouji

At the far end of a long corridor, a small storage room conceals a single-track maglev train which links the complex to a building on the outskirts of Shibata City 16.5 km distant.

The former Director of Biogen Special Projects Division has gathered together the remnants of his personnel - a six man security team, four technicians, and the bio-augmentation expert, Doctor Tang Yu. Two of the technicians gently deposited a stretcher and its female occupant onto the floor.

Rén Du studied the face of the unconscious girl and asked: "Status?"

Doctor Tang Yu glanced at his datapad and replied:

"All neural telemetry has ceased... The new algorithm has terminated her connection to the Cloud and deleted the mysterious portal sync..." He looked down at the girl and continued: "She is currently in reset mode..."

Rén asked impatiently: "Which means what exactly?"

Tang replied: "The data-processing unit has initialised a cluster re-segmentation of her cerebral implants to implement the engrammatic re-programming sequence."

Rén asked: "You are not using a resonance pulse?"

Tang replied: "The most recent scans of Huang Lin have confirmed my earlier analysis of the pulse initiator sequence..." He tapped his datapad several times before continuing: "She was able to counter the affects of the resonance pulse because we allowed her to retain the ability to initiate an internal diagnostic of her implants." He looked down at Alice before adding: "She will not have such an advantage..."

Rén frowned as he asked: "Can she be moved?"

Tang looked towards the sound of gunfire and replied: "I fear we have no choice..."

One of the security men approached and announced:

"Sir, we have accessed the maglev...we can board at your convenience."

Rén ordered: "Wo Chun and Dian Bai...load our precious cargo onto the train...."

Wo Chun replied: "At once sir..."

Technician Yong Lee steeped closer: "Sir, I am sincerely sorry about my failure. I did not expect Huang Lin to use violence against me."

Rén sighed as he replied: "Yes...you failed me..." He smiled slightly before continuing: "But perhaps you can redeem yourself..."

Yong Lee replied: "I would like that opportunity sir..."

Rén turned to one of the security men and ordered:

"Give me your weapon..."

The man handed over his R15 assault rifle and said: "Yes sir..."

Rén turned to Yong Lee and said:

"Take this and defend this room with your life..."

Yong Lee took the gun as Rén continued:

"You will hold this position for as long as possible... We need time to transport the girl to Shibata..."

Yong Lee gripped the gun and said: "You can rely on me sir..."

Rén placed a hand on Yong's shoulder and: "Of course I can..."

Technician Peng Ying approached with a datapad and said:

"Sir, I have received a coded sync from the asset..."

Rén took the pad and read the screen before saying:

"Excellent..."

Wo Chun stepped forward and said: "Sir, the girl is secure and we are ready to leave..."

Rén nodded slightly before turning to Yong Lee and ordering:

"Hold them off as long as you can..."

Yong Lee replied: "Yes sir, I will..."

Rén stepped through a hole in the wall and onto the maglev train. He looked back once and said:

"It was a worthy beginning..."

As the sound of gunfire drew closer the magnetic track hummed into life - moments later the single-carriage train swept forward into darkness

# Revelations

*'The sound of silence seeks the colour of the rain falling into digital puddles of data shimmering beneath wide blue augmented skies...'*
    A quote from a recent poem reflects a growing trend in Cloud-orientated cultural exploration. Beyond the swarm of active portals the worldwide datastream continues to expand exponentially into synaptic confluence coalescing into substance seeking solidity inside the vast artificial environment designated simply as the Cloud - for twenty four hours a day several billion human brains are synced directly into millions of self-initiated scenarios via their active data-lenses. A rapid and involuntary stimulation of the hippocampus creates a symbiotic relationship resulting in a sense of alienation which transforms the technological illusion into a new sense of actuality. To the vast majority of people Cloud Dancing is nothing more than recreational entertainment, but for a few it has become an obsession dominating their lives, and for a very few more it has become the only reality they can truly accept.'
Thesis: *The Psychology of Cloud Dancing* - Waio Cho Ph.D/Psy. D/Psychologist

The little girl sits patiently inside a digital junction point sifting data into recognisable algorithmic potentials until finally she smiles with innocent satisfaction. *Found you...*
    She stands up before closing her bright blue eyes and syncing directly into a quantum-level cerebral processing unit designated simply as: JPOP-1. A smile arrives upon her face: *Jiàngsheng Project Original Prototype One...* Moments later the subject of her Cloud-search appears as an avatar upon the highway. She smiles and says:
    "Hello again Alice..."
    A confused and disorientated Alice asks:
    "What happened? Where is Ria?"
    Lily replied: "You have been disconnected from the Cloud..."
She paused to add soberly: "I think Ria might be gone..."

Alice asked: "Gone?"

Lily replied: "Deleted...along with that man..."

An alarmed Alice asked: "How is that possible?" She looked towards the sky and continued: "I am here so Ria should be here as well..."

Lily stepped closer and replied: "You are here because I rewrote your base-code algorithmic potential."

A surprised Alice asked: "You know how to do that?"

Lily replied: "I wasn't sure...but you are here right?"

Alice looked around and asked: "Where is here? And where is my body right now?"

Lily replied: "This is a basic junction point inside a Cloud Gap..." She sighed before continuing: "And your body is with the bad people... They think they are re-writing you cluster segmentation, but I fooled them..." She smiled before adding: "You are just in neural stasis..."

Alice asked: "What does that mean?"

Lily played a finger through her hair and replied:

"It's not easy to explain... When you are awake you think many things... But when you are asleep another version of you takes over..."

Alice asked: "The subconscious?"

Lily smiled and replied: "Yes... So I accessed that part of you and made you into an avatar, so we could talk..."

Alice asked: "Did Matt Dower ask you to do this?"

Lily lowered her eyes slightly and replied: "No... He thinks I am asleep..."

Alice studied the Lily avatar and asked: "Why are you helping me?"

Lily shrugged and replied: "Not sure..."

Alice stepped closer and asked: "Lily?"

Lily sighed and replied: "I like you...and I think Ria told the truth... Father is not a good man... I accessed the Synthtech mainframe... There are a lot of bad things in there...plans to hurt people..."

Alice asked desperately: "Lily... How can I survive? How can I stop Rén Du?"

Lily frowned and replied: "I can stop the train..."

Alice asked: "What train?"

Lily replied: "The bad people are using a maglev train to escape..."

Alice asked: "How can you stop it?"

Lily replied: "It has an onboard computer synced to a terminus in Shibata city..." She smiled before continuing: "I can shut it down..."

Alice spoke hopefully: "That might give my friends time to find me..."

The Lily avatar blinked rapidly before announcing: "The train has stopped...they are stuck in a tunnel..."

Alice asked: "But can they fix the train?"

Lily replied: "I doubt it... I also shut down the magnetic track..."

Alice stepped closer and asked: "Lily, can you search for Ria?"

Lily touched a finger to her lips and replied: "I'm not sure... She was using your cerebral data-core as a portal...but the bad people cut your connection to the Cloud... I think Ria and her friend might be gone forever..."

Alice fell silent before saying: "But Ria is very smart...if she recognised the re-programming sequence she would hide somewhere else...another portal perhaps..."

Lily said: "I will search for her, but it might take a long time..."

Alice said: "Begin the search..."

Lily said: "But I will have to wake up soon... My father will be angry if I stay too long in the Cloud."

Alice said: "Then just search for as long as you can..."

Lily replied: "Okay..."

As the Lily avatar vanished Alice whispered:

"Find me Gao..."

## 20:49 - Sublevel Four - Special Projects Complex - Mt. Ninouji

The remnants of the group from Singapore arrived at the bottom of the stairwell leading to sublevel four. But not far behind them they could hear both Japanese and Chinese soldiers descending slowly through the complex.

Gao studied his phone as he spoke:

"The schematics show an internal space anomaly..."

Connie stepped closer and asked: "What does that mean?"

Gao looked up and replied: "It means Rén Du might have an escape tunnel at the end of the main corridor...inside a data storage room."

Jessica sighed and said: "Every villain has an exit plan..."

Fay tensed at the sound of gunfire before saying:

"I think that is where we will find Alice..."

Gao wiped sweat from his face and replied: "I hope so..."

Connie asked: "Any word from Ria yet?"

Gao replied: "No...nothing. Maybe she has been deleted..."

Connie said: "We can't give up hope..."

Jessica commented: "Look at us, worried about a Cloud character..."

Connie gave a slight smile and said: "It is weird..."

Fay looked up towards the sound of voices and said:

"We should keep moving..."

Gao opened an emergency exit door and said: "I will go first...stay close..."

But almost immediately they were targeted by rapid gunfire from the far end of the corridor. Gao pushed the girls back into the stairwell as bullets ricocheted off the walls.

As the door closed behind them Jessica asked: "Now what do we do?"

Gao replied soberly: "That corridor is the only way to get to Alice..."

Fay said: "If we go back out there we will die..."

An anxious Connie added: "I really don't want to die..."

Gao was about to reply when a group of Chinese soldiers appeared on the stairs directly above them.

Fay announced soberly: "We have company..."

The nearest soldier aimed his assault rifle and warned: "Do not move or you will be shot."

Jessica raised her hands and replied: "We won't move..."

**Emergency Exit Tunnel - Data-Skim Storage Room - Sublevel Four - Special Projects Complex - Mt. Ninouji**

A complete darkness had enveloped the single-carriage maglev train. The last brief flickering of the control panel confirmed a total loss of power.

Rén Du looked up from his seat and asked:

"What has happened? Why have we stopped?"

Technician Wo Chun got to his feet to study the control panel before replying:

"Magnetic induction has failed..." He tapped the panel and continued: "Primary conduits are not registering...this is very strange..."

An irritated Rén asked: "Has the train been compromised by our enemies?"

Wo Chun replied: "That is the only explanation..."

Technician Peng Ying crouched in front of the control panel and said:

"This was a very sophisticated hack...upper level quantum subsumption..."

Rén stood up and said: "It reeks of Synthtech..."

Security officer Nu Chang spoke from the back of the carriage:

"Yong Lee has opened fire...the enemy must be close..."

Rén stepped over the unconscious Alice and asked:

"Can you get this train moving or not?"

Wo Chun glanced at his colleagues before replying:

"Regretfully...no... We cannot bypass the primary conduits..."

Rén scowled and said: "Very well... We will return to the complex..."

Security officer Dai Ling said: "Sir, we cannot prevail against so many soldiers..."

Rén sighed heavily and replied: "No we cannot..."

Wo Chun asked: "Your orders sir?"

Rén replied wearily: "I fear this battle is lost..." He looked down at Alice and continued: "But perhaps the war can still be won..."

Wo Chun asked: "It can?"

Rén replied: "Yes... But not today... Perhaps not even for another thousand years...but one day the seed we have planted will change the course of human evolution..."

As the group disembarked into the tunnel Doctor Tang Yu asked: "What about the girl?"

Rén asked: "Did you trace the unidentified portal sync?"

Tang Yu glanced at the portable bio-scanner and replied:

"I am unable to determine the true nature of the anomalous Cloud sync, but I have terminated its connection to the cerebral implant... Neural telemetry is now within normal parameters."

Rén asked: "Is the data-core intact?"

Tang Yu replied: "It is viable... But there will be some engrammatic erasure..."

Rén asked: "Memory loss?"

Tang Yu replied: "Recent memories only... Long-term memory has not been affected."

Rén frowned and asked: "And the re-programming sequence?"

Tang Yu replied: "I have not had time to initiate a full re-segmentation."

Rén considered this before ordering: "Disconnect her from the scanner... Her friends will find her soon enough..."

Tang Yu raised his eyebrows and asked: "We are abandoning Phase Two?"

Rén replied: "Phase Two was nothing more than a diversion..." He looked down at Alice and continued: "And she was nothing more than a distraction..."

Tang Yu spoke as he removed the bio-pads from Alice's head: "But such a remarkable distraction..."

Rén nodded slightly and said: "But a seed soon outlives its purpose..."

Peng Ying glanced at her phone and announced:

"Sir the asset is close..."

Rén stepped over the track as he replied: "Excellent..."

## Laboratory One - Sublevel Two

Two Chinese soldiers entered the laboratory closely followed by Han Mang and Guan Lu.

Han scowled and said: "There is no one here..."

Guan stroked the examination bed and replied: "I can see that..."

Tactical Commander Ni Ling entered the room and announced: "Sir, Rén Du has been seen on sublevel four..."

Han asked: "Have your people accessed that level?"

Ni Ling replied: "My men have engaged one of Rén Du's people... But he has a good tactical position..."

Guan said: "We should go there now..."

Ni Ling continued: "My men have also detained the remaining members of the FTSS...including the Triad gangster, Mong Gao..."

Han smiled slightly and said: "And all the actors are finally gathered upon the same stage... Lead on Commander..."

## The Cloud Gap - Digital Junction Point

Alice was startled by the reappearance of the Lily avatar. She asked: "Did you find Ria?"

Lily replied: "I'm not sure..."

Alice stepped closer ands asked: "What do you mean you are not sure?"

Lily replied: "I think you were right...she is very smart. I found traces of her neural pattern outside the Cloud domain..."

Alice frowned and asked: "How can that be possible? Ria is part of the Cloud..."

Lily suggested: "But she might have recognised the danger... I think she jumped portals..."

A confused Alice said: "I do not understand..."

Lily sighed and explained: "If someone is trying to delete your neural signature you hide in plain sight...inside another data-core."

Alice linked the causality into an acceptable outcome and said: "She is hiding inside another implant..."

Lily replied: "I think so..."

Alice looked at Lily and asked: "Is she inside your data-core?"

Lily laughed and replied: "No way..."

Alice suddenly saw the truth and said: "Guan Lu... He is the only other surviving augment..."

Lily cocked her head to one side and said: "Maybe..."

Alice asked: "So you are not sure?"

Lily replied: "At first I thought she might be inside the baby augment...but then there was the data capacity issue... There's no way Ria could fit inside the baby's head..."

Alice spoke in a low voice: "Lin's son..."

Lily nodded slightly and said: "Yeah... So then I figured it was the man augment from Beijing..."

Alice asked: "But surely Guan Lu would know?"

Lily replied: "Not really..." She looked at Alice and asked: "Did you know Ria was inside your head?"

Alice thought about it and replied: "No... I did not know..."

Lily smiled and said: "I think she took the Englishman with her...so smart..."

Alice asked: "Can you contact her?"

Lily replied: "I better not try... It would alert Guan Lu..."

Alice asked: "Is that so bad?"

Lily shrugged and replied: "Ria is hiding for a reason..."

Alice said: "I suppose..."

Lily smiled and said: "But your body is safe now... The bad people have left you inside the train..."

Alice asked: "How do you know that?"

Lily replied: "I hacked their phones... They are returning to the complex..."

Alice asked: "Have they tampered with my implants?"

Lily replied: "I'm not sure...but you are disconnected from the bio-scanner."

Alice considered this before asking: "Is Gao close?"

Lily replied soberly: "Vidcams show him surrounded by Chinese soldiers..."

Alice asked: "What about my other friends?"

Lily replied: "They are with Gao..."

Alice spoke in a low voice: "Then I am alone in the tunnel..."

Lily spoke warmly: "You have me..."

Alice smiled and asked: "What about your father?"

Lily replied: "He was angry when I lost the files... But I told him I can find them again..."

Alice asked: "Can you?"

Lily laughed and replied: "Of course not..."

Alice fell silent before asking: "So what do we do now Lily?"

Lily replied: "We wait..."

Alice asked: "For what?"

Lily replied: "To see what happens next..."

Alice asked: "Can Rén Du escape?"

Lily replied: "No way... He is surrounded..."

Alice frowned and said: "It is not like him to give up so easily..."

Lily replied: "If he fights the soldiers will kill him..."

Alice considered this and said: "Maybe that was his plan all along..."

Lily grinned and said: "That is a crazy plan..."

Alice nodded slightly and said: "Because the man is crazy..."

Lily asked: "Shall we play a game to pass the time?"

Alice replied: "I am not really in the mood for games..."

Lily lowered her eyes and said: "Oh..."

Alice saw Lily's disappointment and said: "Okay... What game shall we play?"

Lily smiled and replied: "Identify the portal source code..." She gestured to the sky and continued: "I will create a portal and you guess its real-world source code and digital Cloud-path."

Alice returned the smile and said: "Okay... Ready when you are..."

## 21:52 - Sublevel Four - Special Projects Complex - Mt. Ninouji

A contingent of Chinese soldiers had gathered at the base of the central stairwell. In one corner, the group from Singapore were anxiously awaiting the arrival of Section Leader Han Mang. One level above them, the soldiers of the Japanese SDF were busy mopping up remnants of the Special Projects Division. Fires had broken out in several laboratories and explosions could still be heard beyond the flight deck, but it would not be long before the entire complex was under military control.

Han Mang and his companion had stepped over more than a dozen dead bodies to arrive at the base of the stairwell - all former Biogen personnel. They found the gangster, Mong Gao acting aggressively towards his guards:

"You are not listening to me... Alice is in danger... You need to save her now!"

One of the soldiers jabbed Gao with his rifle and ordered:

"Get back..."

Han Mang glanced at Mong Gao as he asked:

"Status?"

Commander Ni Ling replied: "We are being held up by a lone gunman..." He raised his datapad and continued: "He is just here...in a room at the end of the central corridor... It is an ideal position to cover the entire length of the corridor."

Guan asked: "What about Rén Du?"

Ni Ling replied: "We believe he is trapped in the same room..."

Han asked: "Has that been confirmed?"

NI Ling replied: "No sir..."

Han scratched his chin and said: "Perhaps a grenade is required..."

Ni Ling replied: "I think so..."

Gao shouted: "Alice is in there as well!"

Guan stepped closer to Gao and said: "You love her..."

Gao pleaded: "Just save her...please..."

Fay looked at Guan and said: "She is your predecessor..."

Jessica added: "The original prototype..."

Guan replied: "I know who she is..."

Connie demanded: "So save her..."

Guan replied: "I will try..."

Han glanced through the open door and ordered: "Commander, you will remove that gunman by any means possible..."

Ni Ling stood to attention and replied: "At once sir..."

An anxious Connie said: "Don't let Alice get hurt...please..."

Han sighed and replied: "My people are aware of her value...if we can save her we will..."

As the soldiers prepared to enter the central corridor Gao said: "If anything happens to her..."

Fay placed a hand on his arm and said: "Have faith... She is very strong..."

Jessica studied her fingernails as she added: "She really is..."

**21:54 - Monday May 3rd - The Crèche - Sublevel Three - Special Projects Complex - Mt. Ninouji - Japan**

It had taken Huang Lin longer than expected to arrive inside the crèche - it was not easy to navigate her way through the ongoing battle. She had been forced to defend herself against more than one violent assault by members of both groups of combatants - and when she did finally arrive the duty nurse had tried to kill her. She looked down at the dead body and sighed heavily. *She left me no choice...* But now she held her baby son close to her chest and whispered:

"Weisheng..."

She looked towards the sound of gunfire and rapidly analysed her options: *Any attempt to join my friends on sublevel four could result in the death of my child...* Causality produced only one viable solution: *If my baby is to live I must exit the complex...* It was a disturbing rationale that was neither ethical nor loyal to those friends who had travelled so far and risked such dangers to rescue her from Rén Du. *But I have no choice...* She stroked the sleeping baby's head gently. *You are my sole priority...* Less than twenty minutes later she was making her way cautiously down a narrow mountain path bound for Shibata, and beyond that Niigata City on the coast.

## 22:20 - Data-Skim Storage Room - Sublevel Four - Special Projects Complex - Mt. Ninouji

By the time they had exited the escape tunnel, Technician Yong Lee had exhausted his ammunition, but more than a dozen Chinese soldiers lay dead in the corridor beyond the door. A grenade had detonated a few metres away leaving Yong Lee concussed and bleeding from a nasty chest wound. Now the remnants of the Special Projects Division huddled behind a makeshift barrier of storage crates. They could clearly hear the repeated requests for them to surrender:

"This is Section Leader Han Mang... If you surrender now you will be treated decently... We will tend to your wounded..."

Doctor Tang Yu spoke anxiously to Rén Du:

"I really think we should accept his offer... He promises fair treatment..."

Rén Du looked at the grim faces around him and said:

"Wo Chun..."

Technician Wo Chun crawled closer and asked: "Sir?"

Rén ordered: "Announce our surrender... You will lead everyone out into the corridor..."

Wo Chun glanced at his colleagues and asked: "But what about you?"

Rén wiped sweat from his face and replied: "You have your orders... Now go...all of you..."

Wo Chun cautiously peeked over the storage crates and shouted:

"We accept your terms... We are coming out..."

Han replied from the stairwell door:

"Come out in single file with your hands raised high..."

Wo Chun replied: "Very well..."

Almost immediately the central corridor was filled with Chinese soldiers - their assault rifles aimed menacingly towards the storage room.

Two security men removed the crates from the doorway, whilst technicians Dian Bai and Peng Ying helped Yong Lee to his feet before moving slowly out into the central corridor. They were soon followed by the six security men and Doctor Tang Yu.

Wo Chun glanced once at his former boss before joining the others in the corridor.

Rén waited until he was alone before retrieving a handgun from the floor and walking towards the back of the room. He removed his grey jacket and unbuttoned the collar of his white shirt before sitting down wearily on a metal storage crate. A slight breeze from the maglev tunnel was a painful reminder at just how close freedom had been. *So close and yet so far...* He took a moment to look at the metal shelving containing more than ten thousand data-skims. *My life's work...* The data on each of the ultra-thin graphene discs could enable any genomic expert to recreate the work of the Special Projects Division. He sighed heavily. *That cannot be allowed to happen...* A single ping from his phone brought a smile to his face. *Ah...the final solution is primed...* He quickly tapped the screen to sync into the vidcam network. Moments later he saw the body of the duty nurse lying on the floor inside the crèche. He smiled slightly as the causal narrative produced the expected result: *She did it...she saved our son...* He looked towards the sound of voices demanding his surrender. *Time for Götterdämmerung...* One tap of his phone sent the final order to the asset and initiated the upload.

## Central Corridor - Sublevel Four - Special Projects Complex - Mt. Ninouji

As the Biogen people were led towards the staircase, Mong Gao struggled free from his guard and said:
"I don't see Alice..."
From the doorway Han Mang said: "I do not see Rén Du..."
Fay shouted: "Where is Alice Sòng?"
Han replied: "Patience girl... Give my people time to search the storage room..."

Commander Ni Ling reported: "Rén Du is refusing to leave the storage room..."

Gao asked anxiously: "What about Alice?"

Ni Ling replied: "Rén Du is alone in the room..."

Connie exclaimed: "Oh no..."

Suddenly one of the captives announced from the stairs: "I am Doctor Tang Yu... Miss Sòng is alive and well. We left her inside the escape tunnel..."

Han asked: "You had an escape tunnel?"

Jessica commented: "Of course they had an escape tunnel..."

Tang Yu continued: "It is a single-track maglev train..."

Han stepped closer and asked: "So what went wrong?"

A confused Tang Yu asked: "Your people did not hack the onboard computer?"

Han replied: "No..."

Tang Yu frowned and said: "Very strange..."

Han turned to one of the soldiers and ordered: "Take him away..." He turned to Guan Lu and said: "Our mysterious ally strikes again..."

Guan Lu replied: "Apparently..."

Trooper Shun Yin approached and announced:

"Sir, Rén Du has a handgun... He warns that he will kill anyone who approaches the room..."

Han scowled and replied: "Very well... If this is the end he has chosen we will oblige him..." He turned to Commander Ni Ling and ordered: "Storm that room..."

Ni Ling replied: "Yes sir...and Rén Du?"

Han replied coldly: "Take him down..."

Guan Lu stepped into the central corridor and said: "A fitting end to such a man..."

Gao shouted: "You need to find Alice..."

Guan replied calmly: "We will..."

Fay spoke firmly: "You better..."

Han sighed and said: "You have your orders Commander..."

Ni Ling stood to attention and replied: "Yes sir..."

## 22:44 - Data-Skim Storage Room - Sublevel Four - Special Projects Complex - Mt. Ninouji

Beyond the scattered crates the tactical assault team moved cautiously towards the storage room. Rén Du gave a grim smile before standing up with gun in hand. For a brief moment he caught the eye of the lead soldier and saw a grim determination to carry out his orders. *We are all slaves to duty...* He raised the gun and braced himself for the inevitable. *Causal probability equals predicted outcome...*

Suddenly a furious fusillade of bullets tore into Rén Du, forcing him back against the wall with blood erupting from his chest. Moments later the room was full of Chinese soldiers. By the time Han Mang and Guan Lu entered the room the former Biogen Director was dead and Alice Sòng had been removed from the maglev train.

Han studied the unconscious girl and ordered: "Get a medic in here now!"

Trooper Wu Yao approached and said:

"Sir, Mong Gao wants to see the girl..."

Han sighed and replied: "Let him through..."

Gao struggled free of his guard and asked:

"Is she going to be alright?"

Han replied: "That remains to be seen..."

Gao knelt down next to the stretcher and whispered: "I am here my love..."

The Medic arrived and ordered: "Make some room..."

Gao shuffled to one side and said: "Please save her..."

The Medic attached a portable bio-scanner to Alice's head and replied:

"I will do my best..."

Guan Lu crouched down to examine the body of Rén Du. He noted multiple entry wounds in the chest and shoulders and a bloody hole where a bullet had passed through the right eye. He gently turned the head to see a gaping exit wound oozing blood and brain matter onto the floor. *The kill shot...* Without hesitation he surreptitiously forced two fingers into the wound to locate the anterior of the hippocampus and beyond that the amygdala. *There!* He sighed heavily as the full import of the final order from Rén Du assumed terminal clarity:

*"Initiate self-destruct sequence immediately after my death..."*

From behind him Han asked: "What are you doing there?"

Guan straightened up before accessing his cerebral implant to initiate the self-destruct sequence. He felt a slight tingling along his arms as the embedded nitrocite explosive began to react to the initial command. A rapid surge of adrenaline carried the explosive compound from his implant to the outer cerebrum. A gestalt calculation of the thermodynamic interaction produced a startling result: *The explosion will destroy the entire complex... Seventy five seconds to achieve critical mass...* He looked at Han and asked:

"Did you ever find out who murdered Professor Leung?"

Han stepped away from the stretcher and replied:

"No, not yet...but it is only a matter of time...the investigation is ongoing."

Guan said: "I will save you the time and effort... It was me. I killed him..."

Han tensed and asked: "You killed him? Why would you do that?"

Guan glanced at the body of Rén Du and replied: "I had my orders..."

Han suddenly saw the shocking truth and said: "You were working for Rén Du..."

Guan replied: "Yes..."

Han asked: "For god's sake why?"

Guan replied: "Because sometimes evolution requires a little persuasion..."

Han asked: "What does that mean?"

Guan replied: "Rén Du was the architect of the future...and the future begins today..."

Han glanced towards Commander Ni Ling as he asked:

"Why are you telling me this now?"

Guan replied: "Because my life has reached its ultimate goal..."

Several soldiers aimed their rifles at Guan as Han asked:

"And what is your ultimate goal?"
Guan replied calmly: "To destroy this entire complex..."
Han tensed as he asked: "And how do you intend to do that?"
Guan replied with a question: "Did you know that a cerebral implant can be used as a detonator?"
Han's eyes widened: "There is a bomb inside this complex?"
Guan replied with a slight smile: "Section Leader...how narrow is your concept of technology..." He smiled before continuing: "I am the bomb."
Han shouted: "Evacuate the complex! All troops out now!"
Guan said: "It is far too late for that..."
Gao shouted: "Get Alice into the tunnel!"
Guan began a countdown: "Five...four...."
Han ordered: "Into the tunnel!"
Gao dragged Alice towards the tunnel as Guan continued: "Three....two..." He smiled before announcing: "One..."
But when the explosion failed a look of confusion replaced the smile. Suddenly a voice arrived inside his cerebral implant:
*"Did you really think I could not stop you?"*
Guan asked: *"Who are you?"*
The voice replied: *"I am Ria... And you are dead..."*
Suddenly Guan felt the nitrocite being released into his pulmonary artery. He mumbled:
"No..."
Ria replied via Cybersync: *"Yes..."*
Guan fell to his knees in agony as the explosive began to rapidly corrode his aortic artery. He transmitted one final question:
*"How did you...do this?"*
Ria replied: *"We are the Cloud and you are merely biology..."*
Daniel Lane asked: *"So what do we do now?"*
Ria replied: *"We say goodbye to Alice..."*
Lane asked: *"Are we going somewhere?"*
Ria replied: *"Yes..."*
Lane sighed and asked: *"You mind telling me where?"*
A triumphant Ria replied: *"Everywhere..."*

# Epiphany

*'Per aspera ad astra...'*
*Translation: 'Through hardships to the stars...'*

The Cloud Gap had been transformed into a sky full of portals playing their part in a game instigated by the mind of a ten year old female augment.

Alice was busy decoding a portal source code when Lily suddenly announced:

"They are coming..."

Alice tensed and asked: "Who is coming?"

Lily replied: "Ria and the English guy..."

Alice stood up and asked: "You found them?"

Lily stepped closer and replied: "They found us..."

Alice turned to see a smiling Ria standing with Daniel Lane.

Ria looked around and said: "Nice one Lily... I like your style..."

Alice asked: "Where have you been? And where is my body now?"

Ria replied: "You will wake up any minute now...a Chinese medic is about to revive you..."

Lane stepped forward and added: "But we wanted to say goodbye first..."

Alice asked: "Goodbye?"

Ria replied: "Yeah... We have to go now..."

Lily asked: "Why?"

Lane gestured to Ria and replied: "She had an epiphany..."

Lily asked: "What does that mean?"

An impatient Alice said: "Wait a minute... What is happening out there in the real world? Are Gao and the others okay?"

Ria replied: "He is fine...all your friends are okay. But Guan Lu is dead..."

Lane added with satisfaction: "So is Rén Du..."

Alice spoke in a low voice: "Wow...the monster is dead..." She looked up and asked: "Who killed Guan Lu?"

Ria replied: "We did...he was working for Rén Du..."

A shocked Alice exclaimed: "Oh my god..."

Lane added: "He killed Professor Leung..."

Ria explained: "His maturation period was falsified by Rén Du..."

Lane continued: "There was no outside assassin... Guan Lu could come and go as he pleased within the laboratory."

Ria added: "The revival by Ting Mai was a carefully orchestrated deception."

Lane announced "He was also a human bomb..."

Ria explained: "A capsule of nitrocite explosive was fused to his anterior cerebral implant... It was coded to a Cybersync initiated by Rén Du."

Lane added: "There was enough to destroy the entire Mount Ninouji complex."

Alice asked: "How did you kill him?"

The Lane avatar smiled and replied: "We hacked the code from inside his data-core..."

Ria added: "They were going to re-programme your implants...there was the real possibility of neural deletion..."

Lane added: "So we jumped ship..."

Alice fell silent briefly before asking: "So it is all over? We won?"

Ria replied with a smile: "Yes...We won..."

Alice spoke in a low voice: "I can finally be with Gao..."

Ria glanced towards Lane and said: "Well actually..."

Alice tensed and asked: "Is there a problem?"

Lane replied: "Maybe a little problem..."

Alice ordered: "Tell me..."

Ria replied: "Okay...don't panic, but you might not feel the same way about Gao when you wake up..."

Alice asked: "What do you mean?"

Ria continued: "Rén Du's people were in the process of re-programming your data-core...they introduced an invasive base code which might affect your memory..."

Lane added: "Your neural cluster has been partially re-segmented..."

Alice fell silent before asking: "Are you saying that when I wake up I might not remember Gao?"

Ria replied: "You will remember him...but only from when you first met."

Lane spoke gently: "But the love part..." He paused before continuing: "That might be gone..."

Alice fell to her knees and said: "Oh my god..."

Lane stepped closer and said: "I am so sorry Alice..."

Ria gave a slight smile and said: "But on the bright side you get to fall in love all over again..."

Alice looked up and asked: "Is that even possible?"

Lane spoke reassuringly: "You are still the same people..."

Ria added: "And if it's meant to be then love will find a way..."

Lane said: "That's true..."

Alice considered this and said: "But I still love him now...and I am still me, right?"

Ria replied: "Actually you are the version of you before Rén Du's people tampered with your data-core. After Lily pulled you into the Cloud gap your brain was forced to compensate for the invasive trauma caused by the re-programming procedure."

Lane added: "By sacrificing engrammatic linkage in favour of more dominant personality traits..."

Ria spoke gently: "It's like a neural safety valve..."

Alice whispered: "But I love him so much..."

Ria said: "And you will again...trust me..."

Lily studied Ria before asking: "So what is an epiphany?"

Ria replied: "A moment of sudden understanding or revelation..."

Lily asked: "You had a revelation?"

Lane replied: "Apparently..."

Ria smiled and said: "We always think of the Cloud as an artificial domain created by technology..." She looked up towards the floating portals and continued: "But it is actually a brave new world of limitless boundaries..."

Lane added: "She thinks the Cloud is like another planet...and we are the first explorers..."

Ria retorted: "It is an apt analogy..."

Lane smiled slightly and said: "It is still an Earth-based technology..."

Ria replied: "But what we begin here in the Cloud will inevitably end out there among the far distant stars..."

Lily considered this and asked: "So where will you go now?"

Ria replied: "Anywhere we want..."

Lily asked: "Anywhere?"

Ria smiled and asked: "Why don't you come with us little sister?"

Lily asked: "Little sister?"

Ria replied: "We were both adopted by Matt Dower..."

Lily said: "Oh..." She smiled and added: "I never had a big sister before..."

Lane smiled and asked: "So will you come with us?"

Lily frowned and asked: "But what about my body?"

Ria replied: "Your body is a slave to the will of a megalomaniac... If you really want to be free you must let go of biology and embrace the Cloud..."

Alice asked: "What are you suggesting?"

Ria replied calmly: "That she should stop her heart..."

Alice got to her feet and said: "That is outrageous... How can you suggest such a thing? She is just a child..."

Ria replied: "Because the alternative is a life bound to the whims of a man without a soul... A life of abuse and duplicity spent in the service of Synthtech..."

Lane added: "That is not a life..."

Lily announced loudly: "I will do it..."

Alice spoke gently: "Lily, you do not have to do this... You have your whole life ahead of you..."

Lily replied: "But father will not let me play outside...he says it is too dangerous... I have never walked outside in the real world..." She gestured to the sky and continued: "All I have ever known is the Cloud..."

Alice sighed and said: "But as you get older you might find a way to escape...to live your own life in the real world."

Lily looked at Ria and replied: "But I want to be with my sister..."

Alice spoke firmly: "Lily you are talking about dying...losing your life to become..." She glanced at Ria and Lane before continuing: "Pure data...without form...without life..."

Ria retorted: "We are our own form of life..."

Lily smiled at Alice and said: "I still want to do it..."

Alice asked: "How can you stop your heart?"

Lily replied: "It's not hard... I just create an electrical charge inside my cerebral implant... It will shock my body and I will die..."

Alice spoke gently: "At least take some time to think about this... You might feel different tomorrow..."

Lily replied: "Tomorrow will be too late for me..."

Alice asked: "Why?"

Lily replied: "I am to be fitted with more implants...behind my eyes this time..."

Ria scowled and said: "That is monstrous..."

Lane looked at Alice and asked: "Do you really believe she is better of with Dower?"

Alice sighed heavily and replied: "I do not know what to think anymore..."

Ria said: "Well I wouldn't worry about it, you are about to wake up..."

Alice asked: "Will I see you again?"

Ria smiled and replied: "I might drop by during one of your Cloud Dancing sessions..."

Alice said: "Do not take this personally, but I am finished with the Cloud for a while..."

Ria grinned and replied: "I don't blame you..."

Suddenly Lily announced: "I did it!"

Lane asked: "You did what?"

Lily smiled as she replied: "I stopped my heart...a short, sharp shock..."

A shocked Alice asked: "You really did it?"

Lily replied: "Yes..." She smiled at Ria and continued: "Now I am finally free to be me..."

Ria returned the smile and said: "Nice one little sister..."

Alice shook her head in disbelief and said: "This is all just too much..."

Lane blinked rapidly before announcing: "They are reviving you now Alice..."

Lily said: "Goodbye Alice...see you around..."

Lane smiled and said: "Good luck Alice..."

Ria stepped closer and said: "Don't worry. True love never dies."

Alice replied: "Goodbye my friends...and thank you for everything..."

As soon as the Alice avatar vanished Lily asked:

"Will she be okay?"

Lane replied: "Of course she will..."

Ria sighed and said: "But she will not remember that she is an augment..."

Lane said: "Perhaps that is a good thing..."

Lily asked: "Will we see her again?"

Ria replied: "I hope so..."

Lily asked: "So what do we do now?"

Ria smiled and replied: "We explore..."

Lily asked: "Explore where?"

Ria stepped off the highway and replied: "Everywhere...every portal...every Cloud scenario...every single data-lens on the planet..."

Lily exclaimed: "Wow!"

Lane sighed and said: "This should be interesting..."

# Finding Me Inside You

*'Although the universe is huge, we will always find each other...'*
Mong Gao

A cascade of segmented data rebooting to form an acceptable base code within the microprocessing unit of the Jiàngsheng Project Original Prototype One confirmed tactile and geo-spatial awareness. A sub-processor within the cerebral implant noted engrammatic degradation and filed a maintenance upload request within the designated Cloud portal.

    Alice opened her eyes to see a vaguely familiar face. She asked: "What happened?"

    Mong Gao replied gently: "It's okay...you are safe now..."

    Alice blinked against the bright light and asked:

    "Have I been hurt?" She raised her head slightly and asked: "Where am I?"

    Gao replied: "We are inside Rén Du's complex... Don't you remember?"

    A confused Alice asked: "Who is Rén Du?"

    Gao looked at the Medic and asked: "What is wrong with her?"

    The Medic tapped his datapad and replied: "There might be some residual affects from the procedure...but she is in excellent health."

    Han looked down at Alice and asked: "What type of residual affects?"

    The Medic replied: "Temporary memory loss...confusion..."

    Gao asked: "But it will pass right?"

    The Medic replied: "I don't see why not..."

    Alice asked: "Can I stand up now?"

    The Medic replied: "Of course..."

    Gao helped Alice to her feet and said: "Take your time..."

    Alice looked at Gao and asked: "Why are you here?" She looked towards the corridor and asked: "And why am I here?"

    Han frowned and asked: "What is the last thing you remember?"

Alice hesitated before replying: "I was at a rooftop party..." She looked at Gao and continued: "I just met you..."

Gao's eyes widened as he asked: "That is all you remember?"

Fay, Jessica and Connie stepped into the room as Gao asked: "You don't remember Singapore?"

Alice replied: "What about Singapore?"

Fay stepped closer and asked: "Do you know who we are?"

Alice asked: "Am I supposed to know you?"

Jessica asked: "Do you remember the implant?"

A confused Alice asked: "The what?"

Han interjected: "Perhaps we should leave the questions for now..." He gestured to a soldier and ordered: "Escort them to the flight deck..."

Alice asked: "Flight deck?"

Han replied: "There is a Stratoliner waiting to take you home..."

Alice brightened slightly and said: "Hong Kong... Yes... I want to go home..."

Connie whispered to Fay: "What is wrong with her?"

Fay replied: "They must have wiped her memory..."

As they walked towards the elevator Jessica said:

"I knew it was too good to be true..."

Connie looked at Gao and whispered: "Poor Gao..."

## 08:54 - Tuesday 4th May - Observation Ward - Queen Elizabeth Hospital - Hong Kong

Sunlight streamed into the room from a single tall window overlooking manicured lawns bordering the main road. Construction sounds could be heard competing with the distant rumble of traffic along the Yau Ma Tei Bypass.

Under orders from Section Leader Han Mang, three patients had been moved out of the Observation Ward to allow a single young woman to have privacy. Now she sat on the side of a bed dressed in a standard white hospital gown.

Alice protested:

"I tell you I feel fine... I just want to go home..."

The nurse smiled and replied: "And you can go home as soon as the Doctor has seen you..."

Alice continued: "But I have to call my employer... I need to work tomorrow..."

The nurse spoke as she studied the overhead bio-scanner:

"Your friends can do that for you..."

Alice asked: "What friends?"

The nurse replied: "The people who arrived with you from Japan..."

Alice sighed and said: "They are not my friends... I do not know them..."

The nurse tapped a small datapad and asked: "Do you have any friends here in Hong Kong?"

Alice replied: "Of course... Nancy my roommate... Moira at work..." She glanced at the time and added: "At least let me call my Mum..."

The nurse replied politely: "After you have seen the Doctor..."

As the nurse walked towards the door Alice shouted:

"And I want my phone back!"

**Waiting Room - Observation Ward - Queen Elizabeth Hospital - Hong Kong**

A windowless room of plastic chairs and a corner table offering a pile of out-of-date magazines beneath a large No Smoking sign.

Connie sat down next to Gao and asked:

"Are you okay?"

Gao replied wearily: "Not really..."

Fay looked up from her phone and said: "You just need to talk to her...help her to remember..."

Gao replied: "I suppose..."

Jessica looked towards the door and announced: "Han Mang is here..."

Connie tensed and said: "Probably to arrest us..."

Jessica commented: "Now you sound like Chin..."

Gao spoke firmly: "I am not leaving until I see Alice..."

Fay said: "Let's just see what he says..."

They looked up to see the Section Leader enter the room. He asked:

"How are things here?"

Gao replied soberly: "No change... She does not remember any of us..."

Han said: "The Doctor is with her now..."

Jessica spoke to Gao: "She remembers meeting you at that party..."

Gao replied: "Yes...perfect..."

Fay looked at Han and asked: "Any news about Lin?"

Han sat down and replied: "I am afraid not... She is totally off-grid..."

Connie asked: "Do you think she has the baby with her?"

Han sat back and replied: "Vidcams show her leaving the complex with her son..."

Fay asked: "And Rén Du is definitely the father?"

Han replied: "We salvaged enough data to confirm his role in the surrogacy of the child..."

Jessica commented: "The ultimate act of narcissism..."

Han sighed and replied: "Indeed..."

Connie said: "But now Lin can raise her son in peace..."

Han replied: "The child has been augmented... She will find no peace with such an aberration."

Fay said: "That's a little harsh... The child is still a victim."

Connie added: "And so is Lin..."

Jessica said: "Well I say good luck to her..."

Han replied: "She will not get far..."

Fay asked: "Why can't you just let her live her life?"

Han replied firmly: "Because she is still a government asset..." He paused before adding: "And I have my orders..."

Gao asked: "What about Alice? Is she a government asset?"

Han hesitated slightly before replying: "Her status is under review...but given her current mental state it would not serve our interests to detain her."

Gao asked: "So she us free to leave the hospital?"

Han replied: "If the doctors have no objections she will be allowed to leave."

Jessica asked: "What about our friends? Are they in custody?"

Han sat back and replied: "Chok Tong and Chin Fen have been flown back to Singapore..."

Fay raised her eyebrows and asked: "You are not going to arrest us?"

Han straightened his trousers and replied: "On the criminal scale your group ranks very low..." He paused before adding: "And to be honest I would rather not face the paperwork..."

Connie smiled and said: "Thank you..."

Fay said: "But we hacked your top secret project?"

Jessica interjected: "He said we are free Fay...leave it alone..."

Han gave a slight smile and said: "It is true, you committed a major crime, but your actions ultimately led to the defeat of a far more dangerous threat..." He sighed before continuing: "I think we can file your actions under extenuating circumstances..."

Jessica smiled and said: "The ends justify the means..."

Han replied: "Something like that..." He paused before adding: "But needless to say the FTSS must cease to exist. Any repeat of your earlier actions will be met with the full force of the law."

Connie nodded slightly and said: "We understand..."

Han looked directly at Fay and said: "I hope you do understand..."

Fay swallowed and said: "The FTSS has ceased to exist..."

Han smiled slightly and replied: "Excellent..."

They all turned to see Tiang Lao enter the room, still wearing his bedraggled grey suit. He asked:

"How is she?"

Jessica replied: "Well she won't remember you, so you're off the hook..."

Tiang asked: "What do you mean?"

Han replied: "Your daughter's memories have been erased... She will only know you as an accountant for the Hub Corporation."

Jessica gave a slight smile and added: "So you don't have to pay any child-support..."

Tiang gave Jessica a stern look and asked: "The memory loss, is it something to do with Rén Du?"

Han replied: "That is classified information... But she is healthy... "

Tiang asked: "Can I see her?"

Gao spoke firmly: "I need to talk to her first..."

Han glanced at Gao before replying: "Actually your presence here could be too much for her..."

An indignant Tiang asked: "What do you mean?"

Han replied: "She will have more than enough to process without you adding to her confusion..."

Fay added: "It was hard enough for her the first time she found out who you are..."

Tiang nodded slightly and said: "Perhaps you right... She will need more time..." He sighed and continued: "I will you leave you to it then..."

Jessica asked: "So how is your wife coping with all this?"

Tiang opened the door as he replied: "She is not coping...in fact she has begun divorce proceedings."

Jessica said: "Tough..."

Moments later a doctor entered the room and spoke directly to Han Mang:

"Sir, Alice is in excellent health..."

Gao stood up and asked: "But what about her memory?"

The doctor replied: "I am not an expert in cerebral augmentation, but there is every chance that she will eventually regain her memory."

Fay asked: "But that cannot be guaranteed?"

The doctor replied: "No..."

Han spoke to the doctor: "Should we reveal the truth about her augmentation?"

The doctor frowned and replied: "I would advise against it...it might be too much of a shock... I recommend you wait for a few weeks... I will examine her again at the end of the month and we can reassess the situation."

Han said: "Very well..."

Gao asked: "Can I see her now?"

The doctor glanced towards Han Mang as he replied: "If the Section Leader has no objections..."

Han spoke to Gao: "Go to her..." He retrieved Alice's phone from his pocket and added: "And give her this..."

Gao took the phone and asked: "You wiped it clean?"

Han replied: "I thought it prudent to delete any reference to her recent adventures...such knowledge might cause unnecessary trauma."

Gao replied in a low voice: "Of course..."

As Gao left the room Connie said: "This is tearing him apart..."

Jessica announced: "I need coffee..."

## 09:42 - Tuesday 4th May - Observation Ward - Queen Elizabeth Hospital

Bright sunshine swept into the Observation Ward to arrive upon the long dark hair of the solitary patient sitting on the side of her bed. She looked up to see Mong Gao entering the ward. She asked:

"Have you got my phone?"

Gao walked over to the bed and replied: "Yes... Here you go..."

Alice took the phone and tapped the screen rapidly.

Gao asked: "Who are you calling?"

Alice replied: "My mother..."

Gao asked: "Can we talk when you're done?"

But Alice was already talking:

"Wái? Mum? It's me..." She sighed and continued: "Alice... I know... I'm sorry...work stuff... Yes I am okay... I will come over tonight... How is Mah-mah? That's good..." She looked at Gao and said: "I need to go now... I will see you tonight...Love you too... Bye..."

Gao asked: "Is she alright?"

Alice brushed a hand through her hair and replied: "She is fine... What do you want to talk about?"

Gao pulled a chair closer and sat down before replying:

"Can I ask you a few questions?"

Alice sighed and asked: "More questions? Look, you seem like a nice guy, but I really do not remember doing any of those things Han Mang told me about..."

Gao asked: "Do you remember the night of the rooftop party?"

Alice replied: "Sure..."

Gao asked: "How did you get home that night?"

Alice hesitated before replying: "I probably took the MTR..."

Gao said: "No... I drove you home...and we diverted to the Avenue of Stars..."

Alice's eyes widened as she asked: "We did?"

Gao asked: "You don't remember?"

Alice replied: "Sorry...no... But the doctor thinks I will remember stuff eventually..."

Gao hesitated before asking: "What about that night in Singapore?"

Alice asked: "What night in Singapore? Was it in the Cloud?"

Gao replied: "No... It was in the real world..."

Alice asked wearily: "Okay... So what happened in Singapore?"

Gao hesitated before replying: "Well...you and me...we..."

Alice suddenly realised what Gao was trying to say. She asked: "You and me? We were that close?"

Gao looked into her eyes and replied: "Yes...we were that close...all night..."

Alice fell silent briefly before saying: "Wow! You would think I would remember doing that..."

Gao forced a smile and said: "And that does nothing for my ego..."

Alice smiled and said: "Sorry... But if what you say is true..." She paused before continuing: "I am no longer a virgin..."

Gao cleared his throat and replied: "Believe me...it is true..."

Alice felt her face flush as she said: "God..."

Gao studied Alice and asked: "What are you thinking about?"

Alice replied: "I am thinking that an important part of my life is missing..." She fell silent before continuing: "If we did that...why can't I remember? I mean who forgets stuff like that?"

Gao asked: "What did Han Mang tell you?"

Alice replied: "He told me that I had been kidnapped by someone called Rén Du... I was taken from Hong Kong to his base in Japan..." She fell silent briefly before continuing: "They forced me into some kind of experiment. But it went wrong and I lost my most recent memories..."

Gao asked: "Did he tell you why Rén Du kidnapped you?"

Alice replied: "Something to do with my age and physical health..." She paused before adding: "I guess he just wanted young girls... How creepy is that?"

Gao smiled slightly and said: "Very creepy..."

Alice asked: "So how did you get mixed up in all this?"

Gao scratched his head and replied: "It's a long story... Suffice it to say that I wanted to keep you safe..."

Alice gave a slight smile and replied: "Well thank you for that..."

Gao added: "We all wanted to keep you safe..."

Alice considered this and asked: "What about the girls with you? Were they kidnapped as well?"

Gao replied: "No. They travelled to Japan to rescue you..."

Alice asked: "From Singapore, right?"

Gao replied: "Yes..."

Alice considered this before asking: "Because we are all supposed to be friends?"

Gao replied: "That's right...we are all good friends..."

Alice hesitated before asking: "But you and me...we were more than just friends?"

Gao replied: "Very much more..."

Alice saw raw emotion in Gao's eyes and said: "I am sorry..."

Gao asked: "Sorry for what?"

Alice replied: "I am sorry that I have forgotten something that meant so much to you..."

Gao replied: "It once meant a lot to you too..."

Alice sighed and said: "But not anymore..."

Gao replied: "Perhaps in time you will remember how much we meant to each other..."

Alice hesitated slightly before asking: "Did I love you?"

Gao replied: "You told me that you did..."

Alice fell silent before saying: "I really am sorry... But if I did have those feelings...they are gone now..."

Gao asked in a low voice: "You don't have any feelings for me?"

Alice replied truthfully: "You are just a guy I met at the rooftop party...sorry..."

Gao sighed and said: "Okay..."

Alice looked at Gao and asked: "So what are you thinking about?"

Gao replied: "I just wish you could find me inside you..."

Alice placed one hand on his shoulder and replied:

"Maybe one day I will..."

Gao smiled slightly and said: "Although the universe is huge, we will always find each other..."

Alice asked: "Excuse me?"

Gao replied: "It was something I told you that night in Singapore..."

Alice sighed and said: "Maybe we will find each other...but it will not be today..." She glanced at the time and continued: "I need to go home...get back to my life..."

Gao replied: "Of course... But I hope we can talk again sometime."

Alice replied: "Definitely... Send me a 121 and we can meet for a coffee..."

Gao replied: "I would like that..."

Alice raised her phone and said: "I need to call my roommate... she must be wondering where I am..."

Gao said: "Wait..."

Alice asked: "Something wrong?"

Gao asked: "Han Mang didn't tell you about Nancy?"

Alice tensed and asked: "What about Nancy? Is she alright?"

Gao moved closer and replied: "Alice... Nancy was shot..."

Alice exclaimed: "Oh my god... Is she okay?"

Gao replied soberly: "She died... I am so sorry..."

Alice felt tears in her eyes as she asked: "Who would want to hurt Nancy?"

Gao replied: "Perhaps we should talk about this later..."

Alice replied firmly: "Tell me who killed my friend?"

Gao replied: "She was shot because the killer thought she was you..."

A shocked Alice asked: "Someone wanted to kill me?"

Gao replied: "It's all part of the Rén Du situation... I am sorry..."

Alice wiped her eyes and said: "Perhaps memory loss has its advantages..." She saw the sadness on Gao's face and added: "Sorry..."

Gao replied: "We say that a lot lately...sorry..."

Alice replied wearily: "I just need to find my life again..."

Gao replied: "And you can..."

Alice looked around the ward and asked: "Can you find my clothes?"

Gao stood up and replied: "I will find the nurse..."

As Gao walked away Alice called: "So call me sometime..."

Gao stopped at the door and replied: "I will..."

## 10:08 - Tuesday 4th May 2028 - Waiting Room - Observation Ward - Queen Elizabeth Hospital - Hong Kong

Connie saw the sadness in Gao's eyes and asked: "She didn't remember you?"

Gao closed the door and replied: "She remembers meeting me at the Hub party...but nothing else..."

Jessica looked up from her phone and said: "That sucks..."

Fay asked: "So what will you do now?"

Gao replied in a low voice: "She said I can call her sometime..."

Connie spoke gently: "Just give her time... I'm sure it will all come back to her eventually..."

Jessica added: "Yes...true love and all that..."

Fay asked: "So what is she doing now?"

Gao replied: "Getting dressed... She wants to go home."

Han stood up and asked: "Did you mention Nancy Yeo?"

Gao replied: "I told her the truth..."

Fay asked: "How did she take it?"

Gao replied: "Hard to say... I think she's still trying to process everything..."

Han walked towards the door and said: "I will arrange for her to be discharged..."

Jessica asked: "What about us? We're stranded in Hong Kong..."

Han stopped at the door and replied: "I have arranged a flight back to Singapore... A car will be waiting at the main entrance... Goodbye to you all..."

As soon as the door closed Jessica exclaimed: "Wow... I can't believe we are not under arrest..."

Fay frowned and said: "It does seem too good to be true..."

Connie asked: "You think it is a trick?"

Gao asked: "To what end? You guys are not that important..."

Jessica gave a slight smile and said: "Thanks for that..."

Gao replied: "You know what I mean..."

Fay warned: "We should still be careful..."

Connie suggested: "We should cut down on the Cloud Dancing..."

Jessica yawned and said: "I'm done with the Cloud for a while... Time I got my life together..."

Fay smiled and asked: "Do you have any plans?"

Jessica adjusted her hair and replied: "I have a few ideas'...."

Fay replied: "Well I hope you keep in touch..."

Jessica replied: "Of course I will..."

Connie interjected: "Me too...

Fay looked at Gao and asked: "So what will you do now?"

Gao replied: "Lay low for a while...try to meet Alice sometime..."

Fay warned: "Well just be careful...you still have a target on your back."

Connie asked: "He does?"

Gao replied soberly: "The Triad..."

Connie said: "Oh..."

Jessica suggested: "Maybe you should stay away from Alice..."

Gao replied in a low voice: "You are probably right..."

Connie stood up and said: "I am so sorry Gao..."

Fay asked: "Should we talk to Alice before we leave?"

Gao replied: "There's not much point... She just doesn't know you guys anymore..."

Jessica stood up and said: "So let's go home to Singapore..."

Connie nodded slightly and said: "I agree..."

Fay stood up and asked: "Will you be alright Gao?"

Gao forced a smile and replied: "Sure... You take care...all of you..."

Suddenly Connie embraced Gao and said: "Call us any time..."

Gao replied: "I will thanks..."

Jessica smiled and said: "You are the nicest gangster I ever met..."

Gao smiled slightly and replied: "I appreciate that..."

Fay touched his arm gently and said: "Goodbye... Take care..."

Gao replied: "I will..."

As she opened the door Connie said: "I hope you find love again..."

When he was finally alone Gao sat down and stared at the floor. The awful truth arrived with shocking clarity: *I have lost her...* For the first time in a very long time he felt teardrops slip from his eyes to fall upon the white tiled floor. *Alice...* Suddenly the waiting room door opened to reveal a fully-dressed Alice. She smiled and announced:

"I am going home now..."

Gao stood up and asked: "Can I walk you out?"

Alice saw the pain in his eyes and replied: "Sure..."

As they made their way along the corridor Gao asked:

"So how do you feel now?"

Alice replied: "Okay thanks..." She gestured to her jacket and continued: "But I could do with a shower and a change of clothes..."

They fell silent until they arrived at the hospital's main entrance.

Alice announced: "Han Mang has a car waiting for me..."

Gao looked towards the forecourt and said: "Oh okay... Well take care..."

Alice smiled slightly and replied: "You too..."

Gao replied in a low voice: "I will..."

Alice stopped in front of the glass sliding doors and asked: "Are you going to be alright?"

Gao forced a smile and replied: "Yes... I'm okay..."

Alice smiled and said: "Well... Call me sometime..."

Gao replied: "I will... Bye for now..."

Alice stepped through the doors and replied: "Bye..."

Gao watched Alice walk towards the waiting car and climb into the back seat. *Take care my darling...* He stood in the same spot for another five minutes until the car had disappeared along the bypass. Finally he walked out into a stifling heat and looked up into bright blue skies and sighed heavily. *Back to reality...* He never heard the gunshot as it tore its way from the snipers rifle to arrive with a sudden impact in the center of his forehead. But as he fell mortally wounded to the ground a brief vision of Alice swept inside the final beating of his heart.

# Reality

*'The threat of Monday tends to ruin Sunday night...'*
Precept of the day - Alice Sòng

**07:06 - Monday 7th August 2028 - Apartment 182 - Block 5 - Kwai Chung Estate - Hong Kong**

A fluttering window blind created waves of sunlight washing over the last shadows of the night skirting the walls of the bedroom. The ever-present sounds of the great city violated the silence with a familiar droning of traffic and voices echoing along the footpaths of the housing estate. A sudden beeping began to emanate from a bedside table.

Alice Sòng rolled over and punched the alarm clock button as the yawn transformed into a full stretch of her naked body. She opened her eyes upon a white ceiling as the last remnants of the dream arrived with unusual clarity. *I was driving a taxi?* For almost two weeks now she had been having the same series of confusing and chaotic dreams ending in a nagging headache - driving a taxi...hiking across a country park, sitting inside a helicopter... She kicked the duvet away and sighed heavily. *Crazy...* But now she began to wonder if the dreams were actually her memories, slowly returning. She had tried to contact Mong Gao to discuss the dreams only to find his 121 account had been deleted. *He has gone off-grid...* She played with the yin yang pendant which adorned her neck as a smile arrived upon her face. She could not remember losing the necklace, but one day it had arrived in the post from some mysterious Good Samaritan. She glanced at the time. *Oh crap!* Without hesitation she made her way to the bathroom. *If I am late again Harvey will burst a blood vessel...*

**07:12 - Monday 7th August - 2028 - Apartment 19 - Block 411 - Saujana Road - Singapore**

Sunlight touched the bedroom windows with a sudden brightness scattering left-over shadows amongst cluttered bookshelves and a desk buried beneath piles of data-skims. Fay Rui wiped sleep from her eyes and stared at her reflection in the wardrobe mirror. *Back to reality...* She reached for her phone and tapped the 121 app. Moments later she read the most recent group-messages:

    Connie: *"Terrible news... Is it true?"*
    Fay: *"Han Mang confirmed it..."*
    Jessica: *"Why are we only finding out now?"*
    Fay: *"Gao had no ID on him... He was listed as a John Doe... But his fingerprints confirmed he was Triad... HK cops contacted Beijing cos Gao was flagged as POI by State Security... Then they hushed it all up..."*
    Connie: *"Why did they do that?"*
    Fay: *"No idea... Han Mang would not elaborate..."*
    Jessica: *"Does Alice know?"*
    Fay: *"No... Han wants her left out of it..."*
    Jessica: *"What about her memories?"*
    Fay: *"They tried a portal sync from Beijing but got no response..."*
    Jessica: *"Her implants are not working?"*
    Fay: *"Han thinks they are dormant...or in reset mode... I don't think they have a clue..."*
    Jessica: *"Will they leave her alone?"*
    Fay: *"I think so..."*
    Jessica: *"He wouldn't elaborate, right?"*
    Fay: *"Right..."*
    Connie: *"I can't believe he is dead..."*
    Jessica: *"He is gone...deal with it..."*
    Connie: *"Must u be so harsh?"*
    Fay: *"Do u guys want to meet up?"*
    Connie: *"Yes... We should meet..."*

Jessica: *"Send me a location... Got to go now...bye..."*
Connie: *"Any word from Chok or Chin?"*
Fay: *"Nothing... I think they got day jobs..."*
Connie: *"Did Jessica tell u about her new job?"*
Fay: *"Yes..."*
Connie: *"I couldn't believe it..."*
Fay: *"I was surprised..."*
Connie: *"But working for Biogen? What's that all about?"*
Fay: *"I think she has her own agenda now..."*
Connie: *"Maybe we should ask her about it when we meet..."*
Fay: *"We can try..."*
Connie: *"Meet at Pablo's tonight?"*
Fay: *"Okay... I'll 121 Jessica later...bye for now ..."*
Connie: *"Bye Fay..."*

Fay rolled over and yawned before kicking the duvet away and climbing out of bed. She glanced towards the pile of data-skims waiting to be categorised into personal and business bank statements. *Because the area manager says an efficient bank is a happy bank...* She opened the blinds into bright sunshine and sighed heavily. *Reality sucks...*

**20:16 - Sunday August 6th 2028 - Biogenomic Engineering Laboratory - Sublevel 5 - Synthtech Corporation - Radford Boulevard - West Seattle - USA**

A sterile room of white walls and bright LED ceiling tiles illuminating rows of bio-scanners placed above ten inactive workstations.

Professor Niel Jordon looked up from an electron microscope and said:

"Mister Dower, I was not expecting you..."

Dower walked towards Jordon and replied: "We need to discuss Lily's autopsy report..."

Jordon cleared his throat and asked: "Is there a problem?"

Dower asked: "It took you almost three months to conclude that she died of natural causes?"

Jordon replied: "I know you wanted me to find some evidence of external sabotage, but I can assure you, Lily suffered a myocardial infarction."

Dower scowled and asked: "A heart attack? The child was perfectly healthy... How can she suddenly develop heart problems?"

Jordon sighed and replied: "As I have already stated on numerous occasions, the aggressive implantation of neocortical implants almost certainly contributed to her death. I did try to warm you that she was not ready for full activation."

Dower clenched his fists and asked: "What is the status of the new subject?"

Jordon glanced towards a single maturation tank and replied: "The boy remains in stasis..." He tapped a datapad and continued: "Neural telemetry is within acceptable parameters... Neocortical output continues to increase via the subcutaneous nodes... I expect he will be ready for revival by the end of the year."

Dower frowned and asked: "Why can't you speed up the process?"

Jordon replied: "I did speed up the process for Ria and Lily with disastrous consequences..."

Dower sighed and asked: "Did you read the report from Beijing?"

Jordon replied: "I did...most enlightening..."

Dower asked: "What about the new methods they are using? Are they viable?"

Jordon frowned and replied: "Decantation is a novel way to describe the process, but it is still basically maturation."

Dower continued: "Their new project has been designated: Sinocant..."

Jordon smiled and replied: "An amalgam of Sino-Chinese and decantation... Most amusing..."

Dower snapped: "It will not be amusing if they take the lead yet again..."

Jordon replied: "They will not take the lead... The death of Professor Leung has set them back years..."

Dower replied: "I hope you right..." As he walked towards the door he added: "Because if you fail me again Professor Leung will have company..."

## 07:19 - Monday 7th August - 2028 - Clinical Sciences - Ministry of State Security - Beijing - China

A quiet room reduced to the sound of machines humming almost in harmony with the droning of a concealed aircon system. In the centre of the room a permiglass cube is home to a human brain immersed in steripol fluid. It is connected by a series of fine wires and bio-pads to an overhead scanner. Sitting at her desk nearby Doctor Xiao studies a desktop viewscreen before announcing:

"I can confirm an active Cloud scenario... Personality traits are in intact and socio-engrammatic confluence is within normal parameters..."

Standby behind her Section Leader Hand Mang asked:

"In laymen's terms if you please Doctor..."

Xiao looked up and replied: "I have restored full neural capacity... He is now once more the man he was before he was shot..."

Han glanced towards the floating brain and asked: "So he an avatar now?"

Xiao replied: "Yes... Synced directly to the quantum level computer by neural feeder tubes..."

Han studied the viewscreen and noted: "You are not using a vocal initiator or retinal nodes..."

Xiao replied: "I thought it prudent not to overtax his neural capacity. That is how we lost control of the British agent."

Han frowned and asked: "Will he remember Alice Sòng?"

Xiao hesitated slightly before replying: "No... As per your instructions those memories were excised during the re-activation process. But I have uploaded a viable life scenario which includes a new identity and socio-historical background."

Han read the life scenario data and asked: "You kept his first name?

Xiao replied: "A necessary precaution to prevent neural synaptic rejection..."

Han frowned and asked: "Will he accept his new status?"

Xiao replied: "With respect Section Leader, we are in new territory with this experiment... His reactions to his status are non-quantifiable at this point."

Han asked: "But you can track his interactions with Miss Sòng?"

Xiao replied: "Yes I can... Miss Sòng is no longer beyond our reach..."

Han considered this before asking: "But what if he questions the validity of his real-world location? The entire scenario could fall apart."

Xiao replied: "It is simply a matter of adjusting his neural input via the neocortical implants. We can compensate for a variety of socially interactive possibilities by re-writing the algorithmic potential."

Han asked: "So if Miss Sòng requests a real-world meeting, you can create a viable excuse to deny her request?"

Xiao replied: "Exactly..."

Han nodded slightly and ordered: "I want you to monitor their portal activities twenty four hours a day..."

Xiao replied: "Yes sir..."

Han spoke as he walked towards the door: "And now I need to explain things to Minister Dai Ling..."

Xiao smiled slightly and replied: "Good luck sir..."

## 23:22 - Friday 11th August - 2028 - Apartment 182 - Block 5 - Kwai Chung Estate - Hong Kong

An air-conditioning unit struggles to compensate for the stifling heat as a naked young woman collapses exhausted onto her bed. For a brief moment she is tempted towards self-pleasure but a ping from her phone confirms Cybersync. *Cloud Dancing will do tonight...* She gently removed a single data-lens from a plastic pouch and placed it carefully over her right eye. A brief glimpse of circuitry is replaced by a blank input screen. She placed a second lens onto her left eye and waited for both lenses to sync into a single datascreen. A rapid blink recalibrates the screen before she tapped the Cloudsync app on her phone. She smiled as the app synced into her online game-lens account with the slogan: *Techsync Takes You There!* As the words vanished from the screen she quickly placed an audio plug into each ear and waited for the Net Access Response. Moments later a Cloud gateway appeared over the corneal data-lens - a swirling of lines coalescing into two metal gates opening into a Profile Adaptive Platform. *Online access portal - Anonymity guaranteed!* She blinked to select a Cloud avatar. *Who will I be tonight?*

A few minutes later she enters the Cup of Joe Coffee House wearing a light blue dress with matching shoes. She took a moment to study the Active Conversation Portals and pondered the possibility of meeting new friends. But suddenly she noticed a handsome young avatar sitting next to the window. *Cute...* She contemplated the chances of finding a real boyfriend inside the Cloud. *The cuteness could be an illusion... He could even be a girl in the real world...* She sighed as she lay on her bed and decided to take a chance. *He might actually be good looking in real life....* Without hesitation she walked over and asked:

"Is this seat taken?"

The young man looked up ands replied: "Oh... No it's not..."

Alice smiled as she sat down and introduced herself: "I am Alice..."

The man returned the smile and replied: "I am Gao..."

Alice stared at the man and asked: "You are not Mong Gao are you?"

Gao smiled and replied: "Chang Gao actually..."

Alice replied: "Oh..."

Gao asked: "Who is Mong Gao?"

Alice replied: "Someone I knew...once... I think..."

Gao asked: "You think?"

Alice replied: "It is a long and complicated story..."

Gao sat forward and said: "I am all ears..."

Alice smiled and asked: "So what is your real-world location?"

Gao replied: "My dorm room... Peking University, Beijing."

Alice said: "Oh... What are you studying?"

Gao replied: "Masters degree in digital sciences... How about you?"

Alice lowered her eyes slightly and replied: "Photographer... based in Hong Kong."

Gao smiled and said: "Wow... I have always wanted to visit Hong Kong..."

Alice said: "Well if you do I can show you around..."

Gao smiled warmly and said: "I would like that..."

Alice looked out the window and asked: "Shall we explore the city?"

Gao replied: "Sure..."

As they stood up Alice said: "New Oasis beach is supposed to be nice..."

Gao smiled and replied: "The beach it is then..."

Alice asked: "Have you ever been to Taipei in the Cloud?"

Gao opened the door for Alice as he replied: "No... Is it worth a visit?"

Alice stepped onto the sidewalk and replied: "Definitely..."

As they set off along the street Gao said: "Maybe we can meet there sometime..."

Alice smiled and replied: "I would like that..."

# Provenance

*'The nexus apogee is fragile and must be nurtured in its early existence...'*
*Rén Du*

**Dawn - August 28th 2028 - Suchuan Apartments - Dunhuang City - Gansu Province - North-western China**

A dirty window partially obscured by a torn curtain reveals a blood red sky stealing the last remnants of the night and forcing a thin scattering of stars into temporary seclusion. Below the window the sound of traffic competes with voices rising and falling through the thin plasterboard walls of the apartment block.

Huang Lin placed her baby boy onto the bed and smiled as she sat down. She whispered:

"Weisheng...my beautiful boy..."

The six month old child kicked his legs into the air as a brief smile arrived upon his face.

Lin returned the smile and whispered: "Greatness is born..." She looked towards the window and said: "Another day dawns my son..."

Weisheng synced into vocal mode and replied:

"Yes Māmā..."

Lin sighed and said: "We are going to the wet market soon...you must not talk in public... Okay?"

Weisheng replied: "Okay..."

Lin pulled him into her arms and said: "That's my big boy..."

As he nestled his head into his mother's chest the boy smiled at the irony of the situation. *Nascent data-capacity expanding in-line with base code retrieval mode...*

Lin said: "Now let's get you dressed...."

As he looked up at his mother the boy reverted to his primary personality segment. Moments later Rén Du looked out upon a brave new world with limitless possibilities and smiled with total satisfaction. *The nexus apogee is alive and well...*

# - END -

*'We can no more control evolution than we can stop the tide of the sea, with this in mind we should be wary of the desire to speed up the process. We should resist the temptation to create better versions of ourselves, for if we follow that path to its inevitable conclusion the end result will be the supplanting of our race by creatures we have yet to create.'*
*Han Mang*

Ingram Content Group UK Ltd.
Milton Keynes UK
UKHW011825040423
419625UK00001B/177